Valdon suddenly stood, almost shaking himself, his mood darkening.

"This has been a most surprising lunch, Mademoiselle Turner, but I'm sorry to say that I have a previous engagement that I fear requires my attention. It cannot be helped."

So jarring was the abrupt shift in conversation that she stared at him slack-jawed, holding his gaze for a beat too long. The air was thick between them. To her surprise, she found that she had been holding her breath. From the look of shock registering on his face, she could see that he felt this connection, too, like static. Somewhere in the distance a clanging metal sound of silverware could be heard from the kitchen.

Valdon struggled feverishly to put his coat on, never once taking his eyes off her. He pushed his hair back and there was a sheen of sweat and the moment was charged. Once the garment was on his shoulders, he seemed out of breath, like it was agony to be in her presence for one moment longer, and yet he did not turn to leave.

Praise for
Constance Sayers

The Star and the Strange Moon

"Be warned! *The Star and the Strange Moon* will cast its spell on you."

—Paula Brackston, *New York Times* bestselling author

"At once a sweeping tale of dark magic, artistic obsession, and a love unbound from the limits of time, *The Star and the Strange Moon* captivates with lush prose and moments of poignant, heartbreaking beauty."

—Paulette Kennedy, bestselling author of *The Witch of Tin Mountain*

"Sayers masterfully weaves a tale of multigenerational secrets, creating an enticing dance between past and present that will keep readers on edge."

—*Publishers Weekly*

The Ladies of the Secret Circus

"Ambitious and teeming with magic, Sayers creates a fascinating mix of art, the belle époque, and more than a little murder."

—Erika Swyler, author of *The Book of Speculation*

"At times decadent and macabre, *The Ladies of the Secret Circus* is a mesmerizing tale of love, treachery, and depraved magic percolating through four generations of Cabot women."

—Luanne G. Smith, author of *The Vine Witch*

"A spellbinding historical fantasy....Fans of Erin Morgenstern's *The Night Circus* will love this page-turning story of dark magic, star-crossed love, and familial sacrifice." —*Publishers Weekly* (starred review)

A Witch in Time

"A captivating tapestry of a tale, *A Witch in Time* weaves together the supernatural, historical fiction, and a humorous present-day heroine while traveling the macabre brambles of a dark curse—through lifetimes—with a compass to the heart."

—Gwendolyn Womack, bestselling author of *The Fortune Teller*

"Fresh and original. A narrative rich in historical detail, brightened by flashes of humor, and filled with colorful characters and fascinating settings. A most rewarding read!"

—Louisa Morgan, author of *A Secret History of Witches*

By Constance Sayers

A Witch in Time

The Ladies of the Secret Circus

The Star and the Strange Moon

The STAR *and the* STRANGE MOON

CONSTANCE SAYERS

This book is a work of fiction. Names, characters, places, and incidents are the product of the author's imagination or are used fictitiously. Any resemblance to actual events, locales, or persons, living or dead, is coincidental.

Cover design by Lisa Marie Pompilio
Cover photographs by Trevillion and Shutterstock

Author photograph by Tyler Hooks for Laura Metzler Photography

Redhook Books/Orbit
Hachette Book Group
1290 Avenue of the Americas
New York, NY 10104
hachettebookgroup.com

First Paperback Edition: April 2024
Originally published in hardcover and ebook by Redhook in November 2023

Redhook is an imprint of Orbit, a division of Hachette Book Group.
The Redhook name and logo are registered trademarks of Hachette Book Group, Inc.

Library of Congress Cataloging-in-Publication Data
Names: Sayers, Constance, author.
Title: The star and the strange moon / Constance Sayers.
Description: First Edition. | New York, NY : Redhook, 2023.
Identifiers: LCCN 2023009909 | ISBN 9780316493741 (hardcover) |
ISBN 9780316493697 (ebook)
Subjects: LCGFT: Fantasy fiction. | Novels.
Classification: LCC PS3619.A9974 S73 2023 | DDC 813/.6—dc23/eng/20230306
LC record available at https://lccn.loc.gov/2023009909

ISBNs: 9780316493758 (trade paperback), 9780316493697 (ebook)

Printed in the United States of America

CW

10 9 8 7 6 5 4 3 2 1

For Mark

PROLOGUE

Christopher Kent
August 14, 1986
Cumberland, Maryland

"It's going to be different this time, I swear it." Christopher Kent's mother pulled the car out of the motel's mostly vacant lot.

She'd gotten a gig singing four nights a week at the lounge in a hotel near the Pittsburgh International Airport. When she told them she didn't have an apartment, the hotel offered them a room free of charge until she got on her feet. It was a new adventure, so she was animated.

"After this job, where would you like to live next?" She used her free hand to shake open the new *Maps of Pennsylvania and Ohio* book as they entered the highway.

She made him nervous when she was manic like this. He studied places like Youngstown, Akron, and Toledo, wondering what each city would be like. Toledo had a nice ring to it. "Guess our fresh start is limited to Pennsylvania or Ohio, huh?"

"Don't be cute," she said as she applied a fresh coat of polish to her nails and held them up to the air vent to dry.

As the sun came through the window, it framed Pamela Kent in a kaleidoscope of light and bouncing shadows, like an angel.

"Never lived in any of these places," said the boy. The idea of a promised fresh start already caused a lurch of anxiety. New places meant he'd have to learn how to take care of them all over again. They'd lasted four months at the previous motel, long enough for him to get a routine, like where to find spare change that had been dropped under the vending machines or in the pay phones after late-night drunken calls. The maids were always the kindest to him, washing his clothes when they saw his pants were too dirty.

The old Pontiac Ventura sputtered before finally kicking into gear with a gasp that sounded like a death rattle. Rolling down the window, she began belting out "Blue Bayou" from Linda Ronstadt's *Simple Dreams* cassette with the intensity of a live performance. It had been a while since she'd been onstage. She was practicing, working up her nerve to sing again and testing to see if she'd done any damage to her voice this time. The acoustics in the old car made her clear soprano sound full and robust. When she was at her worst, her speaking voice was a rumble, and the drinking and the ranting that followed always made her hoarse.

Nearly an hour into the trip and after two rotations of Linda Ronstadt, they pulled into a truck stop for gas and lunch. "How did I sound?"

He gave her a confident nod, like he was her manager. "Just like always."

That's what she wanted to hear from him—that nothing had changed in these months, no damage had been done.

"Wait for me in there." She motioned toward the diner. Christopher shuffled reluctantly to the door, lingering for a moment near the jugs of antifreeze as the door opened and closed, a cool wave of air-conditioning from inside.

Inside the restaurant, he found a booth near the window where he strained his neck to see what she was doing at the pump. A truck driver had wandered over to her. Men like this could be a problem. Several times, she'd ended up with a black eye or a chipped tooth, him too. Moving positions so he could get a better view, he saw her touching the man's bare arm as she spoke. She twirled a stray strand of hair that flipped dramatically across her eyes and leaned against the car. His mother was thirty-six years old but had shaved eight years from her age, telling people she'd had Christopher when she was eighteen. Despite everything, she still looked dewy and beautiful, and she knew it. The man was wiry with a full beard and wore a black T-shirt, but Christopher could see his jeans were dirty. While she paid, the driver followed her to the window. Then the pair ducked behind a line of parked trucks and out of the boy's view.

"Just you?"

Startled, Christopher looked up to see the waitress, pad in hand and eyebrow perked, like she didn't see many children alone in booths. A name tag read MIDGE.

"No, my mom is coming," he said, pointing to the now-abandoned pump where the Ventura sat waiting, just like him. Turning his attention to the menu, he knew what he'd be ordering. The cheapest things on the menu were a grilled cheese sandwich or a hot dog.

"Fries with that?" asked Midge.

"No, thank you," said Christopher, closing the flaps on the menu. "Just the sandwich."

When Midge balked, the boy slid the menu toward her with his fingertips like he was a Vegas card dealer. "I have the six dollars to pay for it."

"Quite the little man you are," said Midge with what was either sarcasm or admiration, he couldn't tell, but it wasn't the first time someone had called him "the little man."

"You aren't like a child," Estella, the maid at the last hotel, used to marvel. Christopher *was* in a hurry to grow up so he could take better care of them. No one took him seriously where his mother was concerned because he was just a kid. But he'd just turned ten last week. Double digits. It felt like an accomplishment.

He helped Estella clean rooms, particularly the bathrooms, which she hated. In exchange, she'd give him a quarter from her tips. If someone hadn't left a tip, she'd keep track of what she "owed" him on an old envelope. At the end of her shift, he'd find abandoned treasures she'd left for him, stuffed animals, army toys, board games, and puzzles with missing pieces. "My little business partner," said Estella with a wink. This arrangement was generous, given that she had two young children of her own to care for. Estella had given him his most valuable possession—his blue hippopotamus finger puppet that had been left in the bathtub by a family on their way to Niagara Falls. It was a treasure with the power to calm him.

His mother blew in from the parking lot, flushed and glowing with a sheen of sweat, her hair and shirt askew and the gold cornicello necklace glistening on her chest. No matter how tight money was, she'd never considered pawning her necklace. Leaning back in the booth, she pushed the errant strand of hair out of the way behind her ear.

Flagging down Midge, she demanded a western omelet with sausage and toast with a side of home fries. When the meal arrived, his mother was wild, almost manic, devouring the omelet while rattling off all the plans of things they'd do. Zoos, museums. From his experience, this was usually a windup of empty promises. Despite her constant array of plans for them, he'd never been to a zoo in his life.

As she paid, he saw a thick wad of new bills in her wallet. There were cycles to her money. Either she was flush with cash from mysterious sources or broke because she was using again. Neither was good news for them.

In his pocket, he felt for the thing that calmed him: the smooth, comforting vinyl body of the blue hippopotamus finger puppet. They would be okay.

Hours later, when they pulled up in the manicured roundabout, Christopher found himself disoriented. There were no cars parked in front of beat-up orange doors or women dangling their arms over the railings. In the center driveway with fresh blacktop pavement sat an imposing fountain surrounded by various hedges shaped into balls and cones. The hotel sign was tucked between some hedges with elegant lighting. It was the first time he realized that you could wrangle crisp geometric shapes from unruly bushes.

Searching for a VACANCY sign but coming up empty, he wondered how people knew they had rooms available.

"Come on," said his mother, her chin in the air, like this was a common occurrence. After check-in, they were directed to a set of elevators. When the elevator doors opened on the sixth floor, he saw a long corridor painted caramel beige with rows of black-and-white photographs perfectly spaced down the hallway—Audrey Hepburn, Cary Grant, and Grace Kelly on one side, Gene Kelly, Carole Lombard, and Sophia Loren on the other. His mother loved old movies—Hitchcock's in particular—so he knew most of these faces. She quizzed him on each as they went by. Kim Novak held court near the door marked 612.

Halfway down the hall, the boy stopped in front of a curious photo of a pretty woman he could not place. The unfamiliar lady in the photo had long, straight hair and bangs that were thick and blunt like the bristles on a new broom. Seated on a leather stool, she'd been snapped mid-laugh, empty liquor bottles lined up in front of her. Unlike the other photos, which were Hollywood publicity "still" shots, this one, a black-and-white candid, was out of place. Peering closer to the frame, Christopher liked how the woman wasn't gazing into the camera, but at something—or someone—that had caught her attention. He followed her eyes and turned around, expecting to find that focal point behind him, but instead, Cary Grant smiled back at him. Immediately, he liked the woman in the photo and wished that he could be on the other side of the camera, making her laugh.

"Bitch." The voice came from behind him suddenly, startling him so much that he jumped. It was his mother, using a tone that she reserved for when he played too close to the motel turn-in or when she was looking for bottles. Instinctively his eyes widened, and he searched the hallway for help.

But the hallway was empty.

Hoping he was wrong, he turned and observed the change in his mother's face. Her beautiful cupid mouth was twisted, her nostrils flaring as she openly gawked at the photo. From somewhere deep in her, a growl began to form. Taking two steps closer to the frame, she stared up at the woman as though she were challenging her. Then she began to frantically rummage through her purse, and Christopher knew enough to take her hand and lead her away, but she shook him off. Then she found what she was searching for and raced back down the hall to the frame.

Christopher heard the glass shatter and saw something dripping from the photo. He ran over and grabbed her hands, turning them over to look for cuts, but instead saw that she had taken a bottle of red nail polish and thrown it at the cheap glass frame, shattering it. Below the mysterious subject's bangs, her face was now obscured by Candy Apple #16. Christopher felt like he'd swallowed stones.

His mother studied the now-macabre artwork and then in one sudden, decisive movement, ripped it from the wall, the little metal wall anchors propelled across the hall like shrapnel. In a fury, she smashed the frame onto the carpet, now dotted with lacquer that resembled drops of blood.

"Mom." The boy picked up her cheap brown pleather handbag, which had been flung across the hallway and now rested at the foot of the picture of Sophia Loren. "Mom," he said louder. "You can't do this. Look at me."

At first, she obeyed, murmuring something he couldn't understand as he guided her away. Listening intently, he tried to make out the garbled words. She gave him one of those blank stares that he feared so much. He was losing her. *No no no.* Searching his mind, he didn't remember what town they were in. There was no one here to help him. How had he let this happen? He'd had a moment of trusting her—trusting that life would neatly arrange itself. The boy wiped sweat from his forehead and could feel his legs shaking. The old motel attendant at the Silver Arms had always known what to do when his mother was like this, giving her some of her "secret medicine" that calmed her for a short while, even though they never had money to pay for it. The old woman at the Arms seemed to take pity on Christopher, but the people behind the desk at this hotel were a different group entirely.

"Mom, we need to go in the room." He could feel tears welling up. This beautiful creature was all he had in this world. His breathing became shallow, and he took small gulps of air so as not to pass out. "Mom."

She pointed at the crumpled bits of the photo now in a heap on the floor. "I never want to see her fucking face again. Do you *hear* me?"

Christopher gazed down at the mess on the floor. No one would ever see the woman's face again. His mother had accomplished that much. He nodded solemnly, like an oath had just formed between them. It seemed easy enough. He'd never seen that woman before today. He could agree to her terms.

"You'll never see her again. I promise. Let's just go to our room. They said we can order one dinner entrée each night. You like fish. It's Friday. Maybe they have fish with tartar sauce." He reached out and took her hand with his much smaller one. "Come on... let's just go to our room... please." He felt himself buckle in two, fold almost. "Please, Mama. Please." Inside his own nervous, twisting stomach, the sandwich he'd eaten earlier had become too much. Christopher lurched forward, vomiting truck-stop grilled cheese all over the new hotel carpet.

His mother staggered to room 612, her eyes vacant, never noticing that Christopher had fallen to his knees as another wave of nausea gripped him.

When the boy managed to stand, he had work to do. After cleaning up after himself and scrubbing the rug with the hotel towels, he began to look for places to hide the shattered photograph. Kids could slide in and out of rooms unnoticed. He could take it down the back stairs and find a dumpster. Maybe they'd never find it. Then his mother would just go on tonight and sing. She'd get a paycheck. He'd meet new front desk clerks, get better vending snacks. He'd take care of them both. First, he just needed to get her away from this painting on the floor. If he did that, she'd return to him.

Despite all his best efforts, she didn't.

For two days, he barely moved, frozen with fear and holding a constant vigil by her bedside, coaxing her to drink water and to use the bathroom. The growling of his stomach was the only sound in the room until the air conditioner kicked in. Anytime Christopher had gone for help in the past, his mother had been furious with him. Outsiders weren't to be trusted. Despite his prodding for her to get up and shower, she missed the Saturday afternoon rehearsal and then the show on Sunday night. Then a terrible pounding began at the door.

He sat on the bed watching her, his own clothes smelling and desperately wanting a fish sandwich. What followed was more pounding, shouting this time. Finally, to his relief, he heard the lock turn, and the door was removed from its hinges even though he'd unhooked the chain. From the looks on the hotel employees' faces when they saw his mother wrapped in the sheet on the floor, covered in vomit and piss and speaking incoherently, he knew things like this didn't happen at these types of establishments. As the ambulance crew arrived, a fatherly hotel manager with a name tag that read ORSON took him to the office.

"We'll need to call your father."

Christopher shook his head. "Don't have one."

The man winced. "Anyone else we can call? Grandmother?"

"I have an aunt."

"You know her number?"

The boy wrote Aunt Wanda's number on a phone pad with the hotel's logo. The man went into his office and shut the door. As he waited, someone from the restaurant brought him a fish sandwich with french fries, and he wondered if he had enough to pay for this meal. Reaching into his pocket, he felt a moment of panic. The hippopotamus was gone. To his horror, he had neither the finger puppet nor any money.

Orson returned to find Christopher pacing. "My puppet," said the boy. "My puppet is gone. It's in the room. I need it. I need it." He began rubbing the leg of his pants before jumping to his feet, looking toward the elevator.

"I'll send them up to the room to find it." The man put a hand on Christopher's shoulder.

The boy waited nervously in the lobby as a bellman was sent to search the room, but the man returned empty-handed.

"He looked," said Orson with a finality that told Christopher the puppet was lost forever.

"It's blue," said Christopher. "Did he know it's blue?" He knew the way things worked. Another maid would find the puppet under the bed or behind the television and take it home to her own child or toss it in the garbage.

The man narrowed his eyes as though his patience was being tested. "It isn't there." His suit jacket was now gone, like dealing with Christopher had taken something out of him.

Six hours later, when Christopher's uncle Martin finally arrived, the manager, who had stayed beyond his shift, presented them with the hotel bill. With a sniff, Martin glanced at the bottom number and reached into his billfold to hand the man a thick stack of twenties "for your trouble." With a nod toward the door, his uncle addressed Christopher for the first time. "Come on."

The boy hesitated, then slid the bill from the desk. Along with damages to the carpet from the nail polish, there was a line item for *Replacement of Gemma Turner artwork*. He couldn't place the name, but something told him to fold the bill and tuck it in his pocket. Like a clue, it would be important later. He looked back down the hallway with one more scan for anything small and blue. But the marble entryway shone.

Nothing had prepared him for a life without his mother. A wave of terror and loneliness hit him, and he stumbled, near fainting before a burst of energy and fear sent him bolting on wobbly legs through the automatic doors to catch up with his uncle Martin.

1

Gemma Turner
April 13, 1968
Paris, France

Already running late when the phone began to blare from the nightstand, Gemma ignored it, shutting the door behind her. Checking her watch, she realized that even the fastest Parisian taxi driver would be hard-pressed to get her to Montparnasse in ten minutes. She'd been warned that Thierry Valdon did not tolerate tardiness and was of the belief that all Americans were *vaches paresseuses.* Now she was in danger of being late. The faint metallic whir of the ringing phone continued until she reached the elevator at the end of the hall.

In the lobby of George V, with its graceful arches, elaborate marble floor, and accents of bunches of green and pink flowers in tall vases, she passed a mirror, taking one last look at her reflection. Gemma was pleased with her outfit, a white wool shift dress with a matching A-line double-breasted coat that came above the knee. Both were Ungaro creations, and the coat, trimmed with a faux-fur collar and matching horizontal fur stripes, made her look like a dessert. The designer had sent it last year when she was still an "it" girl. Back then, boxes and garment bags filled with samples were always appearing at her hotel room with the hope she'd be photographed in them. Now those had thinned as well. As she turned the white enamel toggles to close the coat, the woman who stared back at her with long, soft strawberry-blond hair was a stranger donning last year's fashion.

"Don't mess this up," she said to her reflection with disdain, her lip curling.

Upstairs in her room, she knew her phone would still be ringing. The same person on the other end, Charlie Hicks, would begin another cycle of the same conversation.

"Jesus, Gems. I need you *here.* The fucking record is not going well. Wren is working with the label to dump all my songs." The label had promised Charlie Hicks that the Prince Charmings' fourth album would be focused on his songs, not those of Wren Atticus, the lead singer who had been the band's principal songwriter. Like a naive child or spoiled artist—they really were one and the same—Charlie had believed them. As a result of this promise, he'd been on a particularly prolific streak, writing eight songs that he thought took the band in an exciting new direction. Wren was always his foil, trying to grab control of the band's creative heart. "Seriously, Gemmy—"

"We talked about this last night," she'd cut him off early this morning, twirling the cord and hoping a firm parental tone would shut him up. He hated not remembering conversations with her when he was blotto. "I have a lunch today. It's important to *me.*"

"That wanker perv? If the frog touches you..."

"Charlie—"

"*I* should be the most important thing to you."

"I need this, Charlie." Until she vocalized it, she hadn't even realized how true this was. Her entire career depended upon this lunch.

At one point, Gemma Turner had been the most talked-about young actress in Hollywood. She closed her eyes, trying to recall how easy it had all been. Playing an aloof surfer-girl love interest in

Thunder Beach, followed by a similar role in a beach-themed drag-racing film—*Beach Rally*—had made her famous. It was a jolt, going from a UCLA freshman majoring in English in the fall to a discovery, like there was something magic about her. She'd believed that, once. An athletic girl, she could actually surf, yet they made her use a stunt double. To hype her skills, her manager had her paddle out in the early morning in Venice Beach with press watching her, snapping stills of her on her longboard. The publicity had caught the eye of every studio, and the offers flooded in. At the height of her fame, she'd played veteran actor Stanley Taylor's daughter in *My Hawaiian Wedding*. In *It Comes in Waves*, she was paired in the press with her costar, Bryan Branch. And all she'd had to do was keep making herself available for these beach films, marry another studio actor, and buy a home in Beverly Hills. It would have been so easy.

"Oh, Gemma, you fool." She wiped away a tear and shook herself. Today, she couldn't doubt herself, and she didn't dare let thoughts of Charlie interfere with this lunch.

The hotel was bustling with midmorning activity, and she hurried outside, where she found her waiting car with an anxious-looking driver checking his watch. Her agent, Mick Fontaine, had hired the man with explicit instructions not to be late.

He maneuvered the car quickly along the Seine, and Gemma realized the deep sense of connection she had to this city, as though it were an inherited memory through her mother. Although everyone thought of her as a bohemian child from California, she'd been born right here. Her French mother and her American army lieutenant father had met when the Fourth Army Infantry Division pushed into Paris in 1944. Gemma leaned forward to talk to the driver in perfect French. "Do you like the cinema?"

"Oui," said the driver, his face brightening.

"Do you know the director Thierry Valdon?"

The man made a face. "He makes strange films that they show at night. My wife and I are not fans of Nouvelle Vague. The camera is too choppy." He took his hands off the steering wheel to make a gesture like he had a handheld video camera. "We like American musicals, *Singin' in the Rain*." The driver began humming the theme song.

Out the window she spied the small billboard of herself staring back at her. The poster for the perfume campaign, Joie de Jardin, hung on an untended part of the street, and her image had faded with the wind and rain so that she was a shadow, the paste that had affixed the poster now peeling off on the edges. While she had hoped they would choose her for another campaign, Joie de Jardin had never called again. Yet, it had been this very poster that had caught Valdon's eye.

"That's you." The driver strained to look up at it.

"That *was* me," she said softly, a wistful look on her face as she turned to see her own image staring back at her. She didn't recognize that confident girl anymore.

At the sight of her on the billboard, Thierry Valdon had insisted he "had to have the Joie de Jardin girl in his next film." Thinking she was a French model, the director balked when he found out she starred in American surf films, but Mick Fontaine had pressed the issue to get her this lunch. It was a long shot, but one she needed to take. Her heart quickened and she dabbed nervously at her lipstick. Was it too much? In a panic, she pulled out a compact and began to wipe off a layer with a tissue.

Thierry Valdon was directing a Nouvelle Vague horror film called *L'Étrange Lune*, or *The Strange Moon* in English. The director's career was on a roll, his last three films opening to full theaters and glowing reviews even if they were, as the cab driver had indicated, of a "cult" status that showed in the evenings at the theaters, rather than the matinees.

While Valdon's career was on the rise, hers was on a different path. After four surf films, each script worse than the last, she'd landed a role in the western *The Horse Thief.* The film had been panned, but her performance had gotten mostly good reviews. This led to a role in Jacques de Poulignac's *Through the Lens*, a thriller with Gemma playing the dead mistress. The film was quickly plagued by script and director changes, and the final cut had been so heavily edited that the film was unrecognizable. *Through the Lens* had been widely panned, and as the most recognizable star, she took most of the blame, with one reviewer claiming, "It is good that Gemma Turner spends most of her screen time unconscious."

"It happens," said Mick. "You were the biggest name attached to the film, so you get the brunt of it, but you'll get more parts."

Mick had been wrong.

The embarrassment of that review still stung. Even now, she could recite every line of the worst reviews. She wasn't sure she'd ever been a good actress, but the risks she had taken with her career had backfired, and her self-doubt only managed to thrust her more deeply into Charlie's world, where she could hide. And she did hide for more than a year. Her life was now chaotic, organized around Charlie; his band, the Prince Charmings; and their recording schedule, touring schedule, and partying schedule. She was photographed boarding airplanes and hanging out backstage. The band's partying only made the press worse for her. Four months ago, Mick had warned her that Charlie made it "difficult" for her to be attached to a film. At twenty-two, she was already in danger of being washed up.

The car came to an abrupt stop in front of a café on Rue des Écoles in the Latin Quarter. At first glance, she thought the place was empty, but then she spied a lone man sitting with his back to her behind a pillar. Checking her watch, she was three minutes late.

She took a deep breath and pushed through the doors.

"Pardon," said Gemma.

"You are four minutes late." A vein pulsed in Thierry Valdon's temple.

Sliding into her chair, she looked at her watch and corrected him. "Non. Je suis arrivé trois minutes en retard. Trois." She held up three fingers.

It was well-known that Valdon didn't care for American actresses, rejecting them for leads in most of his films despite some of the most popular being dangled in front of him. A long list of Hollywood ingenues before her had come away from a lunch like this one without a part. And they had all likely been early.

Gemma touched her brow and found, to her horror, that she was sweating, her face flushed from nerves. She tried to steady herself in the cane chair that felt woefully too wobbly. What was she thinking? Had she just corrected Thierry Valdon? Did she just say *trois*? Mick *should* just kill her and put her out of her misery now.

A long silence hung between them while he studied her, his hands folded in front of him and his eyes never blinking. It was unnerving. At one point, she looked away out onto the street, not sure what to do. No one had stared at her this rudely, ever.

The man sitting opposite her was not what she expected. He was younger—forty at most, with jet-black hair tamed by a smooth pomade, one errant lock defying him and heading toward his nose, which was currently flaring with anger. His hazel eyes were a sharp contrast to his thick black brows and dark lashes. She'd read somewhere that his mother had been Spanish and Moroccan, and his father French. Had he been an actor, he'd have played the role of the handsome, swashbuckling, villainous competition to a bland studio actor like Bryan Branch. He was incredibly handsome.

"You have dark circles under your eyes," he said finally, like a verdict, twirling a spoon and watching the rotation. His fingers were elegant and fine boned, like he played the piano.

"I...I was up late last night." Gemma touched her face. She'd thought she'd applied enough pancake makeup to hide any imperfections, and now she regretted wiping off most of her lipstick. Did she look pale?

"Not surprising," he said, catching her eye. "Pain becomes you. Makes you look hungry. Beautiful women can be dull." He waited until the waiter dropped a single menu in front of Gemma and nodded to the man.

His comment felt like a punch in the gut, so she studied her menu intently. Had he just insulted her? Was he implying she was beautiful or dull? Or both? She hadn't thought the inner turmoil inside her had begun to show on her face. Feeling self-conscious and a little dizzy, she looked up at him. Had she missed something in translation?

He tapped lightly on the window with the back of his finger and shifted his gaze to the street. "It was terrible here during the war and then after. While we were occupied, these streets were bare and melancholy. The Germans took from us and gave nothing in return. I came back to Paris in 1946 to find a city as shabby as your grandmother's underwear drawer." People, pulling their coats tight against a windy April day, walked by briskly with briefcases or clutching the hands of children. "The entire city was hungry, many starved to death and looking like walking skeletons. The streets themselves were black with soot, rotten shutters dangled on rusted nails, but look at them now. Everyone on their way to somewhere else. We French are certainly resilient."

"I was born here," she said, hoping that might surprise him, save the lunch, and challenge what was an obvious bias against hiring her. "My mother is French. My father was an American soldier."

"Ah," he said with a stoic nod. "Does your mother miss Paris?"

Gemma leaned forward and tugged at her collar. For more than a year now, she had tried to bring her mother to Europe—to London—for a visit, but her mother refused, likely due to her dislike of Charlie. "She claims not, but I think the idea that she would return to that bleak Paris is too much for her to bear. She's afraid of what she'll find."

"Many people did not come back," he said wistfully, settling in his chair. "They loaded everything and everyone up on trucks. My mother had put me on a train to the Amboise countryside, where I would be safe. I didn't learn my father had been shot as part of the resistance until the war had ended. He died on August 24, 1944. My birthday. Just one more day and he'd have seen the liberation of Paris. Just one day." He placed his hand down on the table, his eyes sharp, the memory gone. He turned his focus to her once again. "Your career is in..." He struggled for the word in English. "Shambles. Oui?"

Gemma was scratching at her neck, feeling it getting warm. If she'd thought the pleasantries would last just a bit longer, she was wrong. Once, she'd been able to charm any director with small talk, but now maybe it was just better to get to the point and bring on the inevitable. "I'm afraid so."

"Why is that?" His head cocked, waiting for a reply.

It was such a direct question that she was taken aback. In Hollywood, no one ever got to the point. Business was handled through intermediaries and bad news softened so much that you didn't often realize your career was over. She'd seen it many times. "Excuse me?"

"Why is your career in shambles?" Valdon nailed the English on this try.

What could she say? That she'd obviously overreached her talent? That the parts offered to her in the surf films were so dull that she couldn't bear to read them anymore, so she'd taken a chance and tried a western and then a thriller? Could she admit to a director that the last film she'd signed up for ended up a mess after editing? You couldn't blame editing; it wasn't professional. The real answer was that she'd foolishly taken chances with her career and her choices had been poor, but she wasn't the sole reason for the failures, although they'd been pinned on her.

"I'm sorry," he said. "I'm being rude."

She didn't disagree; perhaps she should have to be polite, but he wasn't sparing her feelings. "I have pushed myself, Monsieur Valdon, to do better with each film, taken risks. I am proud of the work that I did, but not everyone agrees that my performances were..." She paused with a crack in her voice. "Well, that they were any good." With that, she gazed down at the floor, hoping that he would just end this charade of a job interview and hire Jeanne Moreau instead. She felt herself deflate. It had all been a joke—this meeting, her fame, her entire career.

He leaned over the table toward her and placed his hand on his head. "You know what I think the problem is?"

She shook her head dully, biting her lip, dreading what shortcoming he was about to articulate to her.

"You have *never* had a brilliant director," he said, and his smile was so wide it showed the white teeth of a wolf. There was a hint of an overlap on his front teeth, just enough imperfection to make his entire face memorable.

She looked up, wide-eyed. This was an interesting development, indeed. Her eyebrow rose; she finished his thought. "But with a *brilliant* director..." She let the sentence linger, her chin lifting. Once as a young girl in a dance class, Gemma had been unable to learn the waltz. "No...no...no...," said the frustrated instructor, pointing to her hapless partner. "You are trying to lead; let *him* lead." She'd never understood exactly what the instructor had meant by that observation until this moment.

"Oui," Valdon said. "A *brilliant* director could get the performance of a lifetime from you." His tone was serious now and he drummed his fingers on the table. "Tell me, who was the first director who inspired you? Make it interesting, please. Don't make me regret this."

"Jean Cocteau," she said a little too quickly. What she wasn't expecting was the look of disdain on his face that came next.

"Why on *earth* would you pick him?" He leaned back on the chair and folded his arms like a pensive professor. "Not John Ford or Hitchcock?"

As she sank in the cane chair, her face fell. Every time she felt she'd achieved a connection with this man, she blew it. This role was too important to lose, and the idea of not measuring up to someone worthwhile like Thierry Valdon was unbearable to her right now. She could feel her eyes welling up, and she blinked hard to clear them. She'd hoped this lunch would be a metamorphosis. There would be no returning to London—to Charlie—and becoming *that* Gemma Turner again. Searching Valdon's face, she tried to read what it was that he wanted from her. As an actress—as a woman—she'd been good at this once.

"*La Belle et la Bête* made me want to be an actress. Look at what Cocteau did for Josette Day. He brought out a fabulous performance from her."

His head nodded slowly in a reluctant agreement.

Gemma smiled demurely. "Can I confess something to you?" Mick would be furious at what she was about to say next. He always warned her that she overreached.

He cocked his head, intrigued. "Of course."

She leaned in like she was telling him a secret. "I wrote a little in college, nothing like what you've done, of course." She lowered her eyes at this, intentionally deferring to him. "But I wrote my own version of *La Belle et la Bête*. This time, Belle was the beast."

"You write?" His brow furrowed. "Belle as the beast. That's clever."

This was dangerous ground. She had to be interesting to him without being threatening. "Un peu." She held her fingers together. "It is hard to imagine someone would love a beastly woman, but I love stories that push against the grain. That's precisely what you do with your films, Monsieur Valdon."

She made a grand gesture with her hands, and she could see him preen, nearly expanding with pride right in front of her.

"When I was a boy, we did not get television as quickly as you Americans," he said, raising his finger to make a point. "My friends and I would drive to Tours to watch your filmmakers. Many here in France hate the American directors like Nicholas Ray or Orson Welles. But not me. I rather enjoyed *Citizen Kane*," he said, shrugging. "Funny that you should find inspiration in Cocteau and not one of your own." Without missing a beat, he nodded to the menu. "The duck confit is excellent."

She noticed small tufts of black hair peeking under the cuff of his sleeve. He was so unlike Charlie, who had no angles to his cherubic face and soft blond curls. There were thousands of little details about Thierry Valdon that she was noticing: the snag in his sweater, the perfect nose, the too-busy brows. He caught her eye, and she saw something unexpected in his expression. Thierry Valdon was *nervous.* As an actress, you did get used to jittery fans, but the idea that he seemed flummoxed by her came as a shock.

"You keep doing that." She squeezed the lemon into her water with the newfound confidence of someone who felt the conversation tipping in their favor.

"What?"

"Looking at me." Her eyes moved from the lemon to him.

"That's hardly odd. I called you to lunch precisely to *look* at you, Mademoiselle Turner. I am a filmmaker, a visual artist, and your face was plastered on billboards throughout Paris. I would think you'd be used to it."

The truth was that after all the years of acting and modeling, Gemma had gotten used to all kinds of looks from men, but his soft stare wasn't base, like those of the men who whistled to her on the street or even the photographers who hoped to bed her after a shoot. Or even Charlie, whose hunger for her was almost animal-like. No, his was a gentle gaze, a cerebral hope to connect with her. "You make me nervous," she said with a shrug, peering back at him with the same intensity, the honesty of what she'd just admitted to him being given like an offering to a god.

It was the silence that followed that caused Gemma's stomach to flutter. She placed her hand behind her neck, feeling her cool palm and realizing that she was warm, despite the fresh air that accompanied every door opening in the drafty bistro.

"For the film, I was thinking your hair should be a copper color."

Gemma touched her strawberry-blond hair. It was straight like her mother's, and she was lucky that it was in fashion. As a child, her mother had made her sleep with pin curls and cut it short so she would resemble Shirley Temple. When Gemma had gotten old enough, she'd let it grow down past her shoulders in rebellion. It was thick and heavy, but the color had never been touched, even during the beach films where she thought she'd be asked to lighten it to a sunny blond. For a moment she tried to imagine herself with copper hair.

The waiter returned and cut an awkward silence. Gemma ordered the duck confit.

"I'm trying to get the most vivid color *directly* out of the camera, none of this post-production bullshit," he said, continuing the conversation where they'd left off. "The costumes are sapphire blues and chartreuse greens. A copper color would look magnificent."

No one had ever consulted with her about such matters prior to being offered a role. Directors tended to send orders through the agent, never dealing directly with an actor. From the sound of it, Thierry Valdon *was* offering the part to her. Gemma's pulse quickened.

"I am doing something a little different with this film," he said, leaning in toward her like he didn't want anyone in the empty restaurant to overhear their conversation. "Like you suggested, I'm going against the grain. I'm trying my hand at a horror film—*L'Étrange Lune* it is called, working title. It is a vampire film, you could say. The vampires are metaphorical, of course, but the villagers don't know that."

"Metaphorical?"

"The vampire represents something else—their inner desires and darkness." One loose piece of hair fell onto his cheek. It was long and sat against his cheek, like a rococo swirl.

Her laugh came out like a snort. "I am aware what a *metaphor* means, Monsieur Valdon." He must think she was stupid, but she was used to directors thinking actresses were stupid. Yet, Gemma thought the concept of this film sounded strange. "I'm just wondering how it applies to a New Wave horror film. Do you have a script that I can see?"

"Please." He lifted his hand up to stop her from speaking. "La Nouvelle Vague, not *New Wave*," he said, mocking her American accent, making her sound like John Wayne. "The film depicts danger from invasion. It doesn't take much to see the analogy between my vampires and the occupation. Filming begins in June in Amboise."

Two dishes of duck confit came so quickly that Gemma felt sure they must have been ordered before she'd arrived. It was a small thing, but she felt manipulated. That Thierry Valdon had ordered for her did not sit well with her. "A *script*, Monsieur Valdon?"

He shook his head and began to cut his meat. "Given you write, I would *love* to have your feedback on the shooting script."

"You would?" Gemma's jaw went slack with surprise. No one. No writer, no director in Hollywood or Pinewood Studios had ever, once asked for her thoughts on anything creative. She was like a doll pulled from a shelf and placed in a scene, nothing more.

"Of course," he said. "We French are very collaborative. Mind you, the script is not final, mine never are, but I have notes that I'll send over to you. Where are you? George V?"

She nodded, speechless and unable to breathe. Was Thierry Valdon not only offering her the role, but suggesting that she give him feedback on his script? For a moment, she could see the credits rolling with her name attached to the film, not just as an actress, but as one of its *writers*. "Are you sure you mean it? You really want my ideas?"

His laugh was like a rumble, deep and thunderous. "That is exactly what Nouvelle Vague is all about. Not this Hollywood patriarchal nonsense with the studio bosses demanding those awful tropes. No, your ideas are welcome on my set. I warn you, though: François let me look at one of his scripts last year. I cannot work that way . . . everything done to the line and the detailed notes." He made a face. "It isn't creative. We have a daily script that we're working from, but I want to see the character of Gisele Dumas come from *you*. None of this faithful quoting of it, please. It isn't Ecclesiastes." Valdon cocked his head, awaiting her reply.

Gemma realized the François that he'd just casually mentioned was the director François Truffaut. She did, however, need a script, especially if the film was to be done in French. But she was thrilled. This man *wanted* her for this film.

"I must address something uncomfortable. We have already established that you have not been working lately," he said between bites.

"I moved to Europe. I've been modeling. Dior." She was unsure where the conversation was going.

He waved his hand at her. "That's not quite true, is it? Everyone in Paris has seen the Dior ad, Mademoiselle Turner, but that was more than a year ago. The fact is that you have not worked because of the boyfriend," said Valdon, gravely looking down at his plate as he spoke as though he needed to gather the courage to say what came next. "Will he be a problem? His reputation precedes him."

"No," she said, irritated that Charlie had wormed his way into her professional conversation. "He won't be a problem."

"We'll be filming at my house. I want to make it clear that you will be staying there but *he* will not." His eyes met hers for affirmation.

"Understood."

He took two more bites and pointed his fork at her. "I won't have you being late, either. American actresses think the clock suits them. I won't have it. You were *four* minutes late today." He held up his fingers. "Quatre."

Before she could reply, Valdon suddenly stood, almost shaking himself, his mood darkening. "This has been a most surprising lunch, Mademoiselle Turner, but I'm sorry to say that I have a previous engagement that I fear requires my attention. It cannot be helped."

So jarring was the abrupt shift in conversation that she stared at him slack-jawed, holding his gaze for a beat too long. The air was thick between them. To her surprise, she found that she had been holding her breath. From the look of shock registering on his face, she could see that he felt this connection, too, like static. Somewhere in the distance a clanging metal sound of silverware could be heard from the kitchen.

Valdon struggled feverishly to put his coat on, never once taking his eyes off her. He pushed his hair back and there was a sheen of sweat and the moment was charged. Once the garment was on his shoulders, he seemed out of breath, like it was agony to be in her presence for one moment longer, and yet he did not turn to leave.

"Oh," she said aloud as the revelation hit her that with this film, this man was about to become the most important man in her life. Thoughts like these were silly. The man sharing lunch with her was a known womanizer. Four years ago, he'd even left his first wife with two children for the actress Manon Marquise, now Manon Valdon. She'd heard rumors about him and yet somehow never thought they would pertain to her. In her naivete, Gemma believed that she would be immune to his charms. This had been a dire miscalculation. The pull of him was so strong it shocked her completely. This man wanted her ideas. He wanted to collaborate with her. No other director in Hollywood had ever treated her like this—like a peer. It was intoxicating, and she found herself breathless and dizzy, the room moving. She could barely breathe.

"I find myself speechless," he said with a nervous laugh. "I really must go. I'm sorry. It cannot be avoided."

"Of course," she said, a sad smile forming in the corners of her lips.

He walked away but turned and placed his hands on the back of the chair. "I don't agree with the critics. You were marvelous in that thriller. The film was an editing nightmare. Anyone with any knowledge of film can see that." He bowed quickly as though he were a man from another time when formality was the fashion, then he turned back toward the door. "I'll send the version of the shooting script I have finished to your hotel room." He pointed to the table. "The bill is settled, so please, stay and enjoy yourself."

And then he was gone, the scent of his soap lingering as a wave of cold air rushed into the room.

Gemma's face flushed. She felt like she'd just been abandoned by a lover, and the empty chair across from her made her ache for his presence again. She reached over and touched his dirty plate, anything that still had his mark. Within minutes, the waiter came by and removed the abandoned dish and scraped the nonexistent crumbs from Valdon's place setting as though he'd never been there at all. Except the director had left some indelible feeling with her, like an imprint.

In the distance, she heard a phone ringing. Returning to the table, the waiter looked stricken. "I'm sorry, mademoiselle, but there is a rather angry man from London on the phone for you. He claims to have called every restaurant in Montparnasse looking for Monsieur Valdon and his lunch guest."

Gemma closed her eyes, feeling fury well up inside her. How dare Charlie call around looking for her like some errant teenager? Had Thierry Valdon stayed a moment longer, he would have heard "the boyfriend" was on phone, and it would have ruined everything. She could imagine what Valdon would have done had he heard this news. Certainly, that would have ended her talks with him for the role. She exhaled and gripped the table, her heart pounding.

But luck—or fate—had intervened.

At this point, Gemma didn't care if the script that Valdon sent over was rubbish, although she doubted it would be. She was going to Amboise to star in this film.

She followed the waiter to a wall phone like a prisoner to the gallows. Wearily, she put the receiver to her ear, no doubt who was on the other line. "Charlie?"

His voice quavered with anger. "You get your ass on that airplane and get back here right now, or I swear I'll jump. Do you hear me?"

She pictured him on a ledge in the Savoy hotel back in London, leaping from the Monet Suite—oh, the poor Monet Suite—the hotel's most famous room, which had resembled a junkyard when she'd left for Paris. Yet, she doubted that he'd ever jump from the hotel balcony onto the Embankment below. Charlie was never alone, and he wasn't alone now. Being his girlfriend meant tolerating the women that he claimed "never mattered." All the girls—so many of them—had no idea what it was like to be day in, day out with Charlie. In the end, she thought that he was correct: None of them mattered, including her. She'd just deluded herself that she was different. Beyond himself, no one else mattered to Charlie Hicks.

"I told you. I will be back in the morning."

"Now," he barked. "I want you here, now."

"Tomorrow," she said, holding on to the word for dear life. She knew there were flights back to London in the afternoon, and the old Gemma would have taken one just to quell this man's tantrum.

"Now," he said, slamming down the phone.

When she got back to her hotel, there was an envelope waiting for her at the front desk. Inside were seventy pages of *L'Étrange Lune* with an address and date. Thumbing through the pages, she wondered what on earth shooting a film with someone like Valdon would be like. She closed the door to her room and removed the receiver from the phone.

Throwing herself on the bed, she kicked off her shoes and opened the script to the first page.

2

Gemma Turner
April 14, 1968
The Savoy hotel, London

Gemma Turner crossed the lobby with its checkerboard polished floor, tugging at the black sleeveless belted jumper she'd worn, hoping the skirt length was considered acceptable to gain her admittance to the Savoy hotel's elevators. The hotel had hosted plenty of kings and queens, both real and movie royalty, but the groovy sixties had not yet made their way to the landmark known for its famously strict dress code, stuffy French cuisine, and period furniture. Rather than being seen as a relic, though, it seemed like every bohemian rock star or actor was angling to grace its hallways, as if entrance legitimized them. It was lore that the Beatles had once been turned away at the door for improper dress. This legend was very much on her mind as she pulled the skirt below her knee. "Suite 618," she said to the elevator attendant, who recognized her.

"The Monet Suite, of course, Ms. Turner," he said with a nod.

With its stunning views of the Waterloo Bridge and the River Thames, suite 618 had once been the painter Claude Monet's two-month refuge from France. Now both the hotel and its prestigious suite, along with three others on the sixth floor, were the temporary home to the Prince Charmings, who had taken up residence while recording their fourth album. Despite the band's moniker, the Prince Charmings were anything but.

Charlie had called four times that morning, ranting. The band's fourth album was a mess, and everyone involved—the manager, the butler, the other band members, as well the guests he met on the hotel elevator—were "absolute arses." Gemma was to get to the Savoy immediately to "do something about it."

So she'd flown back from Paris that morning, stopping briefly at their apartment in Mayfair to change her clothes. She had no idea what she was supposed to "do" about the politics around their album, but she was here now. Charlie never once asked her about her meeting with Thierry Valdon, as though it was an unfortunate footnote to their relationship.

Before she stepped onto the elevator, she spied the pay phone at the end of the lobby. "I need to make a phone call first," she said to the attendant. Pulling the door to the pay phone around her so no one would hear her conversation, she dialed Mick's number in Los Angeles and reversed the charges. It would be morning on the West Coast. As soon as he answered, she could hear the elation in his voice.

"Gemma dear! Glad you called. Just got off the phone with Valdon's people. The part is yours," he said in his nasal tenor, the sound of seagulls in the background making her homesick for California. "They're sending over the contract tomorrow. The money is about half your last offer, but these French directors are not flush with cash like the studios here."

"I understand," she said, closing her eyes tightly, almost bursting with excitement. Gemma leaned against the booth's wall to steady herself. Only when her heart missed a beat did she realize that she'd been holding her breath. She'd hoped that the part was hers, but to hear it from Mick made it real. "You're sure the part is mine? You're sure?"

"It's yours," he said. "Of course, you'll need to be available for press in the next few weeks, but I told them you'd be ready. For Thierry Valdon to choose an American actress is big news, so you'll need to make the rounds to the papers here and there. Valdon's thrilled your French is fluent. Filming starts in June?"

"He mentioned that."

"That's seven weeks from now." There was an edge to Mick's voice, a lift at the end that meant he wanted to be sure she got the point.

"I can count, Mick." She tugged nervously on the metal cord with her finger.

"When are you going to tell Charlie?"

"Not right away," said Gemma. "When I tell him, I have to be prepared to go to Paris immediately."

Mick sighed audibly. "That would be wise. Don't let him screw this up for you, kid. I don't think I have to tell you this, but I will anyway. The parts have dried up. It wasn't you, but the director of that last film isn't going to be blaming himself for that mess. It's just the way it goes. Easier to blame the starlet."

"I know," she said, bristling at his comment, even if it was true.

"Do you?" he asked. "I'd hate to see you waiting tables or answering phones at a doctor's office or worse. You gals don't do well when you fall. You understand me? I know you think you can come back here and do the surf films again, but you're not eighteen anymore, and Suzy has replaced you. The studio loves her. She does what they tell her to do."

The Suzy that Mick was referring to was Suzy Hutton, a sweet girl and a good friend who had played her kid sister in two of the beach films. It had been an easy transition to give Suzy's character, Lacey, her own film spin-off when Gemma didn't return.

"The problem with you, Gemma, is you're impulsive and impatient. We had all the time in the world to build your career, but you wanted more and you wanted it fast. I mean, stop with this writing thing as well. You aren't a writer."

"I understand," she said through gritted teeth, knowing he'd be furious that she'd talked about her writing to Thierry Valdon. She was a writer, and Thierry Valdon said he welcomed her ideas. Rather than Hollywood, perhaps the Nouvelle Vague movement in Paris was a place where she would finally be accepted. "Thank you, Mick."

"Always," he said.

After she'd hung up the phone, she considered going back to the apartment that she shared with Charlie and packing everything up—the urge to flee to Paris so great. She had a little savings and had been good with her earnings, but Mick's warning had been dire. If this film with Valdon failed, then she would need to save all the money she had for her future, and renting an apartment in Paris for seven weeks would put a dent in those funds. No, for now, she needed to stay put in London.

Gemma steeled herself and took the elevator to the sixth floor. Outside the suite, she took a deep breath and placed her hand on the door for a moment to steady herself before knocking.

A weary-looking butler let her into the room. No doubt the man was earning his wages tonight. Despite his best efforts, the room was littered with ashtrays and empty beer and Tanqueray bottles that he now attempted to gather. That the butler's name was Serge and that he could play bass was all the room seemed to be talking about. Each time Serge picked up a bottle, it was knocked out of his hand, and he was reluctantly led over to the bass guitar to demonstrate his skills.

Gemma hated these childish pranks. There could be a hidden guitar savant tearing tickets at the train station, but more often, it was fun for them to see how bad a guitar player or drummer could be. It was a cruel game, and Gemma hated the lot of them for it. She could see Serge was in agony and that he needed to clean the suite to keep his job.

They'd been scheduled to record at drummer Gary Wainwright's country house in Salisbury. Unfortunately, he'd fallen asleep with a lit Parliament and caught his mattress on fire, and within seven minutes, the blaze had consumed most of the second floor and, most importantly, his recording studio, which had been his gem. Now the Prince Charmings were cutting the album at the very corporate EMI Studios and camping out here, searching for inspiration.

This change in plans had everyone in a bad mood. The record label had placated the furious hotel manager temporarily, but they were on borrowed time. The foursome had smuggled a full drum kit into one of the rooms, placing a mattress against the wall in a lame attempt to soundproof the walls. Guests complained about the noise, so the hotel cleared the entire sixth floor at the record company's expense.

The root cause of all this angst and bad behavior was that the band felt that their fourth album was pure shit—or "shite," as Charlie Hicks kept declaring as though he were British. That Charlie now used terms like "shite," "arses," and "knickers" amused Gemma. The very American lead guitar player hailed from rural Virginia, yet he adopted an over-the-top British accent to try to fit in with his British band members.

On the dining table was a record player, and Gemma recognized Hank Williams's *Jambalaya*. It was a strange combination: hard-drinking country spinning on the player while a British butler catered to a group of children dressed as grown men.

"Gemmy!" Gemma heard a voice behind her and turned to find Charlie Hicks, lanky frame and all, pushing through the crowd with two young girls hanging off his arms. With Gemma's arrival, she could see the women—Tamsin and Penny—glance at each other to calculate what her presence meant for them. Should they stay? Was this party good enough?

" 'Bout time you got here," said Tamsin, her chin out. Tamsin, the one with the boyish pixie, and her sidekick, Penny, all blond ringlets and cupid-faced, were never far from Charlie these days.

Dressed head to toe in black, Charlie resembled a beatnik cowboy, with his bell-bottomed jeans and western shirt, cowboy boots and sunglasses. If he'd left the Savoy, Gemma doubted he could get back through its front doors looking like that. Even his long, dirty-blond hair was shaped into a loose pompadour like his idol, Johnny Cash. When he was three years old, a dog had ripped into Charlie's face, leaving a scar along his eyebrow that curved downward past his bright blue eyes like an upside-down letter *C*. It was clear that the dog had nearly succeeded in removing Charlie's left eye. Like Mick Jagger's too-big smile, the scar *made* Charlie's look uniquely his own, a masculine trophy that contrasted him sharply with Wren's polished veneer. He had the face of a cherub—full cheeks, perfect heart-shaped mouth, tousled blond hair, and that "magic" that actors and musicians had where they lit up the screen.

It was this magic that had captivated Niles Tarkenton, who had been so impressed with the kid playing Fats Domino onstage in a run-down ballroom in New Jersey that he had called Wren Atticus from a pay phone in the lobby, holding up the receiver so his vocalist could hear for himself.

With Wren Atticus's honey-smooth voice, he had range enough to handle anything thrown his way, but he was no songwriter, and everything he penned sounded like Beatles imitations.

In what would become one of the greatest communication errors in rock history, Niles mistook "sounds great" from Wren on a garbled international phone line to mean he agreed that Charlie Hicks should be added to the band. The misunderstanding between the two would be something that haunted the group for years. Convinced the tall American was exactly the jolt his band needed to stand out, Niles signed Charlie on the spot. While Tarkenton had been right about Charlie's talent, in the end, he'd been terribly wrong about where he'd placed him, and it had cost him. The band had fired their manager at the beginning of the fourth album, replacing them with Kenny Kilgore, whose only experience had been managing a restaurant before taking on the band.

A lit cigarette dangled from Charlie's lips as he navigated a sea of heavy, cluttered furniture to get to her. To her horror, Gemma didn't see an ashtray anywhere near him. Spying the fine rug beneath him, Gemma rushed over to grab one from the side table and slid it under his hand just as a giant ash cluster fell from the Parliament. He looked confused and then sucked the cigarette hard, extinguishing it on the tray. Charlie draped his arm around Gemma's neck and kissed her temple, drawing her close. He was wobbly and drunk. "The girls and I were wondering when you'd get here."

At the mention of "the girls," Gemma halted. She did not want to be compared to groupies, even American ones, *especially* not American ones, and she doubted the two of them had been wondering when she was going to arrive. Is this what Charlie thought she was? A groupie? He didn't seem to regard her as the artist equal to him, but then again why should he? She'd let her own career fall apart. Would he have done the same for her? Move across the world to cater to her every whim? She knew the answer to that.

"It's been a gas," said Penny, taking a drag of her own cigarette and affecting some type of accent to announce her sophistication. "Charlie's songs are brilliant."

"Are they?" Gemma raised her eyebrow. His last song he'd written for the album had been a ballad, "And Yet God Has Not Said a Word," a take on the last line of Robert Browning's "Porphyria's Lover," a macabre poem about a man who chokes his lover by strangling her with her own hair.

"Had you been here, you'd have heard them," said Penny, like proximity to Charlie had made her a musical authority. The longer Tamsin and Penny lingered in the circle, the bolder they became.

"My girl." Charlie held on to her, not only to hold himself up but also like she was some trophy.

Gemma hated it when he called her that. She wasn't *anyone's* girl.

There were about ten people in the room tonight. On the extra-long beige sofa, Gary Wainwright was deep in conversation with filmmaker Topaz Maroni, who had been rumored to be shopping a documentary of the band to a major Hollywood studio. Opposite the sofa in a wing chair sat an odd man wearing sunglasses and dressed like Lord Byron, who watched Charlie with a curious intensity. She recalled that Wren was working with an occultist and thought that must be him. With his period dress, she wondered if he was an apparition of Monet himself.

Gary Wainwright's very pregnant girlfriend, Minerva Smythe, had positioned herself sitting sideways on the decorative chair next to the drapes. Minerva's short, blond geometric haircut was in sharp contrast to Gemma's own long, flowing strawberry-blond locks.

"Oh, thank God, you're here." Minerva looked up and waved her fingers. "I was so fucking bored I was forced to talk to Kenny. *Kenny*," said Minerva with a whisper and a look of disdain. Gemma leaned down and kissed the woman's head. "I'm so puffy, Gems." As if to demonstrate, she lifted her skirt to the top of her thigh and poked it, the indent leaving a white mark that lingered on her skin.

"You're due next week," said Gemma. "What do you expect?"

"I thought I'd have a house to have a baby in, not some ridiculous hotel room. I'm thinking of going home to my parents' house after I give birth."

Gemma had a sinking feeling that Minerva's departure, however temporary she thought it to be, would be permanent. She loved Minerva, but women cycled through the band, their babies, too. Gary already had two other children with another model who lived in Scotland. The impermanence of the group was almost part of the appeal. Like surfers, the people in the Monet Suite were riding a moment and squeezing every drop of fame and excess before it bottomed out. The wise ones knew it would end someday. For the others, the moment was just too intoxicating, like a disorienting fog. Yet, Gemma had a feeling that a toll would ultimately be extracted for this much living.

"Who is that?" asked Gemma.

"Who?" Miranda looked around.

"The guy who looks like he's a funeral director."

Miranda leaned forward to grab a lobster toast. "What did you say?"

"Oh, nothing," said Gemma, studying the curious-looking man with his out-of-place overcoat and long ringlets. Most of Wren's friends fell into this camp. Poor Wren, the heartthrob with his auburn hair and high cheekbones, the light lyricist, the poet, likening himself to Keats, Baudelaire, and Verlaine, and Charlie's greatest foil. What had been supposed to be a collaboration of Charlie filling out Wren's two-minute melodies into more sophisticated music had now become dueling camps.

The discord between Charlie and Wren had produced a handful of catchy studio-led songs. Two years and two number one songs later, and the band was famous despite themselves, but Charlie was tired of being another cover band of sorts, so he began pushing the group musically, trying new styles from America—blues and country. Haunted by the empty ballrooms they'd played early on, Wren, ever the businessman, wanted to keep doing what fans—and studio executives—expected.

"They came to blows twice today," said Minerva with a nod to Wren.

"They need to tour," said Gemma. "Too long in the studio."

"There *is* something to them performing live, isn't there?" agreed Minerva. "It's like a pressure valve that releases all this tension."

Gemma thought Minerva had a point. Time away made the foursome nostalgic for the genius they shared, that rare "magic" that made their band—any band for that matter—work. Gemma had been with them when they listened to the last album, *Flame of Night*, and she'd seen their pride create an amnesia at how hard it had been to record it.

"I think recording an album is like giving birth," said Gemma. "You must forget the pain of birth, or you'll never do it again."

Minerva laughed, rubbing her belly. "I'll let you know how the two compare."

A sound came from the corner of the room. It was a simple A chord. Music was always playing somewhere in the room; that was something that she'd had to get used to. Gemma's world had been quiet, but Charlie filled all the spaces with music or chatter. In the middle of dinner, the meal could disintegrate into a jam session because someone got an idea, but this was a more determined organization of notes. Everyone turned toward the sound at the window.

Charlie had a dining room chair at an angle, and his long legs were stretched to the windowsill. Expertly, he began the first few chords of a song she hadn't heard before.

Your entire life is packed in little suitcases on our lawn

You think it will be easy for me to get along when you're gone

The strings of the electric guitar bent and whirred as his wrist furiously wrestled with the fretboard. Rapt, the entire room went silent. Watching Charlie Hicks perform still gave Gemma chills and always had the unfortunate effect of making her more forgiving of his bad behavior. She couldn't do this again. Time away from him had allowed her to see him clearly. The fact was that everyone in his life—from his bandmates to his manager to his girlfriends both past and present—was only as good as they were *useful* to him. Everything Charlie did was transactional. Once she'd realized his behavior, she couldn't go back. Never again could she trust that his affections were true. Shaking her head, she willed herself out of romantic memories of Charlie's performances lit against the stage.

But God, he was good. She'd remembered wanting to be that close to genius, hoping it would rub off on her. Instead, it had absorbed her. Gary Wainwright slid off the sofa and cleared the coffee table with one sweep. Then, watching Charlie carefully, he began to keep the beat like the furniture was a bongo drum.

Charlie's arms moved fluidly across the guitar's neck, his mop of hair falling over his face as he was totally immersed in this intimate concert. Wainwright joined in the song's chorus of what Gemma now knew was titled "Now You're Gone." This morning, Wren had gotten the producer to cut this *very* song from the new album. That decision had been a mistake. Hell, everyone in the room knew it was a mistake, and Charlie was going to prove it.

She turned to see Wren seething, his hands in his pockets and his eyes fixed on Charlie. There was a tally kept between the two as to how many songs penned by each made it onto the album. This song was beautiful—more beautiful than the others she'd heard and more powerful than anything that came from Wren's clean and tidy songwriting style. If it made it onto the album, it would be an instant hit. It would redefine the band, and everyone in the room right now knew it.

There was something political about what Charlie was doing. Over in the corner, nursing a gin and tonic, was an EMI executive talking to a music critic. If he saw that the rest of the room loved the song, then it put Wren in an awkward position—an outsider in his own band.

Gemma and Wren locked eyes. His face mirrored her own. While she wanted to be loyal to Charlie, she thought that maybe she disliked Charlie as much—or more—than Wren. In a strange way, this unspoken secret was a bond between them. He sighed and turned toward her, stopping just past her.

"It's a good song, Wren," she said in a whisper. "You know that. Let him have this one."

"It just isn't our sound, Gems. It's not a Prince Charmings' song, it's a Charlie Hicks song—we're all just along for the ride, aren't we, luv." Looking over at Charlie, Wren shook his head. "And you can be brilliant without being an asshole about it."

Wren walked out into the hallway, shutting the door behind him.

Charlie was bent over the chair now, lost in his own world of a screaming guitar solo that he reined in and returned to the chorus, Gary beating on the antique furniture of the Monet Suite. The song was mesmerizing. Surprisingly, Gemma's throat caught.

The guitar went silent, and Gemma heard the power go out on the amp. It was Topaz Maroni who began to clap first. "Fucking brilliant, Charlie," she said, whistling. Gemma noticed the music executive looked uncomfortable. Charlie had made his point.

Gemma made her way over to sit on a stool in front of the sofa. Within minutes, Charlie sat down behind her, uncomfortably pawing at his hair, his blue eyes animated. He reached for her hand, and she felt his weathered fingers, scarred from years of guitar strings. If she was telling Charlie about the film in France, she needed to be ready to leave London immediately after. She'd give him these last few weeks before everything changed.

They sat together watching Kenny, Topaz, Minerva, Russ, Gary, and even the two American girls settle into an evening of conversation and drinking.

Circling the room was a photographer with a Nikon camera around his neck, snapping some shots of the band in their clusters of conversation. She'd heard his name was Rick Nash and he was in from the States to shoot the album cover. His face was familiar, and she had a nostalgic pang for Laurel Canyon, where she thought she'd run into him a few times.

There was an ache for Los Angeles right now, where she'd drawn energy. Almost two years ago, in the middle of playing a set at the Whisky a Go Go, Charlie spied Gemma, standing in the back row of the audience. He'd stopped the song, "Run for Cover," and pointed to her, asking for her name. The entire audience turned in waves to face her, waiting for her reply. Gemma felt herself do something she'd never done—swoon. Charlie Hicks—*the* Charlie Hicks—bad boy of the Prince Charmings, had stopped his number one hit to simply get *her* name. It was the most romantic thing that anyone had ever done for her. And he waited, quieting both the band and the audience until she said, "Gemma Turner," their eyes locking.

"I think I'm in love, Gemma Turner," he said, his crooked smile growing wider.

Now she felt an uncomfortable tug, a premonition of sorts that she was seeing the end of something. Not just that she was leaving, but that there was a larger ending, circling and looming. To her surprise, this thought gave her a great pang of sadness.

Back and forth, the band shared the same stories she'd heard dozens of times, and in the middle of a conversation, one of them would get up and grab an acoustic guitar as an idea came to them. A whiff of desperation hung in the air as they clung together tightly that night, their egos thinking they were more than the group, but worried that the music wouldn't be there *this* time. Each member knew that magic was hard to re-create with another band; sometimes it only struck once.

Someone laughed, and Gemma turned her head just as Rick Nash snapped a photo, the unmistakable click and flash directed her way. She remembered being bothered by the suddenness of the photo, fearing she hadn't been properly posed for it and that he had caught her totally off guard.

She felt a presence and looked up to find the man she thought to be the occultist standing behind her. As he leaned down, his round sunglasses lowered enough for her to see his eyes, which were a strange amber color. His voice was soft. "You're making the right decision."

Gemma's face fell, puzzled. "I don't know what you mean—"

"Don't you?" He laughed, throwing his head back, letting his brown ringlets fall around his shoulders. In one quick movement, he was gone. Gemma struggled to get up from her seat, and by the time she turned, she could see him walking through the door with a nod to Serge.

"Wait," she called.

Stepping out into the hallway, she found it empty.

A giggle came from the corner nearest the service elevator. It was Charlie with the girls—Tamsin and Penny.

"Hey, Gems," he said lazily, like it wasn't any big deal, but it was clear she'd caught them. Tamsin was wiping her lips.

"We were just telling Charlie how great the song was," said Penny.

Gemma focused on Charlie, who was sore that she hadn't immediately come over to him to rave about the song. "Did you see a man come out here?"

At the suggestion that Gemma was looking for a man, Charlie bristled, the irony of the situation never occurring to him. "No," he said sharply as his eyes darted down the hall.

"No one has come out but you." Tamsin rolled her eyes.

"I just saw him," said Gemma. "That occultist that Wren is working with."

Serge came out behind her, struggling with a bag of empty beer bottles.

"You just saw him," said Gemma, startling Serge.

"I saw who?" Serge dropped the bag.

"The man with the long hair and the black suit. He just passed you a minute ago at the door."

Serge looked back and forth from Charlie, Tamsin, and Penny to Gemma. "I'm sorry," said Serge. "There was no man."

3

Gemma Turner
May 10, 1968
The Savoy hotel, London

An announcement in the *Daily Mail* forced Gemma to tell Charlie about *L'Étrange Lune* earlier than she'd expected. He responded by taking his prized Fender and smashing it over the antique walnut coffee table in the center of the Monet Suite. When he'd finished destroying the rather sturdy table, he took his weapon and tossed it on the floor. Gemma stared at the instrument, its neck severed and hard body in splinters. Instantly, she dropped to her knees to pick up the shattered guitar parts with no fear for her own safety.

In the corner, Charlie composed himself, straightening the errant blond lock that had fallen across his eye in his fury. Preening like a rooster, he crossed the room, then focused on her. "How could you be so selfish?"

"*Me?*" Gemma snorted, gesturing toward the remnants of the table. "What have you done? I just want to work again, Charlie. I should be able to do that and be with you. It shouldn't be a choice. You're making it a choice."

"Jesus Christ." It was Wren's voice behind her as he surveyed the damage. "You've definitely gone and gotten us kicked out of here now, you stupid, bloody bastard." His tone was acidic. "I didn't think it was possible for you to be any more idiotic than you are, Charlie. Clearly, I was wrong."

"My old lady's leaving," said Charlie, pointing at her as though Wren wouldn't know her otherwise.

"Can't say I blame her," said Wren, shooting Gemma a look of sympathy before crouching down and helping her pick up a piece of the Fender. "Shame. Nice fucking guitar, too."

"She's going to France to work for some fucking frog on a stupid film," bellowed Charlie, half on the verge of tears. "I'm sure she's sleeping with him."

Fury welled up inside her, and Gemma stood, tossing bits of the guitar neck back onto the floor. "Of course, that must be it." Her arms waved dramatically. "It would never be my talent, would it?" She met Wren's eyes, and something in them told her that he, too, would run like hell if he could.

Charlie managed a snort. "Talent?"

Gemma felt like she'd been kicked. "How dare you," she spat.

Charlie paced in front of the window. "How *was* your last film, Gems? Huh?"

"Asshole." It was Wren's voice, a murmur.

"She's gone and ruined the entire album now," said Charlie, kicking the coffee table with his steel-toed American boots, a footwear accessory that Wren detested. "I can't create now."

"What will we do?" said Wren sarcastically under his breath, finally standing and stepping back.

"You keep tossing out my songs, which are better than anything you've ever done. Admit it." Charlie's eyes went back and forth between them. "You two are a pair. Both of you, nothing but has-beens." Wren looked down at the floor. Then Charlie turned toward

Gemma with a low, rumbling fury that told Gemma to back up and head toward the door. "And you."

By the time Gemma backed herself to where she was within an arm's reach of the doorknob, Kenny Kilgore was in the room, trying to placate both Charlie and Wren. A frantic knock startled Gemma, and she was nearly hit by the door swinging wide open to reveal the furious manager of the Savoy. What happened next was a screaming match that was chaotic enough for Gemma to slip out of the room unnoticed and down the service elevator. The last thing she heard was Wren screaming, "You'll be the ruination of us all."

Later, when she knew Charlie would be at the studio, she'd gone back to the apartment in Mayfair and packed her things, which amounted to three Louis Vuitton luggage pieces, gifts from the company for an ad she had done for them last year.

Before she left, she sat on the sofa heavily, overcome with emotion. Placing her head in her hands, she looked around the apartment. Was he right? At twenty-two, was she already a "has-been"?

"No," she said, standing. "He'll see. They'll all see. This next role will change everything for me."

That night, Mick booked her in a London hotel far away from the Savoy. In contrast to the Monet Suite, her room was so quiet that she could hear the clock ticking. A wave of loneliness struck her, and she cradled the phone in her lap before deciding to call Suzy Hutton in Los Angeles.

"Oh my god!" the voice on the other end squealed. "I was just thinking about you. I have so much to tell you. So, I have a new film I'm shooting right now. Have you heard about it? It's about a girl who goes to college and falls for the son of her professor who is terribly mean—of course she has no idea that he's the son. It's really, really funny. They've paired me with William Way, do you remember him? He played the motorcycle gang member in *Thunder Beach* with us.

The Irish-looking kid who they'd given the bad dye job? His hair was black like Eddie Munster, remember?"

"I—" Gemma didn't finish her sentence before Suzy dove back in.

"Anyway, we've kind of started dating.... Well, the studio suggested we attend some things together, and we hit it off." Finally, the girl took a breath. Gemma could picture her on the other end, twirling her chin-length bob. Before her big break as Gemma's little sister in the surf films, she had been modeling for the Sears and Montgomery Ward catalogs; when she landed the part, she earned enough to buy her family a ranch house in the Valley. Now Suzy Hutton had stepped into Gemma's roles at the studio, so Gemma was sure the family would be moving out of the Valley and into Beverly Hills.

"How are you?" Suzy inhaled loudly. "Oh my goodness, are you calling to tell me that you and Charlie are getting married?" The voice squealed again with excitement. "That's it, isn't it? Everyone is getting married but me."

"No," said Gemma with a sad laugh. "We're not getting married." She didn't have the heart to tell Suzy the truth. "I just called to hear your voice."

"Oh," said Suzy with more than a little disappointment. "Are you coming back to LA? I was thinking that I could pitch an idea where Lacey joins Betsy at college for a weekend. Come back, Gemma. It isn't the same without you. I mean, we all still have fun on the set, but...you were my sister."

In Suzy's mind, she'd always thought that she and Gemma were now connected like real sisters. Gemma missed that kind of pure friendship.

"I'm headed to Paris for a film, but maybe after." Looking out the window watching cabs go by, Gemma had never felt so alone. "Tell me what you're doing tonight?" Checking her watch, she saw it was nearly eleven fifteen at night, London time, so it would be a little after three in the afternoon in LA.

"William and I are seeing Dion tonight at the Troubadour. God, I wish you could come," said Suzy, letting out a big groan. "I want my big sister's opinion on William."

Gemma laughed. "What are you wearing tonight?"

Another squeal emitted. "I just got a bunch of dresses from Susie at Bryant 9. They're fabulous. Everyone is starting to wear earthier colors, lots of suede. These dresses are pastel, but the yellow one looks great on me. If you were here, I have one that would look great on you!"

"I wish I could be there, too," said Gemma, a wistful smile on her face.

There was a pause, then Suzy said, "Gotta go, but I'll tell my mom you called!"

"Please do," said Gemma, lingering on the line even after the connection broke.

For a moment, she imagined herself back in Los Angeles, getting dressed and heading to the Troubadour with Suzy and William. Why hadn't that easy friendship been enough for her? Gemma worried that there was some flaw inside her that never allowed her to settle—not settle as in accept less, but settle as in feel comfortable in her own skin, in her own world. Why did she feel alone everywhere she went?

The next morning, on the way to the airport, an incredible wave of guilt struck her. Was she once again packing up and leaving her world behind? Would she get to Paris and regret the way she'd left here, just as she'd done with Los Angeles? Impulsively, she asked the cabbie to double back to Charlie's apartment, and there she found him, not in the depths of despair, but in bed with Tamsin and Penny. If Gemma was, indeed, leaving for Paris, then he required an immediate replacement.

The girls were both nubile like Botticelli paintings, yet neither of them rushed to cover themselves, and seemed blissfully sure they had just secured a prize in Charlie Hicks. Gemma admired their innocence but knew that was also temporary. Charlie would destroy the dewy, wide-eyed way they looked at their new world. That was all he did.

In an odd way, Gemma's discovery of the three of them thrilled Charlie. "Did you forget something, Gems?" he asked. "Leave your key. Don't want you walking in on us again."

Closing the front door softly, she heard them: "Did you see her face?" asked one of the girls, giggling, then the three of them erupted into laughter.

The reaction had been a gift from Charlie to her. She would leave London with a clear conscience. Before she got into the car, Penny made her way out to the street, wrapping the bedsheet around her like a toga. She held the sheet together with one hand and had a lit cigarette in the other. "He says not to come back."

"Tell him that's not going to be a problem," said Gemma, opening the car door. "I'm going to Paris."

"He's better off without you, you know."

"You're not." Gemma snorted with laughter. This young thing had no idea what she was getting into. "Let's go," said Gemma to the driver as she closed the door on Penny. How dare Charlie have the last word, even through a messenger.

The car pulled out of the spot, leaving the girl with the ringlets standing in the street, her toga gaping.

"Drive fast, please. Get me the hell out of here."

Having left London sooner than expected, Gemma would stay in Paris for three weeks until filming for *L'Étrange Lune* began. The company financing the film was keen to get more press for the movie, so they'd sent her a small advance to pay for a hotel in exchange for Gemma doing interviews, preferably in French. Until landing at the airport, however, she had been oblivious to the extent of unrest happening in the country, and no one from the production company had mentioned that the airport was nearly shut down. Making her way through an empty airport, she found a lone cab who was dropping another person at departures. As her cab made its way to the hotel, the shortage of food created long lines outside every shop. This was not the Paris she'd seen just weeks ago.

"What has happened here?" Gemma turned to look out the back window. "I was just here a few weeks ago."

"Strikes," said the cab driver. "Students protesting the Vietnam War, but the police response was fierce, then the workers followed. I'll see how close we can get to Rue des Écoles, but I can't make any promises."

The cab halted at Boulevard Saint-Germain, and the driver motioned that she would have to walk the long block up the hill. Carrying her suitcase and her typewriter case, she began the steep incline toward the little boutique hotel near the Sorbonne that she'd booked under her mother's name, Marie Breton. A woman about her mother's age, was apologetic upon check-in that the maids had stopped coming in to work. "It's fine," said Gemma. "I can wash my own sheets, just show me where the laundry room is located."

The flustered but elegant woman at the desk was clearly the owner of the hotel but seemed unused to handling guest requests. "That is very kind of you. Most guests have left." She presented Gemma with a large brass key that was attached to a large red tassel. Helping Gemma steer her suitcase to the tiny elevator, she gave a sheepish grin. "The bellman is gone, too, I fear."

Gemma was delighted with the spacious, sparsely furnished room, complete with a king-size bed with a tufted red velvet headboard. The opulent bed was in sharp contrast to the small desk where Gemma placed her typewriter case. Pulling back the matching red velvet curtains, Gemma found that the room had a walkout window where she could sit and watch the Rue des Écoles from her balcony.

As night fell over the Latin Quarter, the familiar sounds of the street were replaced by more frequent sirens and a sea of protesters with their rhythmic chanting of "Adieu de Gaulle." The shouting was interrupted by an occasional peppered sound of what she first thought were firecrackers, but after a quick look out of her window and seeing a car ablaze, she realized the sound had been gunshots fired by riot police.

In the morning, Gemma waded through the streets with the rest of the stunned Parisians, finding them littered with overturned cars and garbage piled high because the sanitation workers were now on strike. From the street, she heard a chorus of tense voices as women discovered empty aisles and bins in the markets. For some who, like her mother, had lived through the war, it must have been a bitter reminder of the past.

As Gemma passed barricades of newspaper stands and trash cans, she saw red signs pasted everywhere. One in particular, LA BEAUTÉ EST DANS LA RUE, caught her eye with a stylistic graffiti image of a woman hurling a brick. Taking the small poster from the streetlamp, she folded it and placed it in her purse, something about it stirring her. These kids were about her age and they were angry, the collective unrest like a spiking fever. Had she been home, would she have been protesting the war? Certainly, the studio would have forbidden it.

She'd managed to be in line at the right time for butter, cream, and marmalade. The fruit stand had been damaged, so Gemma picked what she could find that was salvageable before returning to the hotel, where she found the owner putting a meager coffee setting in the dining room. Gemma unpacked the jar of orange marmalade, along with the butter, cream, and fruit. "Pardon, I couldn't find bread."

The woman's face brightened. "It is I who should be caring for *you*, as my guest in this hotel." There was something about her proper manner that made Gemma ache for her own mother. "I am Yvette," said the woman, extending her hand.

"Gemma."

"Oh, I know who you are," said Yvette, her smile widening. "We *all* know. I've seen you in *Paris Match*. You've come to star in Thierry Valdon's new film. My daughter, Bette, who is studying film at the Sorbonne, is quite starstruck. You will see her here. She helps after school, but she has not been able to go these past few days."

The routine at the hotel became the same. At night, Yvette would lock the front doors, and Gemma barricaded herself in her room, pulling the heavy velvet drapes shut. Yvette had given her several candles and a bottle of red wine from the cellar. Pulling the typewriter down from the desk, Gemma sat on the rug farthest away from the window. With the candlelight casting shadows, the room took on a mysterious atmosphere; she could imagine this room in the belle epoque period. What illicit love affairs had taken place in these walls? Her imagination ran wild.

She opened a copy of Andrew Wainwright Collier's novel *The Damsel and the Demon* that she'd found in the only open bookstore on Saint-Germain. Collier had claimed his own book to be damned and had every copy destroyed—well, almost every copy. Unfortunately for Collier, that type of lore was exactly the kind of reputation that made people want to keep a copy, just in case, so as legend had it, the printer couldn't bear to destroy the last copy. Over the years, the novel became essential reading for radicals. The novel's plot featured the demon Althacazur, who is in love with a mortal woman, Aerin, and ruins her marriage prospects, causing her to kill herself. Once in the underworld, she is given to Althacazur as a gift from Lucifer; however, Aerin has retained her memories and now hates Althacazur. Eventually, she is cast out of Hell for being too pure.

Collier's novel gave her ideas for Valdon's script, and she saw parallels between Gisele and Aerin. She took out Thierry Valdon's script notes and began typing while she finished her second glass. Both the wine and the creative rush overtook her as she imagined how thrilled the director would be to get her notes. Gemma stopped typing to recall what he'd said: *Given you write, I would love to have your feedback on the shooting script.* The script she'd received was not pushing any boundaries, but she had some ideas, and Valdon seemed to want them. This...this was what she had left the Hollywood studio system for. More confident than ever, Gemma took a big swig of wine and began reworking scenes with Gisele, writing: *Gisele is used much in the same manner all women are used in all horror films. She's a victim, a pawn. There is nothing new about her.* Taking a scene where Gisele meets the vampire Roman for the first time, she rewrote the scene to have the young woman suspicious of the vampire, not Pascale.

The sound of the keys clapping soothed her as she tuned out the tapping of gunfire and the occasional explosion outside, which was then followed by waves of people running and screaming—always the noise came in waves. With only the candles illuminating her paper, her fingers knew their way around the keyboard enough that she didn't really need light. She began working on more scenes for *L'Étrange Lune*, worrying only that she would run out of paper and had no idea where to find any. As she wrote, she began to feel quite a kinship with this work. She swelled with pride as she created three new scenes that made Gisele Dumas a fresh character worthy of Nouvelle Vague. She hoped Valdon would like them.

Finally, Gemma fell asleep on the floor, her dreams vivid, like the screenplay had begun writing itself. Around five in the morning, the sirens became infrequent and the screaming subsided. From a distance, she saw the first hints of a sunrise, the pink opening at the horizon.

Cautiously, she opened the window to gaze at the street below her. Police cars and ambulances were scattered; people moaned or shouted as they were carried away on stretchers or in wagons depending upon their ultimate destination. Overturned flower carts sat in the middle of the street, and it occurred to her that they'd been dragged from the market blocks away.

Out of the corner of her eye, she spied something that didn't look right. Looking down at her typewriter, there was a piece of paper in the drum that she hadn't recalled leaving there. Pulling the paper out, she couldn't believe her eyes:

Ms. Turner:

In my humble opinion, you've got a good start here, but you and I both know the script is sadly lacking. Mademoiselle Dumas would be intrigued with Roman, not that dull Pascale. Pascale the hero of this story? I don't think so. . . . Push harder. The Damsel and the Demon is an excellent source of inspiration. Push push. . . .

—A

Who had written this? Someone named "A"? In a fit, she searched her room, pulling back the curtains and armoires and searching the bath, but everything was empty. She checked the lock, but it was tightly secured. In her haze last night, she'd left the window open, just a crack for air. Had someone come into her room in the middle of the night and read her draft? Looking down at the note, it appeared someone had done exactly that. A shiver ran through her. *Someone had been in her room.*

"You're losing your mind, Gemma." Recalling the way that Charlie, Serge, Tamsin, and Penny had looked at her when she'd insisted that she'd chased a man out of the Monet Suite, she wondered if she was seeing things. The look of pity as Serge spoke to her was still etched in her mind. *There was no man.*

The only other explanation was that Gemma herself had written this...well...this critique of her own draft. Was it possible that she'd hated her draft and so, subconsciously, had written this? People could sleepwalk. But the idea of sleep typing was ridiculous, and she knew it. She'd been happy with her new scenes for *L'Étrange Lune.*

"Mon dieu." She dressed quickly, needing to get air and to get out of the room that now felt violated.

As she hurried down the stairs, she realized that entering a war zone had made it easier to forget about the battle with Charlie. Through friends, she'd heard that he was now desperate to find her, yet she felt secure that he had no idea of the assumed name she was now living under. Charlie had never bothered to ask nor seemed interested about anything related to her family, let alone her mother's name. It was this small detail that once again reaffirmed for her that she'd done the right thing in the end by leaving.

In the lobby, she found the door still locked, which was curious as Yvette always unlocked it promptly at seven. From the dining room, Gemma heard a shuffling noise and a whimper. Stepping into the dining room, where under normal circumstances there would have been a meager coffee service, Gemma found Yvette lying on the floor, face down. A young girl was crouched on her knees beside her, sobbing quietly like she didn't want to disturb the guests.

"She's dead." Looking up at Gemma, the girl's face revealed several deep gashes, and there were glass fragments in her hair.

Only then could Gemma make out what had happened here. An explosion on Rue des Écoles had caused the front window in the dining room to shatter, sending glass shards like shrapnel into the room where, only moments ago, Yvette had been preparing their breakfast. Pitifully, Gemma saw the woman had found more marmalade, and the jar was in her hand when she'd been knocked out. From the look of her, the daughter had been nearby.

Gemma raced over to Yvette's body and slowly turned her over. Back in

Los Angeles, she'd been a lifeguard for a summer, so she knew basic first-aid training. Listening for the sound of breathing, Gemma did hear a faint sound and could feel a weak pulse. "We need to get her an ambulance."

The girl, covered in debris, shook her head slowly. "Impossible."

"L'automobile?"

The girl shook her head. "The streets are blocked."

Gemma stood and ran to the door and unlocked it, running onto the street to find cars and overturned carts indeed blocking the path. No ambulance could make its way here.

Yvette didn't have much time, so Gemma scanned the street for anything that would help her get the woman to an ambulance. Spying a young man, Gemma motioned for him. "Aider."

Gemma ran through the lobby, opening doors and searching a laundry room and finding sheets in a closet next to the elevator. If they couldn't get to an ambulance, then she would have to take Yvette to help. Gemma laid out two sheets on the floor, hoping they would hold, then she and the man lifted Yvette's deadweight onto the sheet. Then each of them grabbed an end of the material, lifting her like she was on a gurney. Before they began to move, Gemma checked to see that the woman still had a pulse, however faint. "Allez," said Gemma to Yvette's daughter. When the young girl didn't move, Gemma realized she was, herself, in shock.

"What is your name?" said Gemma, kneeling next to her. Lightly, Gemma began to pat her on the cheeks to rouse her.

The girl stirred. "Bette," she said, so weakly that Gemma had to lean in close to hear it.

"Okay, Bette, we are going to get you some help as well." Gemma shot the man a look. "Can you find more help on the street?" Nodding, he let his end of the sheet go for one minute to go back on the street and find help. Gemma made her way back to the laundry closet to find another pair of sheets.

Two more men had joined the group, and they laid out the second makeshift stretcher and loaded Bette onto it. The two groups wove their way down the streets, dodging overturned carts and calling for people to clear the path as they made their way down to Boulevard Saint-Germain, where they had any hope of finding an ambulance.

Yvette was heavy, and Gemma had to make several stops before finally another man motioned for her to get out of the way and he picked up her ends of the sheet. Gemma ran along in front of the group scanning for help.

To Gemma's relief, she found that cars were running on Saint-Germain, and she flagged down an ambulance that double-parked near an overturned cart to quickly move Yvette onto a proper gurney. A second ambulance arrived, and Gemma rode to the hospital with Bette, realizing she had no money to get herself back to the hotel. Only when the paramedic began fussing at her did she realize that she'd cut up her own knees from kneeling on the floor of the hotel. As he dabbed at her injuries, Gemma winced.

"Will she be okay?" she asked, looking down at Bette, who was now unconscious and slumped on the seat.

"She is in shock," the paramedic said, noncommittal.

"And her mother?" Gemma nodded toward Yvette.

"She is worse," said the paramedic, his mouth tightening.

Emerging from the ambulance, Gemma came face-to-face with her own image staring back at her, the peeling billboard for Joie de Jardin perfume hanging on the building across from the emergency department entrance.

The poster, now long faded, had been recently vandalized. Gemma's face had been scratched out. At a diagonal angle, pasted over the old billboard, was the fresh poster of the protestor in red with the words LA BEAUTÉ EST DANS LA RUE.

4

Christopher Kent
April 2, 1991
Las Vegas, Nevada

The heavy old Bell and Howell projector could have been mistaken for a microwave. Christopher pushed the button until he heard the whir of the cartridge advancing, an encouraging sound. For the last week, he'd had the broken machine parts lying on the unused formal dining room table. After several frustrating attempts at fixing the machine, Aunt Wanda dropped him off at the photography shop on the Strip for help on the autoload function. The owner, who had once possessed the same projector, groaned when he saw it. After finding a vintage bulb, they'd gotten the projector to load cassettes. His aunt Wanda peered around the corner. "Are you doing a screening soon?"

"In a few minutes," he said, trying the advance button one last time. The machine whirred to life.

For five years, Christopher had lived with his aunt and uncle and two cousins, Jason and Angela. When his school records were unearthed, Christopher's secret shame was finally revealed to everyone—he hadn't been to school for more than a year, causing him to repeat the fifth grade, which put him in the class with his cousin Angela, who had more friends than anyone he knew. But the transition wasn't easy. Up until that point, Christopher had existed and navigated in a world of adults... his mother's boyfriends, landlords, old women at the laundromat. He had no experience talking with or even playing with other kids, and he always felt the situation was temporary. He kept an eye on the door, a small bag packed, money for a grilled cheese sandwich and a bus ticket if he needed it again.

Aunt Wanda had made microwave popcorn for the occasion. Often, Christopher searched Aunt Wanda's face, looking for anything familiar, but where his mother was blond and ethereal like she was on a permanent soft focus, his aunt Wanda was earthy with heavy, shiny chestnut hair that fell to her shoulders and was tangled in clips, spare knitting needles, or buns, like she couldn't be bothered with the fuss.

His aunt rummaged through the box of film cartridges with names like *July 4th Parade 1967* and *Pamela's Bus Ride to NY 1967.* "Your grandfather got the camera in Japan years before it was available in the US," said Aunt Wanda. "He was a tinkerer like you. The thing never worked properly, though. I think it was a prototype."

His uncle Martin had recently gotten a promotion with the insurance company, and the family had uprooted from Gainesville to Las Vegas, like one hot location was as good as another.

He and Jason and Angela spent their days inside watching cartoons and calling up the weather line to hear the current temperature: *The time is two p.m., and the temperature is one hundred and six degrees.* At dusk, they'd take to the streets, riding their bikes all over the new development. He was almost fifteen. Had he been a year older, Christopher would have been more interested in driving or girls, but he was the new kid in town without a driver's license and bored to tears—that was until he found the old projector and cassettes in a box in the garage.

The cartridge stalled again, and Christopher pulled it back from the loading tray and inspected it, the bulb blasting light into his eyes. "Shit," he said.

"Christopher," said Aunt Wanda, frowning. "Language."

"Sorry," he said, wiping his hands on his pants.

One press of the button and there she was. On the grainy, fast-moving scene, his mother, Pamela Kent, appeared, arranging herself next to his aunt Wanda, who was pushing her sister in front of her. Pamela looked around nervously, the camera pulling in closer and then farther as the cameraman, his grandfather, played with the zoom button. Seeing his mother moving, animated again, took his breath away. A feeling of dissonance swept over him. How could she be healthy and alive there and not here? Film tricked you, bringing the dead back to life. "Mommy," he said softly, some primal part of himself never having fully given up the search for her, wondering where her mind had gone that day. This was the mother he never knew existed—a carefree, younger version moving jerkily on the screen.

"We didn't buy the projector until 1974," said Wanda, watching the film, but also Christopher, the boy feeling her eyes on him. "We had all that film and no idea if the camera ever worked. I don't think I've ever actually seen these."

The muted celluloid grains crackled between scenes as his mother posed with new cars and at Christmas, family reunions, and airport send-offs. In his favorite clip, she was a bridesmaid dressed in a powder-blue halter gown and matching dyed shoes (a point of focus for the videographer).

The Christmas video was jarring. His mother seemed thrilled to be ripping open presents, yet the woman he knew took no joy in the holidays. Nostalgia mixed with melancholy would send her into the bathroom, where she'd lock herself for hours, taking baths. Christopher had been so frightened that she'd fall asleep that, on more than one occasion, he'd picked the lock with the tool the maintenance man had given him and pulled the stopper on the bathtub, letting it drain while she was passed out in the cold tub. She woke hours later, cold, naked and furious, but she'd been alive.

"Jeez," said Aunt Wanda, putting her hand up to block the dizzying image.

He placed his hand over his mouth to stop himself from sobbing. His stomach began to twist like it did in those days with her.

His mother had been dead three years now. After Pittsburgh, she'd been transferred to an institution in Atlanta, but everyone insisted on calling it "the center," like his mom was off on a yoga retreat. It was one of those contemporary buildings with walls of windows that backed up to patches of evergreen trees. The first time that he saw her at the center, she was tied to a chair in the "Imperial Wing." While he'd settled into a normal life and stopped looking under bathroom doors to make sure the tub wasn't overflowing or turning people on their sides to stop them from choking on vomit, she was now catatonic, staring off into a corner at a "Year in Cats" calendar, her mouth slack like she was going to sing a note. She only lasted eleven months there before dying of pneumonia.

He sank in the seat, transfixed by her cherubic blond curls, her upturned nose, and that wide smile. His mother was a ghost beckoning him. Time didn't heal wounds this big. In the end, what filled that hole was a tolerable numbness shaped by missed opportunities and an imagined alternate life he could have had with her. He longed to place himself in there with her. Anything to see her again.

The final film featured the family sending her off as she caught a bus to New York City. Vibrant and hopeful, his mother was not the broken women he had rolled onto her side in so many cheap hotel rooms. The grainy crackling of the film snapped him back into reality, a reminder that the stunning woman with a brown suede fringe jacket was nothing but a long-ago memory. She waved frenetically to her family, the film speed making her look like she was rushing off to an exciting new adventure. There would be no film capturing her grim return, years later.

"What happened to her?" Christopher had never asked Aunt Wanda this crucial question. He'd been too young, too grateful that she'd taken him in, to seek answers.

Her big blue eyes narrowed. "I shouldn't have let any of it happen," she said. "That you hadn't been to school for a year. I heard you scrounged for change to eat."

"It wasn't too bad."

"Yes, it was," she said with a weary sigh. "Pam had trouble with the world as it was. She lived in a fantasy world while the real one chipped away at her until she was...just gone. Pills, booze, men...they were all just ways of her coping, but the seeds of it were there from the beginning. She never fit in this life." Aunt Wanda's face was illuminated by the projector light, and Christopher thought he spotted tears. "I just wish we had been enough for her."

That Christmas, Christopher was given a used Sony video camera as a gift from his aunt and uncle. Even used, this was an extravagant gift for his family.

Jason had gotten a baseball glove and Angela a curling iron. He saw them give each other confused glances at the monetary disparity between the gifts.

"I called the photography shop," said Aunt Wanda. "The owner said you'd had your eye on that one." Christopher had, indeed, been looking at that used camera in the case, wondering what he could do with it and an empty cartridge of film. The new camera still had its original packaging, and Christopher could tell it meant something important coming from them—his aunt Wanda was trying to steer him away from his obsessive watching of the old films and toward a new chapter.

"Maybe you can take some videos of our Christmas," she said, her smile hopeful.

For a budding filmmaker, the Las Vegas Strip provided plenty of fodder. Christopher spent his first few weeks in the spring riding up and down the Strip with Jason, capturing signs advertising the Grateful Dead, Santana, and George Burns. One sign caught his eye at the Sands hotel, THE SURF FILM FESTIVAL.

"We gotta go to that," said Christopher, pointing to the sign. Jason had developed a recent obsession with surfing even though they now lived in the desert and, despite having lived in Florida, had only ever been to Myrtle Beach.

"There might be babes there." At sixteen, Jason had a fixation with "babes."

They pulled into the parking lot, both feeling like adults on a mission. The hotel parking lot tugged at Christopher—it felt like the places where he and his mom used to live. Aunt Wanda and Uncle Martin were big fans of tent camping in national parks, so the last hotel that Christopher had been to was the one in Pittsburgh.

"Do you think we need an ID?" Jason patted his hair in the rearview mirror. He was convinced he looked older than sixteen.

"I think it's a film convention. We should be okay."

"We should try to get into the casino?" He frowned at a rather large zit on his chin, giving him away as a teenage boy.

"Your mom will kill us," said Christopher.

"True." Jason nodded, taking out his comb from his back pocket to run it through his hair that still had a mullet kind of shape to it from the woman who had cut it in Gainesville. Jason had great hair and lots of it, but it was getting long. He handed Christopher the comb.

"No, thanks."

"You sure?"

Christopher patted his short, wavy hair down. "I'm sure."

The wall of air-conditioning hit them as they pushed through the doors, entering the lobby. Following signs for the film convention, they got in the registration line in front of a skirted table with a WELCOME FANS sign. Christopher wasn't expecting to have to pay six dollars to get in, but they'd both gotten their allowances, and neither wanted to turn around now.

A woman with bright red, heavily teased hair handed them their badges. "The talk is in the Grand Ballroom. The Frankie Avalon dinner is this evening, but it is not included with your admission."

"Okay," said Christopher, not understanding any of that. "We don't need to see Frankie Avalon."

Wandering down through the hallway, Jason was captivated by the exhibit featuring movie posters with names like *Beach Blanket Bingo*, *Wipeout*, and *Thunder Beach*. "I need some of these for my room."

"Do you think you'd actually like surfing?" Christopher wasn't sure where Jason's fascination with surfing had come from, but the endless sounds of Beach Boys albums coming out of his room had taken a dramatic turn with the move to Las Vegas, as though Jason was trying to position himself as a surfer from Florida in his new school. It must be hard to have moved in eleventh grade. Christopher had never had any stability, so he'd coped much better than his cousins had with the change in schools.

"I know I would," said Jason, his eyes sparkling.

The *Thunder Beach* poster caught Christopher's eye. One of the actresses in the poster was a familiar face, with her long, straight hair and heavy bangs. Following the poster down to the credits, he saw the name he was looking for: *Gemma Turner.* "No way," said Christopher.

In the move, he'd opened the shoebox he kept with his mother's things, including the gold cornicello necklace, programs from her singing engagements, and the bill he'd kept saved that day from the hotel: *Replacement of Gemma Turner artwork.*

So, Gemma Turner had starred in a surf film.

"I'm bored," said Jason, scanning the festival attendees as they passed. "The babes here are old."

"I want to go to the talk." Christopher's heart started racing with this new information. This woman, Gemma Turner, was connected to his mother. But how? The answer might be in that ballroom. He *had* to get into that ballroom.

Jason shot him a look. "You're kidding."

Christopher shrugged. "Just come back for me."

His cousin made an exasperated sigh and put out his hand. "You owe me six dollars."

"Why?"

"Because this festival is lame."

With a groan, Christopher reached into his pocket. "I only have a ten."

Jason snapped the bill out of his hand. "I'll get you change . . . later."

Christopher rolled his eyes. "I'm never getting change back."

Jason started toward the Copa Room and gave him a backward wave. "I'll meet you in the parking lot in an hour, or Mom will kill us."

"Don't try to go to the casino, Jason."

His cousin spun in the faded hotel carpet, pretending like he was about to sneak into the guarded hotel casino, before turning and meandering back toward the hotel's entrance.

Christopher opened the door to the Grand Ballroom, entering quietly so as not to disturb the session in progress. The ballroom, with its yellow-gold curtain and square ceiling chandeliers, was packed, so he took a seat in the back next to an older, friendly looking woman.

"You're a bit young," she whispered. "I wish my grandson had your taste in films."

"I'm a fan of Gemma Turner," said Christopher, bluffing and hoping to get some sort of reaction from her.

"Tragic," said the woman with a grave shake of her head. "You must be excited about this panel, then."

"Yeah," said Christopher, not wanting to give away that he had no idea who was on the panel or what was so tragic about Gemma Turner. The boy leaned closer to her. "I didn't get my agenda. Who else is in this panel?"

"Besides Suzy Hutton?" The woman's eyes narrowed.

The name Suzy Hutton meant nothing to him, nor did any of the other names the woman rattled off before the emcee took the stage to introduce the next panel moderator.

The woman put her hand up to muffle her voice. "Shame about Suzy Hutton, too."

Christopher looked puzzled but pretended to agree with her.

"The husband, William Way, was killed in that car crash five years ago with his mistress." The woman's eyebrows rose. "Three young kids. Now she has to star on that game show because parts have dried up."

"Oh," said Christopher with a pretend knowing nod. "Yeah, that was terrible."

Suzy Hutton, the poor woman in question, sat in the center of the stage on a soft beige chair with a fake smile plastered on her face. She looked to be about forty, with shoulder-length butter-blond hair that was styled like a newscaster's. Christopher recognized the desperation on her face. He'd seen it before when his mother needed to prove that she was okay. Suzy Hutton was not okay.

"She looks good," said Christopher, lying and watching for the woman's reaction. Circling her face with her finger, she scowled. "Too much work done."

The panel questions focused on what it had been like to star in the surf films from 1963 to 1969. Suzy Hutton was effusive: The scripts were marvelous, the director supportive to a young actress, and the fans—well, the fans were remarkable. The audience clapped and hooted at that response. There would be an autograph signing after the panel.

When the moderator opened up the question-and-answer portion, Christopher raised his hand before thinking. Suzy Hutton had starred in *Thunder Beach* with Gemma Turner. Why had no one mentioned her?

Someone with a microphone wandered over to Christopher. From the stage, the moderator, seeing it was a teenager, laughed. "Our fans get younger every year."

The room erupted in laughter.

"Hi," he said, a quaver in his voice. As all eyes were on him, he felt his face flush. "My name is Christopher Kent." He swallowed, rubbing his hands on his jeans nervously. "My question is for Suzy Hutton."

Suzy smiled and leaned forward on the beige chair like she was captivated.

His face scrunched up. "What was it like working with Gemma Turner?"

The room went quiet. The panelists onstage all lowered their heads except for Suzy, who stared back at Christopher with an intensity that made him think she could see right through him. Her jaw went slack as she stuttered before answering the question.

Looking around the audience, Christopher was confused why mention of Gemma Turner had cast a pall over the room. No one met his eyes. Even the woman sitting next to him was now clutching her throat and staring down at the gold-and-green geometric patterns on the carpet to avoid his gaze.

What on earth had happened to Gemma Turner? Why did no one want to talk about her?

"She was the *most* fantastic actress and person I ever worked with." Suzy's smile faded. "She was like a sister to me. You know, she never received the attention she deserved. Watching her in *Thunder Beach* and *My Hawaiian Wedding*, we all know she transcended those films. And history has shown that *The Horse Thief* was brilliant, and her performance is up there with the greats, despite the film being panned on its release. She was just ahead of her time. It was a shame what happened."

Christopher nodded in her direction, looking grateful for her answer, but wanting to scream *What happened?*

"So tragic, really, what happened to her," said the emcee. "Next question."

His pulse quickened. Looking around the ballroom at the downcast eyes, everyone else knew the answer. The easiest thing would be to ask the woman next to him, but he'd let on he was a fan of surf films, and although it was a stupid thing, he didn't feel like blowing his cover. When the discussion ended, she was up out of her seat scurrying in the opposite direction away from him. People hurried out of the room, and Christopher felt that he'd done something wrong.

He made his way out to the parking lot, hoping to recognize someone from the Grand Ballroom who could give him any insight, but there was only Jason idling in the car.

Christopher opened the door. "If I needed to find out about an actress, where would I go?"

"Dunno," said Jason, adjusting himself in his seat to see what angle made him look cooler. "Is she a babe?"

Christopher considered his question. "Yes. Most definitely."

"The library, then, coz." Jason put the car in gear and pulled out of the Sands parking lot onto South Las Vegas Boulevard. "But Mom will be mad if we're late for dinner, so we'll have to do it tomorrow."

Nodding to his cousin, Christopher rolled down the window and felt the warm air stir.

That both his mother and Gemma Turner had met tragic ends was no coincidence. They were linked both in life and in fate, Christopher was sure of it. And tomorrow, he'd start on his quest to find answers.

The next day, Jason dropped him off at the Las Vegas library. After spending an entire morning searching, the librarian, an older woman who had taken the request as a challenge, finally found something intriguing on microfilm. When Christopher saw the grainy publicity still of Gemma Turner, he recognized the woman's face from all those years ago.

"This is all I could find." The librarian looked perplexed.

But the article she found raised more questions than it answered.

From the *Who's Who in Film Encyclopedia, 1976*

GEMMA TURNER (b. April 12, 1946. Missing, presumed dead, June 10, 1968)

Gemma Turner was a French-born American actress who starred in popular surf films in the 1960s, including *Thunder Beach* (1964), *Beach Rally* (1964), *It Comes in Waves* (1965), and *My Hawaiian Wedding* (1965). She disappeared ten days into filming on the set in Amboise, France, during a night shoot. The subsequent investigation targeted a vagrant, Jean-Michel Caron, who had been arrested in Nice for assault on his girlfriend, nearly killing her. Police cited the resemblance between Gemma Turner and his girlfriend as the possible motive. Ultimately, Amboise police did not have enough evidence to charge Caron, and the man was released, maintaining his innocence. Turner's disappearance remains unsolved, and she was declared dead in absentia in 1975. The film, *L'Étrange Lune*, was finished but never shown. After her disappearance, the film's director, Thierry Valdon, retreated into isolation to his country house, dying in 1972. In a strange development, Turner's former boyfriend, guitarist Charlie Hicks, drowned in the Loire River in Amboise in 1971, three years after she went missing, leading some to speculate that he had some hand in her disappearance, although he was in London at the time, working on the Prince Charmings' fourth album, *Shocking in Pink*.

5

Gemma Turner
June 1, 1968
Amboise, France

They call it the Valley of the Kings," said Mick from the front seat. He was flipping through a guidebook that he'd gotten from the travel agent in Paris. "'You'll find châteaus throughout this region because minor aristocracy were trying to get close to the king who lived here. After the revolution, many estates were destroyed or turned into prisons.'" He looked up. "Well, that's a bit dreary reading."

From her seat in the back, Gemma couldn't shake this feeling of numbness at everything around her. The things she'd witnessed in Paris were still foremost in her thoughts. She'd stayed at the hotel until Yvette and Bette had both been released from the hospital, but she hated to leave them. Both were on the mend from their injuries, and that was all that mattered, but they'd looked frail as she'd said goodbye this morning.

"You're awfully quiet back there," said Mick.

And he was right. For more than an hour now, Mick had been rattling on nonstop while they traveled southwest of Paris, leaving the outskirts, past signs to Versailles, and then they were soon surrounded by golden fields and grain silos. She couldn't talk about what she'd witnessed in the Latin Quarter, not that anyone had asked her. It was so traumatic that she wasn't sure it had been real. Now she was even chalking up the typewriter incident to stress. Given everything she'd experienced, it was likely—expected, even—to *see* things.

"I'm just a little tired from the travel."

"This trip used to take a day by horseback," said the driver, who smiled at her in the rearview mirror. "Thank goodness we have a car."

After what seemed like another hour traveling along the Loire River, she could finally see Amboise, with its grand white Tuffeau stone château, glistening in the distance. The chalky limestone gave the town a pearly appearance, as though they were passing by heaven itself.

"Says here that the Loire is the longest river in France," said Mick.

"*This* river is the *true* heart of France," said the driver with a tinge of annoyance.

"You know da Vinci died here." Mick pointed down to the car like the artist's bones were buried under the road. "I saw the *Mona Lisa* once, tiny little thing," he said, pinching his fingers together for emphasis. "Did you know they once thought Picasso had been one of the people responsible for the heist?" Mick's thick New York accent butchered Picasso's name, pronouncing the *A* in the artist's name as a strong, long sound.

"There is some question where da Vinci is *actually* buried," said the driver through gritted teeth. He gripped the steering wheel until his knuckles turned white, then gazed up in the rearview mirror to meet Gemma's eyes.

She smiled, a small conspiratorial gesture that admitted that she, too, knew Mick was an ass, but at least he'd come this time when she'd called him.

Amboise, with its looming Château Royal, sat high above the

winding river as though it had been lovingly placed there like a child's toy on a shelf. Along the road, Chenin Blanc grapes grew in neat rows.

"Our wine caves," said the driver, proudly pointing to mountains just behind the grapes. "The wine is stored in there. You'll find caves like that throughout the valley."

"They're not as popular as the other ones... Bordeaux?"

"Mick," said Gemma, knowing the driver had reached his limit of tolerance.

The car made a right turn, and within minutes they were winding around a small village where people went in and out of banks and boulangeries; a woman swept the steps of a Catholic church in the center of the roundabout. Gemma turned back to look out the rear window, Amboise shrinking in her view as the car wove through the circles, taking them back out of the town and onto a single-lane country road with nothing but green fields on either side. The entire principal cast would be staying at Château Verenson, Valdon claiming that he preferred a setting where his actors would cloister when not on set and build camaraderie, but she thought that was a ruse for what was a tight budget. Gemma hadn't thought she'd be this far away from town, this isolated.

"We're out here a ways," she said, more than a little alarm in her voice.

"There it is, up ahead," said the driver. "Did your guidebook tell you that this house has a tragic history? The painter Vallery Arnault was killed here." The driver wiped at the windshield. "This is odd. There is a sudden bit of fog."

As the car turned onto a long, winding drive, a thick mist stirred around the car until a giant bronze stag statue came into focus in the roundabout.

Gemma tried to recall the work of Vallery Arnault. "You said Arnault was a painter?"

"Oui," said the driver. "Portraits and landscapes. You'll find them at Château de Chenonceau and Versailles. He was not one of the greats, but had he lived he might have been."

Peeking through the trees was a grand three-story brick and stone house with perfectly clipped moss vines that crawled up past the second floor, engulfing the second-floor windows in greenery. This was Thierry Valdon's country house, Château Verenson. Its freshly painted white shutters were closed tight for the morning, a detail that Gemma found odd. Several newer Tuffeau stone additions flanked the original building, with a long terrace running the length of the front entrance and overlooking a large lawn. Under the mist, the grass was so soft and green that it resembled a carpet. Ornately carved holly hedges were shaped into rounds and obelisks and placed in pots like giant chess pieces on the concrete patio.

Anticipating their arrival, three staffers with starched uniforms approached the car: a butler, a porter, and a maid, their hands clasped in front of them like dutiful nuns.

"Good lord, this is stunning," said Gemma, a surprising croak emitting from her throat. Never had she expected Valdon's house to be—well—an estate! As she got out of the car, she was immediately hit by a fragrant combination of juniper and orange blossoms.

"Bonjour." She nodded to the staff as she stepped out. The trip had seemed longer than two hours. So grateful was she to be out of the car that she had the sudden urge to bend over and kiss the gravel beneath her feet.

A solemn butler with jowls and long ears that resembled a hound dog's led the team. "Bonjour, Mademoiselle Turner and Monsieur Fontaine. Welcome to Château Verenson. Monsieur Valdon welcomes you to his humble country home."

Lifting her hand to shield her eyes from the sun, she took in the vastness of Château Verenson. "Humble?" she said with a laugh. The length of the veranda stretched on as far as she could see.

In unison, the staff surrounded the suitcases and picked them up like a synchronized set of dancers. "Unfortunately," said the butler, trotting ahead with Mick's heavy suitcase, "Monsieur Valdon is on the set today, so he is not here to greet you, but he has given very specific instructions that Mademoiselle Turner get rest before dinner so that she is not tired for her first day on the set tomorrow. As you know, Monsieur Valdon finds tardiness unacceptable."

That Valdon was not here was extremely disappointing. It had been nearly two months since the lunch with him. In that time, her imagination had worked overtime, creating an image of the director that was larger than life, yet the man himself was nowhere in sight. When she'd arrived in Paris, she'd hoped that he'd arrange to meet with her again so she could talk to him about her ideas for the script, but she'd been told that he was on holiday with his wife in the Côte d'Azur.

They were led midway down the terrace that overlooked the lake. A set of double French doors opened to a stunning foyer with a large sweeping staircase and a table with a four-foot-high centerpiece of hydrangeas with green-and-white bunches of blossoms. Above the table hung an elaborate antique bronze chandelier.

"This is the original part of the house," said the butler. "Dinner and petit-déjeuner are served in there." He pointed to the left to an opulently furnished dining room with wood beams and a painted ceiling. "We bring in fresh croissants and pain au chocolat each morning from the village. The cook prepares dinner each night at eight."

"Bonjour," said a breathless voice.

Gemma turned to find a woman slightly older than herself standing before her, tanned and blond, dressed in a white shirt and black pedal pushers with black loafers. She tossed a bouquet of hand-cut flowers on the table. "I'm *Madame* Valdon," she said, meeting Gemma's eyes. In that instant, Gemma knew that her presence both on this set and in this house was seen as a threat.

"It is lovely to meet you, Madame Valdon." Gemma gave a little bow like the woman was the queen.

One of the most sought-after actresses in France, Manon Valdon had been the star of Thierry Valdon's film *Coeur Battant* (*Beating Heart*) five years ago as well as the catalyst for the director's subsequent divorce from his first wife, Sandrine.

"Call me Manon." She turned and pointed toward the right of the entrance. "You and Monsieur Fontaine will be staying in the newer wing through the salon," she said, bending her arm to the left. "The plumbing is better on that wing. Robert here will show you to your rooms."

Mick was only staying for a week, but already Gemma felt a sense of dread at being left alone here. From the window she could still see that the thick mist blocked the view of the lake. She didn't like the feel of this house.

Manon opened double doors to a room anchored by a carved stone fireplace and featuring several elegant seating areas with upholstered chairs, sofas, and chaise longues. The doors that led back to the terrace were framed in silk drapes and rugs. Around the room were antique tables with photos of Manon and her husband tucked between stacks of art books. Gemma saw a candid photo of Thierry and Manon laughing on the set of *Beating Hearts*, caught in an intimate moment.

They were a stunning couple, her earthy beauty a sharp contrast to his dark, exotic polish. Next to the candid was a photo of them that appeared to be at a dinner party, with Manon dressed in a white lace sleeveless dress and Thierry in a dark suit. It occurred to Gemma that this was their wedding photo. Thierry's smile was wide and full of pure joy. Only then did Gemma look up to see animal heads mounted on the wall.

"Oh." She jumped back.

"Yes, I'm quite the hunter," said Manon, following Gemma's eyes to the displays. "The house was...is...a hunting lodge. Originally built to be near the king, but by no means a castle. The ceilings are a dead giveaway." She pointed up. "They're a little over three meters, so the house is designed to be cozier than those large castles."

Despite the deer and boar heads on the wall, Gemma had trouble thinking of this exquisite woman in the thick of the Loire Valley forest, tracking down prey of any kind. Mick and Robert departed through a set of doors on the other end of the room, and she had a sudden desire to run after them.

"It is a stunning home." Gemma picked up the frame. "Is this your wedding photo?"

Manon nodded.

"You look happy," said Gemma.

"I was," said Manon with a tight smile. "Merci, Mademoiselle Turner." A gold lock had found its way across Manon's face, and she brushed it away in frustration. Her entire demeanor exuded exasperation, like this whole arrangement was too much for her.

"Please call me Gemma."

"Gemma," said the woman with an uneasy smile, like the name didn't sit well with her.

"Thank you for your kindness in letting us stay here," said Gemma, turning to follow Mick's retreating figure down the hallway. "I believe Pierre Lanvin will be here as well. I'm such a fan."

She dismissed Gemma with the wave of her hand. "Pierre is already on set. Loren Marantz arrives later today. This week, your scenes are with Pierre." The woman put her hands on her hips and cocked her head. "Look," she said with a small, nervous laugh. "The part in *L'Étrange Lune* was mine. You are aware of that, non?"

Gemma inhaled sharply, then let out a gasp. "The part of Gisele? I had no idea."

"I suspected as much," said Manon with an exaggerated eye roll. "In my own film, I was not aware that I'd been cast in the role of love interest, either, if you get my point." She leaned against a chair, looking both bored and weary. "Understand that the part of Gisele Dumas in this ridiculous horror film will be the *only* thing you will steal from me." She raised her eyebrow. "D'accord?"

Gemma gave a firm nod, feeling like a parochial schoolgirl who'd just been chastised by the head nun. She eyed the exit, where she could still hear Mick's comforting laugh in the hall.

Satisfied, Manon Valdon turned on her heels, leaving Gemma alone in the well-appointed salon. Looking up at the animal heads with their mouths agape, Gemma inhaled sharply before picking up her typewriter case. "I wonder if you all were given a similar warning."

Making her way through the upstairs wing, Gemma found a room that contained the rest of her luggage and assumed this was where she would be sleeping. Placed on the center of her bed was a script with her name. Flipping through it, she found notes and corrections in what she guessed was Valdon's handwriting, sparse, sloppy lettering with no roundness or flourish.

She stretched out on the bed and slipped off her shoes. One look through the script and it was clear that this version was as disappointing as the earlier one, something she never considered from a director famous for his inventive reflections of real life. His body of work was well-known for its beautiful yet tragic stories of middle-aged disappointment, failed families, and lost love. Horror, however, was clearly an unfamiliar genre to him and one that came with certain expectations that he seemed either unaware of or uninterested in learning. Gemma and her mother watched all the films from Hammer, the British company that made cheap and popular horror films, and loved them. If Valdon was going to break genre conventions as he indicated he'd wanted to do, he needed to understand the very rules he was defying. Rather than turning the traditional vampire film trope on its head, this script reinforced them to the point they were silly imitations.

She recalled the note in the typewriter: `You and I both know the script is sadly lacking.`

"It's still terrible," she said softly, a wash of dread coming over her with the realization that if this film flopped, her career would never recover.

She'd written several new scenes in Paris, but now she found she lacked the courage to give those to Valdon. Taking the new draft, she decided to write notes instead and began furiously writing her suggestions in the margins. While Valdon placed her character, Gisele Dumas, at the center of the story as the owner of the château upon the death of her father, he failed to do anything with that power, leaving her a stock victim character. Gisele spent the script's seventy pages acting as a pawn between the vampires and the rather drably written hero, Pascale. Flipping through the action scenes, Gemma expected to find Gisele spraining her ankle in the chase scene but was relieved to find at least that stereotype wasn't included.

In the wrong hands, this film could be laughable. She fell back into the bed groaning. She'd done everything right this time, attached herself to a director known for brilliance and devoted herself entirely to his process. Hurling the pages at the floor, she placed her hands over her eyes.

Sometime later, a loud noise woke her from a rather sound slumber.

Her heart racing, she sat up in bed, waiting a few minutes to hear if there were any shouts or cries of distress, but there was nothing. *I must be hearing things.* Settling again, she closed her eyes but was jolted upright by the sound of a gunshot. While the gunfire that she'd heard in Paris had been frantic, erratic, this was the luxurious pull of the trigger from a shotgun. "Calm down," she said to herself, her heart pounding in her chest.

There was a growing feeling inside Gemma that this film was a mistake. Should she bow out now, let Manon take the role of Gisele Dumas, and fly home to the safety of her parents? She was a bundle of nerves and had started seeing things. The disappointment of her career, the tumultuous end to her relationship with Charlie, and the violence in Paris had all left her with a melancholy that she just couldn't shake. Arriving here, a hollowness had enveloped her. Perhaps a horror film was appropriate for her current state of mind, yet she had a premonition of sorts that this film was going to be the undoing of her.

There was a knock on the door, which opened a crack as a maid peered in before wheeling in afternoon tea on an aqua Bernardaud china tea set. After a bath and a few moments spent agonizing over her wardrobe, Gemma chose a black silk pantsuit for dinner, assuming it would be a formal affair.

At eight, Mick rapped on the door. Opening it, she found him dressed in the same suit, but he'd switched out his shirt and tie, which accentuated his tan.

"I couldn't sleep with all that damned shooting," she said.

Her manager looked confused. "What shooting?"

"You didn't hear it?" She motioned for him to fasten her necklace, a sentimental piece of jewelry that had been one of her first splurges.

"No," he said. "I think I'm in the room next to you, so I should hear shooting, don't you think? It was probably just our dinner being slayed. The wife is quite the gardener, I hear, so at least the salad should be good."

"She's quite the expert shot, too," said Gemma. "All those animals hanging in the living room have her to thank for being mounted on a wall."

Mick lifted Gemma's hair like a doting stage mother, then rearranged it around her shoulders.

"She's angry with me," said Gemma in an accusatory tone, her bangles clanking as she ran her hands through her hair. "She claims I took the part of Gisele Dumas from her." She faced Mick and found him guiltily studying the floorboards. "Did I?"

He looked past her down the hall to make sure they were alone. "I *had* heard that Manon was attached to the part."

"Mick!" Gemma felt fury bubbling up inside her. She would never have taken a role from anyone. "You said the part hadn't been cast."

"Did I?" The agent waved his hands at her in surrender. "It's not my fault Valdon saw your face on the billboard, then you wowed him at lunch. The rest, as they say, is history."

"I shouldn't be here," she said in an urgent whisper.

"Oh, Gemma, don't be daft." Mick rolled his eyes and started down the hallway. "This is all you have. Look around. She doesn't need the part—you do!"

She lowered her eyes to the floor. The truth of his statement smarted. "I never meant to take her part."

At the top of the stairs, he spun to face her. "But now you have it, my dear. Manon Valdon is an actress with an ego, a big one. Do you really think if you abandoned the role now that she would take it?" He snorted. "You've sullied the role of Gisele Dumas for her forever." He took his tone down to a whisper. "If there is something going on between the two of them, that's their business, not yours and not mine." He pointed a finger at her, his tone more unkind than usual. "Keep your head on straight and stay away from him."

"Except they've made it my business by bringing me here."

"Do I have to remind you that this is your last chance?" For the first time, Mick's eyes weren't kind. He waved his hands like an umpire calling a player out. "There is nothing back in Hollywood for you."

From talking to Suzy Hutton, Gemma knew this was true, but still there was the feeling that this film was a mistake.

As they turned the corner at the bottom of the stairwell, the ceiling height dropped dramatically. "Watch your head," said Mick. "Do you know that Charles VIII was killed by running into a beam on his way to a tennis match?"

"That's a terrible story."

"It seems he was quite *tall* for a Frenchman." Mick shrugged and plowed ahead into the parlor.

They found Thierry and Manon Valdon deep in conversation, as though they were actors posing in the parts of a genteel country couple. He was leaning against a wing chair with a glass of wine in his hand, his white buttoned shirt illuminating his olive skin, but as they entered the room, he stood up to greet them. Despite how he'd acted in Paris, this man now looked every bit the role of country gentleman. Manon remained planted on the sofa. There were three conversation areas: one with two facing sofas, bookcases, and a walnut writing desk; another with a carved table that Gemma could imagine hosted many card games; and finally, one with two love seats and a mahogany grand piano. Hanging from the ceiling above them was an elaborate black iron and crystal chandelier, its glass beads dipping like a ceiling bracelet. Gemma was surprised that she'd missed it when she arrived, but the chandelier competed with the animal heads in the room. In fact, it seemed like everything—and everyone—in this room was in competition, giving the whole room a charged air.

"My dear," he said, giving her a quick kiss on each side of her cheek. Freshly showered, he smelled of savory soap.

Valdon's eyes went immediately to her hair, now a vibrant and garish copper thanks to a recommended Parisian hairdresser. He touched a strand, a move so forward that it caused Gemma to step back. Yet, he held on to the lock and yanked an errant strand that was out of place, plucking it from her head. "There. Now it's perfect," he said. "Henri did a magnificent job. I knew he would."

Surprised, Gemma rubbed her tingling scalp.

"It's a cinematic shade," agreed Manon, folding her arms in a manner that indicated it wasn't a compliment.

Manon Valdon's eyes bored through her. Had the situation been reversed, Gemma would have felt the same way, so she understood the woman's hostility, but Mick was right. She felt like a pawn between the couple.

"This must be the American I have heard so much about," said a voice behind her, the Italian accent thick. Gemma turned to find the actor Loren Marantz standing in the doorway, staring her up and down, but there was nothing sexual about his gaze. He might have studied a chair with the same intensity. "You are gorgeous, my dear. Agree about the hair, Thierry."

Living and working in Hollywood, Gemma had learned there were two kinds of actors: The first were smaller than they appeared on-screen both in stature and in presence. These were the quiet actors who shocked people for looking "so different" in person because, like wizards, they tricked the camera into magnifying them. These were chameleons who could slip in and out of roles. The second kind of actors were ones who owned the room from the minute they stepped onto the set, like they were born to be on film, giving the camera no say in the matter. The gravitational pull of these actors was almost infectious—they were larger than any role, film, or studio. Loren Marantz sat firmly in the second category. He was in danger of overshadowing everyone on-screen—or in the room—with him.

Rather quickly, he shifted his attention to the other side of the room, where Daphne Duras, the long-legged, blond Belgian actress, had just made her entrance. "Loren." She gave him a coy smile.

He almost sashayed across the room to meet her as she held out her hand and he kissed it. Daphne Duras was nearly a foot taller than Loren Marantz, and they weren't even from the same country, so the casting was odd, given the two characters, Roman and Avril, were supposed to be twins. Loren quickly began speaking perfect French, and Gemma could see him slipping into his role.

"They're old friends," said Valdon.

"Drinks?" Manon stood and walked to an elaborately carved bar in the corner. As she moved, the full-length silk Pucci dress billowed behind her like a Loie Fuller creation. It became clear that underneath she wasn't wearing a bra, and the dress, being rather sheer, left little to the imagination.

"I loved you in *The Flight of Spring*," said Mick, wandering over next to her.

"Merci," said the woman with a faux-modest nod. "May I offer you a drink?"

"I'd love one of those Loire Valley wines I hear so much about."

"Non," said Manon with a sharp wave of her hand, her posture as straight as a dancer's.

"Tonight's wine is one of Manon's favorites from Rhône," said Valdon with a laugh. "The Languedoc region."

Loren and Daphne, deep in conversation about a holiday in Saint-Tropez, ignored everyone around them.

Thierry joined Manon at the bar and was pouring two glasses from an open bottle. The wine was almost black with just a hint of red when it moved in the glass, like the most beautiful garnet stone. He handed a rather heavy goblet to Mick and then made his way to Gemma.

"Were you at l'Hôtel de Paris again?" Valdon's voice boomed in an effort to interrupt the conversation between Daphne and Loren.

"Non," said Daphne with a scowl. "Hôtel Byblos."

Loren looked impressed. "I was home in Firenze cooking pasta with my mama while she was sailing with Alain Delon and Bardot."

Thierry handed Gemma her wineglass. Until the last few weeks in the Latin Quarter, she'd never been much of a wine drinker, always preferring a Tanqueray and tonic, liking the crisp, simpler taste of a cold cocktail. Taking a sip, she found that the wine was tart, which wasn't her preference, but after the initial pucker, there was something that washed over her mouth. If she could describe it, she would say it was almost a smoky, earthy taste.

As if he could read her thoughts, Thierry Valdon laughed. "You don't like it?"

Gemma looked around to see the rest of the room was eagerly sipping from their goblets. "Oh," she said with a nervous smile, feeling like a rube. "I think it's wonderful."

He made a fist. "In that glass is the terroir of France itself...the soil...the rain—"

"What my husband means," said Manon, interrupting with a deep sigh like it was something she was often forced to do, "is that unlike wines here in central France, where the air is cooler and the limestone gives Loire Valley wine that herbaceous and tart, slightly chalky taste"—she held up the glass by its stem—"this wine is from the south of France, where the grapes are plucked at their *peak* of ripeness in the warm sun. The elements, unique to the soil and the environment, are reflected in the wine's taste—*terroir,* we call it."

She pronounced the last word with a throatiness that was sexy and deep—and condescending. Manon took a sip and held it in her mouth before swallowing, a wide smile appearing on her lips. Then she placed the glass back down on the bar and patted the low chignon at the base of her head. Not one hair was out of place. Gemma felt like an unsophisticated American compared to this woman. And that had been the point. Had Manon played Gisele Dumas, Gemma wondered if Thierry would have made her color those golden strands to the garish copper color on her own head. She doubted it.

"Respectfully, my friends," said Loren, who seemed a bit offended at the wine lecture, "I prefer the *terroir* of Chianti and my beloved Brunello."

"To each his own," said Valdon, giving Loren a hearty pat on the back. "As usual, my wife is correct. Tonight, Loren, I will be forced to make you drink the *very* essence of our humble Languedoc region." He took a sip and met Gemma's eyes. "This is a 1962. Wet year, I believe."

Manon shook her head.

"Non?" He smiled sheepishly.

"Non," said Manon with a sad smile. "It was a perfectly balanced year—not too wet and not too dry. We do have a 1961 Chianti that I will break out just for you, Loren."

"I look forward to it." Loren raised his glass.

Robert opened the doors to the dining room, announcing that dinner was now served. The group moved across the foyer and into the dining room. The grand table seated twelve. Two beautiful bouquets of lavender were placed in the center between candles, and the entire table was awash in candlelight. Thierry and Manon took their seats on each end, Mick and Daphne one side, Gemma and Loren on the other.

"I understand you were staying in the Latin Quarter during the riots?" Thierry directed the question to Gemma as he settled into his chair.

"Non," said Daphne, her eyes wide with amazement.

Mick gave a shake of his head. "Tried to get her over to the Ritz, but she wouldn't budge."

Gemma shot Mick a look. Not once had he called to check on her or move her anywhere else—and certainly never the Ritz—not that she would have gone. In fact, she was glad to have been at the hotel with Yvette and Bette when they'd been injured, wondering, if just for a moment, what twist of fate would have befallen them had she *not* been there.

"What was it like?" For the first time, Manon showed some signs of interest in Gemma, her face illuminated by the candle like she was rapt in a tarot reading.

"It was hell," said Gemma, surprised to hear the words coming out of her mouth. She hadn't talked about what she'd seen. "At night, glass would break and people would scream and chant and shout. The sound of shooting continued until dawn; I was never sure who was doing the shooting—the protestors or the police. The next morning, like a bunch of voyeurs, we would all go see the previous night's destruction. I had not lived through the war but imagine this is what it was like. Garbage was piled high, burned-out cars littered the streets, the markets were empty…the women panicked." As she described the scene from Paris, she watched the color drain from Thierry's face and his jaw tighten. The one detail Gemma found she couldn't speak of was seeing Yvette lying on the floor that morning. That intimate detail belonged only to her.

"De Gaulle fled the country for a day," said Daphne. "Can you believe that? Thankfully we were in Saint-Tropez. It wasn't so bad there, just a few worker protests at the hotel."

"That's what we found as well," said Manon.

"It seems to have settled," offered Loren. "We had our own battle in Valle Giulia in March. There is discontent in the air."

As if on cue, the doors to the kitchen opened, and staff in dinner jackets brought out covered dishes and slid them quietly on the table. This was so different from the meager bits of bread and cheese that Gemma had been able to find in Paris that it was hard to rationalize she was in the same country. In unison, the staff lifted the silver domes to reveal green bowls of spring vegetable stew with artichokes, spring onions, peas, and pancetta with parsley and mint.

"This house is magnificent," said Mick, making small talk.

"It has a rather dark history." Thierry chewed his food, his eyes lit with anticipation.

"Must we discuss it?" Manon fussed with her napkin.

"The driver mentioned something about it, didn't he, Gemma?"

"Oui," said Gemma, wondering if the soup tasted as wonderful as it looked. "Something about a painter dying here."

"Do tell us," said Daphne. "Did it inspire *L'Étrange Lune*?"

Like he was telling a ghost story, Thierry began to spin the tale, shadows dancing on his face from the candlelight. "Before the Revolution, this house was owned by a wealthy farming family who built it to be close to court. The older brother owned the land, while the younger brother dabbled in painting."

"I wouldn't say *dabbled*," said Manon with a snort. "Vallery Arnault was a famous portrait painter in his day."

Thierry waited for her to finish and let a beat of silence occur to let her know that he didn't agree with her assessment of the painter's fame before continuing. "They were rumored to have squabbled over a woman and shot each other in a duel, but not before the woman stepped in front of her lover, taking the shot before him. All three died right on our lawn out there." He motioned toward the terrace.

"*That* story is fabricated," said Manon, shooting her husband a look. "My husband likes to embellish it. Ignore him."

Thierry shrugged. "They say the house is quite haunted—that you can hear the screams of the woman in the night as well as the shots."

At that, Gemma looked up. "Shots?"

"Not in the new wing, though." He smiled and dismissed it with a wave of his hand. "You are all safe."

Suddenly, it was as if Château Verenson itself felt it needed to weigh in on the story. The doors to the terrace began to rattle in their frames and burst open, sending a rush of wind through the dining room, extinguishing the candles and sending the napkins billowing around the table. Gemma jumped in her seat, feeling her heart skipping a beat with terror. The servants scrambled to secure the doors' handles. One of them screamed and ran back into the kitchen with the tray.

Loren, closest to the doors, leapt from his chair to assist the head server in latching the door, Mick joining him from the other side of the table.

Gemma had her hand over her chest, trying to calm her thumping heart. She met Manon Valdon's eyes and could see the woman was equally startled and was clawing at her bare arms, her cool veneer shattered for a just a moment. "What on earth was that?"

Manon shook her head vigorously. "I do not know."

"Valley wind," said Thierry Valdon. "It happens all the time in June."

"It does *not*," said Manon sharply.

"Hell of a valley wind," said Mick, settling back in his seat.

The shaky staff resumed the meal, but everyone was on edge as they served the next course of trout served in a beurre blanc sauce, covered in toasted almonds and a generous helping of asparagus. One server's hand shook as he poured a dollop of sauce. Despite the gorgeous spread in front of her, Gemma kept her eye on the doors, rattled.

"The asparagus is from Manon's garden," said Thierry, winking at his wife, trying to steer the conversation.

"Hopefully no one died there," said Mick with a forced laugh. "The haunted hedge is enough... not sure your doors could take much more."

At this, everyone laughed a little uneasily. Knives scraped plates as Robert reignited the candles.

The wine flowed and the plates emptied as the six of them settled into easy conversation in multiple languages about Jean-Paul Sartre's *Les Mots*, the latest Truffaut film, and the celebrities like Jane Birkin who'd been vacationing in Saint-Tropez. Loren and Daphne had worked with Manon on several films, and Gemma sensed that Madame Valdon had cast most of the film, including Pierre Lanvin, the only principal cast member missing.

"So, Gemma," said Thierry, cutting his trout. "Enough small talk. What did you think of the script?"

"You got a script?" Loren's eyebrows rose.

"Hush," said Thierry with a playful smile to the Italian.

"Thierry gives us our pages each morning," said Loren. "Never a full script."

"You're such an artiste, Loren, you don't need them earlier," teased Daphne.

Gemma met his eyes. While they'd only had one meeting, he looked thinner than before. His face was gaunt with dark circles under his eyes, something the deep tan managed to hide. She placed her napkin to her lips as everyone had turned their attention to her, expectantly. She wasn't in the inner circle of this group, so she needed to tread carefully. "I liked it," she said, returning to cutting her asparagus, studying it intently.

"It's not a pet." Valdon chewed slowly, a tight smile forming.

At this comment, Manon cleared her throat, drawing everyone's attention. "My husband doesn't share his script in advance with everyone, so it was quite an honor that he sent it to you, Gemma. He and Paul Germaine, who is his head scriptwriter, agonized over it. You were happy with the second version, weren't you, dear?"

"No," he said in a calm yet biting manner, like this was a well-trod discussion between them. "I have never been happy with the script. You know that." His speech quickened in what appeared to be an abrupt change of topic, causing Manon to sit up straight in her chair. "Did you all know that I despise the theater?"

The confused dinner guests looked at one another, wondering how the conversation had just veered to the theater, a topic no one had been discussing.

"No," said Loren. "That's a surprise considering your wife is still one of the grande dames of the stage."

"I really don't know how you actors do theater," he continued with a snort. "I mean, Manon over there spent years reciting the same script night after night like a pet parrot."

At his comment, Manon fingered the stem of her wine goblet, her smile gone. The jaws of the remaining dinner guests went slack with surprise at the measured cruelty of his words.

"Sometimes twice a day," he continued. "It's like taking the same bus to work day after day after day as though you were bankers." As if to demonstrate, his head bobbed around in a circle. "After a while, you don't hear words anymore, do you? Just the monotony of the same lines. It's masturbation, really," he said, his tone cutting, patronizing.

"You draw energy from the audience, my *love*," said Manon, choking on the word as a steely look fixed on her beautiful features.

He pounded his fist on the table. "I adore *film* because you can take a script and give an actor a page just before the scene and get something entirely raw and real. *That* is Nouvelle Vague. Not this overrehearsed, stylized bullshit. But I did share my idea with you, Mademoiselle Turner, so now tell me." He turned to Gemma, his eyes fixed on her face and his voice raised to a shout. "What did you *think* of the draft pages I sent you?"

After hearing Valdon's declaration of the superiority of film, Gemma found she couldn't stifle a laugh that came out as a loud snort. Once she'd held Thierry Valdon in high esteem, but despite all his pomposity, his script—draft pages—whatever he called it, was a disaster. Had Loren Marantz been given more than two pages a day, he'd flee back to Firenze. Immediately, her fingers rushed to cover her mouth as another snort emitted.

Everyone around the table was now sitting on the edge of their seats from Gemma's outburst.

"Gemma?" Mick laughed nervously. "Are you okay?"

"Pardon," said Gemma, placing her hand over her mouth to force herself to stop laughing. She waved Mick off. "I was thinking of something else." Gripping the fork and knife until her fingers were white, she studied her dinner plate and tried to piece together a response. Whether the film flopped or she was fired from it, either way, this was her last chance at any career, so she had no good options. Had the Valdon of her lunch been an illusion? Had she been so desperate to leave Charlie that she had made this man into a cinematic hero? Cocteau? Now the comparison seemed ridiculous. Looking around the table, she knew that each one of the actors would suffer if she didn't speak up. "I'm sorry," said Gemma. "I feel the character of Gisele is a bit too familiar, too tropey."

He leaned toward her like he was sizing her up to eat her, and out of the corner of her eye she saw Loren and Daphne exchange worried glances.

"You aren't suggesting I'm making a Hammer film, are you, Mademoiselle Turner?" he asked.

"Not at all," she said, looking for any hints of the connection they'd shared at lunch in Paris, her opinion razor-sharp on the matter. He would be lucky to be making a Hammer film, but she needed to tread carefully. "I see what you're attempting to do: lulling the audience into expecting one horror trope—a familiar one like Hammer's vampires—only to unleash a more insidious, realistic horror underneath it. This is a story of the invasion of a people. That framework is brilliant, Monsieur Valdon. I confess that I'm a fan of Hammer films. My tastes are not highbrow, and in my humble opinion, Gisele is used much in the same manner all women are used in all horror films. She's a victim, a pawn. There is nothing new. But again, that is merely my opinion, nothing more."

Silence fell over the table, and Gemma lowered herself in her chair like a dog about to be struck by its owner. Out of the corner of her eye, she saw Manon Valdon smile.

"Gemma," said Mick, pointing at her with his fork. "I think you need to enjoy your dinner. You haven't touched a thing." He chuckled, showing his teeth. It was a tic of Mick's that she knew well. It appeared when he was angry. "Never mind her, Thierry, she fancies herself a writer. Hell, she totes around this portable typewriter with her all the time, people think she's my secretary." He waved her off like she was insignificant.

Thierry Valdon's jaw tightened. "You are correct, Mademoiselle

Turner. I did ask for your opinion, and I must admit that I agree with your assessment of what appears to be a most *dreadful* script." While it was an olive branch to her, there was real bitterness in his tone. Gemma gulped. She'd gone too far. He was seething.

The corners of his mouth turned up, and she saw the overlap of his front teeth. He resembled a wolf. "You carry a typewriter with you, Mademoiselle Turner?" Thierry addressed the rest of the table, like he was letting them in on a joke. "I'll know who to call if we need a quick retype of it."

So, this was his revenge? Belittling her in front of everyone like she was an intellectual lightweight? He'd just done the same thing to Manon about the theater. Her blood boiling, Gemma placed her knife and fork down and folded her hands. "My mother insisted that I learn to type. During the war, she said that having a skill saved her life. You seem to think it's a frivolous skill. Sorry that I don't share your opinion, nor do I find it *funny*."

"Gemma types ninety words a minute," said Mick, his eyebrow rising.

Gemma's face flushed in humiliation. How dare Mick speak about her like that, especially in front of these people—her peers! Thierry and Daphne chuckled with Mick. Her breath became shallow. *They were making fun of her. She felt like Serge at the Savoy—the joke in the room.*

Only Loren Marantz and Manon Valdon were quiet, not finding humor at her expense. At this gesture of kindness, Gemma felt her face becoming wet with tears.

Then fury welled up inside her as Gemma defended herself, defended her dream. Pride lifting her chin, she met Mick's mocking gaze directly. "I've *written* two screenplays on that typewriter. I haven't *typed* them. Thierry asked my opinion, Mick. I assume he can accept my answer."

"You know what they say about opinions, Gemma." Mick returned to his plate.

Manon frowned, nearly scowling at the agent and his vulgar suggestion. The room quieted, like a family dinner gone wrong.

"I think it's noble," said Manon.

"Yes, well, you think the theater is noble as well, my dear," said Valdon.

"Enough," said Manon sharply, her fists hitting the table.

"My sincerest apologies," said Thierry, turning to face Gemma. "I have a kinship of sorts with your mother, both of us surviving the war here. I am, however, sorry you hate my script."

"She said nothing of the sort." Loren Marantz had bundled up his napkin and tossed it on the table and addressed Manon. "I adore the theater, Manon, and your performances have never been rote." He drummed his tan fingers on the table. "And as for typing. During the war, I worked for the Allies typing battle operation notes that were sent up to Churchill for Operation Shingle because my English was good. I applaud you, Mademoiselle Turner. Now, can we get on to the dessert?"

Gemma gave a grateful nod to Loren. "I don't hate your script, Thierry. It seems you're trying to create a film about the nightmares that still plague you. I'm merely suggesting that you could break more conventions by allowing Gisele to use the power you have given her as owner of the château. Make her your hero. That would be a rare thing for a woman in 1878. Right now, she's an accessory of Pascale and Roman. There is nothing new. She is doomed."

"In the end, we are *all* doomed," said Valdon with a weary smile. He took a long sip of wine, looking extremely forlorn. "Death finds us all, eventually."

"Let's change the conversation, shall we?" Manon slid another bottle of wine toward him.

Ignoring them all, Valdon reached across the table to pour himself another glass and swallowed a rather large gulp. "No other director has done what I am attempting to do—stripping conventions of the horror film and unpeeling it slowly. Almost like poetry." Valdon's eyes shone like those of an evangelical minister—or a guitarist high on dope. Gemma had seen the same look several times, on someone in love with their own voice. The current incarnation of *L'Étrange Lune* was not stripping horror films of their conventions, and Gemma thought she'd made that clear, but she could see that Valdon *needed* this image of himself as a creative genius.

"I want to wrap nightmares in layers," he continued, not caring he was engaged in a monologue and the table was bored. "But your point is a fine one, Gemma. I haven't pushed far enough."

"Well, now, I can't wait to get my pages," said Daphne with just a hint of sarcasm.

The evening ended with baked pears in honey and dark chocolate followed by a cheese course. After dinner, the guests sat on the terrace.

Gemma found Manon and Thierry in the foyer talking in hushed tones.

"You're mad," said Thierry. "It's ridiculous."

"I see them," said Manon, her voice lowering to a whisper. "I hear the shots."

"You're exhausted, my love. The miscarriages have been too much."

"How dare you," said Manon. "You saw what happened tonight with the wind. That was not my hysteria. This place is evil, Thierry. You know it as well as I do."

A chill traveled down Gemma's spine, and she stepped back into the dining room away from them. Pushing through the very doors that had opened on their own earlier, she sat alone in a cold iron lawn chair and thought about what she'd just overheard. Their words supporting what she was feeling. This whole film seemed wrong. A voice in her head kept saying *Run, Gemma*. Lost in thought, she looked up to find Thierry Valdon towering above her.

"You startled me."

"My apologies," he said, lowering himself and pulling up another iron chair to face her. "I sincerely apologize for finding amusement in your toting around a typewriter. I'll be sure to not push you again. I was rude." He put his hand out. "Friends?"

She nodded, reaching to shake his hand, but denying him a full acceptance of his apology, the wound too fresh and deep. Sadly, this man was just like all the other directors she'd worked with in Hollywood. Afraid she couldn't hide her disappointment, she changed the subject. She nodded toward the hedge. "So, the duel happened right here?" At the thought of the painter and his brother lying dead on the grass, she could have sworn she saw something move in the darkness of the night just beyond the hedges.

"Indeed, it did. They say the distance between the brothers' pistols was memorialized by that hedgerow," said Valdon, pointing to a line of boxwoods. From the lift in his voice, she could tell he wanted to change the subject. "Have you written notes on the script?"

"I've *typed* them up," she said, daring him to make fun of her again. "Perhaps I should keep them to myself."

"No," he said, his head shaking furiously. "I would love to see your suggestions for Gisele. You are right. I gave her the ultimate power and yet led her like a lamb to slaughter."

Gemma studied him, seeing just a hint of the man who'd so captivated her in Paris, but she didn't trust him. Which was the real Valdon? The old Gemma would have looked for the good in him, but experience had taught her that people were mostly the compilation of all their sides—good and bad. Gone was her optimism.

Looking out at the hedge in front of this cold, remote estate, she recalled Manon's words. *This place is evil.* Gemma could feel it. In such a short time, this dream film was quickly becoming a nightmare.

6

Christopher Kent
November 26, 1997
Las Vegas, Nevada

Christopher pushed past the people pulling slot machines in the Las Vegas Airport, searching for the familiar face of Aunt Wanda. It was the family's first Thanksgiving without Jason, who'd joined the air force that summer. Without his goofy cousin, Christopher wasn't sure that the house would be the same during the holidays. Jason was the glue, his good-natured enthusiasm for anything sentimental always rousing the family from their separate quarters of the house to go to late-night slots at Circus Circus after the turkey was brining.

He spied Aunt Wanda near the gift shop, looking a little subdued. She was unusually quiet as they navigated their way through baggage claim and then the airport parking maze. Although it was daytime, the Las Vegas Strip neon signs just beyond the long-term parking were on, something that always amazed him.

Wanda pointed south toward Mount Potosi. "Did you know that Carole Lombard died right over there?"

Christopher adjusted his heavy backpack. "Did *you* know that Clark Gable sat for three days at the Pioneer Saloon in Goodsprings waiting for word about her? Spencer Tracy reportedly drove three hundred miles from Los Angeles to sit with his friend. They say the cigarette burns in the bar are from Gable."

Squinting, she gave a proud smile. "I should have known if there was a doomed Hollywood starlet that you'd know about her."

"Especially one so close," said Christopher with a shrug. "Jason and I love the Pioneer Saloon." As his cousin's name left his lips, he instantly regretted it as he saw the smile fade from her face. "It's just one Thanksgiving, Aunt Wanda. He'll be back."

"Will he?" He'd always been tall, but Christopher found that he now towered over her, and he could see how the color of her hair had softened from the threads of silver now woven in it. She clicked the remote on the car and it beeped to life. "You're all scattering. And he looks miserable in his air force photo."

"Everyone looks miserable in their basic training photo."

She sniffed in disagreement. That he'd only be staying two days before taking the Greyhound to Los Angeles to see his girlfriend was another sore subject between them.

"Can you drive?" She tossed him the keys.

"And we're not all scattering."

"You are," she said, opening the passenger door. "I suppose it's normal. Angela is here at least."

A junior at Columbia University film school in New York City, he hadn't been home for three months since he'd left for the fall term. His cousin was a junior at UNLV and living at home. Christopher had gotten used to the East Coast fall and once again found himself overdressed for the desert with a leather jacket and long-sleeved T-shirt. Quickly, he peeled off a layer before getting in the driver's seat.

"Remind me again why you have to go to Los Angeles to see her when you already see her in New York?" Wanda was not fond of Ivy Cross, his girlfriend of nearly a year. A fellow film student, Ivy was the only child of producer Zander Cross, who was famous for the cop drama franchise *City PD*. Syndication of the shows was lucrative, with episodes always running on cable television.

"You don't like her."

"I didn't say that." Wanda let a beat pass. "I think she's bossy."

"I need bossy," said Christopher, putting the car in gear as he blasted the air conditioner. "You're bossy."

Like a fever breaking, a loud eruption of laughter came from the passenger seat, and his Aunt Wanda was over her spell of melancholy. She began updating him on the new family dog and Angela's love life. "She's bringing the new one for Thanksgiving."

"You like him?"

She shrugged.

"I'm sensing a pattern here."

"Oh, be quiet." She pulled the seat belt across her lap.

Living in New York had changed his perspective. Everything was now smaller by comparison. The one thing that wasn't was his childhood bedroom, which was about twice the size of his Harlem apartment. Flicking on the light, he saw the familiar band posters—the Smiths, the Cure, Nirvana—and then finally the thing he always looked for, his framed poster of Gemma Turner.

Gemma Turner, Savoy hotel, April 1968

Leaning against the doorframe, he studied the familiar scene. The tragic starlet surrounded by partygoers. Within two months of that photo being taken, she would be gone. Over the years, after finding out about her tragic end, Christopher had studied every inch of the photo for clues. It was a ridiculous theory, but something about that photo haunted him, even beyond what had happened with his mother. Oh, the power this photo still had over him. He placed his hand to his mouth; seeing it again always took the very breath out of him. What would it have been like to have *been* in that room with her?

"Why her?" The voice behind him broke the spell. He turned to find Aunt Wanda standing behind him, peering over his shoulder. She was now dressed in Adidas running tights and an oversize sweatshirt. While Jason had gotten the framed print for him as a birthday present, no one in the family knew the true significance of this poster—or his obsession with Gemma Turner. He'd never shared the details about the hotel in Pittsburgh, and no one had ever connected the dots.

"Let me show you." Pulling out a box from his closet marked *Fragile* and *Do Not Toss*, Christopher dug deep through a meager stack of magazines featuring anything on Gemma Turner that he could find—and information had been sparse. He'd had better luck with the VHS tapes of her movies and finally found what he was looking for at the bottom of that stack. There it was: the worn, folded bill that he'd kept like a fucked-up memento of the end of his childhood, knowing on some level that the events of that day would mark him forever.

He handed the paper to her and watched her face as she opened it. As she scanned the bill, the details weren't registering. "I don't get it."

"It's from the hotel in Pittsburgh where Uncle Martin came for me that day," he said, waiting until he saw recognition in her face. "You know you never *actually* asked me what had happened that day with Mom."

Looking from the paper to the poster, her face fell. Wearily, she folded the paper and handed it back to him. "So, this has been what all this Gemma Turner stuff has been about all these years?" She sat down on his bed and put her head down. "I went out of my way to *not* ask you about those days—and it was days, Christopher, not one day.

You were in that hotel room for nearly three days while Pammy was catatonic. I just wanted you to forget it."

"I couldn't forget something like that." He was surprised to find her so defensive, and worried as he always did that somehow, he would be too much trouble and she and Uncle Martin would send him away. All his life he ran a constant inventory in his head of his merits: His grades were better than Jason's but not Angela's, who had straight As. While Jason got into trouble regularly, Christopher was never a problem. He'd tried to blend in and disappear between the other two kids, but the knowledge that he was truly alone in this world was never far from him. That fear had stretched into adulthood.

As his aunt gazed up at him, he saw tears had begun streaming down her face. "I failed you, didn't I? We weren't enough, were we?" While it was directed at him, she was also talking about his mother.

Christopher sat down beside her and pulled her toward him. "I've loved it here, but you can't expect me to forget."

"I just wanted you to have a happy life and let it go—"

"You mean let *her* go."

She nodded and pulled away to face him. "Christopher. If you never listen to anything else in your life, listen to me now. You need to let her go." Pointing to the poster, like she was stabbing at it. "This... this is *not* healthy."

She was right of course. It wasn't healthy to keep a framed reminder of the very chain of events in 1986 in Pittsburgh like it held some secret mystery for him to solve. Somewhere in his mind, he believed if he could just rewind the film of his own life to that precise moment and place a *different* photo on that wall, he'd have his mother back. But then he'd found out Gemma Turner had her own mystery, and the pull of it was all too powerful. His aunt Wanda could have asked anything of him—except this—except to forget. He was never letting go of that photo and—most importantly—to its connection to his mother.

Knowing this might be the only moment he had, he pointed at the poster. "She went crazy when she saw this picture. Why?"

Aunt Wanda shrugged. "Who knows, Christopher. She flipped out over a banana sandwich...a red sofa...daisies. The list goes on, you know this. You had to manage all those things. We had to unwind all of that when you came to live with us."

"A banana sandwich?" Christopher smirked.

"What?" She looked confused.

"You're basing my mother's sanity on the fact that she hated a banana sandwich?" Christopher did what he'd always done in tense situations: tried to defuse the tension with humor. He pulled a face.

"Your grandfather made them for us." She wiped tears away from her face and sniffled. "They're all gone, you know. This is a tough Thanksgiving. Mom, Dad, and Pammy are all gone. Now you and Jason."

"I'm still here for two days and then back in four weeks for Christmas." He pulled her close to hug her. "But I know what you mean."

She got up from the bed and smoothed her sweatshirt and wiped her face, grimacing at the trail of mascara on her hands.

"I can't do that, you know," he said. "Forget her. It isn't that you and Uncle Martin didn't give me everything. You gave me more than I could ever have asked for, but you can't ask for that in return. Not that." Christopher debated asking her the next question, but he had to do it. He had to know. "Did she know Gemma Turner?"

Wanda stared at the photo and laughed. "I hate to burst your bubble, Christopher, but your mother had terrible emotional problems and medicated with alcohol and drugs. She was an addict. She did not *know* Gemma Turner. Maybe in her head she did, but not in real life. The one that matters."

He let her words settle. Aunt Wanda liked having the last word, and he was good at giving people what they wanted. While he understood that she needed his mother's story to be a simple one—a sister weighted down by her addictions—Christopher knew in his heart that his mother's true tale had been hidden from him—from all of them. He just had to find it.

Aunt Wanda stepped into the hallway but poked her head back into the room. "When you leave in two days," she said, pointing to the poster, "either take that thing with you or it goes in the trash."

Christopher felt guilty all through Thanksgiving, like he'd broken his aunt's heart, which killed him because she'd been his lifeline for more than ten years now. As he'd been instructed to do, he rolled the poster up and took it with him on the bus to Los Angeles, leaving the empty frame behind.

When she took him to the bus terminal, she held him tight. "Live in this world, Christopher. I worry so much about you." Then she released him and walked away, never looking back.

Rather than the Greyhound bus, Ivy had wanted to send a private plane to Las Vegas to pick him up, but Aunt Wanda refused. "You need to pay your own way with her." Already, Aunt Wanda was worried that they'd be flying back to New York in Zander Cross's private plane.

Arriving in the Los Angeles bus station, he saw all eyes turn as a woman with a Louise Brooks haircut and cat-eye sunglasses made her way across the terminal toward him. Ivy had done her best to leave any hint of the Southern California beach behind her, rejecting everything that looked like her much-hated twenty-six-year-old stepmother, Vera, who was a buxom, tanned blonde. She didn't own anything that wasn't black, from turtleneck sweaters, jeans, and leather biker jacket to her Frye motorcycle boots that squeaked as she crossed the station.

She looked around like the place was a curiosity. "I've never *been* to the bus station," she said, her voice breathless.

"It's not so bad," said Christopher, hoisting his bag over his shoulder.

She eyed the terminal like she disagreed with his assessment entirely.

Ivy lived in a world of private jets and pool houses. Celebrities like Tom and Brad were spoken of by their first names only and were on Zander Cross's speed dial. At any given time, a Zander Cross TV show was being broadcast somewhere in the world, causing Ivy to remark when she saw one, "Oh, there's another Louis Vuitton for Vera."

Christopher was sad he wouldn't get to meet the infamous Vera, who was now vacationing in Bali with Ivy's father.

Ivy drove them down Sunset Boulevard in her Mercedes convertible, pointing out landmarks like the Viper Room and the Whiskey a Go Go as they passed them. The road wound, and she turned off to a street with tall palm trees and a mix of Georgian and Mediterranean-style mansions with gates and elegantly manicured roundabouts.

"You'll love this little piece of trivia," said Ivy, pointing to a modest Spanish-style house. "That was Jean Harlow's house. I think she died there." They pulled up to a gate that began to open slowly. Something caught Ivy's eye, and she opened the door and trotted over to retrieve a newspaper from a lawn attached to a modest two-story brick home. By the time she'd returned, the gate was fully opened and she handed the paper to Christopher. "Uncle Mickey always forgets to cancel his paper when he's out of town."

"Uncle Mickey?"

"Mick Fontaine."

Christopher's head whipped around to get another look at the lawn and the house. "*The* Mick Fontaine?"

Ivy chuckled. "He's ancient. I have no idea what you mean, but yes, he's quite unique."

"No," said Christopher. "You know Mick Fontaine?"

"That is his daily newspaper you are holding in your hands. He is dad's tennis partner and the very culprit who betrayed me by introducing dad to Vera. He knows I think he is the devil for that move."

"He was Gemma Turner's agent."

Ivy shrugged. "Okay."

"You didn't know that?"

"He's a fossil, Christopher. He was probably Jesus's agent."

"Can I meet him?"

"Of course, but sadly, not this visit. He's in Maui this week."

Christopher's heart was racing. Here was an actual connection to Gemma Turner. It felt like a piece of the puzzle falling into place, and he had a feeling none of it was a coincidence.

7

Gemma Turner
June 4, 1968
Amboise, France

Gemma sat straight up in bed, startled. Gunshots. Real or ghostly, the sound of gunfire had awakened her once again. Pulling the pillow over her head, she heard something scratching from across the room. "What now?" Rolling over, she saw a thick bundle of pages appearing under the door. It was today's pages of the script.

Before she'd gone to bed, she'd taken all her notes and given them to a staffer, who assured her Valdon "worked through the night." Once again, Thierry had requested her notes on his script. She had taken him at his word and given him the scenes she'd written in Paris.

Now, flipping through today's pages, she saw that none of her suggestions had been made.

Wearily, she made her way to the bath and her awaiting costume.

"I mustn't be late," she said, looking at her face in the bathroom mirror. The face that stared back seemed to scream *Run, Gemma.*

From her experience, whether it was an American beach flick or a low-budget French film, all film sets were surprisingly the same. A film might begin as a creative endeavor, but it ended up a technical symphony. Equipment—long microphones, lights, and cables—fed a film shoot. While the pastries were better on this film, it was the same waiting game—waiting for the perfect light, the best angle, the traffic to clear. If you were an actor, you were always waiting. Grabbing a café au lait, she paced back and forth while the grip crew set up for today's scene in the old town on the south bank facing the Loire River.

With its rustic half-timbered buildings and clock tower, old town Amboise could have played the part of medieval village or Shakespearean square. A good crew could scrub the looming castle and block off the modern cars from the shot to re-create the quaint Eastern European towns that were so popular in horror films. On the next square over, idling beyond the alleys, were two carriages without horses. As if on cue, a trailer carrying live animals pulled up behind the carriages. Given the tight budget, this was the only location shoot; the rest would all take place at Château Verenson.

There was no costumer on set. Five costumes, each freshly pressed and in plastic garment bags, had been placed in Gemma's closet with each scene and date on them. For today's, she was dressed in a bronze princess-line satin dress with a yellow skirt and sandals. Underneath the dress was an uncomfortable corset not yet pulled tight.

Francine Delon, the production manager, made her way over to Gemma, croissant in hand. "Precends ça," said Francine, pushing another pile of papers into Gemma's hands with not so much as a smile. It was yet another copy of revisions on the shooting script.

"Wait," said Gemma, but the woman had already walked away.

Thumbing through the script, Gemma could see that this was the same version that had been delivered to her room. It was dreadful.

Gisele sees Pascale in town. There is a strained passion between them. Pascale is with another young woman in the village, and he is helping her and her mother, but it is clear that he longs to be with Gisele. They speak briefly and she watches him walk away, desire clear on her face.

The rest of the pages contained a scene in the square between Gisele and Pascale that had dialogue so wooden it was worse than any cheap horror film she had seen. Grimacing, she read it aloud in French: "'Desire clear on her face.'" Rolling her eyes, she crossed the street to the souvenir shop and bought a pen and some writing paper. Taking a seat on the bench facing the square, she began to rewrite her lines.

"You're out of bed awfully early," said a voice behind her. It was Mick.

"Who could sleep with the gunshots?" said Gemma.

"Again?" Mick looked puzzled.

"You didn't hear them?" She was still furious with Mick from dinner, so she was terse. He knew it; trying to make small talk was his way of apologizing.

"I think you're hearing things," said Mick. "I'll give you that the dinner was weird—all that talk of the theater, with the doors blowing open."

"It was like some fucked-up séance. The whole place gives me the creeps."

"I'd agree with you that it might be wind from the great beyond, but the Valdons are both so strange, I'm not sure it wasn't just theater for us."

Taking that in, Gemma turned to him, shocked. "You think they staged the door blowing open like a pair of Victorian mediums? Why?"

"Dunno," he said with a shrug. "Effect. I think they're a strange couple."

Recalling the exchange between Manon and Thierry, Gemma shook her head. "I'm not so sure I agree with you, Mick. I overheard them talking. She was terrified and says the place is evil. I have to say that I agree."

"I'm just saying I'd bet on those two before I'd think the ghost of the hedgerow did it."

Gemma wasn't so sure. She was hearing gunshots, then there was the note in the typewriter back in Paris and the man who wasn't there at the Savoy. She was seeing and hearing things. It was time to face that perhaps the stress was causing her to crack. She swallowed, getting courage to broach the subject. "I've been thinking. Maybe I should go home," she said quietly, waiting for Mick's response.

"To London?"

"Los Angeles."

Mick shook his head. "That's a terrible idea, kid. You walk away from this film, it will look bad for both of us. Finish this. Then you can come back."

"I have a very bad feeling about this place... this film."

"It's all in your imagination." Mick came around and sat next to her on the bench, fanning himself with a straw hat. Looking up at the sun, he squinted. "It's going to be a scorcher."

"And look at me dressed in this long-sleeved gown." She pulled at it.

"Well, you said you were tired of beach films."

A commotion among the crew signaled that Thierry Valdon had finally arrived.

Taking the script from Francine, Thierry placed himself behind Claude, the cameraman, who was fixed with the camera in the center of the square. Then he spent twenty minutes walking back and forth between the camera and the proposed shot, angling the camera, the boom, and the lights.

"What do you think of that?"

"That's a hell of a lot of time to set up a scene," said Mick with a whistle. "Maybe he is a genius after all. Or he's crazy?"

"They often go hand in hand," said Gemma under her breath. Audiences had no idea the hours that went into minutes of celluloid, but this was something different. Most directors Gemma had worked with were not this precise.

"You be careful with him," said Mick. "I'm only trying to protect you from yourself."

"When have you ever protected me?" Gemma spun to face him. "You certainly weren't protecting me last night." The mere suggestion that Mick looked out for her was infuriating. Mick had *never* protected her interests. Far from it. He'd have been content to keep doing beach films until she was thirty years old as long as it paid for his house in Beverly Hills. When Charlie Hicks came along, Mick could have intervened, but he thought Charlie would be helpful to Gemma's celebrity status. And then, in the last film, *Through the Lens*, when it was clear the shoot was going off the rails, Gemma had frantically called Mick, but he couldn't be bothered to come to London. The other actors, knowing the film was a bust, had their agents on set leveraging the disaster to negotiate more lucrative contracts with the studio, protecting their clients' interests long-term. Mick had a tennis tournament that was more important than those meetings. In the end, it was no surprise the film's failure had largely been pinned on Gemma's inexperience. She'd been the only one who hadn't been protected.

He wagged a finger at her. "I got you this role when no one was returning my calls. And as for last night, I was trying to save you from yourself. I don't know where this crazy idea that you're a writer has come from, but you nearly got yourself sent home."

With a frustrated sigh, she looked out at the set to see that Pierre Lanvin had joined Valdon in the square. Tall and gangly, Pierre nodded politely while Valdon gestured wildly and paced back and forth like he was demonstrating the proper way to walk.

"You know why he is not staying at Château Verenson, don't you?"

Gemma shook her head.

"He slept with Manon." Mick nodded toward her costar for the morning.

"How do *you* know?"

"Rumor."

Gemma snorted in disbelief. "If it were true, then why would Valdon hire him to work opposite his wife?"

"He wants to get rid of her."

She raised an eyebrow. "You're not a very nice man, are you, Mick?"

He placed his straw panama hat on his head. "No, Gemma, I am not, but you don't pay me to be."

"I don't pay you at all, really. You just take a pound of flesh."

"Have you read today's pages?" Mick snatched them out of her hands.

Pulling out his reading glasses from his front shirt pocket, he scanned the pages. "Did you know this was in French?"

Gemma blinked incredulously. "Did you think this was an English-speaking film?"

Mick was silent.

"Mick? You have no idea what this film is about, do you?"

Pushing the script at her, he asked, "What does it say?"

Gemma translated the words for him. She watched Mick's face absorb each line.

Her agent pulled his mouth tight. "The dialogue sounds like a stag film."

"I think even *they* have more detailed scripts."

"Maybe it's different in translation?" He smiled weakly, then lowering his voice. "Do your best, kid."

"He asked for my notes," said Gemma. Placing her sunglasses on, she focused on her notebook. "So I sent them to him. He clearly has not read them."

From a distance, she heard, "Silence, moteur, action!"

"Gemma." Mick's face had turned a bright red.

"He keeps saying he wants my help with the script."

"He doesn't." Mick shook his head gravely.

"Gemma," Valdon barked as if on cue.

She got up and shook her skirt, taking her notes with her. Mick grabbed her hand and jerked her back.

"Please stop declaring yourself some kind of writer, will you?"

As she walked past the cameras, she found Pierre standing by the carriage, smoking.

"We haven't been properly introduced," she said, placing her hand out. Up close, he was much taller, with sideburns that were half-natural and half created by makeup. His blond hair was curly and styled stiffly with hairspray. He was known for his masculine looks, and Gemma thought his jaw was the most angular she'd ever seen.

"Gemma Turner." He extended his hand and chuckled. "The American Gem. You are so rare and valuable, it seems, so rare that you replaced Manon." He gave a belly laugh like the idea was preposterous.

Gemma raised her chin and pushed past him. She had dealt with difficult people on sets before. This one was no different.

He was still chuckling when Thierry approached them, sensing some tension.

"Pierre," he barked. "I need you back down at the carriage."

The actor shrugged, taking one last deep drag from his cigarette before tossing it on the ground.

"What was that about?" Valdon watched the actor amble over to the cameraman.

"Nothing," said Gemma. Startled, she felt a tug and realized that the hair and makeup woman had come up behind her and was tightening her corset. Another tug and she heard another woman exclaiming that Gemma's hair needed tending. "Did you get my notes on the script... the additional scenes? I sent them last night."

"Did you get mine?"

"You... you mean what was delivered today? I thought you had agreed that the structure needed to change so that Gisele's—"

"I agreed to nothing." Defiantly, he stuck his jaw out, meeting her eyes, daring her to cross him.

"I thought..." Gemma struggled to gather her rewritten pages and gave them to Thierry Valdon like a child would give artwork to a parent. He glanced down at them, placing his hand up to stop the hair and makeup people, who were itching to get at Gemma's face. Then he ripped the pages up, letting them scatter on the cobblestones below.

Gemma stared down at her notes, speechless. Her emotions ranged from confusion to rage.

Valdon leaned close to whisper like they were the only two people on the set. "You have this story in your soul, like I do. Now, I want you to throw out those notes and feel the lines you wrote. Have confidence. I don't care if you flub your lines. In fact, we'll do twenty takes to get you into the character. I don't want you reading lines, no matter how well you recite them. D'accord?"

"It isn't the lines, Thierry. It's the scene itself. There is nothing new here. No way my ad-libbing lines is going to change that," she said with a protest, and it was clear to her that this man had never seen a horror film in his life. "Have you seen an actual horror film? *Nosferatu*?"

He flashed her a look that confirmed her suspicions. He had no idea what he was doing. The arrogance of the man was astounding.

"We will talk about your *little* notes later." He smiled, motioning for the crew to take her away. "We keep the framework I set up in the script, but feel free to change up the dialogue, of course. No riding the bus, am I right?" He made a masturbatory sign with his right hand. "We'll talk tonight after dinner."

Gemma stopped walking, her mouth agape as the crew laughed at his hand gestures. What had she gotten herself into? She had seen this look countless times, the condescension, the humoring. Everything he had said last night had been for show. She looked around the set. Did everyone else know this was a terrible film?

Like an army general in battle, she knew she would have to deliver the performance of her lifetime to even make a dent in this piece-of-shit film. The best she could hope for was for critics to say *Gemma Turner does the most with every scene she is in*. She bent over to pick up her notes. Changing the lines of dialogue didn't fix anything. Her head held high, she lifted the hem of her skirt and walked over to join the waiting hair and makeup crew.

That night, she claimed exhaustion and ate dinner in her room. After her tray was cleared, there was a knock at her door. She found Valdon leaning against the doorframe. "Come. I want to show you something."

"No," she said as she began to close the door, realizing that it was his house and the gesture was rude.

"Please," he said in exaggerated English.

Reluctantly, she followed him down the stairs and out the door toward a long path shrouded by dramatic twisted oak trees. As he led them away from the main house, Gemma raised her eyebrow suspiciously. She didn't want to be alone with Thierry Valdon.

"I just want to show you where I lived when I was young," he said. "For a small period of time during the war, this was a home for boys."

"I didn't know you actually *lived* here as a child." This revelation surprised her, though it made sense somehow that he would seek to buy this place as an adult.

He walked ahead of her, hands in his pockets, his linen pants and untucked white shirt flowing with the slight breeze. After a few steps, he turned to see if she was following. When he saw she hadn't moved, he stopped, like a parent patiently waiting. "This is the only place where I feel safe."

They walked along in silence, the sounds of night insects loud. It was the first time Gemma understood how vast these grounds were. Midway down the path, he turned onto a secondary track. The light from the house was still visible, and Mick's loud laughter could be heard carrying in the air, giving Gemma a moment's reassurance.

They reached a stone building that appeared to precede the house by decades. Valdon opened a metal door that was attached to a structure that had been built into the hillside, like a bunker. As she stepped into the building, the cooler temperature hit her instantly. From beneath her sandals, she could feel the damp earthen floor.

"What is this place?" She hesitated. Being alone with him in a secluded spot, far away from Mick and Manon, wasn't in her best interests. She was already having bad feelings about the house and the film. Valdon had also proven to have a volatile and cruel streak. In the past she had forgiven men for their cruelty and focused only on their kindnesses. Usually, it was based on wishful thinking, and she'd learned the hard way that the cruelty in someone was often the more defining characteristic, not the lesser one. She backed away from the door.

"It's a wine cave. Well, I guess it was a cave for other things, but I use it as a wine cave now." He flicked on a lamp, and pale yellow light from a dim bulb washed over the space. Another flick of a switch and a line of scones illuminated a pathway of rows of barrels. "You like it?"

Her eyes explored each corner and she gave a nod. Above her, the cave's ceiling had been carved out quite high. This building did not feel like her grandmother's cramped root cellar.

"I come here sometimes, to think." He motioned to a table and chairs. Pulling a bottle from the shelf, he began working the cork. He motioned her in.

When Gemma didn't move past the threshold or sit in the chair, he stopped. "Please."

In the light with the dramatic shadows, he appeared gaunt; his cheekbones, already high and regal, now stood out sharply. She knew directors who lost weight during filming only to regain it after the wrap, yet Valdon's seemed too drastic. Then again, Gemma had only met him once before, and her memory of him had been unreliable. She was studying him intently, wondering why he'd brought her here, the urge to flee never far from her thoughts. *Run, Gemma*, said a voice inside her.

"This is a Chenin Blanc and Chardonnay blend. My own creation." Placing two glasses on the table, he poured the wine, turning the bottle to stop the flow.

Taking the seat opposite her, he seemed lost in his thoughts, touching the stem of his wineglass. "People stored their valuables here during the war. They told us children to come here and hide if the Germans came through the line. Every day, we children lived in fear of that happening. We always knew the nearest cave. I can't tell you how often I played hide-and-seek in this very space. Of course, it was a terrible hiding place because everyone hid in here as well." He gave a hearty laugh, but his eyes betrayed him. There was no joy in him tonight, and the laugh faded quickly enough and was replaced with a somber, thin smile. He was deep inside his memories now. "I would hide right over there where the rock dips back a bit." He looked down at the wineglass, avoiding her gaze. "You are angry."

"I'm confused." Blurting out the truth felt freeing.

"Why?" He was fixated on something, twirling something in his fingers, never meeting her eyes.

"Why?" she nearly shouted. Her voice finally caused him to look at her.

"What do you want?" His face was inquisitive, like a child's.

"I beg your pardon?" Gemma felt herself pull back in the chair, thrown by the question, but also furious at his audacity.

He looked surprised and squirmed in his seat.

She leaned forward, her fury driving a clarity that she had never quite felt before. "Why do you ask 'What do I want?' like you're some philosopher? Don't you dare dangle dreams in front of me. I was very clear with you about my dreams. I want to *write.* You fed into that dream, sent scripts to my hotel, promised me I would be a collaborator with you—'the Nouvelle Vague way,' you said. Then I arrived here, and you mocked me as typist in front of everyone who matters in this film. You played with me like a cruel barn cat, coaxing me to send my notes to you. Like a fool, I wrapped them up and sent them to you in the night. Not only have you ignored my meager pages, but you ripped up my 'little notes' in front of me. They may not mean much to you, but they're *everything* to me. If they weren't good, just say so." Folding her arms, Gemma sat back, feeling like a burden had been lifted from her.

"Like you, I want to create worlds," he said, "Sex, fatherhood, food, alcohol, love—nothing has truly pleased me in this life, so I am constantly compelled to create another world. Why is this current world so unbearable that I need to manipulate another inside of it? Replicate it as a god would? I don't know, but I am compelled to do it."

Gemma felt herself tighten. She couldn't bear another monologue from this narcissistic ass. He was toying with her again, and she was done—done with this film and him.

Valdon studied her as he'd done at the Paris café the first time they'd met. "Your hair, for example; I made it more vibrant than it is in real life. It was beautiful. Why do I feel the need to create a reality that is not my own?"

"Oh, I don't know, Thierry. From what I've seen of your work, I think you're running from your past."

"We artists are always running from our past. The art we create is simply a reaction to where we've been, whether we know it or not. So that is what I had once wanted most in this world. To create worlds where this one has fallen short." He held up a finger. "But what we should be doing is running from our future."

She gave him a confused look.

"We think we're always running toward something better, but we're simply running toward our own end." He took a long sip of wine and placed the glass back on the table. "I'm sorry, but I cannot give you what you want."

Her brow furrowed, and it felt like she'd been punched in the gut. "Is my work not good?"

"It's quite admirable, actually." His voice quickened, something Gemma noticed he did when he was nervous. "Your instincts are great. You see, in Paris, when I made the offer to you to be my collaborator, I was being sincere, but I was also being generous. I felt I had time to give, more films to give the world. Now, you see, what I want the most is time." He looked down at the dirt floor, then nodded like he was happy with his answer.

"Time?" Gemma was wondering if the wine had gone to her head. He was talking in riddles.

"My idea for this film began with the image of the character of Pascale after he is drained. It was the same emptiness in the eyes of people during the war. They were subjugated and humiliated, or they had sold their souls, so to speak, to get along. It was that image of Pascale drained on the bed at Avril's hands that was the genesis of *L'Étrange Lune.* I saw the twisted white sheets and their naked bodies, hers invigorated, and his a husk. But then I saw you on that billboard... that look you gave the photographer over your shoulder. It was there that I envisioned Gisele. Everything just snapped into place—all the pieces."

"But—"

"Please let me finish. You are angry with me, and I owe you an explanation." His eyes slowly left the glass and refocused on her. "When we finally met, I could see our future so clearly. First this film and then after..." He let the sentence fall, and Gemma looked away, blushing. "And I could see from your face that day that you could see it as well."

He waited for a response, but she refused to give him one. Any childish dreams she'd had about him once were gone. And they had been killed when she met Manon. She would not be "the other woman."

"If you recall, I had to leave our lunch early in our first meeting. I fear the news I got that day was not good. *L'Étrange Lune* will have the distinction of being my *final* film."

Confusion registered on her face. Was he finished directing films? "I don't understand."

"I'm dying." As soon as the words left his lips, he looked depleted, like the gravity of them had just finally sunk in.

From the hollow look on his face and the weight loss, Gemma knew he was telling the truth. In a moment, she calculated the loss of him—both to her and the world. He had been correct. Once, she had seen them together, their fates entwined. Somewhere in her mind she had let the seeds of those ideas germinate within a walled garden.

The two of them would create beautiful films together, their connection fusing them together both professionally—and then of course—personally. She had to admit that even if she might have never acted on it. She'd thought it. In that make-believe world, she felt the loss of that dream, however far away it had been or however unreal and complicated it might have been for them both. She met his eyes. "I'm so sorry, Thierry."

"I want time," he said. A sad smile formed on the corners of his lips. "But I won't get it."

She placed her hands on her face, then reached over to touch his hand. "I don't know what to say. Is there something—anything—you can do? Treatment somewhere? Switzerland?"

"Not for the type of cancer that I have, I'm afraid." He straightened as though he'd said too much. "I apologize. I shouldn't have shocked you like this, but I know you feel that I have taken something from you, and you deserve an answer. The truth is that I have nothing to give you."

Gemma blinked, trying to make sense of what he was telling her. "What does Manon think?"

"She does not know."

Gemma nearly choked at this revelation. The order of things was all wrong. His wife, Manon, needed to know first, before a total stranger like Gemma. Her spine straightened and she pulled her hand back. This felt wrong. "Surely, you've told her. Thierry, you *need* to tell her. She's your wife."

"Manon and I have stopped looking at each other, Gemma. It's always the way with couples when they fall out of love. They stop seeing each other."

"This isn't about a tiff with Manon, Thierry, or a romantic idea of love. You *need* to tell your wife." The idea that he was keeping this type of news from his wife was childish and selfish. Gemma felt herself recoil.

"I haven't told anyone," he said. "Except *you*. I have always been a man of great passion, but I've been accused of being a man who reveals little of himself. That day was so cruel because I saw our future so clearly and then, later, the demise of it. If I tell Manon, she will insist I spend my final days in Saint-Tropez turning myself into a raisin as if the sunshine and surf will make my death any easier. I'm not sure she's in the emotional state right now for more. It's been a tough time for her."

"And it is going to get tougher." The burden of this horrible secret felt as though it were too much for their relationship. They were colleagues, yes, but they weren't friends. There was no deep history between them. What they had been was a possibility to each other, nothing more. Why had he shared this terrible secret with her, a stranger?

He rubbed his face, his gaze far away like he was thinking of the next thing to say. The wistful smile on his face gutted her. "So, you see, if this is to be my last film, then it must be *mine*, not yours and not *ours*, no matter what my dreams for us had been." He leaned forward. "I want to make this film, and I don't want anyone stopping me from creating my unique vision. I appreciate what you are trying to do with all your notes and your scripts, but it must be my legacy, so I demand total control over it. You will have other opportunities to create films, but I will not." He stood and placed his hands on the back of his chair, leaning heavily.

"I could help you." Gemma was beside him, touching him lightly on the arm.

"With your vision of my film?" The way he said it was like it was distasteful. He stood facing her, resembling a cornered animal, his eyes wide. He was breathing heavily like he had been running, his chest rising and falling. Then, with a fury, he grabbed her, pulling her toward him, and kissed her, nearly lifting her off her feet. For his gaunt appearance, he was strong, their bodies crashing against each other and the chairs hitting the floor. As he pushed her onto the table, his body heavy on hers and wineglasses scattering from the table, Gemma had several thoughts. The first was that this was a very, very bad idea. The second was that she'd felt with his confession that he'd manipulated her with this forced intimacy. Her mother used to tell her cautionary tales of soldiers shipping off to war using their mortality and potential tour of duty at the front to prey on vulnerable women's sympathy to do things they wouldn't normally do in the wee hours. Was that what he doing now? No matter how hard she tried, Gemma found she couldn't trust his motives.

But the most powerful thought, the one that sent her hands pushing him away, was that he'd made certain that while her body was welcome, her *mind* was not. In that regard, he was like every other director she'd ever known.

Scrambling to her feet, she did what her mind told her. *Run, Gemma.* Out the cave she bolted, her legs pushing her down the path through the canopy of trees until she found herself running parallel to the haunted hedgerow and then inside the house and up the stairs to her room, where finally her legs gave out, and she locked her door behind her.

8

Christopher Kent
June 8, 1998
New York

It was pouring rain outside the packed Hungarian bakery. Christopher managed to find a table for four with only two chairs. Looking around, he saw that the rest of the chairs were being used by a chemistry study group. Like a breeze, Ivy Cross shook off her leather biker jacket and arranged herself in the precariously wobbly seat opposite him.

"This chair is messed up." She teetered, her bracelets clanking.

"I know," he said, brushing back the shock of auburn hair that curled across his face. This reminded him that he desperately needed a haircut, but his final short film on photographer Rick Nash was late, so it would have to wait a bit longer. Rolling up the sleeves on his shirt, he shrugged. "They picked off the best ones for that table over there."

"Is yours better?"

"It is," he said.

"Then give it to me, asshole. Be a little chivalrous, will you?'

Christopher stood and bent like a knight for Ivy to take his better chair.

Once settled, she leaned over and spoke rather breathlessly as she flipped through her notebook, wiping away raindrops from the paper. "I don't even know how to tell you this."

He shot her a look. God, she was dramatic. Returning to his own notebook, he grinned. "Give it a try."

"You're going to lose it," she said, with a slight uptick of her crimson lip that reminded him of Elvis. "I mean, you're not going to be able to handle this news."

This was her tell when something was important. Whatever she was about to say was going to be big, so he closed his notebook and focused all his attention on her. "Hit me."

"I got an invitation to see *L'Étrange Lune*. I think I can get you in as well." Leaning back, she awaited his response and inhaled with excitement, holding her breath.

He felt her go smaller and then come back, like a real-life *Vertigo* moment. The room seemed to spin under him. He blinked. "What did you just say?"

"I'll speak slow. I. Have. A. Ticket. To. *L'Étrange Lune*."

"My *L'Étrange Lune*?"

"Well, I wouldn't say you *owned* the film," she said with a snort.

"You mean the film that I'm obsessed with. The one that I talk about constantly."

"Incessantly," she corrected him. "Yes, that one."

"You have a ticket." *L'Étrange Lune* was Gemma's final film. It was the only film of hers he'd never seen—no one had seen it. There were rumors of a mysterious bootleg version of the film shown every few years, but there weren't many details, and it was just a rumor on the message boards. Scant mention on an AOL room about a filmmaker, Anthony A, who might have had a copy, but no one could find him.

Christopher was itchy all over. He *had* to see this film. No one knew or cared more about Gemma Turner than he did. "Where did you get this ticket?"

"My dad," she said, a rare sheepish look.

"Why does your dad have a ticket?" He was more than a little annoyed that she was being so coy.

"I—I don't know." Ivy was at a rare loss for words. "I don't think he was permitted to talk about it. He's quite cagey about the whole thing. There's a weird version of it that plays. He said he saw it ten years ago and that it was strange, like it lives... exists." Her brow furrowed. "Why are you being such a dick about this? I thought you'd be happy. My dad knows you're obsessed with Gemma Turner and thinks he can get another ticket for you."

"How?"

"He says he's one of le Soixante-Quinze?"

"The what?"

"It's a group of seventy-five people who get to see the film every ten years."

Christopher's head was swimming with all this new information. He'd been hoping to talk to Mick Fontaine the next time he went home with Ivy. Vera was now pregnant, and Zander was insistent that Ivy attend the baby shower next month. Ivy was refusing to go unless Christopher went with her to offer emotional support. She couldn't hear anything about her new half sibling without breaking into sobs.

Ivy rolled her eyes. "It does appear that you are correct in your paranoid, crazy theory that no one discusses the film."

"I knew it," said Christopher, recalling the rumors about Anthony A having the only version of the film. He began rubbing his jeans nervously. "It's probably just outtakes someone found, or fan art."

"Stop doing that." She pointed to his hands with a disgusted look.

"Like I said, he really won't talk about the film, which is odd, because he yammers on about everything, but I think he's afraid. He said he was shaken when he saw it, that there was something wrong with it. He'd know if it was simply fan art."

Zander Cross was many things, but the man knew film. If it was a hack job, Zander Cross wouldn't give the film the time of day. "He was shaken by it, and yet he still thinks you should see it?"

"He *thinks* it's a rite of passage for me to see it, as the child of a Hollywood producer," she said slowly to emphasize her point. "Also, Vera's birthday is the day of the screening. It's become a 'thing' between them that he be there for her party, and now she's big as a house." She rolled her eyes.

Sometimes he wished Ivy could hear herself. Hatred for Vera aside, she had *one* ticket. There was the possibility of a second, but she didn't currently possess a second one. These weren't tickets to a sold-out Cure concert; this was fucking *L'Étrange Lune.* True, he didn't own the film, but it was his film... his obsession. Hours... hours he spent on AOL chat rooms and buying up old Gemma Turner memorabilia. She knew this about him. Even knowing how much he'd put into researching Gemma Turner and the film, he knew that Ivy would take the ticket for herself and never give it a second thought. She was spoiled that way, and he resented her for it.

It was partly his fault. He'd never told her the story of his mother and his connection to Gemma Turner. The only person who knew that information was Aunt Wanda. It wasn't Ivy's fault that she thought this film was some childish fancy, not a primal longing to find some connection between his mother and Gemma Turner. Sadly, he had no desire to share that part of himself with her or anyone again.

So anxious was he about getting a ticket that it was impossible to focus on anything else but the film. Christopher called Ivy six times that night to check on the second ticket. Finally, his calls went straight to voice mail.

In the morning she called early, her voice low. "Something happened to one of the Seventy-Five."

"What do you mean?"

"A ticket has become available." Her voice was thin and tense.

"How does a ticket become available, Ivy?" That familiar lump was back in his throat, and his heart was beating wildly. Christopher felt his heart sink, a sense that his desire for the ticket had sent something negative into the universe.

"My dad thought it was strange, too. It was almost like you asking for a ticket..." Blessedly, she didn't finish the sentence.

He had a connection to *L'Étrange Lune*, he just knew it. The film *wanted* him to see it.

"Did I kill someone, Ivy?"

"Oh God, Christopher. Stop it! You do not own this film. You have no cosmic connection to it no matter how much you want to have one," she said, but he could hear something in her voice that told him she was lying. "Anyway, the screening is in Rome," said Ivy. "Is your passport up-to-date?"

In a moment of panic, Christopher realized he didn't own a passport. No one in his family had ever needed one. When he was quiet, she sighed.

"Who doesn't have a passport?"

"A rube," said Christopher, confirming her suspicion.

"Let me call my dad."

Within the hour, Ivy's father had arranged for a passport to be expedited, but it required them to fly to Tallahassee to secure a copy of Christopher's birth certificate.

"We'll have to fly commercial," said Ivy with a groan. "Dad's secretary got us two flights out of LaGuardia, but we leave in an hour. He found someone who can turn your passport around in a few hours, but we can't miss our flight back to New York. Dad's plane will be waiting for us the minute we get the passport."

He was going to buy Zander Cross a nice bottle of Scotch when he got back.

Twelve hours later, sitting at the Tallahassee airport with his birth certificate in his hand, he studied the paper, surprised the father *unknown* field on his birth certificate stung more than he'd expected it would. The lack of a father was always something he'd known, but to see it there in the official paperwork defined him in ways he'd never thought of before this trip. There it was in black-and-white. He was the bastard child with no father to claim him.

"Your mom was short and blond, right?" Ivy peered over his shoulder, almost reading his mind. "So that means we're looking for a tall, red- or auburn-haired gentleman, maybe even brown-haired."

"Huh?"

"We're on a quest to find your dad," said Ivy, her voice low. "He must balance out the tiny blond woman who was your mother. You're solving an equation by looking for the missing variables—height and hair." She turned his chin toward her. "Your eyes are this funny gray color. What color were your mother's eyes?"

"Blue."

"Hmmm."

"So it's like algebra." He turned in the line and pulled the document close to his chest.

"Just like algebra," she agreed, leaning up to kiss him.

"My mom's hair was wavy, like mine," said Christopher. "So he could have had straight hair." What other traits had he gotten from his mother? Like all college kids, he'd struggled with depression, but he worried that it wasn't just stress from finals, but that melancholy was in the dye for him. If she stayed long enough, would Ivy be looking under bathroom doors for him?

Had that been what Aunt Wanda had warned him about? Living this life? Was he in danger of going adrift like his mother?

He and Ivy had never gotten along better than they had these last two days, co-conspirators, trying to get a glimpse of a forbidden film. In the last two days, she had been kinder than normal. He hadn't found her to be a sensitive sort, and that was partly why he'd been drawn to her. She was the torque he needed to propel him on; otherwise he'd begin to list, like a rudderless boat. He drew energy from her certainty. Ivy Cross knew her place in this world, and through her Christopher found his place.

The passport took three hours to process and cost him five hundred dollars, which he put on his credit card. Zander Cross's jet was idling in Newark, and they took off hours later, having just a morning to catch a few tourist sights—the Colosseum, the Spanish Steps, and a museum. While they knew the screening was in Rome, they were waiting for information on the location. Looking down at his watch, Christopher saw that it was one in the afternoon. They had ten hours to go.

When they got back to the hotel room, the phone in their room was already ringing. Ivy grabbed it, expecting the front desk, but immediately Christopher knew it was the call they'd been waiting for. Even from across the room, he could hear the crackle on the line and the strange voice. It was like the invitation was in song, the sound on the other end a hypnotic lilt.

Ivy's posture straightened and she looked—frightened. Whatever was on the other end wasn't engaging in conversation.

As she placed the receiver back on the cradle, she looked ashen. "We're to go to the door."

Christopher slid off the bed and opened the door to find a box in the hallway. It was surprisingly light, and they opened it tentatively, finding two gold masks and heavy black robes inside. The robes were thick, like they'd been constructed from upholstery velvet.

"That voice," said Ivy, shaking her head. "I can't get it out of my head."

"I heard it from across the room," he said. "It was in song."

"Not exactly," said Ivy. "It was like spoken word, but the voice was unusual, like a toy's voice. It didn't sound human, Christopher."

He lifted a robe from the box.

"It's June," she said, taking hers. "I'm going to be sweating in this."

Surprisingly the robes were constructed to fit, Ivy's six inches shorter than Christopher's. The instructions were clear: They were to wear the cloaks and take a cab to Campo de' Fiori to a desecrated chapel and then don the masks immediately upon exiting the taxi. The identities of the viewers were to remain anonymous, and no written or photographic record of the screening was permitted inside the actual theater.

Christopher placed the mask on his face to test it out. As it touched his skin, he felt a prick and then a wave of sorrow wash over him, the emotion so intense that he tossed the mask onto the floor, and the clatter caused Ivy to look up, startled.

"What's wrong?" She raced over to it. "Don't break it! It's made of some kind of porcelain."

"That thing," he said, looking at it like it was a haunted relic. "Something is wrong with it."

"This entire thing is dark," she said with a sigh. "You're just getting freaked out now that you see that we have to wear some kind of Skull and Bones getup?"

"No," said Christopher, sure of what he'd felt. "There is something wrong with that mask." He pointed at it, upturned in her hand like some startled Guy Fawkes mask.

"I'll give you it's creepy," said Ivy, taking hers and placing it on her face. "Ouch."

Taking her mask, he tried to pull it off her face, but it felt like it was pulling back.

Finally, Ivy removed it and rubbed her chin. "This thing cut me."

He studied the line of blood near her jawline. Turning the mask, he spotted what looked like a rough part of the porcelain.

"You see," she said, taking the mask from his hand. "It just wasn't polished well enough."

He placed the mask on the bed next to his own. While Ivy was trying to convince herself everything was fine, Christopher wasn't sure. *What were they getting themselves into?*

At ten thirty, they took a cab to the square and found the chapel down a small side street as instructed. As they drove through Rome, Christopher found himself fretting that somehow, after all this anticipation and fuss over the robes and clandestine theater, he and Ivy wouldn't be admitted or, worse, that the film itself would be a letdown. What if it was a hack job, an amateur film that was brilliantly promoted as some underground screening? What if it was just some corny French slasher film with Technicolor tits and cherry blood bombs?

Arriving fifteen minutes early, they could see people standing in the shadows, but not speaking to one another. When the doors opened, he looked down at his robe and mask. Hesitating, he placed the mask back on and felt the same pinch that Ivy had described. Checking his jaw, he found that he, too, had a puncture wound.

"They probably made them in batches," said Ivy, shaking her head. "Stop being such a baby."

"You don't feel it?" They crossed the street as a line of people formed in front of the doors—all dressed in robes and masks.

"Feel what?"

"Sorrow," he said.

"No," she said, taking his hand and leading him inside the chapel alcove, where cloaked ushers with gold masks allowed them in. "You're being melodramatic."

"How do they know who we are?" asked Christopher.

"I'm not sure they care as long as you have a robe," she said, looking around and taking the scene in.

Behind him was a line of cloaked patrons who, with their costumes, were reduced to mere sizes and shapes. Tall with small, thin with round. "Do you want to turn back?" Suddenly Christopher was terrified that the film would be a turning point that would doom him forever.

"Hell, no," said Ivy, her voice muffled inside her mask.

"The film is only ninety-six minutes long in this viewing." She pointed to a sign written in elegant calligraphy. "It was eighty-four minutes during the last viewing. The projectionist is allowed to tell us how long the film is. That way you know how the films have changed."

"What do you mean 'changed'?"

Masked faces turned to them. Heads shook in warning. One put a finger up to its lips. "Shhh."

He felt his stomach sink like it did before he got on a roller coaster. Furiously, he began rubbing his wet palms against the velvet robe.

Ivy placed her hand out to stop him. She pulled him close, her voice a whisper. "There isn't only one version of the film. My dad said it was different in 1988. They'd added footage. There was some disagreement about whether the scenes were possible since Gemma hadn't been there for them."

He didn't know what to do with that information. Until he saw this film, he couldn't fully grasp how a missing starlet could be in scenes she never filmed.

Inside the former chapel, all religious symbolism had been removed except for the stained-glass windows. It smelled of old, musty stones, and the pews were shiny, like someone had recently attempted polishing them. There were hundreds—perhaps thousands—of candles burning in the church.

The scene reminded him of his mother's funeral and the image of the casket closing. He turned to Ivy and leaned down to whisper into her ear. "What are you thinking right now?"

"About how the sun looked the afternoon my father told me my mother had been in a car accident and was never coming home." Her voice was smaller, and he could hear a quaver.

"Are you sure you don't want to turn back?"

She shook her head. Instinctively, he reached out to touch her hand. And for a moment he smiled, the sorrow passing.

The door opened and a swift wind put out all the candles in one swoosh, causing the audience to fall silent except for an occasional cough or throat clearing.

Then the film began to roll.

9

Gemma Turner
June 10, 1968
Amboise, France

"You'll never get away with this, Roman!" As Gemma spoke the line, her foot caught, and she knew the emphasis on *never* was all wrong and Valdon, riding in a customized Citroën with the camera bolted to it, was going to require another take.

The night shoot had gone on painfully long as she finished her next line, running rather half-heartedly, her ankle boots hitting the cobblestones, nearly causing her to stumble again. The alleyway they had selected for this scene was harrowing, with the loose stones under her feet. If she fell, that would really blow the scene, but she kept running anyway, waiting for the impatient "Coupé" order from Thierry.

They hadn't spoken since she'd fled the cave. He'd arrived on the set just before shooting, avoiding her entirely. Gemma could hear the whispers among the crew that he'd gone to the Amboise Hotel bar until the wee hours and had been nursing a terrible hangover.

"He's in a foul mood," said Claude Moravin, placing the film in the camera.

"Pierre and Manon are at it again," said Jean-Luc, the makeup artist. "It has him in knots."

Of course, Gemma knew the truth, but she thought that Thierry would prefer the rumor of an affair of his wife and his leading man to the truth that he was hiding. While the staff thought he was nursing a hangover and had gone home to sleep it off, Gemma could see he was looking frail. If the illness progressed this quickly, then Thierry's secret would be out soon enough.

When no order to "cut" came, Gemma turned around to find the alley dark. In night shoots, it wasn't uncommon for someone to trip over a wire, causing the whole set to lose power. She sighed, almost folding herself over. Cradling her arms over her head, she muttered "Shit" to herself and began the long journey back down the alley. In the dark, Gemma found herself feeling for the stone walls. "Some light, please," she called. No one answered.

"Lights," she yelled again, a little more impatient this time. Finally, she stopped walking, waiting for the crew to yell back to her how long to expect. Nothing.

The alley was eerily quiet, except for the sound of faraway hoofbeats, which was odd. Gemma hadn't seen any animals or their handlers out for tonight's filming. Feeling her way down the alley, she emerged in the square, finding it empty. Well, not empty exactly, but *changed*. The crew was gone, as were the cafés and gift shops. There was no Thierry, no Claude, no cameras, vans, or food tables. Nothing she recognized. Spinning around the square, Gemma felt her breath catch.

"Thierry! What on earth is going on?"

Silence.

"Claude?"

A woman hurried past, her head down and her long skirt dirty. Okay, thought Gemma, this middle-aged woman was an extra she didn't recognize, but obviously connected to the film due to the grim period attire. Yet, the dirty hem was a strange detail that caught Gemma's eye.

The costumes were usually cleaned after each shoot. Shaking off the thought, she sighed. At least someone else was in the street.

The woman pushed past her strangely.

"Hello," said Gemma, trying to catch her eye.

She stopped in front of Gemma and stared. Gemma was used to such behavior from fans, so she smiled. "I'm wondering where everyone went."

"You shouldn't be out here. It's too dangerous. People have gone missing."

Hmm. Gemma hadn't read that line in the terrible script, but okay. Maybe Thierry was doing some improvisation tonight.

"You haven't seen anyone?"

The woman nearly recoiled. "Seen anyone? It's late, mademoiselle. I'm on my way home, and it would be wise for you to be, too."

"Yes, I know," said Gemma, rather bored with the line. What was Thierry doing? A pungent scent wafted behind her. This woman smelled like some peasant farm worker.

The woman made the sign of the cross, pulled her cape tightly around her neck, and bolted from the square. Again, Gemma waited to hear "Coupé." Glancing around, she noticed gaslights. She turned in a 360-degree circle to take in her surroundings. Where did that prop come from? There had been a newsstand on the corner. Gemma made her way over to it and found the store was now not a newsstand at all, but a tobacco shop. Reaching into her skirt pocket, Gemma pulled out the postcard she'd purchased there earlier that day. Along with the postcard was a receipt from the cash register with the date and time keyed in. The proof was in the purple ink on the receipt: Just thirty minutes ago, this *had* been a newsstand. But how?

No. It had been this door, this shop. The shops were all wrong. The streetlights were gone. The square, different.

Nothing about this square looked familiar.

Where was she?

10

Gemma Turner
June 10, 1968
Amboise, France

The furious pounding of hooves on stones made Gemma look up. Entering the square was a team of four black horses pulling a sleek black coach. It looked like the same coach from yesterday's scene, but the horses had been white. Maybe Thierry had decided white horses were too cliché and changed them.

A man sat on the perch, and he jumped down. "Pardon, mademoiselle."

She glanced around the square searching for a camera, getting increasingly confused and irritated. Were they still filming? Was the crew hidden somewhere, playing a trick on her? She felt tears welling up in her eyes. If this was something to make fun of the "American Gem," it wasn't funny anymore. The lights, the missing crew, the newsstand. She felt like a kid playing hide-and-seek in the woods, but the other kids had left her alone in the forest.

"Where is Thierry?" She hated that her voice was high-pitched with desperation.

With his top hat, Gemma could see the man's outline, but not his face. He cocked his head. "Thierry?"

"Thierry Valdon, the director," she said.

The man attempted to lead her inside the carriage. "You must come with me."

Gemma sensed that he wanted her out of the square sooner rather than later. He was another extra she didn't recognize. While his costume was clean, it looked worn, like the woman's had been. Wardrobe must have just made his breeches, yet they looked weathered, like the ones in museums. Everything about this man looked…wrong. He was a little too in character.

Raising her chin, she did a little stomp with her boot. "I demand to see Thierry."

The driver nodded, motioning toward the open door of the coach. "Château Dumas."

"No," said Gemma, tired of whatever game this man was playing, "Château *Verenson*."

Château Dumas was the name of the house in the film, not the house's real moniker, not the house she had been staying in.

"It's late, Mademoiselle Dumas. I suggest you get into the coach." He looked around nervously. From a distance, the clock chimed. She counted twelve. When they'd started shooting, it was nine. How had it gotten to be midnight?

"Mademoiselle," said the man with a hint of concern. "I *insist*."

He'd called her Mademoiselle Dumas, so this was definitely an improvisation Thierry had cooked up. Some revenge for her rebuffing his advances. Gathering her skirt, Gemma refused the man's help with the step and pulled herself into the carriage. This was ridiculous, riding around in character. She'd find Mick once she got back to Château Verenson and give him an earful.

Despite her anger, the rhythmic pounding of the horses made her drowsy, and she leaned against the window. There was little light anywhere. Was Thierry Valdon powerful enough to extinguish all the light in the Loire Valley?

It appeared he was.

Morning light streamed through a sheer curtain. Gemma studied her unfamiliar surroundings. Gone was the simple four-poster bed with the chenille bedspread and pom-poms adorning the hem. Instead, she was almost encased in a heavy canopy bed with velvet drapes at each post and embellished cream-and-pink silk damask linens. The dresser was missing, replaced with an ornate carved armoire. What had happened last night? How had she gotten to this strange bed? The last thing she remembered was riding in the carriage.

She leapt out of bed and ran to the armoire, throwing it open, looking for anything from her suitcase. Instead of her shift dresses and capri pants, she found nearly a dozen dresses—long dresses—old, period dresses. Pulling one out, she studied it carefully. Were these costumes? They didn't resemble costumes, which tended to look good on-screen or from a distance, but whose details were always disappointing up close: the buttons cheap or the lace of poor quality. These dresses, from the silk sleeves to the rich colors of salmon pink and cornflower blue, were exquisite. These hooks and mother-of-pearl buttons were designed to last longer than a six-week film shoot.

A gunshot rang out, and Gemma ran to the window, pulling back the curtain. It was an unfamiliar scene outside—the front of the house. This room was in the original part of the mansion, not the new wing where she and Mick had been placed.

The door opened partly, and a young woman—a maid—peeked

her head around. Realizing the bed was empty, she seemed to startle and almost leapt when she saw Gemma's stare fixed on her.

"Bonjour, mademoiselle." The woman walked fully into the bedroom and bowed. Her apron was a crisp white, and her dress was a delicately striped blue-and-white cotton. The woman's uniform was longer than the ones she'd seen the staff wearing before, like she was donning a period maid costume.

"Is Manon out shooting?"

"Certainly not," said the woman. "*Bernard* is hunting pheasant for dinner."

"Pardon," said Gemma coolly. "Where on earth am I? Is this the other side of the house?"

The woman stuttered. "You're...you're...in your room, Mademoiselle Dumas."

The girl fussed with a baroque candelabra at the bedside table. Only then did Gemma notice there was no light switch or overhead light fixture.

What on earth was going on?

"This really isn't funny anymore," snapped Gemma. "My name is not Mademoiselle Dumas. I'm Gemma Turner. *Surely* you know who I am."

The woman's face registered a look somewhere between confusion and abject fear. In her hands, she held a mocha-colored silk dress, and as Gemma spoke, she dropped it onto the floor, a stricken look on her face. The girl gazed at her wide-eyed and placed her hand to her mouth, shocked.

"I know who you are, mademoiselle. So, it *is* true. Bernard said you were talking strangely last night, asking for someone called Thierry Valdon. There is worry downstairs that you might have the fever, but I didn't believe it."

"The fever?" Gemma's voice rose like she was speaking to a child. "That's absurd. I'm not *someone* else, I'm Gemma *fucking* Turner. I'm an actress, and the character that I play in *L'Étrange Lune* is Gisele Dumas. She is a *character.* Thierry Valdon is the director of the film."

There were stories of people—fans usually—who confused characters with the actors who played them, but Gemma hadn't experienced this phenomenon until now. Was this woman one of those lunatic fans who mistook actresses for their parts or wished so badly that a character was real? "Is Monsieur Valdon awake? I need to see him immediately."

"I don't understand a word you are saying." The maid displayed the same puzzled look as the carriage driver had done the night before. "Who is Monsieur Valdon? Who is Gemma Turner?"

"*I* am Gemma Turner." Gemma reached down to pick up the dress, shaking it off. Like the others, this material was fine and heavy.

"No," said the woman. "*You* are Gisele Dumas."

Gemma clutched her throat. She needed to calm down. This was clearly a prank. A bad one. Leaning in close, she lowered her voice to a whisper. "Listen to me carefully. Gisele Dumas is a character... *in a movie.*" She stepped back to wait for the truth to sink in.

The woman sucked in air, horror registering on her round face. "I'm so sorry. There is no one by the name of Monsieur Valdon here. Perhaps you are confused, mademoiselle." She backed toward the door like Gemma was contagious.

"Really?" Gemma's eyes bored into the woman, and she tossed the dress on the bed. This was getting annoying. "Thierry Valdon? Ring a bell? Dark hair, penetrating stare, strikingly handsome man with a patronizing attitude? Pays your salary? Chain-smoker? Barks orders at all of us? Nothing?"

The woman shook her head furiously, the door stopping her from retreating farther. A sweaty tendril of brown hair had managed to come loose from her tight bun.

Mick would need to straighten this out quickly. "Tell me. Is Monsieur Fontaine in his room?"

The woman's eyes grew wide once again. Letting out a squeak, she grabbed Gemma's wrist conspiratorially, her voice low. "They said last night as they put you to bed that you were babbling, asking after this man called Valdon, saying you needed to..." The woman paused with a confused look, her mouth twisting. "...*telephone*...someone named *Mick*."

The sound of the name seemed foreign to the young woman's tongue, and Gemma noticed that her two front teeth were overlapped.

"Yes, exactly. I *do* need to see or phone Mick." She looked around the room at each of the bedside tables. "So, where is the telephone in this place?"

The woman lifted her arms in supplication. "I do not know what a *telephone* is, mademoiselle."

Gemma lifted her hand to mimic a receiver. "You know...a phone? Hello?" She rotated her hands like she was fake dialing.

The woman squawked like a duck. "You must not say these things. It is as I feared. All the excitement from your father's death. Bernard said he found you, wandering around alone at night in Amboise like a vagrant. If you don't stop speaking like this, Monsieur Batton will send you away. As you know, he is not fond of you, and your father is not here to protect you any longer. It only takes a few people gossiping that you are strange for them to take you away. Those places are terrible, and you'd never come back."

"I don't understand." Gemma blinked. "Thierry Valdon owns this château. He bought it when his first film was a success."

"No, mademoiselle," exclaimed the woman, reaching out to

Gemma. "*You* are the owner of this château. After your father died in the winter, you inherited it. Do you not recall that?"

This poor woman had obviously gotten ahold of this dreadful script and was now living out this fantasy that Gemma was Gisele Dumas. Why couldn't she have picked *Citizen Kane* or something better? Her awful dialogue was lifted from Thierry's shooting script.

"Oh, that is funny. You fooled me. What is your name? Are you an extra?"

The woman choked down a sob. "I'm sorry, mademoiselle. My name is Bridgette. I have been your maid for *five* years. I would like to think we are also friends. How could you not remember me? Me?" The woman snuffled and turned her head away.

"What about Manon?"

At this name, Bridgette's face brightened. "Oh yes, Manon. She is downstairs. Shall I call for her?"

Gemma felt a sense of relief wash over her. Thank God for Manon. "That would be lovely," she said with a loud exhale, almost feeling the tension leave her body. Surely Manon would not conspire with Thierry. The timing of this little prank was poor after the news Thierry had shared, but she'd get Mick, who would straighten everything out. Valdon hadn't been specific about his illness, just that it was cancer. What if poor Thierry had a brain tumor of some kind? Maybe that explained this strange change in the script and his moods. With sweaty palms, she wiped at her dress. She could feel her heart beating wildly.

Bridgette left the room, and Gemma could hear her heavy footsteps recede and then come back up. She entered the room, bringing an older woman who was wearing a black high-necked gown with a severe bun. This was not the Manon that Gemma had been expecting.

"You are Manon?" Gemma studied the tall woman who looked to be in her fifties with her hair pulled back into a tight chignon. She had the spare, modest appearance of a nun, not the revealing dresses of Manon Valdon.

"Manon," said Bridgette, presenting the woman, beaming. "Mademoiselle Dumas asked for you."

"Did she?" The dour woman's tone was measured and curious, like a cat sizing up a fat mouse.

Gemma's heart sank, surprised at how much hope she'd placed on Manon Valdon being the mistress of the house. This woman's—this Manon's—hands were clasped in front of her, waiting for Gemma's reply. Something told Gemma that she needed to be cautious and to act the part of Gisele Dumas, mistress of the château, until she figured out her next steps. Mick was scrappy, and he would find her. She just needed to play along.

"Are you well, mademoiselle?" With her straight back and perfect posture, Manon gazed down at Gemma with the countenance of a crow.

"I'm much better, Manon. Thank you," said Gemma with a thick smile. The older woman snapped the brown silk dress off the bed and passed it to Bridgette in a movement that seemed swift for a woman her age.

Out of the corner of her eye, draped across a chair, Gemma spied the dress that she had been wearing last night on the film shoot—it had been the last thing she remembered before everything went topsy-turvy. The idea that *this* dress had been with her *before* provided some comfort. If this truly wasn't a joke at her expense, then something malevolent was going on and Gemma needed to remain calm and keep her head about her. These people might be dangerous. At this thought, she physically stepped back from the maids.

"Are you hungry, mademoiselle?" It was Bridgette.

Gemma *was* famished. As if on cue, her stomach began to rumble, loudly, and she tried to recall when she'd last eaten. Before the shoot, she'd grabbed a piece of baguette and a few slices of cheese from the crew table. She *was* hungry, but she didn't know these people and certainly didn't trust them. Would they drug her? Had they drugged her already? Is that why she had no recollection of them changing her out of her dress? One minute she was riding in a carriage, and then this morning she'd awakened, thinking that it had been a dream.

Perhaps they were right and she had a fever—"the fever," as they referred to it around here. Perhaps this was a fever dream of some sort? She looked down at the rug. Was it spinning? Clutching her stomach, she could hear Bridgette, but couldn't answer. *Yes*, she wanted to say, *I'm hungry.* Instead, she felt herself begin to lean, and then everything went black.

"Oh dear, mademoiselle." Gemma opened her eyes to find Bridgette sitting on the edge of her bed. Once again, Gemma was lying down. As if on instinct, Bridgette put her hand on Gemma's. "We moved you. You fainted. Do you remember it?"

Gemma nodded. "Hungry." It was all she could muster in terms of conversation.

"I knew it," said Bridgette, slapping her hands on her legs. "Madame Pflouffe said that you had the fever." The woman's hand moved to Gemma's forehead. "But I said that you were fine. You were just hungry, that's all. We'll fix you right up, mademoiselle. Don't you worry. Bernard got a lovely bird this morning, and they're plucking it now as we speak. I'll be back with some duck, cheese, and bread from the kitchen."

The maid patted her on the leg and quietly scampered out the door. Gemma listened for Bridgette's receding footsteps and then sat up and placed her feet on the floor. She was still a little dizzy, so she steadied herself with her hands. Once she felt stable, Gemma looked under the bed, lifting the silk bed skirt. There had to be a phone line or a hint of where a phone line had once been tacked to the boards.

Crawling on her hands and knees, Gemma looked behind furniture, but found nothing but pristine baseboards. Hearing the maid's feet on the stairs, she moved swiftly back to the bed. Feigning that she'd been attempting to sit up, she made a dramatic attempt at rising before falling back. *After all, she was an actress.*

"You need to stay right there in bed," said Bridgette with a nervous chuckle. "I found you some soup. Nothing like soup to get that mind humming again."

She brought the tray around the bed and put it on the table, then helped Gemma pull back the sheets and plucked the dress from the edge of the bed.

"My dress," said Gemma, reaching for it.

Lifting it, Bridgette frowned. "I've never seen that one before. It's rather shabby, mademoiselle." Bridgette pulled at the lace distastefully. "Look at the lace. Poor workmanship."

Gemma examined the cheap lace embellishment that was coming apart from the sleeve. "Please don't get rid of this dress, Bridgette."

The woman frowned. "It's certainly not up to your usual standard, mademoiselle."

"I know, but I like it. S'il vous plaît?"

Bridgette studied the nightdress Gemma was wearing and bent over to look at her shoulder. "Mademoiselle?"

"What?"

"What is this thing you're wearing?"

Gemma looked down to find that Bridgette was referring to her bra strap. "It's a bra, Bridgette."

"You normally wear corsets and crinolines, mademoiselle. This is..." Her voice trailed. "I don't understand *what* this is?"

Something occurred to Gemma. The lack of lights or phones, the dresses.

"What year is it, Bridgette?"

The woman eyed Gemma suspiciously. "Oh, mademoiselle."

"Humor me, Bridgette. I swear I don't have *the fever*." She needed to play along and see what she could find out. Putting her hand to her forehead, she feigned faint. "Since Father died, it's just been so difficult."

"It's been hard on all of us, mademoiselle. Him dying so suddenly. Why, it's 1878, mademoiselle."

"1878?" Gemma heard the shock in her own voice. Of course that was ridiculous. It was *1968*. Gemma found she didn't have to feign weakness. This was the year that *L'Étrange Lune* was set. This entire scene was a reenactment of the film.

Plus, Gemma was so hungry. While Bridgette looked on approvingly, she finished the soup quickly. Next, Gemma started on the duck and cheese, devouring them like a child who had come in from the wild.

Silently, Bridgette collected the empty plates and took the tray away. Gemma waited until she was gone to get up from the bed. She walked over to the window. The room felt steamy.

Bridgette returned and began fussing at the bed. Gazing over at the dress that the maid had laid out for her, she noted the heavy cotton and couldn't imagine wearing a long dress in this heat. Looking out the window again, what struck her was that the mist was hanging over the valley. So thick was the area with fog that the lake that she knew was beyond the yard wasn't visible. Directly beneath her windows were blue-tinged evergreen trees. While hot, there had been a rain, and it smelled fresh and sharp and savory like pine or juniper.

A carriage rounded the front of the house with two unfamiliar horses—this pair was as dark as ebony piano keys, and their coats glistened, their manes dark and flowing. The normal horses on set were white.

"Where are the other horses, Bridgette?"

"What?" The maid looked up.

"The two white horses."

"White horses?" Bridgette made a face. "I've never seen such a thing, my lady," she said with a snort. "Horses aren't white; everyone knows that."

Gemma gave her a look of contempt. It was ridiculous that this woman, obviously an actress, was making her go through this mundane conversation about two animals on the film set.

"The *white* horses." Gemma lifted the white sheet for emphasis.

Suddenly, the maid erupted, bursting into tears. "I don't know what you're rattling on about, mademoiselle. There are no such things as white horses. I've never heard of such an animal."

Gemma's voice was even, yet there was a quaver that gave her away. She was frightened. "There are white horses, black horses, bay horses . . . that's brown . . . there are spotted horses . . . gray horses . . . hell, even a striped horse if you count zebras."

Tears flowed down the maid's face. Taking her apron, she wiped her eyes with a corner. "It must be the fever, mademoiselle, but now you're just being cruel."

It was hard to take in everything she was seeing—or not seeing. This house, this maid . . . none of it made sense. Placing her hand on her forehead, Gemma realized that she was sweating. Maybe they were right, and this was an illness. All of this was simply a fevered dream, and she'd awaken back on the film set. That was the last thought she had before she fainted once again.

In the dark of night, Gemma woke. The lack of a lamp beside her bed meant that the strange world had sadly not been a dream at all. Defiantly, she threw back the covers and grabbed the robe that was placed on the foot of her bed. As she crept down the stairs with a lit candle, she realized she knew the layout. The house was familiar and yet it wasn't. Instead of Manon Valdon's family photos in black-and-white frames arranged on the staircase walls, she found small paintings. Gemma raised a candle to get a closer look at one of the paintings and gasped. A familiar face stared back at her. It was herself as a little girl wearing a long dress with her hair in ringlets. And yet, Gemma had never posed for this painting. How could this be? Had Thierry gotten one of Gemma's childhood photos and copied it into a period setting? But why go to all this trouble for a joke? Unnerved, she moved down the stairs at a clip, listening for any sounds.

She stopped dead on the landing, frozen in fear. Somewhere on the second floor, there was a scratching noise, like the clawing of a frantic animal. There hadn't been a dog, at least not one that she'd seen, but then again, she hadn't left her room. The scratching stopped, and Gemma convinced herself that she was hearing things again. Pushing on down the stairs, she stopped at the bottom.

Holding up her light, she gazed to the left—the parlor—where Manon and Thierry had made drinks for everyone. Peering into the room, she found it was the same room, but the decor was different. The bar was gone; the piano had been replaced with a pianoforte. It was as though a set designer had come in and aged the room back to . . . 1878.

Making her way back to the foyer, she passed the elaborate table with flowers and tiptoed to the dining room, where she found the doors closed. Opening the French doors, she winced as a hinge squeaked, sending the noise up the stairs. Panicked, she held on to the door, listening for any sounds in the house. While she hadn't seen it during her stay at Château Verenson, Gemma had a vague idea of where to find the kitchen. What she discovered was a kitchen lost in time. A modern stove that would have been acceptable for a house this affluent was missing. In its place was a stone fireplace that spanned the length of the wall with two coal-fired ovens. In the center of the kitchen was a giant wooden island with mortar and pestle sets and other kitchen tools. Along the wall were hand-carved drawers and shelves, all neatly organized. Quietly, she opened drawers, which were filled with fine silver, flatware, and serving pieces as well as linen napkins, several tablecloths, and candlesticks. As she stepped past the kitchen, she heard a board creak and stopped in her tracks. Convinced she was alone, after hearing no further noise, she crept down the hallway to the mudroom, where she found bed warmers and scrubbed chamber pots, but no sign of a single modern convenience, no phone wire, no gas lamp.

Fear was setting in. She had to find a phone. How long had she been gone? Two days? Mick had to be frantic wondering where she was. Looking around the room, she couldn't make sense of it. Where would he look for her? She was in the same house that he was. Yet, she wasn't. It was like a twin of that house. A twin world.

She stopped, frozen. Was that it? Was this a twin world? She shook the idea off.

Undaunted, she began opening doors, until she found one with a bolt. That likely meant it led to a basement. Pulling it hard, it popped, and in front of her she spied a flight of stairs heading down to darkness and the scent of mildew confirming that this was some type of cellar. Certain that she would find a stash of modern supplies like Coca-Colas and secret phones, she took a step, holding the candle in front of her to lead the way.

There was a damp draft coming up, making Gemma shiver. She

half expected to find a video crew in hiding, taking part in a little hazing of the "precious" American actress. But the thick dust on the steps revealed no one had come down here for a long time. She swallowed and kept going, the space getting darker. She nearly missed that the final two steps had been rotted away. Her foot stepped on the unstable wood, sending her tumbling, but before either she or the candle tipped over, she gripped the textured stone wall to steady herself, letting the candle illuminate the room. It was much cooler down here, and Gemma spied old wine bottles and a loom, but nothing resembling a telephone or junction box or any sign of modern life.

A heavy sense of dread filled her. What was this place?

"Mademoiselle!"

Frightened, Gemma looked up to find Bridgette standing above her, dressed in her nightclothes, pulling her robe tightly around herself.

"What are you doing down there?" Her maid's voice was an urgent whisper.

"I...I..." Gemma hadn't rehearsed an excuse if she got caught. She scrambled to concoct a story. "I wanted wine for dinner tomorrow and was hoping that I could see some of Father's vintages."

"You wanted wine for dinner *tomorrow*?" From her vantage point she could see Bridgette's head was now deeply cocked in concern. "Mademoiselle, it is *three* in the morning."

There was suspicion in Bridgette's voice, and Gemma took a step toward the maid, contemplating how to answer that question. She was behaving strangely, but if Gemma was the lady of the house, she needed to act less like an American bohemian and more like the mistress of a nineteenth-century country château. She'd done enough research for her role to know how to behave. Ladies of the château felt they were beyond reproach. Walking up the crooked stairs, Gemma steeled herself when she'd safely reached the top. She feigned fury as she pointed toward the dark stairwell. "I could have died from those steps. They need to be fixed, Bridgette."

"But, mademoiselle, Manon or Bernard would have gotten the wine for you. I've never seen you use the stairs. Ever." Bridgette's eyebrow was raised in alarm.

"I won't have things falling into disrepair in this house. It's a disgrace." Trying to recall who Bernard was from the script—he had a bit part—she settled on him being the caretaker and groundsman, the one who did all the shooting. "See to it that Bernard looks at the steps immediately. I want to be able to go wherever I want without fear of breaking my neck."

Pushing past Bridgette, she headed back to her room, shut the door, and leaned heavily on it as the room spun. So many questions were racing through her brain. She gripped her head as she rocked back and forth, trying to calm herself. Gemma wasn't prone to hysterics. She always faced the truth, however unpleasant, but she could feel panic clawing at her again. Taking deep breaths, she was desperate to calm herself. Nothing about this place made sense. It was the first time that Gemma felt tears ready to flow. Alone and utterly defeated, she let them run down her face.

Wherever here was and whoever these people were, she was a prisoner.

11

Christopher Kent
June 10, 1998
Rome, Italy

In the darkened theater, Christopher was on the edge of his pew, trying to memorize each image on the screen so he'd recall it later. At its heart, *The Strange Moon* was a rather simple horror story, but was a visually stunning masterpiece. Each scene was packed with vivid color, like it had been painted in the editing process. While tempting to say Technicolor, even that wasn't saturated enough to describe the feast of the eyes that was *L'Étrange Lune*, with its reds and blues and greens. Most French New Wave films were spare, gritty creations shot in black-and-white film with a handheld camera. Valdon's final film leapt off the screen with its lushness.

The sad beauty of the film hinged on Gemma Turner's performance. He'd seen her films thousands of times, and while she'd been a good actress, at twenty-two, she had yet to come into her own, and her performances were never deep. He imagined she walked on the set and stepped into whatever character without much thought, and that made sense for *It Comes in Waves*. While Gemma had all the youthful dewiness required of a horror film lead, there was something wizened behind her eyes that had never been there before in her previous performances.

"Something horrible happened to you," he whispered into the

darkened theater. In the role of Gisele Dumas, she was not the same actress. He had the same feeling as when he watched the home movies with his mother. Had the same camera been there when his mother stepped off the bus years later, her face would have displayed the same cautious weariness that Gemma Turner did in this film.

There were no credits at the end of *L'Étrange Lune*. It was as though the film was ripped out of the camera, resulting in a disorienting blur and roaring sound, followed by blackness. Jarred viewers jumped in their seats. Softly, the candles that illuminated the exit flickered back to life as though they were on a circuit somewhere, and the ushers, moving like stiff automatons, began releasing each row one at a time like a midnight wedding. The Soixante-Quinze members quietly moved out of the pews.

Christopher went to speak, but Ivy shook her head, her voice a whisper. "My dad was clear. They don't want people talking about it among themselves."

Deep in thought, he followed Ivy until an usher blocked him with their arms out. "Your robe and mask, please." The sound of the voice was chilling; he could almost hear what sounded like an old audiotape inside the thing. If he pulled off their mask and robe, he wondered if there would be anything *in* there. Both he and Ivy removed their masks and robes, and the usher pointed for them to exit across the street.

Once they stepped outside, Christopher looked back at the old church. "If we aren't supposed to discuss it, then why show the film at all?" He was tired of all the creepy theatrics. His brain was buzzing and he was dying to discuss it.

"What did we just see?"

Ivy rubbed her shoulders, and he saw her shudder. "I don't know." She was quiet, subdued.

"Are you okay?"

"I don't know." She put her hands in her jeans pockets and shrugged as she began searching for an open restaurant at this hour, her eyes not meeting his. "I want dinner." She walked on away from him in a daze. "I was surprised you could understand it."

"What do you mean?" He was irked. While she was the top student in film school, he wasn't far behind her.

"The film was in French, idiot." She spun and gave him a confused look. "You don't speak French." She paused. "Do you?"

"It wasn't in French," he said with a chuckle, like she was daft. At her curious statement, he stopped walking. Something about what she just said made sense. It was as though he'd been in a trance or in a dream in the theater. While he had no difficulty understanding the dialogue, he was trying to remember what language his ears had been listening to. The film made you dizzy, unsure of what you were seeing—or hearing.

"I thought so," she muttered.

Across the street, he saw several men gathering outside a café. "I think they were at the screening. Come on." He pointed to the group. As an old clock struck one, he took Ivy's hand and led her toward the café. "Let's see what we can find out."

They found a seat about six feet away from the group, who were French. Instead of food, he was concentrating on the men. He adjusted his chair to get closer to them. "What are they saying?"

She gave him a look. "Thought you just understood every word of the film we watched?"

He sighed and she relented. For a few minutes she listened intently, straining to hear. Each time he went to ask, she held up her finger. "They're talking about the cousins. In tonight's film, Gisele sent them away. That was a big deviation from the last film. In the first version, she lets them in the house and they wreak havoc on the village."

"I don't get the big deal," he said.

She listened a bit more. "They're going over the differences between the versions of the film. I'm not sure what they mean because you and I have only seen this one, but there is a version where Gisele does not banish the cousins, which was, of course, in the original version. The one we saw tonight was quite different than the previous version. I think they're wrong."

"About what?" Christopher was rapt.

"The scenes don't matter. They're tracking the differences between each, like a close reading, but I don't think that is what is important here, but again, I've only seen this version."

"Yeah, Valdon probably had a bunch of outtakes he never used."

"No," said Ivy, leaning closer, her lipstick still smudged from the porcelain mask. "Gemma was only on the set for ten days. She was not there when those scenes were shot. They're saying it's as though a ghost is filming those scenes, but there is more...." Her voice trailed as she leaned in to listen.

Something about that comment hit Christopher square in the gut. "It's her performance. That's what's been bothering me so much. I've seen her acting so many times. In this film, she is like a ghost. I can't shake this feeling that something terrible has happened to her."

"Something terrible did happen to her," said Ivy, playing with the saltshaker. "She died."

The blunt truth of what Ivy said settled on him. It was true that Gemma had been declared dead, but her body had never been found. "But that doesn't explain how those scenes got there. A dead woman can't make films."

Ivy kept listening to the four men, who were arguing now. "They're saying that they can't get caught talking about what they saw. It's too dangerous. Before the film, Valdon had been pursuing dark themes." She shook her head. "Something about an abrupt change in this work in those last few months that were driven by darkness. The film is evil." She sat back in her chair. "On that, I agree with them."

A waiter interrupted them, and Ivy ordered a glass of Nebbiolo, a rucola salad, and puttanesca pasta. "Don't even think you're sharing my pasta," she said.

"For me, it's like the Zapruder film," said Christopher. "You could analyze it frame by frame looking for clues, but its tragic, inevitable outcome hangs over the film. I can't see *L'Étrange Lune* the same way as I would *Thunder Beach* because this one was so closely linked to her doom. Every scene is like a countdown clock to her end."

"It's nothing like the Zapruder film," said Ivy. "We can't analyze this film frame by frame. Hell, no one is even permitted to talk about it, so why the creepy underground clandestine viewings? For some reason these screenings happen every ten years, but whoever is doing this doesn't really want you to see it, and certainly not talk about it. It's a film at odds with itself. Solve that mystery, and I think you get closer to finding out what happened."

"The editing is the key to understanding it." He kept studying the men from a distance. They had ordered food, and pasta dishes arrived as they argued. He could hear words like *Valdon* and *Gemma Turner.*

She took a big sip of wine. "I knew you'd run to the editing. You're such a technician."

That was meant as an insult. She was the writer and the director, and him, the cameraman. But technical expertise was like craft, and while Ivy couldn't be bothered framing shots, Christopher understood composition. For him, film was technical; for Ivy, it was theoretical. His passion was pushing the medium technically, something he'd learned to do at an early age. For Ivy, film was the family business, but a business nonetheless. "Don't you think the new scenes have a strange intimacy with Gemma? They aren't like the earlier scenes where she's getting out of the carriage to see Pascale or even the one where she is running away from Roman down the alleyway. I'd say there is a different person behind the camera."

"You're right," said Ivy. "She is not filmed in the same manner. Also, I'm struck that the focus shifts away from being an ensemble cast to where the other actors don't appear to be big. It's like they're stunt doubles. The film goes out of its way to not show them, or they're soft focused."

"She's the focus," said Christopher. "There is a different hand to the new scenes."

Ivy closed her eyes. "I can't shake the sorrow."

"Me too," said Christopher, "I felt it the moment I walked into the chapel."

"I haven't thought of my mother for ages, and I can feel that way I did when my dad told me she was never coming back. I see the sun framed behind his eyes."

"You said your father knew Charlie Hicks. Did he know Gemma?"

"Other than the obvious?"

Christopher wasn't following her.

She folded her arms and began to slowly shake her head. "You really don't know, do you?" Pushing her salad plate—a large one overflowing with rucola—over to him to share, she began to stab at her greens. "My mother and father were extras on *Beach Rally* and *Thunder Beach*. My mother, Anne Cross, was famous for dying."

She blinked back tears.

"You don't have to talk about this." He put his hand on hers.

"She was the one in the car with Suzy Hutton's husband, William Way, when they were both killed in a car accident on the PCH. They'd been having an affair for years. My father doesn't know that I know this, but after my mother died, he took a sample of my DNA to prove that I was his child. I mean, what would he have done if I hadn't been his? Both my mother and William were dead."

"I'm so sorry, Ivy," he said, realizing how much she had to have suffered at this knowledge. His own story felt small compared to what had to be a very public loss to her.

"I don't want to go there again. We had reporters and photographers on our lawn. My mother was branded a whore by the press, so I felt I was never able mourn her. Only Uncle Mickey understood. He loved her like I did, and he forgave her. When I needed to cry, I'd cry to him. Hell, everyone was screwing everyone else in Hollywood. I'm not justifying it, but it's just Mother who got killed in the act." Until this moment, she'd been avoiding his eyes. "You often think that Vera is what I'm running from, but it's not her. It's my mother. Take the black dye off my hair and I look just like her. I've become the opposite of Anne Cross. It's intentional." She tossed her napkin on the table. "If it's okay with you, I want to fly home tomorrow."

"Sure," he said, meeting her eyes. It was the first time he felt he'd gotten to see the real Ivy.

The men in the nearby table stood up, finished with their drinks. As they passed the table, Christopher stood. "Bonjour."

They studied him warily and walked on.

"We just saw *L'Étrange Lune*, like you did."

His eyes darted to Ivy. "Tell them we just saw the film. What did they think of it?"

He watched as their faces fell. A few looked around the room nervously. None of them spoke.

She tugged at his arm, attempting to pull him back into his seat, but he stood there, gazing at the balding, old men. "I don't think they're interested in talking to us."

The men regarded one another and headed toward the exit. The last one to leave was compact, tan, and muscular, like the aging photos of artist Pablo Picasso. He took Christopher's wrist firmly, like a father might do to a son. In perfect English, the man spoke. "You would be wise to not run around asking about the film. It prefers to live in the shadows."

The next morning, they left Rome on Zander Cross's private plane. Ivy didn't say much the entire flight. When they got close to Newark, she said, "We have to refuel here, but I'm going on to Burbank."

"Do you want me to come with you?"

"No," she said. "I need you for the birth of Vera's spawn, next month. I can't handle that on my own, but I need to be alone right now."

What she'd told him about her father getting a DNA test to prove she was his daughter gave new context to everything about the arrival of her sibling, which they now knew to be a boy, but he felt reluctant to leave the airplane. The film had shaken her, and Ivy was rarely caught off guard.

"Are you sure?" he asked.

He stood in the airport, watching her plane take off again, feeling guilt that he'd gotten them into this mess to begin with.

In the weeks after returning from Rome, he made another attempt at researching the film in other interlibrary catalogs at Columbia, but found very little on Thierry Valdon or *L'Étrange Lune*. Alongside his contemporaries who had decades of films with critical acclaim, he was the director and writer of only a handful. In a film book devoted to French film history, there was one entry about *L'Étrange Lune*: *After the disappearance of its star, Gemma Turner, on the 1968 film set, Thierry Valdon's* L'Étrange Lune *was left unfinished and, despite rumors of secret screenings, has never been viewed by a wide audience.*

The film certainly lived in the shadows.

He had more luck locating a few more articles on the disappearance of Gemma Turner and the police investigation that followed. He also found an article on the 1972 death of Thierry Valdon, which made mention of *L'Étrange Lune* being Valdon's final film. Next, he tried AOL and found an online chat group devoted to Thierry Valdon that seemed to be run by an avid fan. Christopher wrote: *Saw the most recent screening of* L'Étrange Lune *as a newbie. Looking to connect with others.*

Later that day, he found a reply.

What you're doing is extremely dangerous. This isn't how you go about this. Don't draw attention to yourself or the Seventy-Five. Wait for signs. —A friend

A few days later, checking his AOL account, he received a printable gift certificate to a coffeehouse called Roasted on the Upper East Side. It was from "A Friend." The gift certificate was sent at exactly 3:00 p.m. Was this the sign?

At 3:00 p.m. the next afternoon, he walked through Roasted. Scanning the room, he saw three people: Two were students, not completely something to be ruled out but also not necessarily his target. An older man was there with a small, fluffy white dog. He set his sights on him.

As Christopher approached the cashier, he checked to see if the man with the dog watched him, but the man's eyes never left the book he was reading. Christopher ordered an iced coffee and an almond and chocolate croissant that looked like it had just been freshly baked. When the cashier rung him up, he reached into his pocket and said, "Oh, I have a gift certificate."

This seemed to surprise the ponytailed cashier, who eyed the printed certificate with interest. "I'll be right back."

She did not return; instead, an older man with an apron came to the cash register and shoved a folded piece of paper into Christopher's open hands, then turned and retreated into the kitchen before he could be asked any further questions. When no one returned to the register,

Christopher finally left. Deciding it was best not to open the paper on the street, he ducked into a Duane Reade.

On the paper was typed:

Library of Congress Special Collections: Cartoons of the Twentieth Century. Volumes 1 and 2: RL265721

Was this a joke? Christopher studied the paper and turned it, looking for something—anything—else. *Cartoons of the Twentieth Century*? As he looked around the aisles at the drugstore, no one seemed to be following him. He shoved the paper deep into his jeans pockets and went and got a Starbucks.

Back at Columbia, Christopher went straight to the library.

To his surprise, there was a hit. Indeed, a book with this name, featuring original cartoon illustrations. There was one copy of it in the entire world, and it was at the Library of Congress in Washington, DC.

"This is how you communicate," said Christopher, pocketing the paper and booking a ticket on the next train to Washington.

Entry into the Library of Congress was typically reserved for doctoral students and professors only. Given he was still an undergraduate student at Columbia, Christopher didn't meet the requirements for admittance on his own and phoned one of his professors to see if there was anything to be done to expediate a day pass. The professor, thrilled at Christopher's sudden scholarship, called back to say that permission had been granted, but that he would need his student ID for admittance to the reading room.

The idea of traveling again exhausted him. Since he'd returned from Rome, he hadn't been feeling well, the deep melancholy setting in. He'd begun to fixate on his mother again, viewing the home movies obsessively. Ivy had called him from Los Angeles, sounding distant, saying it had been good "to sleep in her old bed," but saying something strange to him before she hung up. "Since I've gotten back, I can't shake the feeling that the film itself is a vampire feeding on all of us who saw it.

I'm now a hollow version of myself." Since she was a semester ahead of him and was graduating, he wasn't sure when, or if, she'd be returning to New York, and she didn't offer anything.

While the sorrow seemed to drive Ivy away, it was what drove him onward toward answers. They were wired differently that way. This was a mystery that needed to be solved. Had his mother known about this film? Was that what had driven her mad? He had become convinced that her illness was connected to this film. He'd follow the trail to Hell itself for answers if he had to.

When he got to the Library of Congress, a somber-looking security guard pushed a button letting him through the gate. Taking a flight of stairs up to the reading room, he found a library from another time. Massive and circular, the room was decorated with inlaid wood and fixed desks, smelling of pungent lemon furniture polish from a futile attempt to keep dust at bay. Apart from the occasional cough or shutting of a heavy fire door, it was nearly as quiet as death itself. Soft daylight came from above, making the place a librarian's heaven. He followed the signs to the information desk.

"Can I help you?" An older woman with glasses hanging on a chain leaned forward. She had long gray hair in a ponytail down her back. Her badge read INGRID TAYLOR-BURTON.

"I'm looking for this." He pointed down to the printed sheet where *Cartoons of the Twentieth Century. Volumes 1 and 2: RL265721* was written, now weathered from his constant studying of it, sure there was hidden meaning somewhere.

She handed him back a form. "You need to fill this out. Are you a first-timer here?"

"I am." He clicked his pen and began to fill out the information.

"Once the form is completed, if we have the volume here, put your desk number and we'll bring it to you within the hour. If we don't, we'll have to pull it from another site, and that could take several weeks."

His face fell. He hadn't expected that the book might not be on the premises.

"Is that unusual to have to pull a book?"

She put her hands on her hips and raised her eyebrow. "We have more than one hundred and seventy million items belonging to this library. Do you know how expensive DC real estate is?"

"Pretty expensive," he said, his voice soft.

"You just go out to the reading room there," she said, pointing beyond the door. "And find a place to sit. On the desk, you'll find a number. Put that number here." She pointed to the blank field on the orange card. "Then go back and sit at *that* desk and wait. Got it?"

"Got it," he said, ambling past the copy machines back into the reading room. If he got a volume of cartoon illustrations, he would be sorely disappointed and feel foolish the entire way back to New York. His credit card was already hurting with the hotels from Rome and the train ticket to DC. He'd done some freelance video work—two weddings—to pay the expenses, but he was going to have to go back to the city and do a bunch of corporate video work to pay his card off. At least he had a skill that kept him from having to wait tables.

He sat quietly at the desk listening to the sounds of reading: coughing, books dropping, and desk light knobs being snapped on.

There was a loud thud, and he looked up to see that two small boxes like the kind that good department stores used to have for shirts had been dropped on his ledge. The boxes featured beautifully illustrated covers: *Cartoons of the Twentieth Century*, volume 1, and *Cartoons of the Twentieth Century*, volume 2.

Opening the lid to volume 1, however, he did not find a book containing rare cartoon illustrations inside. Instead, he found three black leather volumes.

Le Soixante-Quinze
L'Étrange Lune *Viewing One: 1978*
L'Étrange Lune *Viewing Two: 1988*
L'Étrange Lune *Viewing Three: 1998 (NEW)*

The comments were in both French and English. Each volume was an account of the three screenings of *L'Étrange Lune*.

On the first page of the leather volume marked *I*, he found a handwritten letter in beautiful blue script.

Dear Soixante-Quinze member:

You are here by invitation as a member of le Soixante-Quinze, who are the exclusive screeners of Thierry Valdon's unfinished film, L'Étrange Lune. *As a member, you have seen the film, so you know that it is a peculiar entrant into cinema history.*

On June 10, 1968, on the ninth day of filming, L'Étrange Lune*'s star, Gemma Turner, disappeared mid-scene. A police investigation followed but failed to uncover any trace of her. It was as though the actress had disappeared into thin air. Tainted by rumors of scandal, including that his actress had met with foul play at his hands, Thierry Valdon retreated to his country home, Château Verenson, where he lived in seclusion until his death by suicide on November 26, 1972.*

One could argue Valdon's death should *have been the end of* L'Étrange Lune. *Except, on June 10, 1978, the Odeon Theatre in Tours received a strange letter promising a copy of the film. The following day, an unmarked box containing a film canister arrived. The proprietor of the theater was told it was the unfinished film* L'Étrange Lune. *At the same time, seventy-five patrons, largely journalists and academics, received an invitation to the screening. The Odeon, had it decided to not show the film, would have been hard-pressed to turn away the group who lingered outside at 11:00 in the evening, not sure of what they were seeing, but knowing that "for one night only" they wanted a peek at Valdon's unfinished masterpiece, one he'd guarded so fiercely. They were, after all, voyeurs who wanted to witness the very thing that ruined him. The Odeon also had a special place in Valdon's history. As a teenager after the war, he had come to the theater with his friends. In other words, the Odeon felt it was a part of Valdon's history and, therefore, obligated to run it.*

The first film was seventy-four minutes long. The canister and the film contained inside of it disappeared after the screening, much like Gemma Turner herself.

Nothing much happened after that screening. People called around asking if anyone knew where to find the film, and no one seemed to have an answer. Finally, interest died down until 1988, when another box appeared, again at the Odeon.

Those of us who had received that first ticket were notified of a second chance at screening this film. And we took it.

What no one was prepared for was that the second screening was different than the first one. Given the fact that the director was dead, this was an impossibility. Now eighty-four minutes in length, the film had changed in very significant ways. There were more scenes involving the film's missing starlet and a storyline that did not match the final shooting script on file.

This became a recurrent theme—the film evolves *on its own as though it lives.*

L'Étrange *Lune continues to turn up every ten years. In 1998, a ninety-six-minute version showed up in Rome, since the Odeon had burned down in 1990. Given we only get a glimpse of it every decade, it has become imperative, I believe, to write down its significance—or insignificance—in both Valdon's oeuvre and the horror film genre in general. The film's distribution method does not allow for an honest discourse of this film, causing it to be shrouded in both mystery and conspiracy. Who sends the film? Who alters it? Where is the footage from Gemma Turner coming from? These are questions that perplex us as we leave the theater, and the answers have proven elusive.*

Here we share what we saw in these films. It is a secret forum to discuss what we think is going on and to pose questions to one another. If you have the ability, please translate the comments. It seems that most of us speak English and French. If we could try to keep the languages to those two, it would be ideal.

My apologies for the cloak-and-dagger around this process, but there has been a desire by whoever sends the film that we not talk to one another about its contents, so this forum unfortunately requires secrecy. Please contribute, translate, and share your feelings. If you feel comfortable, please write your name so we have some sense of who you are and what films you've seen.

I feel we are an honored group with a uniquely shared experience, but like the blind person who touches only a small part of the elephant, we are each seeing only one piece of this puzzle, not the entire landscape.

Sincerely,
Elizabeth Bourget, film critic at Le Monde
Member, le Soixante-Quinze

Christopher spent the next four hours poring through the books, reading the English entries with various theories like "Thierry Valdon is not dead and is secretly behind the films." He dug through his pockets to find enough change to get a photocopy card so he could make photocopies to translate from French later with Ivy's help. The entries included a detailed synopsis on each of the three films.

Viewing One

June 10, 1978

Considered the original, this seventy-four-minute version is the director's cut, with the additions of Manon Valdon serving as a stand-in for Gemma Turner in the scenes she had not completed. The group agreed (with confirmation from cinematographer, Claude Moravin) that this was the version closest to the shooting script that they had seen. Valdon kept this version secret until his death.

Viewing Two

June 10, 1988

This second screening was ten minutes longer than the 1978 version and featured Gemma Turner as Gisele refusing the cousins Avril and Roman. This plot twist was a big departure from the first film, where she has no idea they are vampires. A cat-and-mouse game between Gisele and the cousins dominates much of the film. That Gisele is not a damsel in distress is a very different representation of the character. That she is also played full-on by Gemma Turner, versus Manon Valdon in profile, is notable.

Viewing Three

June 10, 1998

This ninety-six-minute version shows the same scenes as viewing two, but there are six minutes of footage of Gisele that are very controversial because while she was the hero in the 1988 version, Gisele appears to die at the end, having been killed by the vampire Roman.

There wasn't as much written about the film that he'd seen a few days ago. He imagined that this volume would continue to expand with theories, but Ivy was right. Most comments were based on close readings of the differences between the scenes themselves and not bigger ideas of who was behind the film.

He took the last Northeast Regional Amtrak train back to New York and spent the time reading all the theories. More importantly, he now had names. Other people who had seen what he had. He needed to talk to them, even in the shadows. Looking down through the list, he saw Elizabeth Bourget, who seemed to be the organizer of the group. Included within were the names of six other members of le Soixante-Quinze: Daniel Brillion, Fabienne de Winter, Michel Alto, Justine Winthrop, and Anthony A (no last name given). This curious detail caught his eye. He'd seen that name before. There was a rumor that a filmmaker named Anthony had a bootleg of the actual film.

"I'll start with you, Elizabeth Bourget," said Christopher, circling her name. "What do you know that you're not telling in these pages?" He had a hunch many of the answers could be found with her.

12

Gemma Turner
"1878"
Amboise, France

When the fuss over Gemma having "the fever" had died down, she played the part of Gisele brilliantly. As the days dragged on, it was the mornings that were the most difficult. At dawn, as sunlight streamed through the curtains, the realization that nothing had changed through the night often sent her spiraling into deep fits of despair. Never in her life had she been so nostalgic for a lamp or a light switch.

An idea struck her, and she asked Bernard to take the carriage into town one morning. What she knew was that the house and the grounds as well as the square were largely unchanged, but they had appeared to go back in time—to 1878.

When the driver was out of sight, Gemma found the alleyway from the night scene she'd been shooting. Peering through windows and turning doorknobs, she found there was nothing unique about this rather plain street. When no one was looking, Gemma ran down the alley just like she'd done the night "the thing" had occurred. And what *had* happened? Had she fainted?

Turning around, she ran again. "You'll never get away with this,

Roman," she called, saying the line just like she'd done in the scene. "You'll never get away with this, Roman." She doubled over, overwhelmed, tears flowing down her cheeks. "I'll *never* trust you again. I'll never trust you again. I'll never trust you again."

Over and over, she kept repeating the words, first in fury and finally despair. And what was she expecting? To get magically transported back to—her world.

Wandering back to the square, she found Bernard standing next to the coach just where he'd said she could find him.

"You were running in the alley, mademoiselle?" There was no judgment in his face, only concern and pity.

Leaning on the coach beside him, she felt breathless. "I just needed a few moments to myself...to work some things out."

"Oui," said the man with a nod. "I find the woods help me the best, but I can't rule out an alleyway. Whatever works for you." He winked.

There was a low hum around them. The villagers were animated, gossiping in clumps.

"What are they doing?"

"Ah, l'étrange lune," he said, his eyes wide with excitement. "It's a bloodred moon. When the moon changes, it causes the sky to turn a wonderful blue color. Supposed to stop the hunters. The last time I saw it, I was a child. Scared the bejesus out of me. The ladies there are imagining all sorts of things the devil has planned that night. And they could be right."

He motioned for her to step up into the carriage. From the script, it was the strange moon that foreshadowed the arrival of her cousins; she knew that Thierry had planned work with a special effects man to create a fake red moon using a model and a fog machine. Gemma wanted to say that their treacherous moon was created in a lab in London that made puppets, but she bit her tongue.

Back at the house, Gemma opened the window to allow air into her bedroom. From the gardens below, she could smell the scent of summer—the sweet grass baking in the warm sun and the sharp, crisp smell of juniper—make its way up to the windows, petals and stalks ripening with the heat. On cue, the locusts' rhythm began fading in and out. Despite the strangeness of everything, it was beautiful.

Across the tree line, she spied something odd—a canopy of trees leading to another property. From the distance, she could see a stone château looming. While she hadn't taken note of every detail on Thierry's country house, she did not believe there had been a château next door. At least that would be something for her to explore today. She needed to find things to do with herself. It didn't appear that Gisele had any interests and just lazed about. Gemma couldn't abide that. She needed something to keep her mind off her plight.

As she passed by the foyer on the way to the gardens, she was enchanted by the new flowers in the decorative vase on the table. Nearly two feet high, the bold blue Chinese pattern now held soft green and blue hydrangeas. The entire arrangement was so overwhelming that Gemma nearly missed the envelope leaning against it.

She knew this envelope.

With shaking hands, she plucked it from the table. This scene was familiar—too familiar. A few days ago, she'd shot it twenty times. Peering around, she searched for a hidden camera, but the rooms were all empty. From the coming of the red moon to this envelope, the plotline from the film was unfolding exactly as the script had been written. If she opened the envelope, she knew from experience, there would be nothing but a blank piece of paper inside. It was a prop, and a separate scene with the contents of the paper in beautiful script would be shot from Gisele's point of view in postproduction.

Taking the envelope, she had to admit that the paper's texture felt different than it had on the set. This envelope was constructed of a heavier cloth paper. It felt like everything else in this house—real. Ripping it open, she found the note inside did, in fact, have handwriting, a beautiful blue script. The contents of the note were the same. It was her solicitor telling her that her Italian cousins, Avril and Roman, had recently fallen on hard times and were requesting to stay with her.

Gemma let the paper fall to her side. This was a peculiar development. Was it possible? No, she pushed that thought out of her mind. But the thought nagged at her. Was it possible that she was somehow living not in a twin world, but in the film? From the exquisite embroidery on her dresses to the heavy paper, this world was both the same as, yet different from, hers. It was like a real version of what the film had been trying to replicate. It made her uneasy. Was *this* fiction now reality?

Pacing, she tried to play this out. If she were somehow in the film, for whatever reason, she was aware of the script while the others were not. This made her think she must have injured herself and was in a coma of some sort, like Dorothy in *The Wizard of Oz*. Yes, that was the only logical explanation! A hit on the head and now she thought this was her new reality. She had to follow the yellow brick road to wake up.

But what did that mean? Should she follow the script? Invite the cousins to stay with her, pretending to be unaware that they were vampires who traveled from town to town posing as "lost relatives" fallen on hard times? No. Dorothy was forced to improvise to get home. If she followed the script, then everyone in the house but Gisele would fall under their spell and have their life forces drained. In the end it was hinted that even Pascale and Gisele were the final victims, becoming vampires themselves. No, that wouldn't work at all.

Perhaps she could rewrite the script as she'd wanted to do. It was *her* reality after all—her fevered dream—her Oz. In her script, Gisele had been the hero. A little smile formed on her lips. Had this been in America, her mother would have booked the destitute cousins into the nearest Holiday Inn and been done with them after a dinner and a small handful of cash, but in Europe in the nineteenth century, there seemed to be a whole cottage industry of penniless relatives occupying wings of country estates. Gemma considered that most of them were vampires in one form or another.

Gemma didn't feel like playing the role of damsel in distress. Gisele Dumas was unaware of her cousins' intentions, but Gemma Turner was not.

"Bridgette," called Gemma, excitement in her voice.

The maid appeared a few moments later with a beautiful tray of pastries and fruit.

"Bonjour, mademoiselle. Today's paper has not arrived. Café?"

This felt like a trap. What did Gisele Dumas have for breakfast? Tea? Bending over to pick up the letter from the floor, Gemma said, "I'll have my usual," wondering what on earth Bridgette would bring her. Thanks to Thierry's poor writing, Gisele had little backstory. When they'd shot these scenes, the mugs usually had stale water in them.

In a few moments, Bridgette returned with a tray carrying coffee with milk. Apparently, Gisele drank a café au lait, which was fabulously in character with what Gemma Turner drank. As she took a sip, she was grateful for the little reminder of home, even if this was all a dream.

She began to plot. "I forget," said Gemma. "Do I have writing paper?"

"Of course, mademoiselle." Bridgette turned with the precision of a dutiful toy soldier and returned shortly with a tray carrying paper, a candle and seal, and a pen with a pot of ink. This was going to be a production. Gemma hadn't counted on having to learn how to use a fountain pen and inkwell. "I'm sorry, mademoiselle, usually this is done in your father's office."

"I know," said Gemma with a mischievous smile, "but the view here today is so *groovy*, isn't it?"

Bridgette made a face that was altogether unpleasant. "The view is 'groovy' from your father's office as well, mademoiselle," said the maid, shaking her head at the word. "It overlooks the back gardens that you love so well. *Your* gardens."

"*My* gardens?" Gemma let out a guffaw and covered her mouth with embarrassment at her outburst. "Oh, I think not."

"Vos jardins," Bridgette muttered, nodding gravely as if to indicate "the fever" was terminal.

"Remind me who owns the château next door to my gardens." Gemma rolled her eyes. "I've been so forgetful lately."

The woman sighed as though Gemma were the village idiot. "It is Monsieur Thibault's estate, but of course you know, it is forbidden to go there."

"Forbidden?" Gemma raised her eyebrow. This Monsieur Thibault was not a character in the script, nor was there a forbidden garden. Well, that was an interesting change in detail. She would be paying this Monsieur Thibault a visit for sure, forbidden or not. Gemma slid out a piece of heavy cotton writing paper and then sipped her coffee. It was a fabulous rich blend of coffee and cream. "That will be all, Bridgette."

After a few failed attempts, Gemma finally got the feel of how to dip the pen into the ink bottle to get just the right amount. It felt like a small victory in this strange world.

Dear Monsieur Batton:

Thank you so much for the letter informing me of my cousins' dreadful situation. While I am sure you would agree that I am extremely charitable and sympathetic, I must confess that I have gone through Father's ledgers and can find no record of these relatives. I'm sure their intentions are nothing but honorable; however, I think you would agree that a woman of means, alone in a house, cannot take in strangers. Therefore, I would find it most unsettling to have strangers in my home so soon after Father's death. Please send them my regards, and if you feel it is appropriate, you may send them a small charitable amount. We must do what we can in these times.

Yours truly,
Gisele Dumas

If Monsieur Batton was writing to her on behalf of Avril and Roman, then he was already under their spell. She would await the cousins' next move.

Gemma spent the rest of her day in the garden, trying every angle to get a glimpse of Monsieur Thibault's mysterious gardens while pretending to prune the roses. After much trial and error, she found if she stood on the stone step, she could get a glimpse of his perfectly tended vines. There were hundreds of neat rows of them. "So, Monsieur Thibault is a vintner."

For the first time, she fell into bed exhausted from working in her garden, and sleep came quickly.

The furious pounding of hooves up the stone pathway early the next morning woke Gemma from a wonderful dream. She roused herself, pulling back the curtain nearest the roundabout, where she found a middle-aged man with a crisp top hat and black suit emerging from his cab, pulling his sleeves to settle his suit over his broad shoulders.

"Well, hello, Monsieur Batton." A sly smile formed on her face.

The solicitor would have received her letter last night by courier. He lived in Amboise, so the fact that he was here first thing in the morning meant that she clearly wasn't getting rid of Avril and Roman so easily.

Within minutes, an intense knocking began at her bedroom door. She opened it to find Bridgette standing in the hall with a crazed expression on her face. The maid did a once-over at Gemma's dress, seeing her mistress was still in her cotton nightgown.

"It's already hot," said Gemma in defense. "Those dresses are oppressive."

"You must get dressed, mademoiselle."

"What is it?" Gemma studied her dismayed maid's face.

"Monsieur Batton is downstairs, mademoiselle."

"Everyone thinks I have the fever anyway; I might as well just receive him in this." She plucked at the skirt of her gown, which was the only article of clothing that didn't make the heat unbearable.

Horror flashed across Bridgette's face. She led Gemma away from the door and spoke in hushed tones. "You must be careful. That man is dangerous. He has attempted to have you sent away several times since your father's death."

"I'm kidding, Bridgette. Tell him that I'll be down in a few moments." While she seemed light and airy, almost dismissive of Bridgette, the news that Monsieur Batton had plotted to have her sent away had not been in the original script, and the idea sent chills up her spine. Gemma knew that she needed to tread carefully. There was little doubt that Monsieur Batton would send her away to an institution if he could, if for no other reason than to pilfer funds from her estate. Without a husband, Gisele Dumas was in a very precarious position.

Gemma surveyed her dresses in the armoire, looking for the coolest one. The bronze silk day dress might be the most comfortable. She knew enough about the period dress to look at the train. All of these gowns were elaborate silk and velvet creations. Only the lengths of the trains seemed to divide the day dresses from the evening ones. She certainly would not be wearing stockings or a corset, but the sleeves on the one she selected were capped, allowing her arms to be free. Plus, the bronze gave depth to her red hair. One look in the mirror told her the garish copper color on her hair hadn't faded, either. The color was still as vibrant as it had been the day Valdon's hairdresser applied it. Twisting her long locks into a low knot, she surveyed herself in the mirror. It would do.

As she descended the stairs, she found Batton in the foyer puffed up like a rooster pacing the floor, his hat fumbling nervously in his hand like he was reciting lines in his head. He looked exactly like his actor counterpart in the film. He was a supporting player in the script, dressed like an undertaker with his high-buttoned black morning suit with gray tie. This was a man who did not like to be kept waiting on the whims of a silly young woman. In Gemma's true time, women demonstrated by burning their bras, and free love was everywhere. It would take some getting used to the idea that while she was the owner of the estate, she was still a vulnerable woman in 1878. Oh, how she longed to hear the word *cut*.

"Monsieur Batton," she said with a weary sigh. So rapt was he in his thoughts he hadn't even noticed her arrival. Gemma was not about to apologize for keeping him waiting. Clearing her throat finally caused him to look up.

"Gisele," said Batton in a tone that infuriated her, too familiar and condescending.

"What a pleasant surprise to find *you* at my doorstep this morning, Monsieur Batton." She walked past him toward the dining room. "Have you eaten?"

"I received your reply," said Batton, nearly falling over himself to catch up with her as she made her way through the French doors to the beautifully set breakfast table.

"Coffee?" She pointed to the elaborate breakfast display in front of them.

"Yes... yes... about your letter."

Gemma faced him. "We will discuss my reply after I have had my coffee, Monsieur Batton. Surely you are not so rude as to walk through my door and begin making all kinds of demands." She pointed to a chair. As she did, she smelled the lovely scent of something like honeysuckle or linden trees wafting through the open door. "Please sit and enjoy some coffee."

Coolly, she took her place at the head of the table, arranging her napkin on her lap, and patiently waited for Monsieur Batton to do the same. The sight of Bernardaud china on the table made her feel that she wasn't lost from her old reality completely. Sometimes she would stare at a cup thinking it could propel her back to Thierry Valdon's dining room. And yet, she was still here, wherever that was, and her solicitor was sitting opposite her at the breakfast table. Why hadn't someone rescued her? Why hadn't she woken up yet? Gemma stifled a frustrated sigh. She pushed a glass plate overflowing with shortbread cookies and pastries toward him. "Almond croissant?"

"Non," said Batton, gruffly fiddling with his cup. He had tufts of hair on his knuckles and wide fingers that seemed to struggle with the fine china, barely fitting his forefinger in the cup's delicate handle.

A door opened, its hinges creaking, and Manon arrived, placing a café au lait in front of Gemma, who gleefully sampled the first sip, finding she was grateful for the woman's presence. There was something deeply comforting about Manon being seemingly as unhappy as Gemma to be there, like they were both prisoners of whatever this world was—either real or in her mind.

"About your reply, Gisele." Monsieur Batton placed his cup back on the saucer without so much as a sip. "You simply cannot turn your cousins away. Impossible."

Gemma chewed her croissant slowly, plotting her next step, "But I don't know them." She blinked innocently, trying to catch his eye.

"I assure you, mademoiselle, they have provided the appropriate documents." He waved his hands like the matter was finished.

"These documents," she said, her voice raised in an innocent lilt. "You've read them?"

"I have." He bowed his chin deeply to affirm his conviction.

"How are they related to me again?"

"They...they are on your father's side. Yes," he said, a flush appearing on his face. That he wasn't prepared for this question shocked her. He wasn't expecting any resistance to his request at all.

"I thought you said it was my mother's?" Gemma kept her tone light, almost flirty.

"Yes, yes, my mistake." His baritone was deep for such a small man. "Your mother's side, of course. They are from Italy."

"Germany," said Gemma, amused that he wasn't even trying to be believable. She was just expected to play her part. "My mother was German."

He shot her a look of fury. "Then, it is your father's side of the family. They are Italian."

"Well, either German or Italian, my dear father is not here to corroborate their claim, sadly."

He pounded the table with his fist. "As your solicitor, my word should be good enough."

Gemma jumped in her seat and studied the man's face. It was an unremarkable face, with thick, rough skin and a bulbous nose, small blue eyes and thin lips. He looked like a rock that had sprouted eyes. "I would think that as my solicitor, you would be more concerned with my worries, yes?" With him, she was beginning to master the art of the rhetorical question. It felt gentler than just disagreeing with him. "I don't know these people. I've never heard my father mention them at all. If I may speak frankly, Monsieur Batton?" She paused.

"Of course," said the man gruffly.

She smiled sweetly. "I doubt their claims. Surely you agree that as a woman without the protections of a husband, I'm vulnerable to all kinds of deceitful machinations. I'm happy to pay them a small sum to find another relative to live with. As a young woman living alone, surely you can understand. It would be unwise to take them in." With that, she picked up her cup and took a sip of her coffee, having to choke down her feigned helplessness.

"That you are a young woman alone is enough reason to have your family surrounding you." He sipped his coffee, then placed the cup back on the saucer with a heavy slam, nearly sending the saucer flying. "Since we are speaking so frankly, I hear you have not been well, Gisele. Nightly ravings about something called a 'movie' and demanding to speak to a man on the 'telephone' named Thierry Valdon. I hear you've begun calling yourself *Gemma Turner.*"

So, the staff was talking to Batton behind her back.

As if he could read her thoughts, he added, "The staff has been concerned about your... well... unorthodox behavior... since your father's death. I feel these relatives would provide some comfort to you, Gisele. Dare I say, they could help you during this difficult time, until you find a husband, of course. Negotiations with Pascale are moving along in that regard."

"No," she snapped, both at the disregard for her feelings and also the news about "negotiations" of marriage with that dreadful lug Pascale. "I won't have them in this house. Do you understand me?"

She could see visible panic on the man's face. Returning without an invitation for Roman and Avril was not an option for him. In the film, her cousins were dangerous vampires, disguising themselves as nobility. They would kill him if he failed.

"I fear that I may be too late in responding to them," said Batton, folding his napkin. "They were planning on departing on the train this morning."

"Then you need to stop them. Wire them or whatever you do. Send a carrier pigeon, I don't care how you do it, but I don't want those strangers in my home."

The solicitor stood and placed his arm on the chair. "I hope you are well, mademoiselle. I must admit I didn't believe the tales that I was hearing about you. But now..."

He was threatening her. Gemma's heart skipped a beat. If this thing went way off script and she went to one of those terrible institutions, she might never get home. She would be locked up, stripped of every right. Cursing herself for pushing too far, she tossed her napkin on the table. The damage had been done. Now she needed to gain back some control.

"But now you think that because I don't want strangers in my house so immediately after the grief of my father's death, that I must be a raving lunatic? Have I summed it up correctly?" Gemma forced herself to stir her café au lait calmly, looking up at Batton only after she'd finished speaking. Her eyes met his, and she was surprised to find what certainly resembled fear.

"I will do my best to try to stop their arrival." Sliding his chair back, Monsieur Batton stood up from the table. The man who left the room was not the same man who'd entered it. His exchange with Gemma had shaken him, and she could see that he gripped the chair a little firmly for support before nodding and taking his leave.

"See that you do," said Gemma. "Good day, Monsieur Batton." Even though this was dangerous, she felt a swell of pride. She'd played Gisele Dumas the way she'd wanted to portray her. In this strange world she found herself, it was the one bit of control that Gemma could take back.

After Batton had left, Gemma walked the grounds around the house in a desperate need to find calm. Increasingly, she found herself falling into fits of crying, stress and fear wearing her down. The garden soothed her and was somewhat out of earshot to the staff. She would have to be more careful now that she knew they were spying on her and reporting to Batton.

Taking a right from the house, she walked down the long path covered with twisted white oak trees, moss tendrils hanging down like tinsel on a Christmas tree. This was the same path she'd taken with Valdon to the wine cave, yet it felt like another world. It was another world. As she reached midway, she saw the cut that led to the cave. One of the few pleasures she had was this walk each morning. Taking the path and back twice could pass the time between petit-déjeuner and déjeuner. Beyond the trees, she could make out the form of an enormous creature grazing in the field, oblivious to her. It was a stag.

Watching the deer graze brought back a memory from childhood of her and her father observing a ten-point buck in the field outside their home in Colorado, before they moved to California. Her father had motioned for her to keep quiet so they could observe the animal. "You're too impatient," he had said. "Just sit quietly and take it all in. You want everything too quickly." If she closed her eyes, she thought she could hear her father's voice. Sobs erupted uncontrollably, her shoulders shaking violently. Looking up, gulping for air, she saw that her crying had frightened the stag, the animal's hooves cutting through thick brush. She missed her father, her mother, her world. It was a primal ache, and the fear was creeping into her thoughts. "No," she said, shaking herself. "You'll get out of here. You'll get back home."

When she'd composed herself enough, she wandered back to the house, staring up at the orange brick mansion covered in moss and the white-shuttered arched windows.

Manon was waiting for her at the door.

"I was walking," she replied, not liking the woman's scrutiny. Would she be reporting back to Monsieur Batton that Gemma went for walks in the woods?

"You must not travel to the woods alone," said the maid. "People disappear."

"If only I could be so lucky," said Gemma under her breath. To her surprise, Gemma found the dining room buzzing with activity. "What is going on in there?"

"Your dinner." Manon's tone was weary, like this was just one of the many things her mistress had forgotten. "Surely you haven't forgotten that as well."

From the script, Gemma knew that the cousins appeared at a grand dinner, the element of surprise in their favor so Gisele invited them in. If she were, indeed, having a dinner tonight, then it was likely Roman and Avril would be making their first appearance.

An idea struck her. Should she cancel the dinner? It would give her more time to prepare against Roman and Avril. She needed to be ready for them. "Is it necessary to entertain? It's just so sudden."

Bridgette entered the room, an elaborate black dress in her arms that Gemma knew must be what she'd planned to wear. Immediately, she and Manon began communicating in alarmed glances. It was Manon who finally stepped forward, her hands folded neatly in front of her.

"Mademoiselle Dumas. It has been six months since your father's death. While I would have waited a year, you decided—quite enthusiastically—that it was time to reenter society."

"Manon thought it was an appalling idea," said Bridgette, as if the woman's feelings on the matter were secret.

The older housekeeper shot Bridgette a look. "I felt it was too soon and I expressed my concerns, but you would not hear of them, so the invitations have been sent and food has been prepared. It would be very improper to cancel at this late hour, regardless of whether you have forgotten about the dinner." She bowed her head, a rather dramatic gesture. "However, I will cancel if you insist."

Bridgette gawked at Gemma. "You've forgotten about the dinner?"

Gemma tut-tutted at Bridgette's alarm. "I simply changed my mind," said Gemma, reading the room. She suspected the true reason was that everyone wanted her to find a husband. A single young lady with an estate was a suspicious creature in the country. "But I see quite a bit of work has been done, so we will proceed."

At seven, the clock chimed and the sound of horses rounding the drive became constant. The house was now illuminated with candles and gaslights, making everything flicker and shimmer. The formal dining room, set for twelve, had been transformed when she walked through the French mullioned doors. Three clusters of flowers—all cream, blue, and soft green—were at the center of the place settings. In addition to Gemma and Monsieur Batton, and his wife Hélène, there was Pascale, as well as three more couples from the village, listed as "Couples, 3, 4, and 5" in the script, plus extended family members. The scene was exactly as it had been filmed, down to the china.

This déjà vu was dizzying. Was she acting? Was any of this real? She traveled around the room, making tweaks to flowers and doing a final change of seats, anything to play the part of Gisele Dumas.

The seat opposite her sat empty in honor of her father, a lovely touch from Manon that Gemma had not considered. Gisele had been very fond of her father, but this posed an issue for Gemma, who only knew the actor who played him in a brief flashback. To gin up the proper amount of nostalgia, Gemma had found herself thinking of her own father that entire day. What did her parents think had happened to her? Normally, she'd have called her mother by now, reversing the charges, something that her parents had insisted that she do even when she made far more money than her father ever had as a career army colonel. What would they do when she missed several calls? She didn't want to be a worry—a burden—to them. Her mother had been through so much in the war. Like Aunt Em in Oz, was her mother standing over her in the other world while she was in some deep coma?

"Mademoiselle?"

Deep in thought, she looked up to find Pascale staring at her expectantly. He was as handsome as the actor who'd been playing him, maybe even more so since Gemma hadn't much cared for Pierre Lanvin. She wondered if this version of Pascale was as dull as his film counterpart.

"It's wonderful to see you," said Gemma, taking his hand with forced smile. The idea that this man was in talks to marry her like she was chattel was revolting.

A sudden commotion in the foyer caused Gemma to spring from

her seat. From her vantage point in the dining room, she could make out two figures. Monsieur Batton, seated next to her, looked down at his soup.

"You said you'd tell them not to come," she said through gritted teeth.

The solicitor never lifted his gaze from the bowl. "I said that I would try to stop them. I didn't say that I could actually *do* it."

So, now she had vampires in the house. Gisele, being the dimwit she was, had no idea they were vampires, so she'd welcome them graciously. But Gemma was determined to get them out of the house like she might a rat or any other vermin.

Pascale was attempting to rise to assist her, but Gemma held up her finger for him to remain in his seat. Funny how he was assuming *he* was the hero of this story.

Avril and Roman stood in the foyer looking bored. It was like an interesting recasting. While both had similarities to their film counterparts, there was a wolfishness to Roman that was both frightening and exciting. This Roman was every bit the aristocrat. Avril wore an ice-blue cape that tied with a silk ribbon at her throat. Both the cape and the ribbon accented her eyes. Her hair was the same platinum blond, piled high on her head like a 1960s Brigitte Bardot interpretation of a Victorian hairstyle.

"Bon soir," said Gemma, not extending her hand. "I'm Mademoiselle Dumas."

The man spoke with a deep, thickly accented voice. He looked weary from travel, and his hair and suit were rumpled. "We are your cousins; this is Avril, and I am Roman."

"Oh dear," said Gemma sheepishly. "I'm so afraid there has been some dreadful mistake. Didn't Monsieur Batton tell you?"

Confused, Roman looked at Avril. She shook her head.

"Non," said Roman. "He said nothing."

"I'm afraid that my father has no record of you. In fact, no one has any record of you, so it would be highly inappropriate... particularly you, Roman...to stay in my home. Also, frankly, we have no room." Looking him up and down, Gemma thought that had Roman not been a vampire, she would have *loved* to have him in the house.

Gemma swore she saw Manon smirk.

"Is that true, Manon? We have no room?"

"That is correct," she said with a submissive nod.

"But..." Avril shot a look at Roman.

Gemma quickly interrupted her. "Manon. By chance did you invite these two dear souls into the house?"

"I let them in," said Manon. "In fact, the girl charged into the house like she owned the place."

Gemma could see the dinner guests now gawking at the commotion. Pascale's mother exclaimed, "Who are they?"

"Would you shut the doors to the dining room, Manon?" As the maid closed the French doors, Gemma returned her gaze to the cousins. "Tsk, tsk. You know the rules as I do. If you weren't invited here by the owner, then I suspect you can't come into the house. Isn't that correct?" She was hoping that film vampire rules were universal, at least in this strange world. Vampires had to be invited. These two hadn't been.

And they knew it. They'd come through the door with Manon inviting them in, but she was just a tenant, not the owner.

"And as the owner, I do not invite you into the house." As if on command, Roman and Avril began struggling like bugs in a jar, grabbing at their throats. As though the air in the foyer was burning them, they both ran from the house. Once on the terrace, the two bent over, struggling to regain their composure, their skin bubbled but then quickly replenished into a youthful sheen.

"I'm so sorry, mademoiselle. What are they?" It was Manon whose mouth was agape as she made the sign of the cross.

"Evil," said Gemma, shutting the door. "Pure evil."

"If I wouldn't have seen it with my own eyes..." Manon blinked. Holding her stomach, she looked like she was about to vomit.

"You didn't know," said Gemma. "They tricked you to get through the door, but they cannot remain in the house without my invitation. They knew that." She leaned in to whisper. "But you mustn't look at them, Manon. They can mesmerize you."

The vampires stood on the other side of the glass, their strength fully regained. Roman gazed at Gemma with fury and something else—hunger. He stepped forward, just to the door, his fingernails clawing at the glass playfully. Instinctively, Gemma stepped back. Then a crooked smile formed on his lips as he pointed to Gemma and mouthed *I'm coming for you.*

The vampires turned and slipped into the night. Gemma felt a shiver and reached up to reassuringly touch her throat.

"I don't like them, mademoiselle." The maid's dour expression was gone.

As Gemma brushed past her to return to the dining room, she leaned in close to whisper into Manon's ear. "Keep your doors and windows locked. Do you have a cross?"

The woman touched her chest, alluding to the necklace under her dress. "Of course."

"Wear it. Tell the others to do the same."

As she returned to the table, Pascale jumped to slide out Gemma's chair. "What was that business?"

"Never you mind." Gemma smiled at each of her guests, hoping to smooth things over, but as she returned her focus to the dinner, she felt Monsieur Batton's eyes on her, watching her like a guard dog might. She kept her face neutral, not allowing the smallest smirk to cross her lips.

"Have you been well, Gemma?" he said, clearing his throat. "There is a doctor that you might want to visit in Tours."

"Certainly not," said Pascale indignantly. "I know of the place you are referring to, and I assure you, it is not a place for Mademoiselle Dumas."

With heavy-lidded eyes, Monsieur Batton shot Gemma a hard look filled with promise. In sending away Roman and Avril, she had made an enemy of him tonight. And that was a dangerous thing.

Later that night, she was wide awake listening for every noise. A floorboard outside of her room creaked, and she jolted up in bed. Quietly, she slid out of the sheets and tiptoed across the room, placing her ear against the door and clutching her crucifix. On the other side, she could feel the presence of something—or someone. Had Roman and Avril returned?

Whoever or whatever was on the other side seemed to sense her presence. The sound began at the top of the door—claws or nails—running down the length of the board. The scrape was deep, and Gemma thought that there were surely marks pushing through the wood. She jumped back from the door, her heart racing.

To her horror, Gemma saw the knob turn, but it was locked. Still, the knob began to turn the other way, and all that stood between her and whatever was on the other side was a simple skeleton key. Racing over to the window, she slid a heavy chair at an angle under the doorknob to block the door from opening.

All night, Gemma sat on the bed watching the door until she finally fell asleep as the sun rose.

In the morning, she made her way downstairs, exhausted from lack of sleep. Whatever had been outside the door had not come back. As she passed the vase on the way to the dining room, she stopped dead in her tracks. Leaning against the vase was an identical envelope to the one from the other morning. Addressed to *Mademoiselle Dumas*, the script was in the same blue ink from Monsieur Batton's pen. Recalling his threatening stare, Gemma grabbed the heavy envelope, frantically tearing it open, almost expecting to hear that she would be going away for treatment for her "fever."

Odd. The contents of the note were *the same* as the note she'd received two days ago. Once again, it was her solicitor telling her that her Italian cousins were requesting to stay with her.

Squinting, she checked the envelope carefully. It was the same letter.

Was this some joke? Just last night she'd sent the "cousins" away, uninviting them from Château Dumas. The contents of this letter seemed to indicate the scene from last night's dinner had not occurred at all. A strange déjà vu swept over Gemma, and she looked around the room.

The sun was streaming in just as it had the day before. The same flowers were in the vase, the same envelope and letter from her solicitor. In a moment, Bridgette would come breezing by, saying today's paper had not come.

As if a director stood on the other side of the door cueing her, Bridgette breezed in maneuvering a heavy silver tray. "Bonjour, mademoiselle. Today's paper—"

"—has not arrived." Gemma finished the line like an understudy. She knew it well.

"How did you know?" The maid set the tray on the dining room table, where just the night before an elaborate dinner had taken place. Yet, there was no hint that this room had been the scene for a dinner for twelve.

Gemma held out the letter. "Did an envelope like this one arrive for me two days ago?"

"Non," said Bridgette.

"Think, Bridgette," said Gemma. "I asked you for ink and paper so that I could write a reply to Monsieur Batton two days ago."

"Non," said Bridgette, alarm in her voice rising. "This is the first time a letter like that has arrived in quite some time from Monsieur Batton."

Frantically, Gemma thrust the letter in Bridgette's face. "Look at it."

The maid's shaking hands clasped the paper. Scanning the letter, she looked up at Gemma's pleading face. "I don't know what you want from me. I've never seen this letter before. Monsieur Batton just got back from Italy yesterday. He has not written to you in months." Her voice was quieter now. "Please, please, mademoiselle." Bridgette's voice was thin. "Stop this madness."

Gemma looked up at the ceiling in exasperation. "Or Monsieur Batton will send me to the hospital in Tours."

"That's not even funny." Yet, Bridgette's face told her that the hospital had been discussed.

"He threatened me with that hospital over dinner, last night." Gemma pointed to the table. "Right here."

"Non, mademoiselle," said Bridgette, her face suddenly brightening. "The dinner is tomorrow night."

A terrible dread washed over Gemma.

She knew exactly what this was. "This" was a retake.

13

Christopher Kent
August 2, 1998
Paris, France

Checking into a hostel-level hotel in the Latin Quarter, Christopher Kent searched the phone books for Elizabeth Bourget. Finding a phone number, he left a message for her saying that he'd read the *Cartoons of the Twentieth Century* collection at the Library of Congress and wanted to meet with her to discuss them. He'd thought it was a long shot, but his phone rang.

"The café across from Palais Brongniart in thirty minutes."

Unfamiliar with Paris, he had to find what she meant and barely got there on time. He didn't have to wonder who she was. A woman in her late forties or early fifties, she had gotten there early. She had straight blond hair that fell to her collarbone and cat-eye sunglasses. Even though it was a sweltering August morning, she wore a black jacket that looked expensive. Her red nails were glossy. A glass of white wine was sitting in front of her with traces of red lipstick on its rim.

She looked up. "At least you've stopped posting on message boards, thank God."

Christopher sat next to her, facing the Palais. "That was you."

"Oui," she said. "I see you've been to the Library of Congress."

The waiter arrived to refill their water glasses, so she'd stopped talking. They sat side by side like two spies in the Cold War.

"Café au lait." It was just before noon, and Christopher wasn't about to start drinking wine. He had to be at the Louvre at four to set up for when they started filming after hours. From the looks of the list of scenes, he'd be there all night.

She lit a cigarette and offered him one, but he shook his head. Only when the waiter left did she speak. "What do you do?"

"I'm a film student at Columbia. I got a job assisting a filmmaker on a documentary being shot at the Louvre."

"Interesting," she said with a hint of surprise.

"Why?"

"Nothing. Just odd that they gave a ticket to a mere student who works as an assistant on other people's films." She inhaled the cigarette and held it out between her fingers in that elegant way 1940s actresses did in films.

"Ivy Cross is my girlfriend. Her father—"

"Ahhhhh, Zander Cross," she drew out, connecting the dots. Glancing down, she picked at imaginary lint from her coat.

"He gave her his seat."

She kept her eyes on the Palais Brongniart and watched some children running through the square. "That means you got Jacques de Poulignac's spot, then. He died days before the last screening. Kind of a waste if you ask me."

It took him a minute to register that she'd just insulted him. He bristled at the rudeness, shocked by what seemed to be unwarranted hostility. "Why would you say that? What makes you *so* sure I'm not worthy of the spot?"

"What makes you so sure that you are?"

She didn't like him, and the feeling was beginning to be mutual. He put his hands in his pockets and slid down in the chair, which wasn't comfortable at all.

"How many of us do you know?"

"Only about thirty of the seventy-five."

"That's all?"

She laughed, then took a long drag and extinguished the cigarette in the ashtray. "Some people don't want to be discovered. Others aren't repeat viewers, so you can hardly know them all."

If he had been hoping that she would be more forthcoming with information, he was disappointed. "Why all the secrecy? Don't you wonder about the film?"

She scowled. "Jesus. Of course, I wonder about the film. Why do you think I've gone to all the trouble to gather us under the radar for knowledge? I've done more than anyone in the scholarship around the film." She gave him an astonished glance, stopping short of an eye roll. "And after all this time, I still don't know who's behind the film. That's the biggest secret of them all. The wizard behind the curtain. That's what we're all seeking."

"Well, who *would* be behind the film? Who benefits? Dark forces? No offense, but you're making this film sound like the Kennedy assassination. I'm not sure there is a vast conspiracy or someone projecting from the grassy knoll. I'll give you that the robes and masks are a bit much. High theater."

"Did you bleed?" There was more than a note of annoyance in her voice.

"Pardon me?" He was so taken aback by her question that it took him a minute to understand what she was referring to.

"When you placed the mask on your face the first time. Did you bleed?"

He touched his cheek.

"And the sorrow. When you stepped into the church, did the feeling of sorrow follow you? Does it follow you still? Right after you see the film it is always the worst, of course. It will subside, in time."

The look on his face must have spoken volumes, because she smiled sadly.

"What does it all mean?" he asked.

"I don't know, but the sorrow I felt the first time I placed that mask on my face was something that I never forgot. I'm glad you're so sure dark forces aren't at work," she said, visibly tensing. "Because I'm not."

The waiter returned with his coffee with cream.

"Merci," said Christopher. "It's probably that filmmaker, Claude..."

She faced him and gripped the back of the cane chair, her cheeks turning bright red. "What are you? Twenty-two? I've seen all *three* films, have you?" She held up her fingers. "How many have you seen? Un? Now you're an expert? How dare you come here and tell me things about which you have no idea. Have you even *met* Claude Moravin?"

Christopher's eyes were wide. Elizabeth faced him, and he could see her brows were knitted with fury. The elegant sheen was dropped; this woman was mad as hell. "Have you?"

"No," he admitted.

"I'll spare you the detective work. Manon Valdon showed him the final cut after Thierry's death. After viewing the second film, he was the first to say that something was wrong with it. Claude found me in Paris and told me that he did not film any of the additional scenes with Gemma Turner that were in that film. He walked me through frame by frame what he could remember. There are scenes in the second version shown in 1988 and this year's version that he didn't film as well. No one knows how they got there."

"So there's another cameraman finishing the film?"

"With a star who doesn't age?" She snorted and gathered her bag. "This was a waste of my time, as I knew it would be. You're a lightweight." She stood up and placed the bag on her shoulder.

Christopher felt gutted by her comments. "Sorry," he said, jumping up from his seat, trying to placate her. "I didn't mean to come off as arrogant. I'm sorry. I just want to help. I may not be Jacques de... de..."

"Poulignac." Her tone was cool, but she was still there, listening.

"I may not be Jacques de Poulignac, but I *am* a filmmaker who has access to a lot of more current editing techniques. What I can tell you is that Gemma Turner's performance is the key to this, not the differences between the films. True, I've only seen one film, but there is a distinct difference in the scenes shot while she was on the set and the ones where she is attempting to thwart Roman and Avril. I edit film all day long. It's like the scenes have different directors."

She smiled and adjusted her handbag on her shoulder. "There are theories that it is a Gemma Turner double, but everyone who was associated with the original film says that it's her."

"It's not a double. Of course, the problem is that none of us do have access to the film to go frame by frame. And that's the whole purpose of this Soixante-Quinze thing. We're supposed to *see* the film, but just not look at it too closely. Why?"

"And you have a theory?"

He swallowed. This one was a bit personal, but he'd been forming a theory about his mother. "I think we all have a connection to Gemma Turner. It's not the film, it's her." While he didn't know how his mother was connected to her, it was that connection that bound him to the film. He was sure of it. When Elizabeth's face fell, he knew his hunch was correct. "I'm right, aren't I?"

When she didn't answer, he continued. "I think we need to start asking bigger questions. All the comments about the differences between the versions are like a close reading. I'm not sure the differences are the point. Why would anyone go to all the trouble to create this film in the first place? It took me a while to pinpoint what bothered me so much about Gemma Turner's 'performance' in the scenes with Avril and Roman," he said, forming air quotes with his fingers. "In my opinion, she's afraid in those scenes. I've spent years watching her in those surf films, and there is a rhythm to her performances. In this film, it's not a performance at all. And the dialogue, it's strange. Well, it's real."

Elizabeth Bourget reached into her bag and pulled out a file folder. "You asked how you can help? You can help me by monitoring the Library of Congress conversations. It's been harder for me to get to Washington these days. Is your French any good?"

He grinned. "Mon français s'améliore." He'd enrolled in a French class at the New School for the fall.

She frowned. "You can call me, but we need to talk in code. Alert me if there is anything that I need to see for myself. And keep on that line of thinking... about Gemma. You're right. We've gotten lazy talking about the parts and not the whole." She pulled away and began to walk down the street.

"Can I ask you a question?"

"Of course." She spun and hugged her handbag.

"What *do* you think we're seeing?" Christopher was buzzing now, feeling like he might be so close to answers... answers about the film and his mother. "I mean, I have so many questions."

She was silent for a moment. For the first time, seeing her straight on, he noticed that she was a striking woman; perhaps she'd been a model in her youth. Deep in thought, she tensed her jaw. "I'm not sure I want to answer you."

He sank a little. This woman knew more than she was letting on. "I think you haven't answered a lot of my questions. Perhaps indulge me just one." He thrust his hands deeply into his pants pockets. What could spook a woman like this? A sudden wave of paranoia swept over him, causing him to survey the street for the first time.

She must have felt it, too, because she took two steps toward him and gazed down at her shoes like she was mustering strength. He had to strain to hear her.

"Over the years, this film has become an obsession of mine," she said in a whisper. "I've explored every possibility, chased down every lead, and wandered down all paths, from fan art with a Gemma Turner lookalike to a secret filming between Thierry and Gemma that no one knew about. There are many theories. Like your Kennedy assassination analogy, all can be refuted. Nothing quite fits."

He was afraid to say anything for fear he'd break her train of thought. This, *this* was what he'd come for.

"There is something *wrong* with that film. There is a palpable sadness to it that seeps out and infects those of us who view it, not unlike the very draining that happens to the villagers in the film. We are the villagers."

Ivy had made the connection between the plot of the film and the sadness that seemed to cling to the viewer, like an infection. And Ivy had been so rattled that she'd remained in Los Angeles.

"Once you've seen it, you become touched," she said softly. "I don't mean anything happens to you per se, but the melancholy clings to you, feeds on you. There is a feeling emanating from the script like the smell of someone sick with the fever. Do you know what I mean?"

"I do," he said.

"If you see another one, it just gets worse, like it compounds, leading me to believe that what you're seeing with *L'Étrange Lune* is a film that comes from Hell itself. You're quite possibly damning yourself by watching it."

With a nod she turned, her heels clicking as she walked away, the cut of her jacket making her look like an elegant military general as she walked down the street. From over her shoulder she said, "So think carefully if you want another ticket?"

14

Gemma Turner
"1878"
Amboise, France

"You are mistaken," said Bridgette. "Monsieur Batton just returned from Italy. He has not written you since Christmas."

Gemma held the envelope in her hand, like evidence. "Returned from Italy?" Gemma let this detail sit with her for a moment. Roman and Avril were from Italy. That must be where Monsieur Batton had encountered them. "And the dinner party?" She already knew the answer.

The maid's face brightened. "Demain!"

"Demain," said Gemma wearily.

"Oui," said Bridgette, alarm in her voice. "You have not forgotten."

"Hardly," said Gemma dismissively, hating that concerned look that Bridgette constantly gave her. Her mind was racing. Trying another angle, Gemma laughed carelessly. "Remind me again who is coming to dinner... Pascale..."

"Monsieur Batton and his wife, of course; Monsieur Claremont and his wife; Pascale and his mother; Monsieur Fournier and his wife and daughter; and Monsieur Lambert and his wife. There are twelve. Manon was very careful about the guest list since this is your first dinner since your father's death." The maid always bowed her head in deference when she spoke of Gisele's father, like he was the king.

It was the same guest list. This was a retake of last night's dinner scene, where she'd been certain she'd banished the cousins. It seemed to have worked for the moment. But it hadn't. In film, a retake happened when the director wasn't happy with the previous scene. She'd changed up the scene the way she thought it needed to be written. Now she was doing it again. Her head was swimming. If it was a retake, then that meant that she was inside her film, a theory that she had considered because everyone was running around in character. If this was a film, where were the cameras? She'd searched every inch of the house, and not only were there no cameras, but there was also no electricity. And who was demanding retakes? The idea that she was being judged inside of this strange set by a hidden entity infuriated her. "I think I'll take breakfast in my father's office," said Gemma, waving the envelope. "I have to answer Monsieur Batton, and the view is so *groovy* from his old office."

Bridgette giggled, trying on the new word for herself. "The view is *groovy*."

There was a tinge of something... sadness? Surrounded by staff who were busily getting ready for the social event of the season, Gemma felt so alone. She couldn't trust the staff, fearing they were providing Monsieur Batton with an accounting of her strange behavior. She'd thought she'd known the plot of this film, but now nothing was certain, not even loyalties.

Sitting in Monsieur Dumas's old office, she was surrounded by books and etchings—all very masculine, with the leather and the brown frames. Sliding the inkpot closer, she lifted the pen and dipped it, finding it much easier than it had been a few days ago. "That's why we actors rehearse," she said aloud.

Dear Monsieur Batton:

Thank you so much for your letter. It sounds like a dreadful situation, but I'm not sure there is anything I can do. My father made it very clear that we did not have any relatives. While I am sure you would agree that I am extremely charitable and sympathetic, I fear they have mistaken me for someone else. I'm sure their intentions are nothing but honorable; however, I think you would agree that as a woman of means, it would be inappropriate for me to take in strangers without a chaperone.

Twirling the pen, she considered her next line. An idea came to her quickly.

I feel that Pascale, given his intentions of matrimony, would find another unmarried man living under my roof a completely untenable situation. If you feel it is appropriate, you may send them a small charitable amount. We must do what we can in these times. Please make haste in communicating with them. Neither Pascale, nor I, would want them coming here expecting to be taken in.

Yours truly,
Gisele Dumas

She would use Pascale's affections to her advantage. If Monsieur Batton would not listen to her, then perhaps he would listen to her potential husband. It was worth a shot. This was a retake, after all.

The next morning, as the light peeked through the drapes, the familiar sound of hooves pounding up the stone pathway was both expected and alarming. Opening the curtain, Gemma found Batton shaking off his top hat before placing it over his head. Last time, she witnessed him pulling on his suit. She paid close attention to everything he did, wondering if every detail was significant. His suit was the same black of yesterday.

On cue, an intense knocking began at her bedroom door. That would be Bridgette to inform her of Batton's arrival. Gemma swung it open to find the maid mid-knock.

"Oh," said Bridgette, visibly deflating as she glanced at Gemma, as though she'd been expecting an entirely different scene. Instead of discovering her mistress lounging in her bedclothes, she found Gemma standing in the doorway in her bronze silk day dress.

"Let me guess." Gemma leaned against the doorframe. "Monsieur Batton is in the foyer waiting for me?"

"Oui," said the maid with a puzzled expression. "But you are already dressed."

"You must seize the morning, Bridgette," said Gemma with a pump of her fist as she brushed past her, hearing the ruffling of her skirt on the floor as she moved.

Bridgette seemed to struggle speaking. Gemma stopped and turned. "What is it?"

"I . . . I . . ."

"Spit it out," said Gemma.

"You must be careful," Bridgette whispered, pointing to the stairs. "That man is dangerous. He has attempted to have you sent away to the hospital several times now." As the words erupted from Bridgette's mouth, she looked visibly perplexed to hear them.

There had been nothing to prompt the line, and yet Bridgette had been compelled to say it anyway, like she wanted to protect Gemma. By getting dressed and ready for battle with Batton, Gemma had altered the morning's events—she had changed the script, ever so slightly.

"Yes, I know he is dangerous." Indeed, Gemma knew to tread carefully. "Tell me, does he inquire about me?"

Bridgette hesitated before looking down, ashamed. "He says we are to tell him when you act strange. It is to help you, but I don't think it is."

"Thank you, Bridgette."

"He is not groovy," said the maid with a sweet smile.

"No," agreed Gemma with a wink. "His *vibe* is terrible."

Bridgette's giggling could be heard down the hall as she rehearsed the word *vibe*.

Once again, Gemma found Batton pacing in the foyer puffed up like a rooster.

"Monsieur Batton," she called with a weary sigh, rushing toward him, embracing him. "It is so wonderful to see you this morning." She took both of his sweaty palms in hers and caught his eye, batting her own. He pulled back, studying her in confusion, expecting a more hostile greeting from her.

If they were doing a retake, she would play the scene differently today. She recalled what Thierry Valdon had said. *No riding the bus.*

"Gisele," he said gruffly, his posture straightening.

She led him toward the dining room. "Have you eaten?"

"I received your reply about your cousins," said Batton, nearly falling over himself to catch up with her as she made her way through the French doors to the beautifully set breakfast table.

"Coffee?"

He frowned, annoyed by her adherence to good hospitality. "Yes... yes... about your letter."

"Oh, please," she said demurely. "Let's enjoy some of Manon's excellent pastries." Taking a pain au chocolat, she held the pastry up to him, inches from his mouth, almost suggesting he eat it from her hand. For a moment, the solicitor looked as confused as Bridgette. In some sense, Batton knew the script—the words he was to say—he just didn't *know* he knew it. Reluctantly, he took the pain au chocolat from her hand. She waited until he tasted it. "Isn't it delightful?" she said, clapping her hands like a fool. Pointing to the chair, she said, "Please sit and enjoy some coffee."

Today, Gemma decided to play Gisele needy and weak. Picking up an almond croissant, she took a dramatic bite. *She was a good actress.*

Unlike yesterday, she gave him the place at the head of the table—the one that had been reserved for her father—and she took the seat to his left and began arranging her napkin on her lap and then patiently waited for Monsieur Batton to do the same.

She pushed a glass plate overflowing with shortbread cookies and pastries toward him.

"Non," said Batton, gruffly fiddling with his cup.

The door from the kitchen opened, its hinges creaking, and Manon appeared, carrying a tray of coffee in her hand. Thrown by the switch to the seating arrangement, Manon stopped in her tracks and then placed the café au lait in front of Gemma with a loud thud. Gemma watched as the woman's arm made several attempts to place the cup where it expected Gisele Dumas to be seated, struggling to improvise even the smallest changes, like a switch in seating.

Gemma took the tray and helped guide the cup to her place at the table. As she met Manon's eyes, the woman gave her a grateful smile.

"About your reply, Gisele." Monsieur Batton picked up his cup then placed it back on the saucer without so much as a sip. "You simply cannot turn your cousins away. Impossible."

Gemma chewed her croissant, plotting her next step. In the last scene, she'd pushed hard against the cousins' arrival. Obviously, whoever was directing this strange film did not care for that version, so she would try another. She blinked a little, rather innocently, trying to catch his eye. "Pascale..."

"I spoke to him this morning," said Batton. "He agrees."

She nearly choked. "You what?"

"Yes, yes," said the man, pursing his lips. "I stopped there before I arrived here. He is quite fine with the arrangements as they are relatives."

"You're sure?" Gemma's voice, face, and stomach dropped, in that order.

"Sure?" He pulled back from the table.

"My mother never mentioned them. I find the whole thing suspicious."

What now? She could challenge her solicitor again, but there was something about his manner that indicated that while he wasn't aware he was replaying the scene again, he seemed to have some residue from the prior take, like an imprint. He was wary today, less defiant, like he knew in some primal way that he'd been outwitted by her before. And for Roman and Avril? She had other ways of defeating them—garlic, crucifixes, and stakes through the heart. Thierry Valdon's original ending had made it clear everyone was doomed. Since it appeared she was now living in this plot, Gemma didn't want the same ending for herself for all eternity. Surely, she was meant to defeat them. Otherwise, why was she here with this awareness? "Have you seen documents?" she asked, her voice raised in an innocent lilt.

"I have." He bowed his chin deeply to affirm the conviction of his answer. "The staff has been concerned about your... well... your unorthodox behavior... since your father's death. I feel these relatives would provide some comfort to you, Gisele. Dare I say, they could help you during this difficult time, until you find a husband, of course. Negotiations with Pascale are moving along in that regard, especially given my talk with him this morning."

"I see," said Gemma—and she did—clearly. Pascale had agreed to the cousins living here with Batton's assurance of matrimony. Fury welled up inside her. Her plan to use Pascale had backfired. By implying that she agreed to marry Pascale, she was now one step closer to actual matrimony. And then what? Pascale would have control over

Château Dumas and her fortune. Taking a deep breath, she decided to choke out the next line. "I'm sure you and Pascale know best."

"We do," he said, as though the matter were settled. This was the Gisele he had been expecting. He did have a hide of a skin on him, twice as thick as her own. His bulbous nose overwhelmed small, watery eyes and thin lips as though the rest of his features simply couldn't compete, so they'd just withered away like flowers under a thick tree. She watched as his shoulders softened, realizing that there would be no more refusal from her.

"Almond croissant?" Gemma held up the pastry plate with a sickening smile.

After seeing him to his carriage and insisting she was grateful for his protection, Gemma needed a walk to clear her head. She found herself in the garden behind the house. Bees hurried by her, their buzzing noises loud on the way to the overflowing lavender pots. In the center were planted yellow daffodils, orange daisies, and white jasmine. From the garden, she could see the elusive Monsieur Thibault's roof as though once, the two properties had not been separated by the gray stone gate, but she couldn't see past the giant oak into Thibault's own garden. She turned and surveyed the garden. The setting was perfect—too perfect.

"What is this place?" She didn't expect an answer, but the mere idea that the scene was being reshot meant there was a director, and if that was the case, there was a way home. Her heart skipped a beat as she tried not to think about it. All she wanted was to go home. Home to the world she knew—pay phones and miniskirts, guitars and beer bottles, and light switches—oh, how she missed the simple act of flicking on a light switch.

If she shook things up enough, then maybe the world would reveal itself to her like the wizard behind the curtain. In changing one crucial detail, Gemma had altered the guest list for tonight's dinner. Unbeknownst to the staff, in addition to a letter to Monsieur Batton, Gemma had sent an invitation to tonight's dinner to Monsieur Thibault.

She was interrupted by a voice clearing. It was Manon. "This has come for you," said the woman holding something heavy. "There was no note."

Gemma turned to find the woman carrying a powder-blue suitcase, but not just any case; this one was familiar. Her eyes lit up. "My typewriter." Nearly pulling it out of Manon's hand, Gemma took the case inside and up to her room, where she placed it on the empty desk and opened it to find her familiar Smith Corona SCM Corsair manual typewriter. Like the dress she'd worn on the night she came to this strange world, her typewriter was from her world and her time. Touching it brought on another wave of homesickness. At times, this world made her doubt that there had once been another place, but this object grounded her like no other.

"Hello, old friend."

"What is it?" Curious, Manon had followed her to see what was inside. She bent down to study the instrument, poking at keys that snapped against the drum. "Strange."

"It's a typewriter," said Gemma, stroking the instrument. "You didn't see who sent it?"

"No," said Manon. "It just appeared at the door."

Looking around the room, Gemma found a composition book and ripped out a page. Winding it around the drum, she advanced the paper, then typed.

`Where am I?`

The feeling of the keys against her fingers made her giddy.

"Can't you just write that on a piece of paper?"

"I could," said Gemma. "But this is so much neater and faster."

"It's the devil's instrument," said Manon, pulling her shawl tighter around her neck before turning to leave.

"Oh, it could very well be the devil's instrument," said Gemma under her breath. This was just like the odd connections of a dream—objects from your waking life colliding with your dream world, almost like anchors to remind you that you're not lucid. Again, Gemma typed.

```
Where am I?
```

After waiting for almost an hour, there was no reply from the keyboard, and she had no choice but to play her part—once again.

For the second time this week, Gemma greeted her guests promptly at seven. Dressed in a sapphire-blue silk gown with a corded bodice and lace sleeves, she looked like a waterfall as she walked. While none of the staff were aware, they had once again decorated the house with candles and gaslights, making everything flicker and shimmer, the formal dining room transformed with colorful china and florals—vibrant arrangements from her garden—at the center of a place setting for *thirteen* guests.

"Mademoiselle?"

Looking up, she found Pascale staring down at her with a new confidence gained from the deal he inked with Monsieur Batton that morning.

She smiled sweetly, figuring she could simply throw the vampires out of the house again if she wanted to do another retake.

"Who is seated there?" Pascale strained his neck to read the place card.

The card had been left blank, and the thirteenth place setting remained empty. Monsieur Thibault had not replied to her invitation, nor had he made an appearance. While it was rude, Gemma found the gesture more curious than ill-mannered. It was as though he was avoiding her. If he wouldn't come to her, she would pay him a visit as soon as she could.

The dinner began with smoked salmon terrines over a bed of cucumber and lavender. The second course was a fresh truffiat pastry with potatoes, leeks, and herbs from the garden, as well as local cheese.

There were two main courses: pike with butter, followed by poulet en barbouille, with its wine cream sauce thickened with chicken's blood just before serving. The aroma of onion, garlic, and thyme was immediate as the staff lifted the serving lids as they flowed through the room.

"Magnificent," said Batton with a smile toward Pascale.

Pascale seemed to expand with pride at Gemma's hostess skills and ordered the staff to fetch the Chenin Blanc and Cabernet Franc as though he already owned the château.

Looking up at the clock, Gemma nearly found herself rising in her chair in anticipation of the front doors swinging open. When she heard the familiar commotion in the foyer, she leapt out of her chair, motioning for Pascale to stay. As she pushed through the French doors, she saw two people in the hallway with Manon. Once again, the housekeeper seemed taken aback by their rude arrival, and this little detail warmed Gemma's heart.

Like well-rehearsed actors, Avril and Roman stood in the foyer, looking a little bored. Avril even studied a fingernail and appeared to yawn. Roman wore the same long black jacket, and Avril wore her ice-blue cape that tied with a silk ribbon at her throat. Once again, her platinum hair was piled high on her head like a 1960s interpretation of a Victorian hairstyle, an inkling that neither she nor Gemma were strictly in their correct time periods.

"Bon soir," said Gemma, not extending her hand. "I'm Mademoiselle Dumas."

The man spoke with a deep, confident voice. "We are your cousins; this is Avril and I am Roman."

In the original script, the one Valdon had written, Gisele welcomed her "cousins" warmly with no inkling she was sealing her doom, so it killed her to have to pretend to welcome them. "I'm so delighted to have you here," said Gemma sheepishly, laying it on a bit thick. "I did not expect you so quickly. As you can see, we are in the midst of dinner. Oh," she said, placing her hand to her mouth. "I do have some poulet en barbouille. The sauce is finished with chicken *blood*."

Confused, Roman looked at Avril.

"Blood?" It was Avril who spoke, her voice rising with interest.

"Oui," said Gemma. "Some people don't dig the dish—you know—it makes them squeamish, but you two strike me as people who could handle it." She winked at Roman. "Am I right?"

"We like blood," said Avril, her accent thick. "But we are not hungry right now."

"Maybe later," said Roman, a crooked smile forming. At this moment, Gemma wondered if he had looked like this before he was made a vampire. He was quite handsome.

Shaking the thought, she turned to Manon and lowered her voice. "Do we have room in the house, Manon? The old wing?"

Manon smirked at her suggestion that they give the cousins the most uncomfortable, stifling rooms. They were on the east side of the house, so they were the sunniest in the morning. While Gisele might agree to take these "cousins" in, she had no intention of making their stay comfortable. "We do have rooms in that wing."

"You have arrived." The booming voice was from Monsieur Batton, who burst from the dining room, throwing open the French doors. "I do hope you will find Mademoiselle Dumas to be hospitable." Batton gave her a sharp warning look. "I fear she has been unwell lately." The matter decided, he looked down at his hand, where he cleaned a bit of dirt from under his fingernail. "Aren't they welcome in the house?"

Everyone turned to look at Gemma. She let the pause go on a very long time as she studied Roman's features, his messy dark brown hair and heart-shaped face that was elongated by his beard. "Of course, you are most welcome." The words of invitation felt like they burned her tongue.

Pleased, Batton nodded and made his way back to the dining room.

Roman eyed Manon hungrily. "You could show us to our rooms?"

"No." Gemma stepped in between them. "I will come as well." Prepared, she pulled out two silver crucifixes from the décolletage of her dress. She heard a yelp from Manon that indicated she found pulling something from one's bosom unladylike, but she quickly reconsidered decorum when Gemma handed her one of the crosses. "For you."

At the sight of the silver cross, a low hiss began to emit from Avril. Roman, more composed, averted his eyes from the bounce of light off the silver.

"Put this on," said Gemma to Manon. "And don't take it off."

"I already wear one." Manon placed her palm on her chest.

"Then wear *another.*" Gemma wasn't in the mood for argument. As she led them back across the hall to the stairs, Manon followed closely behind.

"I don't like them, mademoiselle." Manon's warm breath was on her neck.

"The soup was marvelous, Manon." Gemma addressed her loudly. Then in a whisper, "Keep your doors and windows locked. Don't take off that cross."

The woman touched her chest and nodded. "Of course."

"Tell the others. Do we have garlic?"

"We do," said Manon.

"Feed it to Avril and Roman if they request food from the kitchen." She glanced over her shoulder to find Roman smiling at her. It was a sickly sweet smile, like he was tasting her.

"No need to worry about us for dinner," said Avril as she breezed past them into her bedroom. "We'll be eating later." With a flick of her wrist, she shut the door.

And Gemma felt a shiver up her spine.

In the middle of the night, she awoke to the sound of her typewriter. Bolting up in bed, she was terrified someone was at her desk. She'd shut the windows tight and fashioned a wooden cross in front of it from tree branches. But the little Smith Corona moved on its own as though it were operated by invisible fingers. Springing up from bed, she peered down at the paper.

Mademoiselle Turner:

As you can tell, I wasn't pleased with the first version. Dracula won't be written for another nineteen years, so using modern vampire vanquishing methods is just plain cheating! In other words, "a no-no." Roman is a worthy adversary for you, so I'd like more scenes with him. Do what you can with Pascale. He remains dull, sadly.

Letting out a frustrated sigh, Gemma typed:

Who are you?

The keys moved on their own, like a Ouija board.

A friend

Gemma laughed at this, typing:

Hardly. I'm a prisoner here.

The machine seemed to ponder for a moment before responding:

`That's a matter of opinion`

And then it was done. Gemma waited for an hour before typing:

`Are you there?`

But there was no response.

Hours later, Gemma opened her eyes and ran down the stairs in her nightclothes to find the foyer table empty. That the cross was still in place upstairs and the foyer table empty seemed to indicate she would not be replaying the scene again. Yet, she wasn't entirely sure that was a good thing, for it meant the cousins were in the house and she was to have more scenes with Roman.

"Pardon," said a voice. It was Manon, carrying an envelope in her hand. "This just came for you."

Gemma felt the color drain from her face. Not again. Reluctantly, she took it from Manon's hand as if possessing it gave it some power. The handwriting was not one that Gemma recognized. Ripping open the envelope, she saw the paper was also different this time.

Gisele,

Mother and I would love to have you as our guest for dinner tonight. We have much to discuss.

Pascale

She groaned audibly. The last thing Gemma wanted to do was spend an evening in the company of Pascale and his mother, but she needed to nip in the bud the idea that they would be wed. Yet, not even Pascale could ruin her sudden good mood. The scene had moved on. Not only that, but she'd also gotten a note from whoever was keeping her in this strange world. If she could communicate with whoever or whatever was doing this, then perhaps she could negotiate her way home.

"I'm having dinner with Pascale this evening," said Gemma, beaming with joy.

"That is wonderful," said Manon. "I am more concerned with our houseguests. The entire house staff are now wearing crucifixes, and I have instructed the cook to add garlic to everything." Manon tugged at her collar. "But our guests were not in their rooms this morning. Their beds had not been touched. Rude, really, if you ask me. Are they sleeping in the woods like animals?"

No, thought Gemma. They just needed to be invited into the house; they didn't plan on sleeping there. In the film, their coffins had been placed in the cellar.

"Did Bernard say that they brought any trunks, luggage?"

"Nothing," said Manon. "It is all highly unusual."

"We should check the cellar."

"The cellar?" Manon gasped.

Gemma didn't answer her, but a quick search of the house found no traces of Roman, Avril, or their luggage, including coffins.

Bridgette, in a rush, had returned from the market with Bernard and placed her basket down, peering into the cellar. The maid was breathless. "They say that there is something wrong with the baker's daughter in the village. She has gone silent and just moves around the room in a state. They've called for the priests and have tied her down. Tied her down!"

"Quit gossiping," said Manon sharply.

Yet, Gemma knew the baker's daughter was only the beginning.

That evening, Gemma's carriage pulled up to a well-lit but modest stone home. Pascale's mother was known for her small but fine garden, and the grounds were indeed impeccable, topiaries in every shape and size in front of the entrance.

The maid took Gemma's gloves and wrap, almost unwinding her from the garment. When the maid spied Gemma's short-sleeved gown, she inhaled sharply.

Pascale and his mother were waiting for her in their small parlor. Only Pascale rose to greet her. With his long black waistcoat and white silk tie, he was overly dressed for a dinner with only three people. His mother, Genevieve, wore some type of lace veil over her face and remained perched on a chair. Gemma had heard she wore the veil because she detested the wrinkles on her face. Once, according to Bernard, she had been the most desirable woman in the valley. "But she married poorly," said Bernard with a grave nod. In the original script, Pascale's mother was conniving to get Gisele's money by securing a marriage for her son.

Pascale offered Gemma a seat next to him on the sofa. Was that his hand briefly on her leg? Gemma gave him a look of disgust, and he slid it back over to his own leg.

"Your gardens are beautiful," said Gemma to the birdlike woman.

"We are pleased with them," said the woman with an insincere smile. "You may call me Maman."

"Oh, I couldn't," said Gemma, thinking the last thing she would ever do was call this manipulative creature *Mother.* Given the woman's tenure in the valley, she might be able to provide more insight on her mysterious neighbor. "Have you seen the gardens of my neighbor, Monsieur Thibault?"

Pascale and his mother exchanged glances, like Gemma was the village idiot. "My dear, *no one* has seen them."

"Why?"

"He never comes out, and no one is invited in," said Pascale with a bored sigh as he flicked at some dirt on his shoe. "And why are you so fascinated with him? I heard you sent an invitation for him the other night." He rolled his eyes dramatically.

Both Pascale and his mother erupted in laughter.

"You aren't curious?" Gemma glanced over at him, awaiting a reply, but he sat there with a vacant look on his face. "His vines are beautiful, impeccable even, yet no one tends them."

"No one has ever met him," said Genevieve like the matter was settled.

"Surely someone has met him. You've lived here all your life." Gemma found this detail very curious. "No one has stepped foot on his property or attempted to visit him?"

"Good god, girl, no." Pascale's mother was lit up now. "It is forbidden. People have gone missing near the grounds. Gemma had heard the rumors of people going missing. "Forbidden by whom?"

"Monsieur Thibault, of course." Pascale was looking at her now like she was ill.

"So, he has told you himself that it is forbidden?" Gemma found their lack of curiosity infuriating until she realized they were simply minor characters, and since nothing about Monsieur Thibault had been written for them in their script, they had no curiosity about him.

"It has always been forbidden."

"And you never wonder?"

"Wonder?" Genevieve seemed at a loss for words. "About Monsieur Thibault? Why would we do such a thing?"

"Excuse us, Mother," said Pascale, reaching for Gemma's hand and leading her outside to the pathway beyond the parlor. "We need to discuss our future." Out of the earshot of his mother, Pascale spun her. "You must quit speaking like that in public. Saying crazy things.

There are all kinds of stories coming out about your state—they say you have the fever."

"Do I look like I have the fever?" Gemma took a step back from him, peeling her hand away.

His blond hair flopped over his eye, and he brushed it back, but he did not answer her.

"Mother will never agree to a wedding if they think you are touched with the fever."

"Oh, I doubt that," said Gemma under her breath. She found this comment insincere. Surely, a mad wife with a fortune would be exactly what this greedy family would want. "Who says I'm looking to be married?"

He put his hands on his hips like a catalog model. "Well, what would you suggest? That you become an old maid?"

A deep laugh escaped from her belly. "I'm only twenty-two."

"A marriageable age," said Pascale, his lips pursing with a pious certainty. "Need I remind you that from twenty-two, the slope becomes steep—and quick. Monsieur Batton agrees—"

"But I'm hardly spinster-worthy," said Gemma, cutting him off.

"What happened to the sleeves of your dress?" Pascale touched her bare shoulder, peeking out from her wrap. The dress had once had long bell sleeves.

She shrunk from his second attempt at touching her this evening. "Oh, I cut them off. I don't know how women stand to be so hot all the time. The corset went, too."

"Gisele!" Pascale grabbed her arm, yanking her back, but whispering so his mother could not hear. "What has gotten into you? You sound mad."

"Can I ask you something?" Gemma pulled free and rubbed her arm where he'd held her a little too tightly. "If I sound strange now, what was I like *before*? Tell me. What has made you so fond of me?"

"Well," said Pascale, stuttering and gazing up at the trees as though they held the answers. "You are kind."

"Kind?" She almost snorted with laughter.

"Why, yes. You loved animals... dogs... bunnies."

This man, this slug, had *no idea* who Gisele Dumas was. Well, there was no Gisele Dumas, really. She was a wooden character in a terrible horror film. Still, Pascale could've been a bit more inventive in his description. Had this man truly cared for Gisele, he would have been more observant. "You make me sound like a child, Pascale."

"You *are* sheltered," said Pascale. "Your father's death affected you very much. He protected you. I could quickly take his place as head of this château if only you'd come to your senses."

Gemma heard Pascale's mother squealing with delight over something.

"Oh, it is our guest," said Pascale, moving quickly back to the parlor.

Gemma trailed him and found Roman standing in the parlor.

"We simply must hear of your cousin's adventures in Italy," said Genevieve, preening over the vampire.

"I was looking for you earlier, cousin," said Gemma, folding her arms. The neck on her own gown was high, but Roman's eyes shot to the giant crucifix in the center of her chest. "Where is Avril?"

"She is dining elsewhere," said the vampire with a cock of his head.

As he peeled off his leather gloves and removed his cape, Roman shot her a look of desire. To her horror, she found it had an effect on her. Was he glamouring her? Vampires could do that. Blinking to close her eyes and break any spell, she opened them and noticed his large brown eyes. God, he was magnificent. Gemma found herself straightening her posture and tilting her head. *Snap out of it*, she thought. *This is what they do before they kill you.*

And then it hit her. Just like Pascale and his mother didn't stretch beyond their characters, her own character was written to fall for Roman. She was also playing to type. As the horror of this predisposition hit her, she immediately stiffened and looked away from him.

They took their seats, Pascale and his mother at each end of the long table, with Gemma and Roman opposite each other. Had Roman wished, he could have reached out and grabbed Gemma by the throat. The thought made Gemma finger her crucifix reassuringly, but another part of her found her heart quickened at the danger.

"I was thinking that a fall wedding would be festive," said Pascale's mother, sampling the asparagus soup. "Perhaps at Château Dumas?"

"I think that is a lovely idea," said Roman, raising his glass to Gemma.

She shot him a disgusted look.

"I should also say welcome to the family." Roman raised his glass again to Pascale and his mother.

Oddly, Pascale and his mother had begun eating. Well, *eating* wasn't the word for it. Both had their heads down and were slurping soup from their spoons.

"The soup is delightful," said Pascale.

Gemma looked around and thought it rude these two were eating when she and Roman had not yet been given bowls.

"Oh dear," said Pascale's mother. "Look at our manners. I couldn't see the table for the flowers."

Roman waved her off. "No worries, madame. I'm sure our soup will be here shortly. Please enjoy."

Slurping noises resumed as Pascale and his mother seemed to devour the soup with the eagerness of dogs. Gemma had to admit she was hungry.

"Oh," said Pascale's mother with a sigh. Gemma turned to watch the woman fall forward into her bowl.

"Mother," said Pascale, who raised his head with a look of concern before falling face down into his own bowl.

"Pascale," said Gemma, jumping up.

Roman watched him fall with a disinterested look. "Fools," said Roman.

He turned to her. "You may be seated."

"I will not," said Gemma.

"It is best if you are," he said. "And now, my dear, you and I can have a more enjoyable evening." Roman studied his hands and appeared concerned with something on his finger. God help her, Gemma could imagine those fingers sliding down her spine. Moving in her seat, she shook herself to push the thought away.

He put his finger to his lips, and Gemma realized, to her horror, that it was bloody.

Cold fingers touched her back, and Gemma jerked away to find the maid behind her. With a quickness Gemma hadn't expected, the woman had undone the clasp, and the crucifix fell to the floor, making a vibrating noise, like a coin does when it hits a hard surface.

Too late, Gemma reached for her throat as Roman moved with supernatural speed up over the table, clearing the giant floral arrangement that had blocked Genevieve's view.

"How?"

As Roman's firm hands—warmer than she'd expected—gripped her shoulders, she was oddly concerned with the details. What had gone wrong? This was a retake.

"I mesmerized the maid." His lips were on her neck. High at first, just under her jaw.

"She poisoned the soup." Gemma closed her eyes, filling in the details of his plot, magnificently orchestrated. He was a worthy adversary.

"Oui," he said. "They are both quite dead, which isn't much of a loss. They were horribly dull."

"It wasn't their fault," said Gemma. "They were written that way, just as you and I are." She felt a wave of pity for the two of them, both lying in their soup bowls.

If these were to be her last moments, then Gemma wanted to take in everything—the bright pinks and blues on the pair of paintings on the walls, a landscape that she swore could have been a Jean-Honoré Fragonard. Inhaling, she caught the lingering scent of lilies from the hallway. From a distance somewhere, the sound of the clock ticked. *Or was that her heartbeat?*

Could she die in this world? Was this it? Or would she wake up back in her old world?

Gemma felt herself sway as he pushed her head back. His touch was ecstasy, satisfying a hunger she never knew she had. His lips traveled down toward her collarbone, and she felt the tip of his tongue as he licked what she knew to be the vein he'd selected.

It couldn't end this way. She'd fought too hard for Gisele not to be a victim for it to end like this. "No," she screamed, springing back with a strength she didn't know she had. The force of it shocked Roman and threw him off guard, just for a moment. She stumbled but began to run. She took two steps before his hands grabbed her and twirled her around like they were doing an intricate tango. She spun right into his awaiting lips, and then she heard it.

The sound of her flesh ripping away as he devoured her.

"I'm dying," she said. Or so she thought because her damaged throat was beyond words. Yet, there was no pain, just the draining of her life like a candle finally extinguishing in the dark night.

15

Christopher Kent
August 10, 1998
Los Angeles, California

When he arrived at the Cross mansion in Los Angeles, Christopher was greeted with an array of blue balloon bouquets. The house had been transformed into a pastel landscape of blues and creams.

"There's a stork ice sculpture on its way," said Ivy, who was unwrapping cupcakes in every shade of blue. She held one up as if to demonstrate. "She particularly loves aqua blue with soft green. If she asks you to see the nursery . . . run. Trust me."

True to brand, Ivy was dressed from head to toe in black. If he'd been hoping that she would be in a better mood since her exile in Los Angeles after seeing the film, he was wrong.

He put his arms around her and felt her relax.

"You just want a cupcake," she said, teasing.

"Are you okay?" He nestled his nose near her neck, which smelled like gardenias.

"It's taken weeks to shake that feeling."

He did know the feeling she was describing. He'd just now felt like he'd broken free of the film's spell. "I met someone who has seen the film."

She turned to face him. It was a look that told him he'd said exactly the wrong thing. "I don't want to talk about that thing." She fed him a cupcake in pieces. "And Uncle Mickey is home and waiting to talk to you, so you're welcome." She checked her watch. "He'll see you at eleven. Take your camera. He said you can film him."

Suddenly aware of his hands on his thighs, he lifted them and started cracking his knuckles.

"This is exactly why I didn't tell you earlier." She leaned against the counter, stretching out her long, lean legs, which were punctuated by Alexander McQueen patent-leather combat boots. Unwrapping a cupcake from its wrapper, she began to munch on a blue teddy bear confection. "I knew you'd freak out."

"Look, he's Uncle Mickey to you. To me, he's a legend. And after what we just saw?"

Suddenly her eyes were wide with panic. "You can't tell him you saw the film, Christopher. Just don't tell anyone. Don't talk about that film. Do you hear me? I'm not even sure we should be discussing it with each other."

Recalling the look that Elizabeth Bourget had given him in the square, he thought Ivy might have a point.

At five minutes until eleven, Christopher, carrying his camera bag, walked past the three houses down North Palm Drive to Mick Fontaine's rather modest two-story brick house with an immaculate lawn and cherub garden ornaments.

The man himself answered the door wearing tennis whites, and Christopher suspected that servants were long gone. Mick hadn't had an A-list client for years.

"You must be the boyfriend?" He let the door start to close and was already through the foyer.

"I am the boyfriend," said Christopher with a small head bow before following Mick past the entrance with its dramatic curved staircase into the kitchen. Inside, the house was done in the Spanish style with terra-cotta tiles and worn carpets. There was a smell—an unpleasant combination of wood and stale dinners. The kitchen had knotty pine cabinets and old white appliances, giving the place a dated look, like he'd stopped fixing it around 1978. At the center of the kitchen island, a green drink was waiting in the blender. Once, this kitchen had been grand. Now the Formica countertop was stained.

"I'm eighty-two, you know, and I still play tennis once a week. You gotta stay in shape. Zander getting ready for the new addition?"

"The house is very blue."

"Yeah, I heard it's a boy. How is our girl feeling about having a little brother?"

Christopher shrugged. "It depends on the day."

"She had a rough time when her mom died. The scandal was hard on a kid, and Zander can be an ass," said Mick. "I know Ivy hates Vera, but she has a positive influence on him."

As Mick poured the drink into an oversize glass, he lifted it in a dramatic salute. "I've always said that Ivy missed her calling. That girl was better off in front of the camera than behind it." He pointed to his own face. "I have an eye for talent, you know."

"Well, she was the top student in our film class."

Mick frowned and spat out pulp into a nearby napkin. "Film school. In my day you didn't need school. You learned it like a craft. Did Howard Hughes or Orson Welles study film?" His voice rose to a surprising boom. "She could have stayed *here* and learned everything she needed to know from her dad." He held up an empty glass. "Kale juice?"

"No, thanks." The juice looked like cleaner. Christopher was bursting with questions. This man *had known* Gemma Turner. He imagined a scenario where Mick confided his theories about her disappearance. Perhaps he even had a theory on how Gemma was connected to his mother.

Pleased with his drink, Mick led them through a set of French doors out to a patio with cracked concrete and a covered pool. "Ivy said you want to know about Gemma?"

"I do," said Christopher. "She's been a near obsession for me for a long time. I've decided to do a senior documentary on her, so this isn't anything that will run on television. I just did a short film on Rick Nash."

"Another one gone too soon," said Mick. "You know he took the famous picture of Gemma at the Savoy."

Christopher's heart skipped a beat. "I do know."

As a warm breeze hit him, Christopher was suddenly a bundle of nerves. Sliding a little too heavily into the wicker chair, he felt it give and fumbled over his notes, unable to find his list of questions. Panic hit him. Where were his notes? This was his only chance to get answers from the one person who knew Gemma well, and he'd left his notes somewhere. Stalling, he smiled sheepishly while he searched through his notebook.

To his relief, two of the notebook pages were stuck together. It was a silly moment of panic, and he forced himself to take a deep breath. His subject was so familiar that he didn't need a list of questions to know what he needed to ask Mick Fontaine—once he calmed down.

In one big gulp, Mick drank half of the green drink and held up his finger for Christopher. Age and sun had not been kind to a man who seemed to once have had a ruddy complexion and red hair. Pushing himself up from the chair, his knees creaked as he pivoted and turned toward the door and into the house, returning with a worn photo album. Christopher saw personal photos of Gemma Turner that he had never seen before as Mick turned the pages: stills of her on the beach, many of her looking bored. "I spied her at the Santa Anita racetrack in sixty-three in the stands. I mean, she really stood out." Mick waved his hands. "Long, straight hair...the color of an apricot...Kewpie doll eyes. Well, I was always on the lookout for talent, and I knew this doll would look fabulous on camera. I slipped her my business card. Told her that I could find her work at a studio. A week later, she called me. Her mom, a real French beauty, drove her to the office to meet me. I had her cast in three films the following year."

Christopher was rapt and put his pen down. He'd waited years to hear these kinds of stories. "What was she like?"

"Stubborn," said Mick with a snort, traces of his thick New York accent still lingering. "Too smart for her own good. Certainly, too smart for Hollywood. She'd gone to UCLA for a year, but the schedule was too much for her while she was filming. I think she thought she could leverage her job as an actress to get something more."

"Like a director?"

"A writer. She wanted to write, but she was forced to act. That's how she saw it. You know she toted a typewriter around with her everywhere? She caught a lot of grief for it."

Something about this memory was clearly painful, and the man wiped at the far corner of his eye. None of the articles, the stacks of *Life* magazines, had given Christopher any sense to the real person behind the face that haunted him for so many years. The visual of Gemma Turner carrying a typewriter was not one he'd anticipated.

"She was a smart-ass," said Mick, pointing to a photo of her on a surfboard. "Never, ever backed down from a challenge. Women in Hollywood weren't like her back then; she was a trailblazer."

Christopher pointed to his camera bag. "Do you care if I film you?"

"Not at all," said Mick, motioning toward the living room—a

Spanish-style room with beams and stucco and an elaborate fireplace. "Better light in there." Mick excused himself, and Christopher began to set up in the living room. Returning a few minutes later, the agent had changed into a royal-blue button-down and had slicked back his gray hair. "I only have about thirty minutes for this, but let me show you some other things." He pulled out a box with a collection of videotapes: Gemma's interviews on *The Mike Douglas Show* and *The Merv Griffin Show*. "You can take these for your film."

Christopher balked. "You don't want them?"

Mick Fontaine smiled wistfully. "I think it's time to pass them on to someone else."

Knowing he only had a half an hour, Christopher set up the camera in a hurry. There were four pages of questions, and he was only going to be able to get through less than a page. Focusing the video camera on Mick's face, he could tell the man had applied foundation to even out his skin tone, causing the man to look a little too cakey.

"Why Gemma?" asked Mick. "Aren't you a little young?"

This was the moment that Christopher had been hoping for, and he gazed up from the camera viewfinder. "I think my mother, Pamela Kent, might have known Gemma." He watched the agent's face, looking for any sense of recognition, but the man sighed like he was a little bored.

"Pamela Kent?" Christopher pressed.

"Never heard of her," said Mick with an uninterested shrug, "but then I didn't know everyone Gemma knew."

Christopher felt a sharp pang of disappointment. He'd hoped that Mick Fontaine could connect his mother to Gemma Turner. Until this moment, he hadn't realized how much he'd wanted some clue from this man who seemed to know everyone. His hands heavy, Christopher tested the light, trying to keep himself moving. Christopher asked about the beach films, why she'd quit, and then they moved into different territory. While everything to this point had been like a pleasant memory, the man sighed wearily at what was coming next.

"And the last film. You want to know about the last film, don't you? Everyone wants to know about that one, *The Strange Moon*."

From somewhere, a cuckoo clock began to chime, causing Christopher to look around for the source of the noise. "I can stop the film for a minute."

Mick waved him off. "No. It's just hard. Even after all these years, it gets harder, not easier, to talk about her." Christopher understood the misconception all too well—that grief faded with time. Mick rubbed his eyes and asked for a glass of water.

Christopher went to the kitchen and rummaged around through the cupboard until he found the glassware. He put the glass on the stand next to Mick's chair, but the agent never touched it.

Not missing a beat, Mick continued. "Over the years, I think critics have seen those last two films in a new light, and her legacy is as an actress who challenged herself, but in 1968, she had no other options. No one—and I mean *no one*—was calling to hire her, except for one person: Thierry Valdon. Mind you, I had no idea who in the hell Thierry Valdon was, but *she* did. Valdon just zeroed in on her. I didn't really think that anything would come from the meeting between them. I mean, he could have had a Deneuve or Bardot for the role, but he chose an American. Jesus, can you imagine how that went over? It was a French New Wave film. I had hoped that filming in nowhere France would let things cool down between her and Charlie Hicks. He'd caused problems on her last two sets, showing up and being a nuisance."

Recalling the surf festival the spring before he turned fifteen and the way the place went silent when her name was mentioned, Christopher knew what he had to ask to get to the thesis of his film. "Why does no one speak of her? Why has she just disappeared?"

Mick flexed his jaw but didn't speak, and rubbed his eyes again. "She wanted to leave *The Strange Moon*. Didn't have a good feeling about it right from the beginning. I might have pressed her too hard to stay—told her that there was nothing back here for her to return to." Mick Fontaine hung his head and took two deep breaths before facing the camera again. "When she went missing, none of us knew what to do. I was at the house, packing up to leave the next morning. Thierry and Manon Valdon were frantic. Everyone driving up and down the back roads, people combing the fields looking for..." He snorted. "A body, I guess. But they found nothing. She just vanished into the night. After that, she became a cautionary tale for actresses who got too demanding, wanted too much from the studios, or didn't know their place. I'm ashamed of my part in her story. I didn't listen to her. No one talks about Gemma Turner because we all failed Gemma Turner, and we're afraid to look at ourselves."

Christopher felt time stop, and he met Mick's eyes, seeing the pain and regret the man lived with. He felt closer to Gemma Turner and her story, as though he'd known her himself. "You say she disappeared on camera." Christopher leaned forward on her chair. "I know they say that, but it's impossible."

"Have you seen the footage? Go see Claude Moravin, the videographer. Nice man. She's in the frame one minute and not in the next. They've ripped apart that film. Experts have weighed in. It wasn't tampered with. She just vanishes in front of your eyes."

"They arrested someone?"

Mick made a face. "It was all for show. The French police had a public relations nightmare on their hands."

"What do *you* think happened to her?"

Mick stared at something on the wall for a long time; his Adam's apple moved up and down like he was struggling to get out the words from this throat. "I think something awful happened to her. There are all those rumors of that underground version of the film."

While Christopher wanted to confess what he knew about the film, he heeded Ivy's warning. Because quite suddenly, just like Elizabeth Bourget had done, Mick began to look increasingly uncomfortable, pulling on his microphone like he didn't want it on his collar anymore. "I've got to go. I'm sorry."

The agent looked at the camera light, and instinctively Christopher knew that if he wanted an answer to this question, the camera needed to be turned off. He went to cut the power off, but Mick waved him off.

"It's time that I speak. I owe her that much."

The agent leveled his eyes at Christopher. "About ten years after Gemma disappeared, someone came to me...told me about this film they'd seen with her. I thought they were crazy. What they described to me just wasn't possible. I was on that set with her, and I know what scenes she filmed before she vanished." He looked up at the ceiling. "Then her parents heard that she was appearing in new scenes in this film. They called the Amboise police. They got their hopes up....It was cruel. Well, I tried to find out; I starting asking around about this film. I heard about a man rumored to have the film."

"Anthony A?"

"Yeah," said Mick, surprised to hear the name.

"Did you find him?"

Mick rubbed his face. There was something weighing on him. "No. I never found him. He didn't want to be found. You have to understand the hole she left when she disappeared." He looked around his own living room like he was seeing it for the first time. "I was never the same after she vanished. Everyone who touched that film regretted it. I loved film . . . once." He let his voice fall.

"Until *L'Étrange Lune*." It was a statement.

He nodded. "I must have asked too many questions. I made a lot of phone calls about this 'bootleg' version. One day, I get this letter with a book. Inside was the obituary of the man who'd told me about the film. A message."

"Do you still have it?"

Mick went into a drawer and got a dog-eared paperback of *The Damsel and the Demon*, and inside was an obituary for a man named John Weatherly. "This book was Gemma's. She'd written a damned screenplay about the thing." Mick flipped it open. "Those are her notes. John Weatherly had been a very famous film critic. He was killed in a small plane crash."

"I've heard of him." Taking the book, Christopher saw her handwriting for the first time. The ink had faded a bit and the pages yellowed, but the feminine loops of her cursive were flowery.

"You think this is a message?"

"Damned right. It's probably dangerous talking to you, but I can't help it." Mick Fontaine leaned in close, so close that Christopher could smell his toothpaste. "I think the question you should be asking is: How are people seeing fresh scenes in *The Strange Moon* when its star vanished long ago?"

What Mick didn't know was the haunting pall that hung over every one of her scenes. Christopher decided to spare him that detail. The man looked like he'd had enough nightmares.

16

Gemma Turner
"1878"
Amboise, France

Like a drowning victim, Gemma searched for air. When her lungs finally, blessedly were infused with breath, she sat up in bed, gasping.

Clutching her throat, eyes wide, she searched the room. The wooden cross was still in front of the window. The scene looked the same as yesterday. Yet, everything had changed.

Roman had killed her. Yet, she was still here.

How was that possible?

She was both overjoyed to be alive and disappointed to be back in this room. Had she thought dying would free her?

Outside her door, Gemma heard creaking as something moved across the floorboard outside of her door. Sometimes a clawing sound commenced, deep in the wood, only for her to find that in the morning, the door was untouched. Convinced that someone was on the other side—Roman, Avril, Monsieur Batton—she quietly slid out of bed and put her ear to the door.

It was a sound, not unlike the wind, but familiar. "You."

Jumping away from the door, she heard the keys on the typewriter begin to clatter.

Mademoiselle Turner:

Well, that scene was certainly exciting! Bravo! Of course, we can't have our heroine dying, so we'll need to do it again, but I think you're getting the hang of it. Squeeze every bit of drama out of your performance. That's what your audience wants!

The sound at the door ceased, likely chased away by the sound of the typewriter keys.

Leaning over the desk, she typed:

Fuck you.

Immediately, the typewriter responded:

Tsk, tsk. We can all benefit from constructive criticism. Unfortunately, your previous performance was flat. Try again. You keep thinking you know the outcome of the story, so you aren't giving your portrayal of Gisele your "all." That is hubris, and we can't have it. Remember: Flat performances cause repeat performances.

—A

"I'll show you a flat performance." She sniffed. Until dawn she paced, finally deciding how to play the scene today.

She dressed as a soldier would, her clothes leaden with a weary sense of upcoming battle. Gazing at herself in the mirror, the woman that stared back at her had hollow eyes, as though she'd been sickly for months. Finally, with a heaviness in her bones, she descended the stairs slowly.

"There you are," said a voice. Manon carried an envelope in her hand. "This just came for you."

Gemma paused, studying the maid's face, looking for any signs of déjà vu from the woman. Taking the envelope, Gemma tried to prompt her. Did anyone else realize they were doing scenes again and again? "What did you do last night?"

"I read the Bible," said Manon. "Said my devotions. Locked my windows, as requested by you."

"Good," said Gemma. "Do it again tonight." She slid the letter off the tray and studied the familiar handwriting. Before she opened it, Gemma held it to her head like a stage medium and closed her eyes for dramatic effect, "Let me guess, this is Pascale asking me to dinner."

"You have not been over to his house since your father died. It is good to see you back in the social season, mademoiselle. What dress can I have Bridgette prepare for you?" Manon headed toward the kitchen.

"One with a high neck," said Gemma.

"Very well," said the maid, puzzled.

Scanning the letter, Gemma saw that it was the same as yesterday.

Gisele,

Mother and I would love to have you as our guest for dinner tonight. We have much to discuss.

Pascale

While yesterday's scenes were lacking, she'd learned one valuable thing about the rules of this strange place. *We can't have our heroine dying.* Maybe not dying, but Gemma's throat was still sore. If she had any ideas that being bit by a vampire would be like in a Hammer film, with two tiny fang marks, she was wrong. Touching her skin, which was again intact, she could still hear her flesh tearing as Roman's teeth ripped into her neck. He'd do the same thing tonight if she let him. Closing her eyes, she sighed and gripped the side of the foyer table to steady herself. Even though she was alive today, her body knew it had been wrecked and put back together again with some magic. She wasn't ready to face Roman again.

Gemma screamed in frustration, ripping up the letter and letting the pieces fall to the floor.

"Fuck, fuck, fuck." Gemma got to her knees and began shredding the small pieces of paper into even smaller pieces, as if reducing the paper to confetti would somehow make this all go away. "I cannot do this again. I cannot."

A pair of ankle boots appeared in front of her. Looking up, she saw that Manon had returned from the kitchen and just witnessed her outburst. "I'm not sure I'm ready for social activities so soon after Father's passing," she said.

"It appears not." Manon held out her hand to help up Gemma from the floor and bent over to pick up the little pieces that had found their way across the room. When Gemma had regained her composure, Manon continued as though she hadn't seen anything. Whether she would report this incident to Monsieur Batton, Gemma could not be certain, but the maid seemed to not be dwelling on Gemma's behavior this morning.

"We must discuss the houseguests, mademoiselle. The entire house staff are now wearing crucifixes, and I have instructed the cook to add garlic to everything—the rillons included." The maid tugged at her collar. "Curiously, our guests were not in their rooms this morning. Their beds had never been touched. Rude, really, if you ask me."

So that's what had caught Manon's ire this morning: the houseguests. "Of course they're not in their beds," snapped Gemma. "They're out spreading destruction in the village."

"So you keep saying." Manon's lips tightened to a thin line, as it often did when she disagreed.

"Have you checked the cellar?"

"The cellar?" Manon gasped.

"Let's check every area of the house again and start with the cellar."

Manon led the way through the kitchen and into the mudroom, knowing the rooms would be empty. As the housekeeper walked, she sorted through a heavy set of keys before finding the one she wanted.

As if on cue, Bridgette swooped in from the market with Bernard, placing her basket down at the door and peering down into the cellar. "They say that there is something wrong with the baker's daughter in the village." Her voice was breathless, like she'd run all the way from the stables just to tell them the news. "She has gone silent and just moves around the room in a state. They've called for the priests and have tied her down." Bridgette's eyes were wide. "Tied her down!"

"Quit gossiping," said Manon sharply as she descended the stairs.

Gemma smiled. It was the same response that Manon had exclaimed yesterday.

She wondered what would happen if she stayed in bed all night, sending regrets to Pascale and his mother. "I'll just have to do it again tomorrow," she surmised.

As Gemma headed out for dinner, she felt like she was headed toward her own funeral. Once again, as she and Bernard took off in the carriage, she found her heart was racing. She felt along her leg, reassured when she found the small wooden post she'd sharpened and tied to her shin in case she needed to use it.

As it had done the previous night, Gemma's carriage pulled up to the well-lit, modest stone home. She steeled herself to go in. "I don't want to go in, Bernard," she said.

"That's pretty obvious, mademoiselle." He took his cap off and scratched his head. "We can go somewhere else."

"Paris," Gemma whispered.

"That's a bad idea," said Bernard. "The road to Paris has been closed for a few weeks."

"I was just wishing aloud." Taking a deep breath, she tried to gather strength, postponing the inevitable. She had to walk in that house. The star couldn't die, but each scene took something out of her. Refocusing on the house in front of her, she recalled what Bernard had told her before. "You said Pascale's mother came from money?"

Bernard looked at her curiously. "I told you that?"

"Yesterday," said Gemma before she remembered Bernard had no memory of their conversation yesterday. "Sorry, I must have overheard it somewhere," she said, tutting him.

"Oui," said Bernard with a grin. "Once she was the belle of the land."

"And now?"

He hesitated. "She's a bit of a climber. Wants to improve her station again. Being the mother-in-law of the mistress of Château Dumas would suit her aims."

"Thank you, Bernard." Before departing for the house, she turned back. "You take care of yourself while I'm in there. If you hear anything, take off and come back for me later."

"Mademoiselle?" He gave her a curious look.

"If you see Roman or Avril, you need to take the carriage back to the house."

"Manon tells me they're dangerous. I won't be leaving you here, mademoiselle."

She gave him a weary smile as she started up the lawn toward the house. Knowing her mark, Gemma waited for the stoic maid to open the door.

"Bonjour," said Gemma, breezing into the foyer, peeling off her gloves and wrap to give to the meek woman who greeted her. This poor creature with her head bowed like a toy soldier was a reminder to Gemma that, in the days since she'd arrived, she'd seen a change in her own staff. While at first, they had interacted like wooden, stock characters, "Maid #1" or "Head Butler," they were now Manon, Bridgette, and Bernard to her. Even when she told Bernard to leave her behind tonight if the cousins arrived, he'd refused.

Peering into the parlor, she did not find Pascale or his mother seated as they had been yesterday. She dreaded the small talk she would have to engage in with them. As she entered, she looked around for someone to help her but saw that the family did not have the means that the Dumas family had, so the staff was lacking. Gemma turned to the right and stopped in her tracks.

Seated at the head of the dinner table was Roman.

She wasn't prepared to battle him this soon. Pascale was on his left, his head down, staring intently at his empty dinner plate. Opposite him was his mother, also looking blankly at her own plate. Blood from a bite mark on her neck oozed down over her strand of pearls. In a panic, Gemma turned to run back out of the room, but the maid blocked her way.

Pascale's mother began to spoon the soup into her mouth while staring off into space.

While she couldn't die, could Gemma, the heroine of the film, be turned into *this*? The idea sickened her.

"I was trying to get your attention," said Roman. "This worked nicely, don't you think?"

"Did you poison the soup this time?"

He gave her a confused glance. Like yesterday, those brown eyes seemed to soften her resolve, and she felt her legs wobble a bit. Then the stake tied to her upper thigh dug into her skin, waking her up from his charms.

Scanning the room, Gemma tried to think how she would flee. The maid, obviously under his spell, would attempt to stop her, and Roman would be able to reach her from across the room instantly. And then...The thought of what came next sickened her. How did this happen? It was nothing like the scene yesterday. She had to know if Roman was like her. He'd seemed confused by her soup remark, but she wanted to be sure. "I thought you would have had your fill of me from last night's dinner."

He gave a throaty, deep laugh. "While I would have loved to have entertained you, we were sent straight to our rooms by you." He gave her a puzzled look. "But you need not worry. I am not here to drain you. I'm quite full already."

He picked at his teeth, a move that made Gemma want to retch.

Thierry Valdon's idea of a vampire was someone who drained the life force from their victims through their blood, essentially making them zombies. Pascale and his mother looked as if they'd been placed in their chairs like dolls. A fly circled Pascale's forelock, and he made no attempt to swat it. Knowing her eyes were wide with horror, she tried to think clearly. She needed to keep her head—literally—this creature had nearly ripped it off yesterday.

"What do you want from me?" She felt herself suddenly unable to catch her breath.

"An excellent question," said Roman, motioning to the empty chair opposite him. "Sit."

Hesitating, she shot a look at the maid, who was now hovering over the doorway, her blank stare fixed on Gemma. There was a cloudiness to her eyes, like that which happens in death. Lowering herself in her seat, she turned her chair so that the maid was not behind her. This time, she'd worn two crucifixes—one hidden inside her dress and the other visible.

"Very wise. Under my influence, she can snap your neck," he said with a nod toward the maid. Gemma noticed drool coming from the poor woman's mouth.

Placing her hand over her crucifix, she could feel her heart pounding.

"Look at me." It was a command, and to her horror everyone's heads—Pascale's, Genevieve's, and the maid's—all turned to face him like synchronized swimmers.

Gemma's eyes slowly rose to meet his, afraid that he would attempt to mesmerize her. There was something about the way he had his arm around the chair that told her he was irritated. Something about this scene wasn't to his liking, yet he'd set it up with careful planning. His eyes were striking—large, round brown eyes with heavy lids, like a sleepy child's. Only then did she notice something—he wasn't breathing, no rhythmic rise or fall of his clothes.

"Oh God," she said, surprised to say it aloud.

"Your choice of jewelry is most unfortunate," said Roman, nearly turning his head away in distaste from the crucifix. Contrary to the long traveling coat he wore yesterday, today's Roman was dressed in a black shirt with a ruffled collar and waistcoat. He nonchalantly took a sip from his cup. "This one here," he said with a nod to Pascale as he began swirling the liquid from his cup around in his mouth like a sommelier. "There is no passion." Then he picked up a second cup and took a generous, satisfying sip. "But her." He pointed to Pascale's mother. "Such a love of life... music, food... flowers." He smacked his lips and ran his finger across the rim of the glass, which glistened with a garnet-colored droplet. "It flows through her blood." He closed his eyes, savoring the taste.

Gemma felt the bile rise in the back of her throat. "What do you want?"

Roman shrugged rather simply. "You."

Gemma's eyes darted toward the maid. "You've made it clear that if I attempt to run that you will have her snap my neck."

"But what fun would that be for you or for me?" asked the vampire. "You mistake my intentions. I do not wish to drain your essence as I have done theirs." Smoothing his hair, he placed his elbows on the table and leaned closer to her, like he was doing a business deal. "No, I want you to be my companion."

Of anything he could have said, this was not the response Gemma had expected, and as a result, she stammered. "But... you already have one of those?"

Roman scowled. "Regrettably, Avril was an impulsive decision of mine in Paris," he said, his Italian accent thick. "As I'm sure you've guessed, we're not twins."

"You're not my cousins?" Her tone was sarcastic.

"We are not. Avril is dull, nothing like you. You have energy, imagination, anger... wit and intelligence."

Roman continued. "I could drink your essence, yes, and I would absorb it, but it wears off so quickly. The essence of you would be fleeting—and I would regret that even more."

"You could rip my throat out," she said, recalling what he'd done yesterday and wondering what had driven him to such violence. Pascale and Genevieve had the stereotypical neat puncture wounds in their necks, and the blood drop from Pascale's mother was nearing the bustline of her dress.

Something about her comment stirred him and unsettled him. "That rarely happens; only when I lose control." He put a finger up. "Which is not something that I do often."

"I see," said Gemma, wondering what made him lose control yesterday.

"When I was as you were, I had a cat, a beautiful thing; she paraded through the house as though it were hers, but if you tried to touch her, she would scratch your eyes out."

"Smart cat," said Gemma.

"Not really." Roman toyed with a signet ring on his finger. "Interesting cat... beautiful cat, but not a smart one."

"What happened to her?"

"I strangled her, but I regretted it. I've tried to not lose myself like that again." He took another sip from the glass and held up a finger to make a point. "I regret it still. She was my greatest companion." He scratched at the table, contemplating something. The stillness of his body without breath made him appear waxen. "Avril is not a great companion. We will go our own ways after we leave here."

"You want to make me like *you*?" Her face registered disgust, then fear. She swallowed hard and felt her own breath leave her.

"Do you wish to insult me?" He laughed, his smile wide and teeth like ivory. She could see the elongated incisors, like a tiger's. "It is not so bad. I was once like you, but now I—"

"Steal the lives of others, yes," said Gemma sharply. "I don't see the appeal. Bad vibes."

"Bad vibes?" He scrunched his face, not understanding. "What are 'vibes'?"

"The essence you give off." Out of the corner of her eye, Gemma saw the maid wobbling like she might topple. Pascale and Genevieve also swayed, like Roman's grip on them had let go only for a moment.

Gemma wondered, if she bolted, if she could make it past the maid. The doorknob would have to turn smoothly, but then there was the front lawn. She would never make it to the carriage without Roman reaching her first.

"Would you rather have spent your short life with this dull creature?"

Roman stood up and moved behind Pascale, where he lifted his head by the top of his hair. Pascale's face was flaccid and his expression blank, not much different from his typical one, but she still didn't like the way Roman was handling his head.

"I would never have married him," said Gemma with a look of disdain.

Roman was making his way toward her slowly. In two small movements, he would be upon her. Curiously, she could smell something like juniper on him. Once, she had smelled the same scent on Thierry Valdon. It had the odd effect of making her nostalgic for her old world. She shook herself. Not now. This was deadly serious.

Like a snake, Roman slithered closer. Then his hand slid across the back of her chair. Quickly, his mouth was next to her ear—so close to her neck.

"You could take off the necklace," said Roman softly, his smell up close intoxicating. She could feel them fitting together in an embrace, like a missing puzzle piece. His nose nuzzled her hair. "Mademoiselle Dumas, you are a magnificent creature. Your hair…I've never seen anything—or smelled anything—like it."

Gemma leaned closer. It felt like no one had touched her for ages. As Roman ran his hand down her bare forearm, she was repulsed by him. But a part of her hungered for him. *This was wrong.* Shaking her head, she tried to snap out of it, but she felt she was in a trance. He was mesmerizing her, his voice lulling her into submission. His voice was beautiful, and it echoed through every vessel and pore in her body. Clutching her crucifix, she squeezed it and felt a stab of reality. She needed to get away—fast.

His hands were on her hair, careful to not touch the necklace, but she felt his fingers on the back of her neck. She expected a quick jolt if he was going to snap her neck, but instead he—his touch surprisingly warm—stroked the spot on her upper back where the dress stopped.

"Take the necklace off." His lips and breath were in her hair. She felt herself move with him, realizing how easy it could be to do what he said. Clutching the crucifix until she felt it cut into her hand, she leapt from the seat, using the chair as a barrier between them.

"No," she said with a desperate croak.

She'd surprised him. She could see it in the narrowing of his eyes. Pascale, his mother, and the maid raised their heads and turned them in her direction like zombies waiting to do Roman's bidding.

Roman's head cocked and he smiled. "As you wish . . . for now."

Moving away, he gave Gemma ample room to leave. He nodded, encouraging her to go. The maid had also ambled into the foyer, giving Gemma a clear path to leave the house. Yet, it felt like a trick. All the talk of cats had Gemma wondering if he was toying with her. Letting her go only to pull her back and finish her off. Pushing the chair in Roman's direction for an extra barrier, Gemma raced out of the dining room into the foyer.

"Mademoiselle Dumas?" Roman called out to her.

She paused, her hands feeling the doorknob give and open.

"Tonight, as you sleep, you will think of me. Soon, you will think of nothing else but being with me—being possessed by me . . . of becoming a sole creature with me. I will make you hunger for me. I will make you beg for me."

Glancing back at him, she felt a tug, pulling her toward him. A bead of sweat rolled down her cheek. Their eyes met, and she had a moment of déjà vu of Thierry Valdon telling her that they had been destined to be together. Like she had done that day in the wine cave when he had kissed her, Gemma ran.

Gemma ran until her legs gave out in the yard. Then she crawled to the carriage, ripping and staining her dress until she could see the outline of Bernard slumped against the carriage door. At first, she thought the worst, but she threw herself on him and shook him awake.

"What in Mary's name has happened to you?"

"We need to leave," she said, jumping up to the front of the carriage. "Now, Bernard!"

"What?" The older man paused.

"Go, go," said Gemma, jumping up onto the carriage where the driver sat.

Bernard took the seat next to her, taking the team of horses at a quick clip back to Château Dumas.

The next morning, she awoke to the sound of Bridgette screaming.

17

Christopher Kent
August 12, 1998
Los Angeles, California

It was that time of morning on North Palm Drive when the sprinklers were waking, pumping, and spraying water across the carefully manicured rosebushes and lemon trees. The jarring sound of sirens caught the attention of everyone—the rich and famous coaxed out of their mansions to see where the ambulance had stopped. Vera Cross, heavily pregnant, with bathrobe barely covering her bump, stepped out onto the lawn, rubbing her lower back.

"Zander, Ivy," she screamed. "It's Mickey. Come quick."

The blue lights flashed several houses down from the Cross mansion, causing Christopher, who had just stepped out into the lawn, to feel a lump in his throat.

Ivy was ahead of him, moving down the street in her short bathrobe, Christopher following close behind in his bare feet over the wet grass.

The paramedics stopped them at the door, but Ivy, used to getting her way, insisted on talking to someone. "We're his neighbors."

"Does he have family?"

Ivy shook her head. "We're like family. In LA, that means family."

The paramedic was in no mood. "Does he have any *actual* family?"

"None that I know of," said Ivy, pulling her robe tightly around her as the morning chill finally hit her.

Just then, an older woman emerged from the door, clutching a tissue or paper towel in a tight wad. Her purse dangled over her other arm.

"Inez," called Ivy. The woman's face lit up at the sight of her. "What happened?"

"Oh, Miss Ivy. He's gone," said Inez, shaking her head gravely. "I came in to clean this morning and found him on the floor in front of that blender. Kale juice everywhere." The green all over Inez's arms, and her purse demonstrated the extent of the kale juice's travels. "He was cold, so cold." The woman scowled and motioned back to the house. "They're doing all sorts of things in there, but he's gone." She looked up at the sky and made the sign of the cross.

Ivy put her hand to her mouth. "Uncle Mickey. This is awful."

Mick had made an appearance at the baby shower, bringing an expensive gift of a Bugaboo pram with a sun canopy filled with blue toys. "I'm Uncle Mickey," he said, wheeling the pram dramatically around the cupcake station.

"I was the last person to talk to him," said Christopher quietly, his jaw slack. "I mean, really talk to him." Mick Fontaine had given him the tapes of Gemma as well as the photo album as though *he knew* something bad was going to happen.

"True," said Ivy. "There was no intelligent conversation at Vera's soiree."

"Had he been sick?" Christopher posed the question to Inez.

"Well, he'd been told to stop playing tennis." Ivy seemed to bristle that he hadn't asked her. "He was like a hundred."

Just then, the door opened, and the paramedics wheeled out a body covered with a thin sheet. A chorus of murmurs and gasps could be heard from the nearby lawns.

Ivy came close and whispered in Christopher's ear. "Did he say anything to you?"

"Just that you didn't need film school and would be better off in front of the camera, not behind it."

She laughed at that, but then tears welled up in her eyes and she poked at the corner of her eye with her fingernail. "He taught me to swim in his pool. Dad was too busy after Mom's death.... Well, let's be honest...Dad thought I wasn't his daughter. Mickey heard I was going to camp and hadn't learned."

"Ivy," said Christopher warily. He focused on the swaying palm trees above him, not meeting her eyes. "Don't you think it's a coincidence that yesterday I filmed him talking about Gemma Turner and then today he...died?"

She rolled her eyes. "The world doesn't revolve around your little Gemma Turner mystery, sorry to say. He was an eighty-two-year-old man with a heart condition who played tennis like he was twenty. Geez." Pushing past him, she headed back toward her house.

As they loaded the body onto the ambulance, the sound of a rapid camera snap caught Christopher's attention and he saw that two freelance photographers were in cars, obviously tipped off.

Ivy was wrong. The look of fear on Mick's face had been real. Had Mick Fontaine died because he talked about Gemma? No. Mick had talked about Gemma for years. Mick Fontaine died because he talked about *that film*.

As the ambulance pulled away, he had the sinking feeling that he'd just uncovered the first layer of the mystery. But answers would come at a cost.

18

Gemma Turner
"1878"
Amboise, France

Bridgette stood over the stable boy, a son of one of Bernard's relatives. The boy—only a child—had failed to show in the morning to muck out the stalls and brush the horses. Bridgette had found him in the cellar, where she'd been looking for spare water jugs.

"What does this mean?" Bridgette handed Gemma a note that had been pinned to the boy's shirt. " 'Est-ce que je vous manque?' "

"It is for me," said Gemma, touching the boy's shirt collar and finding the familiar two bite marks with blood trails beneath his collar. " 'Am I missing him?' "

"Missing who?" Bridgette scratched her head. "Who would write such a thing? Who would *do* such a thing?"

"Roman." Something in her stirred about this detail and made her feel responsible for this boy's condition. She needed to drive these creatures out of her house. Roman had done this under her roof to get her attention. What *had* Roman done to her last night? Left his mark on her? Mesmerized her? All she knew was that she felt like had she stayed another moment in his company, she would have fallen under his spell forever. And she wasn't sure she'd come back. Whoever was "directing" this strange world didn't want her dead, but that didn't mean she couldn't be turned into Roman's companion. She felt certain she'd rather be dead than be his companion.

Like Pascale and his mother, the boy now stared blankly, and a blue tinge had begun to form on the skin at the corners of his mouth and his eyes were clouded, like he was beginning to rot, yet he was not dead. When Bernard placed him on a soft chair, the boy attempted to stand, trying to go about his work, gray veins mottling his skin and a sickly sweet stench surrounding him. The boy's appearance was faithful to Thierry Valdon's description of his vampires. Gemma recalled the extras on the set who were fresh out of the makeup chair looking exactly as this boy did. When the sun from the kitchen touched his skin, it smoked softly like it was cooking, yet the boy kept moving even as his flesh burned.

"He needs to be out of the light," said Gemma, leading him into the dining room and pulling the drapes.

"What has happened to him?" asked Bernard, fury in his voice. "I saw the look on your face last night when you came bolting out of that house. This is what you saw at Pascale's?"

"It's what he did to Pascale and his mother," said Gemma, meeting Bernard's eyes. "This boy is now a vampire, or becoming one in any case. His essence is drained. They do it by drinking the blood."

"I thought you were talking crazy last night," said Bernard, a softness forming in his eyes. He believed her. "But you were right."

"It's the work of a vampire," said Gemma, turning the boy's neck to show the two puncture wounds, "A walking-dead creature that feeds on the blood or—in this case—the essence of a living thing."

"This vampire... is it an animal?" He took his cap off and scratched his head.

"No," said Gemma. "It—they—look human."

"Is there anything we can do?"

"Well, that depends," said Gemma. "Has anyone seen Avril or Roman this morning?"

"No, mademoiselle. I don't believe they've ever been in their rooms," said Bridgette, a worried edge forming in her voice. "You don't suspect them, mademoiselle?"

Bernard read Gemma's face perfectly. Their eyes met and Gemma knew, for the first time since she'd arrived in this strange world, she finally had an ally.

"You don't have any wooden fence posts, do you? The only way to save this boy—and Pascale and his mother—is to stake Avril and Roman through the hearts." Given that they didn't breathe, she was hoping this worked, but it was the only shot they had. What Gemma did not say was that to save herself she desperately needed to kill Roman, or risk being turned into his concubine for eternity.

"Stake them? As in, put a stake in their hearts? You are not suggesting we *kill* our houseguests?" Manon's sudden entrance startled Gemma; her nerves were still frayed from last night.

"I am, indeed." Like a general trying to rally troops, she turned to Bernard, Bridgette, and Manon and sized up her army. "You must believe me. If we don't kill them, they will pick off each one of you one by one. I've seen this... well, this story... before." Gemma stared down at the boy, who'd been placed back in his seat. He was not more than thirteen years old. Looking up, she found the staff staring at her, wide-eyed.

"That is madness, mademoiselle," said Manon indignantly.

"Are you sure you feel well?" Bridgette reached to feel her forehead, but Gemma batted her away.

"Look at him," said Gemma, holding the boy's collar open. "You tell me what did this if not a vampire."

"Perhaps a dog?" Bridgette turned to Manon.

"Yes," agreed Manon, "a dog."

"A dog?" Gemma's voice rose, and she threw up her hands. "You really think a dog did this?"

"A vicious one," said Bridgette.

"No," said Bernard. He stood alongside Gemma and pounded his fist into his hand. "No dog bite would turn a child into that. You both need to hear the truth."

"Have you lost your senses, Bernard? Crosses and garlic are one thing," said Manon. "As a Catholic, I will not be part of stabbing anyone in their heart with a fence post while they slumber in their bed. Non." With this, she clutched her own chest and backed up a few steps. Once a bit player in the film, Manon now seemed a little high on the histrionics, but then the moment did call for it.

Bernard shrugged. "I didn't like them much, so if you say they're vampires, then that's good enough for me." He left the room, returning a few minutes later with two picket-fence boards. "Would this work, mademoiselle?"

Gemma slid one from his hand and held it firmly in her grip, feeling its weight. Her thoughts raced to the scene. It was a good one—a rallying of the forces of good. The scene last night between her and Roman had been quite dramatic, and she certainly didn't feel her performance was flat. She really didn't want to do another retake. And, worse, if she failed and was turned into a creature, would she come back to try again? Turning to Manon and Bridgette, she could hear the pleading in her voice. "Would you join us?"

"I certainly will *not* be joining you," sniffed Manon. "I want no part of this."

Bridgette simply sobbed, shaking her head repeatedly. Gemma realized it was up to her and Bernard. She sized up the man, feeling grateful to have someone who finally believed her, but racked with guilt at the danger ahead of them, knowing they were poorly matched to do battle with Roman and Avril. "Can you do this?"

The older man nodded. "If you say they did that to him," he said, pointing the stake at the boy, "then your word is good enough for me."

Gemma smiled. "If we kill one of them, it will help drive the other one out, I believe."

"Have you gone mad?" Manon attempted to pull the post from Gemma's hands. She was a much taller woman than Gemma and incredibly strong, so it only took a moment for her to wrestle the stakes from Gemma's grip. "You'll be hanged. Listen to me, please. You cannot *kill* the houseguests."

Gemma pulled the post free, sending Manon nearly stumbling over the boy. "If we do not, they will kill all of us. One by one. You must believe me."

"I do not, miss." Manon spun on her heels and walked to the foyer. "Bernard, you may do as you wish, but I hate to see what will befall you if you follow her madness."

"Have you seen the boy, Manon?" Bernard's voice rose. "Look at him, woman! Do you believe an animal attacked him and didn't kill him but left him in the cellar to die? The cellar. No. Mademoiselle Gisele is right. If you can explain something different, then tell me now."

There was a long silence before Manon bowed her head in defeat. "Blessed be they're not in the house right now."

"You're just going to let them kill you?" Gemma felt strength with the stake in her hands. "Because they might not be here now, but they're coming for all of us."

Manon seemed to consider her words, but then walked on through the foyer.

"Where could they be, mademoiselle?" Bridgette's eyes were wide with fright.

She considered the original film. Given the admonishment from the director that she shouldn't assume to know the script, she wondered where she would have placed them had she written this scene.

Gemma and Bernard spent all morning searching the grounds. The rumblings of an approaching thunderstorm caused them both to look up.

"I better tend to the animals," said Bernard.

"Take your stake," said Gemma.

"Oui," said the man with a wink.

As she watched him walk down the path, Gemma recalled Thierry's wine cave. While the path was there, no one had mentioned that there was a wine cave, and she wondered if it existed in this world as it had in hers. She turned left at the hydrangea bushes toward the hill, recalling the stories he had told her. Once, it had been a great place for a child to hide. It could also be a great place to hide if you were a vampire.

Ahead of the line of fragrant, blooming linden trees, she spied a change in the land, an incline with a thick forest that bordered Monsieur Thibault's property. She walked around the stones and found the entrance that she'd been searching for. Opening the door and ducking under the entrance, she felt the cool temperature hit her almost immediately. Unlike the time she'd been here with Valdon, where there had been candles illuminating the cave, the interior was pitch-black. Cold, dank air emitted from the stones. Gemma backed up, suddenly not trusting the dark space in front of her nor the entrance behind her. The hairs on her neck prickled. Like a bolt, she ran, tripping over the stones and sending herself hurtling onto the dirt path. Not stopping to look behind her, Gemma got to her feet, her ankle smarting, and ran down the canopied path back to the house.

"It looks terrible," said Manon, lifting Gemma's foot, which now resembled a bloated eggplant. "I'm just thankful you didn't fall on that ridiculous stake and impale yourself."

A sprained ankle? Gemma was furious with herself. She'd become a helpless heroine—a stock character. Now, as the killers loomed, she was as useless as a lame horse.

"Well, hopefully this stops you from running around the château with this crazy notion your cousins need to be killed." Manon didn't even try to disguise her disdain.

"Have you seen them?" Gemma was suddenly alarmed. Had they come back to the house?

"No. And I'm glad I haven't since you and Bernard saw fit to run about the property with sharpened tree branches." Shaking her head, she propped Gemma's injured leg on a pillow. "I'll send Bridgette up with some lunch."

"Make sure it has garlic in it," said Gemma, inching closer to the edge of the bed.

Manon sighed heavily before shutting the door behind her.

Falling back on her pillow, Gemma studied the canopy, lined with a striped silk pattern, above her. She was wildly off script and running on pure instinct now. She would not succumb to a vampire—no one else in this village was going to be turned if she had any say in it.

A few minutes later, there was a knock on the door. It was Bernard. Given his role as a caretaker and groundsman in the household, his presence in her bedroom was highly unusual, but it spoke of the new camaraderie between them.

"I heard you had been injured." He stood back, knowing his place.

"It's true," said Gemma, pointing to her foot.

Catching a glimpse of the pillow, he winced. "That looks painful. Did that myself once."

"I need something to wrap it with so I can walk." Motioning for him to step closer, she began to whisper. "I think I know where they are."

Bernard leaned down to hear her, turning his head like he had a bad ear. "If it is anything like my injury, mademoiselle, you cannot walk." He opened his bag and pulled out a string of garlic. "I found this in the market this morning. I've gotten several for the house."

She took the offering from his hands and clutched it. "Thank you, Bernard."

"We'll try again, when you're better."

As he left the garlic hanging on her doorknob, Gemma worried that her stupid injury might have doomed them all. While she was exhausted, she had a fitful night of sleep, sure she heard scratching at the door. Even sleeping, she was in character. In this strange world of the film, she was always Gisele Dumas. She longed to hear the word *cut* so she could break character and just go kick back drinks with the crew. What peace she did have was plagued by something lurking just outside her door. After tossing and turning for hours, she finally fell asleep.

The next morning, it was Manon's scream that woke the house.

Hobbling down the hallway, Gemma found Manon in her bedclothes, her long hair undone and standing over Bridgette's lifeless body. Blood dripped down the girl's neck. Her chest rose and fell. She was still living, but she had been turned.

"Where is her cross?" Gemma couldn't see the gold necklace that normally hung from Bridgette's neck. "It's odd that she would remove it."

"I heard a scream from outside." Bernard stopped in his tracks. Spying Bridgette, the man's voice fell. "Oh no."

"Oh, poor Bridgette," said Manon, sobs erupting from her. When she reached over to touch Bridgette's hand, a hissing sound emanated from her as Manon's crucifix came close to her body. "I shouldn't have doubted you, mademoiselle."

"Have you checked on the boy?" Gemma asked.

Bernard shook his head. "The horses won't let him in the stalls with them. They tried to trample him. His skin...looks like he's rotting."

At this, Manon's shoulders began to heave.

"I think I know where they are," said Gemma. She began to limp toward the wall for support, aware that in this condition she was in little shape to fight two vampires.

Manon locked eyes with her. "Where?"

"I think they're hiding midway between here and the end of the path."

"Do you have a knife?" Manon directed the question at Bernard before removing the shawl from around her shoulders.

"I do," said Bernard, taking what looked like a small penknife from his pocket and holding it out to her.

Manon took the knife and sliced the silk fabric of her shawl down the middle. Turning to Gemma, she looked at the state of her foot. "You'll need that ankle wrapped." She ripped the fabric into three long pieces. Motioning for Gemma to sit on Bridgette's chair, she tied the fabric firmly around the ankle. As she tucked the final sheath under Gemma's arch, she admired her work. "My father was a doctor. Try it." She motioned for Gemma to place her foot on the ground.

While it hurt, Gemma could bear the weight at least until they could get the job done.

"It's good," said Gemma, shifting her weight. "I believe they're in the wine cave."

The two of them looked at her with blank expressions. "The what?"

It was Bernard who had scrunched his features like he'd tasted something sour, the man's bushy eyebrows knit together.

"Midway down the path, there is a rock with a door in it. There's a cave for storing wine."

"I've lived here for forty years," said Bernard with a firm head shake. "I've never seen anything like a cave. For wine, you say?"

"Well, I'm not sure if it is used for wine now." Gemma stammered, not sure how to explain that in the future, in another world, it would be storing Thierry Valdon's extensive collection.

After making sure Bridgette was in her bed and there was nothing more they could do for her, the three of them headed out the terrace and down the twisted oak path toward Monsieur Thibault's property. Midway, Gemma left the path and headed toward the stone fence.

"We can't go there," said Manon. "It's forbidden."

"Says who?"

"Thibault," said Bernard, nodding in agreement.

Gemma turned, resting her stake over her shoulder. "And you both have met Monsieur Thibault and heard this from his lips?"

"Can't say that I have," said Bernard.

Manon shrugged in agreement. "I recall my mother saying that no one ever came back from there. People go missing, you know."

"Well, I'm not suggesting we hoist ourselves over the fence," said Gemma. "I'm just saying we go here." She pulled back some branches to reveal the old door.

"I'll be damned," said Bernard, who took the handle and wrestled the door open. Peering into the dark space, he stepped back. "Can't say I much relish the idea of going in there, either."

Manon made a sign of the cross.

"I'll go," said Gemma. While she hated to set the cave on fire, she thought it was the best way to lure them out, rather than risk all of them going in there, where they could be ambushed in the dark. "We'll need to set it on fire."

"Are you sure, mademoiselle?" Bernard asked, his face scrunching.

"No," she said honestly. "But I think a fire will drive them out."

"And then what?" Manon looked down at her stake, realizing the plan. "Are we just going to toss torches in there? That's the plan?"

"Do you have a better one?"

"One that won't kill us?" Bernard frowned but began gathering some kindling around the cave.

From memory, she knew that the cave had a long corridor beyond the front room. "I'll go in and toss it."

"You'll do no such thing," said Bernard. "None of us are going in there." Using a thick branch, he wrapped the twigs around it and secured it with a small piece of rope. When he had three makeshift torches, he crouched down and tried to start a fire with some flint. Within minutes, he had a small fire the size of a candle and was able to catch the kindling. He positioned himself at the threshold.

"You'll need to throw them long, Bernard. I bet they're in the far room. That's where I would be if…" What she wanted to say was if she were writing the scene, which, in a way, she felt she was.

Bernard threw the first torch. It hit the cool dirt and extinguished immediately.

Manon sighed and bent over to gather more kindling to make torches. "We're going to need hundreds of those." Rolling a few stones into place, she started a small campfire with some of the twigs.

Peering into the cave, Gemma recalled the table and chairs where she had sat with Thierry Valdon. Beyond the table and chairs had been barrels. "Is there anything in there? Furniture? Barrels?"

"It's empty except for some chairs," said Bernard. Taking the next torch, Bernard aimed for one of the chairs, but again the flame extinguished immediately. "The fire isn't taking hold. It's too damp."

Just inside the entrance, Gemma spied what looked like a small table and single chair. "Can you light the table?"

Manon handed a lit torch to Bernard, who threw it, but again, it extinguished.

"Here," said Gemma, taking one. "I'll go inside and light the chair."

"And what if that thing is right at the door?"

Gemma recalled what happened the last time Roman had killed her. If she died, she'd be back again tomorrow perfecting the plan. "I'll be quick."

Taking the torch, she kept the chair in the direct sunlight from the open door, hoping that would at least slow Roman down and give her time. She held the torch to the chair leg, but it took forever to catch. Almost reluctantly, the old chair began to smolder. She then carefully placed the chair by its legs on top of the table and then scurried out of the cave. From the outside, the three watched as flames from the chair began to lick the table, setting it ablaze.

Bernard shut the door to the cave, leaving it open only a crack to fuel the fire. The three of them waited outside with stakes in their hands.

"We don't even know they're in there," said Bernard with a chuckle. "What if we just cooked some squirrels?"

"You say if we kill them, Bridgette will be okay?" Manon gripped her stake.

While Gemma didn't know for sure, it was the only hope they had in curing Bridgette. "I hope so."

From inside the cave came a terrible wailing sound, like that of an animal.

Gemma felt her heart quicken. Her foot throbbed, but she found she was ready to pounce the minute something came out of that cave.

The door flew open, and Avril emerged, shrieking once the sunlight hit her. Attempting to go back in the cave, she realized she was trapped. The creature's eyes darted, hunting for an escape, but her path was blocked by the three of them, who had circled the cave's entrance.

She hissed like a cat.

"Watch her," said Gemma. The three banded together as a unit, moving closer to the fire that Manon had built. "They move fast."

Avril began to chant, and Gemma felt the words force her hands to loosen her grip on the stake. Avril was attempting to mesmerize them. Gemma screamed, "Now," and leapt on Avril, while Bernard lunged at her. To Gemma's surprise, Avril was strong, even as her skin appeared to be boiling. Despite feeling like her arms were weighted, Gemma held them out, keeping Avril's fangs from her neck.

The creature began twisting her neck like an angry dog. She screamed, and Gemma realized that Manon was beside her holding her crucifix and forcing Avril backward, where she fell into Bernard's stake.

The loud screeching and hissing noises stopped as Gemma saw the tip of the stake protrude from Avril's chest. Her face went slack like a doll's. Within seconds, gray veining appeared all over her porcelain skin, and then her entire body began cracking, hairline seams forming and then shattering.

"Where's the other one?" Manon looked around defensively, pulling her stake closer.

In a swift movement, a second figure emerged from the cave, coiling itself around Manon like a snake. Holding the stake against Manon's own chest, Roman pulled the maid's head back, exposing her neck. As he did this, the vampire began to smolder like a cigarette in an ashtray.

"Let her go," said Gemma, stepping forward. Suddenly, the stake in her hand felt hot, like it was burning. Tossing it to the ground, Gemma looked at her hand, which was still smooth and untouched.

The vampire's face flushed, and he smiled. "Come to me, my darling."

"Let her go and I will," said Gemma, feeling the pull of him. He was in her head. Clutching her crucifix, Gemma tried to shake the tug toward Roman. Against her will, she took slow steps toward the vampire.

The billowing smoke from him became more pronounced. Sensing he was weak, Bernard raced toward Manon, who Gemma saw had produced a knife—the silver knife that she had used to cut her shawl. Stabbing Roman in the leg, the vampire screamed, freeing the maid, just as Bernard landed on him.

Roman tried to bite the man. The break in attention caused Gemma to shake out of the spell, and she reached down for her stake just as Roman began overpowering Bernard. Thick smoke billowed from the vampire, and he winced in pain as Manon pulled him off Bernard long enough for Gemma to drive a stake directly through his chest.

The vampire looked down at his chest in surprise. The familiar gray veins made their way up his neck and to his face as his skin seemed to harden and crack before shattering. For a long time, the three stood looking at the two piles of ash, but no one spoke.

Finally, Bernard broke the silence. "It seems we've killed the houseguests."

The next morning, as the sun streamed through the curtain, Gemma opened her eyes with apprehension. Pulling the covers back, she ran to the typewriter but found only a blank piece of paper. A wave of disappointment washed over her as she looked around the room searching for signs that today was any different. Was she going to go downstairs to find no one recalled yesterday and that Avril and Roman were still running around the village? There was no bloodcurdling scream from Manon, so perhaps the scene had advanced, but she couldn't be sure.

Gemma crept down the stairs to the breakfast room expecting something—anything—to happen. While she knew it was crazy, would she find Mick and Thierry Valdon seated in the chairs, sipping coffee, all of this a joke at her expense, punishment for her absurd claims to be a writer?

She'd portrayed Gisele Dumas the way she'd felt the part should have been written. Hell, she'd *become* Gisele Dumas. Yesterday, she had even vanquished vampires. Swelling with pride, she couldn't help but think that her version of the script had been better than Valdon's. Just imagine if that version would have played in theaters, it would have defined horror film conventions at the time. And yet she was still here.

Wandering from room to room, she found them all empty.

She took her seat at the table with the sound of the grandfather clock ticking, staying focused on the door, willing it to open. Yet, when it did, it was Manon, her maid, who entered, not Mick or Thierry. Gemma could feel herself tense as Manon brought her a café au lait and almond croissant on the same Bernardaud china as always. Somewhere in the distance, Bernard could be heard shooting and whistling with delight.

"Bridgette's her old self, thank God," said Manon. "I'm keeping her in bed for the day, but you'll likely see her arranging your dresses by this evening." The maid headed back to the door but stopped. "Mademoiselle Dumas?"

Gemma could feel herself exhale with joy. Bridgette was going to be fine, and they'd truly gotten rid of the cousins. "Yes?" Gemma blotted her lips with her napkin, so grateful that Manon appeared to know what she was talking about.

Manon smiled and bowed a little. "We all owe you a debt of gratitude."

Nodding quickly, Gemma felt tears forming. Finally, she had earned the respect of her staff. And yet, she couldn't help but be disappointed. Why was she still here? She had traveled her brick road, and yet she was still no closer to being home. Wherever she was, hadn't killing the vampires earned her escape?

She had no idea what this world was, but it was *real.* Monsters here were real. Then the looming truth. She had gotten something terribly wrong.

No one was coming to rescue her.

19

Christopher Kent
May 2000
New York

The box sat on the bottom step. That the parcel was dry was a miracle, given there was a downpour. Christopher scanned his brain, trying to recall if he'd ordered any tapes or equipment...or, God forbid...records. He'd ordered the Sasha and Digweed *Northern Exposure* LP with the sole purpose of listening to God Within's "Raincry," but the box was too big for that. Obviously, the owner of the new Thai restaurant he lived above had dragged it in from the rain, and for that he was grateful. He recognized the familiar flowery printing, and instantly, he knew its contents: an old sweater, two even older sweatshirts, and his only running shoes. These cast-off possessions were heavier than expected, so he knew that Ivy had included all the photos of them, as well as some wineglasses, to make a point that she was purging herself of all memories of him. These were things that could have been tossed, but she wanted the last word. Ivy always did.

As he opened the door, he was hit with the poor ventilation between his apartment and the restaurant below. The garlic, basil, and coconut smells that wafted up through the old floorboards were a distinct change from the scent of ginger and cloves of the Ethiopian restaurant that had previously been here. He placed the box on his tiny kitchen counter and turned on the living room lights.

Surveying his apartment, he realized just how spare it was. With his upbringing, he learned to live with very few material possessions. He wore nothing but Levi's and black long-sleeved T-shirts, Dr. Martens boots, and an old black leather jacket that he'd found at Goodwill. So far, though, his biggest extravagance had been a laptop and video and editing equipment, but in the past few years, he'd purchased a few record albums that had grown into a serious collection. Owning possessions made him nervous, though, as if he still expected to have to flee in the middle of the night for an unpaid bill.

After all these years, the poster of Gemma Turner was still the most precious thing he owned. He'd gotten it reframed a few years ago and learned more about this famous photo, taken by rock photographer Rick Nash, who'd flown to London to photograph the Prince Charmings for their fourth album. It had been one of the last assignments that Nash had done before an abrupt shift in his career, when he left behind a career as a sought-after photographer to volunteer for Vietnam, where he was killed in 1970. Christopher's senior film about Nash had gotten a great deal of buzz, and he'd just heard that he received an $80,000 grant to expand it to a full-length feature.

He'd also kept up his work at the Library of Congress, checking the editions of *Cartoons of the Twentieth Century*, volumes 1 and 2, but after the death of Mick Fontaine, he'd distanced himself from *L'Étrange Lune*. He was sure that his curiosity had killed a man, and he wasn't going to be responsible for anyone else's death. Elizabeth Bourget had called him when she was in New York, and they had drunk until the bar closed, him finally confessing what had happened to Mick Fontaine. To his surprise, she didn't reassure him he was being paranoid.

"You said he was frightened? She listened to the play-by-play on his conversation with Mick, but she never once asked to see the video he'd filmed that day. And he had never looked at the tape, either. He couldn't bring himself to watch it.

The film had proven to be a divisive force between himself and Ivy. After they'd seen the film in Rome, she told him she never wanted to discuss it again. Despite her protests, he knew that she believed he'd had something to do with Mick Fontaine's death. They'd been broken up six months now, and she'd moved back to Los Angeles, so he didn't have to worry about running into her on campus anymore. Christopher was now in the master's program in film. He still loaned himself out on other films both for experience and for income, and he was headed to France to be a cinematographer on a feature-length documentary called *The Mona Lisa Mystery*; the original cinematographer had taken ill. While he'd excelled in directing and screenwriting, his first love was the technical aspects of the camera. He was a gear man; his knowledge of camera techniques and editing often made him the first call of many of his former classmates when they needed help on their own films. Wedding and corporate videos paid the bills, but he tried to limit those to the best-paying jobs.

The Mona Lisa Mystery would require two days of shooting in Amboise and the Loire Valley. Christopher would be handling all the location shots at Château du Close Lucé, where an actor was playing Leonardo da Vinci in several narrative shots.

The appeal of this job had been that it would take him to France. Like a scab he'd picked over and reopened, the very idea of traveling to Amboise had opened the mystery of *L'Étrange Lune* once again. No matter how hard he tried, *L'Étrange Lune* kept drawing him back.

The buzzer sounded, and Christopher looked out the window to see who was standing below in the rain. He couldn't make out the person's face, but the red umbrella was familiar. "Shit."

Ivy Cross gazed up at the window and saw him peering down at her. He hardly recognized her: the once severe, bobbed black hair was now shoulder-length and softer, though her lipstick was still crimson.

He motioned her in and stood at the top of the stairs. "I got your package today."

She gave the umbrella two shakes before setting it near the door. "I dropped it off earlier, but you weren't here. It was heavy." She steeled herself before placing her foot on the first step. He knew how much she hated his apartment. "I can't *believe* you still live here. I've got a house in Larchmont now."

Christopher had no idea of Southern California real estate and what that meant, but he knew he was supposed to be impressed. "So, how is Los Angeles?" This was what she was here for—to gloat that she'd moved on, which clearly she hadn't, if she was back here in the first place. He wasn't sure he had the emotional energy to deal with her today. Unless he had class, days would go by without his talking to anyone.

"It's great," she said.

"How is your dad...and...," he said, stumbling to recall her little brother's name.

"The baby is named Zeke." She snorted, not believing he forgot that detail.

"Vera?"

She gave him a puzzled look. "Who cares how Vera is." Sizing up his apartment after all these months, she clutched her handbag like she wanted to run out of the place. "I'm working as an assistant director on one of my dad's shows. It's so different than what we did at school. You should definitely think about moving out there."

He did a quick translation in his head: *Different than what we did at school* meant that she was learning more than him in the master's program at Columbia, and that he should *definitely think about moving* was that he would never be successful in New York. To the entire Cross family, film only existed in Los Angeles. While he'd craved it early in their relationship, her certainty in the direction of his life was a trait he did not miss.

Leaning back against his refrigerator, he folded his arms in front of him protectively. "Thanks for bringing my stuff by. You didn't have to go out of your way."

"Here." She reached into her bag and handed him two notebooks. "Those were the plans for the Gemma Turner documentary, weren't they?" Touching the old notebooks, he realized he hadn't looked at them again after Mick's death. The questions he'd asked the agent were scribbled inside that book.

She frowned, looking around. "Do you realize that nothing has changed for you? Same futon, same black shirt..."

"I'm a creature of habit," he said with a shrug. "What can I say? Looks like the full-length documentary on Rick Nash may happen. I got approved for the grant."

"If you were in LA," she said, steering him back to conversation where she felt superior, "you wouldn't need to be grubbing around for all this public broadcasting funding. You'd be able to make better connections in the industry to get your films produced for television."

"Probably so," he said, "but I like to control my own films. You know that."

"You just never realize your full potential."

"Okay," said Christopher, putting his hands up in defeat. "I appreciate you bringing my stuff by and all. It was nice for you to go out of your way, but this isn't a license to begin going down my list of faults. You lost that privilege when you cheated on me."

Christopher recalled the day a mutual friend let it slip that Ivy had developed a "close" friendship with a theater major named Trent. Growing up with his world in flux, he had an extra sense to know when something was wrong. She said she was studying, but Christopher instead found the two having a "romantic" dinner on her rooftop.

"I just wanted your attention," she said, exasperation in her voice. Throwing up her arms, she gathered her purse.

"You had my attention."

"Nothing was ever the same after the film, and you know it." She stared at the Gemma Turner poster with disgust. "And her. You're so obsessed with her that she's who you're really having a relationship with."

In a flash, he saw the same look of hatred pass over Ivy's face that he'd seen on his mother's face at the sight of Gemma Turner's photo. A chill ran down his spine at the memory. "I'm not going over this again. We weren't a good fit for each other, okay? I'm sure the other guy—"

"Trent," she said, cutting him off. "His name is Trent. He's an actor."

"Okay," he said with a shrug. "I'm sure that Trent is probably a better man for you. You *did* choose him, after all," he said, surprised he could hear the bitterness in his voice.

"We were kissing, but nothing else had happened. You stormed out and threw away three years of our relationship."

"You blame me?" His voice rose, and it thundered in the room, shocking him at how forcefully the statement had come out. "Jesus, Ivy. Had I come in ten minutes later I'd have been in the middle of a porn film. You're right. Everything changed with that film…and Mick Fontaine. You blamed me for his death."

"Maybe." She looked around the apartment like she would a dollar store. "You need to grow up, Christopher, and move past your fucked-up childhood. No one wants someone who is emotionally unavailable."

Anger welled up in him. How dare she judge him. "Thank you for your wisdom, Ivy. I'm sure you're glad you don't have to deal with all my faults anymore." He motioned toward the stairs, hoping she'd get the hint.

She threw up her hands like there was nothing more she could do for him. "Take care," she said, sliding the purse from the counter once again.

"You too," he said, moving from the refrigerator to the stove and gripping the handle behind him. He held it tightly while he heard her boots on the stairs.

When the door closed, he closed his eyes and felt nothing but relief. Despite her judgment of his childhood—and she wasn't wrong—it was *his* history, and however messed up it was, it belonged to him, defined him. Was he emotionally unavailable? Thinking back to the last six months of casual sex and frenetic work, he would agree with her, but he didn't have the emotion to deal with anyone anymore. His distance protected him, insulated him from the outside world.

Ivy Cross had chosen him because he didn't look like anyone she'd known in Los Angeles. The intensity that first attracted her to him waned as their relationship grew and she realized she didn't care for the origins of his drive, the dark folds in the fabric of his life that made him who he was. For his part, she provided structure for him, something he'd liked with Aunt Wanda and Uncle Martin. People without guardrails, like his mother, scared him too much. After enough time away from her, he wasn't sure he'd ever really loved Ivy.

Looking around the room at his meager things, yeah, he could try harder with his apartment—buy a new sofa, new plates, have people over for dinner, and get a new girlfriend, but this was his life and his choice.

The trip to Amboise next week was coming at a perfect time. He needed to get out of New York for a while. He'd sent Elizabeth a note that he'd be in France for a week, hoping they could connect in Paris, and to his surprise, she'd sent him an email to call her.

When she answered, she got right to the point. "The cinematographer of *Cartoons of the Twentieth Century* wants to speak with you... on the record."

Christopher bristled at the suggestion. "Why me?"

"It appears your Rick Nash short has made you famous here. You said in an interview somewhere that you wanted to do a documentary on Gemma Turner next. Claude read that and took it to mean you want to talk about the film."

"You talked to him?"

"No. He sent a message through a friend."

"I'll talk to him, but not on the record."

"You mean you won't film him?"

"That's exactly what I mean." After what happened to Mick Fontaine, there was no way Christopher was ever letting another person talk about *L'Étrange Lune* on film again.

"You should talk to Claude. We'll never get closer to the truth."

"It's too dangerous for him."

She was silent on the other end, and he could hear her breathing. "He's dying."

"Oh," said Christopher working out how that information changed things. Was this a deathbed confession of sorts? "You still need to warn him. I'll talk to him either way, but he needs to know the risks... of filming his story."

"I will."

The following week, in between shoots for the *The Mona Lisa Mystery*, Christopher found himself face-to-face with Claude Moravin, Thierry Valdon's chief cinematographer and the last person to ever see Gemma Turner. As soon as the man greeted Christopher at the door, it was clear he was gravely ill.

Pulling a thick cable-knit cardigan tightly around his bony frame, he directed them to his study. "Emphysema," he said as he proceeded down the hall, stepping heavily like the effort was almost too much for him. "I saw your short," he said over his shoulder. "It was magnificent. Rick Nash was another genius gone too soon."

Christopher followed him, touched that this famous icon of French New Wave film had even seen his film, let alone liked it. Christopher put his camera down and surveyed the small study. "I only brought the camera if you wanted to talk on video. Did Elizabeth explain to you?"

"The risks?". He nodded as he settled stiffly into a chair. "This might be my last chance to talk about it all." The man laughed a wet smoker's laugh. His skin was thick like a hide, and everything about him was compact. "Set up your camera there." The seasoned cameraman pointed to the best position in the room for light.

As Christopher unzipped his equipment and began removing his camera, Claude leaned over to look at the light filters. "I heard you started with an old Yashica, my friend."

"My mom wasn't well. Her old home videos were very precious to me, so I learned to fix the old Yashica and the Bell and Howell projector. I was a tinkerer first." Christopher clipped a microphone on the man's shirt. When he was satisfied with the setup, he hit the record button. As he pressed it, a wave of guilt hit him. Was he sealing this man's doom with this interview? "You're sure about this?"

If Claude was worried, he didn't let on. He sat back in the chair and settled himself. "We all come to this through something else. In 1952, I was sent to Vietnam in *our* war there. I'd had some experience with cameras, so they made me a war photographer, mostly stationed in Tonkin. While it may sound easy—carrying a camera, not a gun—I was often...how you Americans say...'in the thick of it.' I did one tour and returned to Paris, where I was doing fashion shoots and paparazzi-type work for *Paris Match* and others."

"How did you meet Thierry Valdon?"

"Thierry had been ahead of me two years in school in Tours." The man pointed at the window behind him as if the town of Tours was magically visible to the west of them. "We ran into each other in Paris and found that neither of us was happy. I had never worked a video camera, and he had never written anything, but we did that first film together."

"*Mastermind*," said Christopher, recalling the well-received dark thriller about the Vichy government.

"Oui," said Claude with a chuckle. "The jump cuts were not art. I couldn't use my camera very well. Back then, everyone started with black-and-white films; they were very bleak—I think we felt that the color had been drained from us during the occupation. Everything Thierry wrote was about the occupation. He never got over it."

Claude reached over and slid a thick file from the surface of an end table. "I almost forgot. You can have this."

Opening the file, Christopher found the original script to *L'Étrange Lune* as well as several stills of the set and early photos of Thierry Valdon. There was a final photo, a night shot of Gemma Turner standing near an alley, dressed in a period costume with hands on her hips. Claude was standing on the Citroën holding what Christopher thought was an Arriflex camera.

"I do believe that is the last photo ever taken of her," said Claude, a wistful smile forming on his lips.

Christopher's heart leapt as he touched the glossy picture.

"Have you ever been an actor?" asked Claude.

"No," said Christopher, never taking his eyes off the photo, once again wishing he could transport himself into that very moment and stop whatever happened next to Gemma Turner. "It never had much appeal."

"I pity actors. They must erase themselves to fit into the whims of a script and a director who remakes them for each role. The camera is their judge. Their words aren't their own. We mold them into someone else. No wonder they're neurotic as hell. Some actors like that... to be erased and remade like human canvases. I've always suspected a void lurks beneath that kind of talent, especially the best ones. Others bring themselves into the role, and you can't see the role for the actor."

Christopher wondered if Claude was talking about Gemma. Which of the two categories did she belong to? He positioned himself again in front of the camera and placed his headphones on.

"Am I in the frame?"

Christopher nodded and gave a thumbs-up.

"Valdon was an actor's director. There was a script of sorts"—he motioned toward the file—"but he loved improvisation. It would drive his actors crazy, especially the ones who needed to memorize everything and had written all kinds of notes. He was famous for doing up to twenty additional takes where he'd make them improvise repeatedly, rapid-fire. We had major stars break down in those scenes, which could be intense. The result was a more natural feel to his films. Compare his films to those of his peers. I would argue that they feel different, like his actors are *alive* inside his films."

"How did Gemma Turner react to this type of direction?" asked Christopher.

"Not well, I'm afraid," said Claude. "She thought the framework of the script was horrible, so there was no point in improvising. If the hull of a ship was damaged and sinking, there was no point in painting it."

That was a surprise to Christopher. He hadn't heard she'd clashed with Valdon. "What did you think?"

"Of the script? I agreed with her," he said. "Everyone on set agreed with her. It was a silent agreement, of course, but the outline was a mess. No one would ever cross Thierry. He didn't have a good handle on what he was trying to do, and Gemma was correct about one thing." Claude held up a weathered finger. "He'd never watched a horror film. The man was so arrogant to think that he could make a better film without knowing what rules he needed to break in the first place. Hubris. Frankly, the original cut of *L'Étrange Lune* was terrible, which reflected what was going on behind the scenes. Manon knew it and so did I. By the time she vanished, Thierry despised Gemma. If he could have fired her, he would have, but he was in too deep with the shooting. That doesn't mean he wasn't a little obsessed with her as well. It was obvious to everyone, but she appeared to rebuff his advances. He wanted rid of her so badly those last few days that some small part of me worried that he had done something to her. It was crazy, of course. Thierry didn't have a violent bone in his body, but he was not himself on that set. He'd gone to dark places with that film. The darkness continued after, as well. It would kill him to know that now his legacy is so entwined with Gemma Turner and *L'Étrange Lune*...his other work largely forgotten. Now Thierry Valdon is a curiosity, never mentioned with the greats of Nouvelle Vague, and that is wrong. But you don't talk about Thierry without talking about Gemma."

Christopher was seated on the arm of the sofa, rapt in the story. Like the tale Mick Fontaine had spun, he felt like if he closed his eyes, he could see these people: Thierry Valdon and Gemma Turner. "What happened that night?"

Claude looked down at the rug to compose his thoughts. The hint of a scar across his trachea was red and raw, like it was recent. "So often, I look back upon that night as the end of it all. Of course, I didn't know it at the time. It was the craziest thing I have ever witnessed. You know, I still have nightmares of it. I was following behind Gemma. She had some line like 'You'll never get away with this,'" he said, waving his hand in the air like the words were irrelevant. "You've walked the spot?" He studied Christopher's face.

"No."

The man's eyes widened. "No? You must see it. The cobblestones were uneven and would send you tumbling. I was terrified I'd break the camera. We drove behind her instead on this Citroën that Thierry fitted with an open top. It was dusk, not exactly night, but that didn't matter. At first, we all thought something had just happened, like she ducked into an alcove or alleyway. We stopped the shoot and waited for her for a few minutes. Then Thierry began to throw a fit and paraded up and down the alleyway, banging on doors and calling for her. We sent someone back to Château Verenson to see if she'd gone back."

"Why would she go back to the château?"

Claude shrugged. "We did not know. We thought she might have taken ill or stormed off and gone home. She'd been threatening to leave the film."

"She'd go without telling anyone?"

"There was such confusion." He put his hands to his face. "The crew looked in restaurants and shops, the cathedral. Even now, my heart aches at that feeling of doom that began to creep over us as every turn was empty. After an hour, we called the police, and they took over. When she didn't come back the next day, they realized they might have a publicity nightmare on their hands. Her agent..."

"Mick Fontaine?"

"That's the one. He was throwing around many accusations, mostly at Thierry, but I could tell Thierry was greatly disturbed by her disappearance. From that moment on, he was never the same. He never worked again."

"Did the police ever actually suspect him?"

"The police suspected *all* of us. I was under suspicion for being the last person who saw her, but fortunately, I had a camera in my hand that proved my innocence. You could see that one minute, she was there, and the next..." His snapped his fingers. "My eyes have played tricks on me in strange ways, but nothing like that."

As Claude Moravin spoke, Christopher was surer than ever that the only way to have a crack at solving Gemma Turner's disappearance was talking about it, gathering information from people who didn't even know they knew something.

"After Gemma, we finished the shoot. Manon, a saint if ever there was one, stepped in to substitute for her. Thierry used some footage he had of Gemma Turner, but frankly all of us were grieving. The whole film had the stench of death on it."

"But you didn't see the final cut of the film?"

"Well, my camera was taken away by the police."

"Was it an Arriflex?"

"Good eye," said the man, winking. "I missed that camera—you remember all of your cameras, even the bad ones, don't you?"

Christopher chuckled. This was true. He still owned every camera, even the bad ones.

"The police even called me a few months ago to see if I wanted the old camera back. The case is closed and cold, but I didn't see much sense. It's a relic now, as am I."

"Did you see the director's cut?"

"I did," he said. "Manon let me see it after Thierry died." He closed his eyes and shook his head gravely. "It was terrible and we both knew it. He spent nearly three years in seclusion editing it. The man went mad; there's no other explanation. The film was unwatchable, which was a shame given the importance of it to his legacy."

Christopher inhaled deeply, considering the multiple ways to ask the next question. "What about the version of the film that is screened every ten years?"

The silence was thick in the room. Claude gave a measured smile. "You know about that one?"

Christopher nodded.

"Then you know that to admit you've seen it is dangerous. The Soixante-Quinze must remain silent." For a minute Claude didn't speak, weighing the consequences of what he was about to reveal on camera. He sighed, almost resigned to his fate. "Like you, I'm a cinematographer. My craft is my native tongue, so to speak, so I know that the hand is different in those new scenes. The ones I didn't shoot."

Christopher's breath left him for a moment. This was the same theory he had about what he'd seen. "That's an interesting phrase.... You say *the hand*... not the camera."

"I'm not sure there is a camera... at least not how you and I think of it." A glimmer of something—fear—seemed to wash over the man's face. His entire countenance shifted.

"You have no idea who is showing these films?" Until this visit, Christopher had always nursed a suspicion that Claude Moravin was behind the screenings, but this man was not creating any bootleg film.

This was a deathbed confession. If Claude had done it, he would admit it now.

Claude laughed like he'd been punched in the gut and began to cough, holding up a finger for Christopher to hold a moment. Finally, he composed himself, wiping his face with a handkerchief. "It wasn't me, and I don't know who else could do it. Gemma is gone. Thierry too. I suppose Manon, but she hated the film, so why keep it alive? No. I'm not one for technology anymore, but the only way those elements get added to the film is if they're added by special effects or by the devil himself."

"What about Anthony A?" Christopher felt the weight of the name like he'd dropped a bomb in the center of the room.

"How do you know that name?" The man fingered the arms of the chair nervously, and for the first time he was not looking into the camera, and Christopher wondered if he was regretting inviting him into his house. If they destroyed the tape now, would the man live another few weeks until the emphysema caught up with him?

"I saw it somewhere," said Christopher.

"No one knows exactly who he is. I've heard he's a famous film director—Italian or Greek. He's been with the Soixante-Quinze from the beginning, though, so if you want to find him, find him quickly. We're all getting old."

"Could Thierry Valdon be behind all of this? Maybe he didn't die."

"And he's living in seclusion filming new scenes with a Gemma Turner lookalike?" Claude sat up, and his words had a new conviction. "I've heard all those crazy theories. Valdon is dead, very dead. Something went very wrong on that set, something evil. That *thing* they call a film isn't my film—certainly not the film I shot and not the director's cut that Manon showed me. I know I probably won't live to see it again. And that's a good thing. Lives were destroyed by *L'Étrange*

Lune. Looking back, I think we all felt doomed from the start, and not one of our careers—or our lives—was ever the same after it." Claude looked weary from the story. In the corner, there was an oxygen canister, and the man eyed it hungrily. He rose slowly from the chair and unfastened the lapel microphone. The interview was done. "Do you have what you need?"

"I do," said Christopher. After packing his equipment in silence, Christopher followed Claude to the door.

"And you. Take care of your back and your knees. Get a better dolly," he said, pointing to Christopher's equipment. "You get old quick."

"I can erase this interview." Christopher motioned toward the bag on his shoulder.

Claude Moravin shook his head, then took both of Christopher's hands in his. "Promise me you'll do something with that tape. Don't hide from whoever is doing this. Find the answers. People don't disappear into thin air. That awful night deserves answers, and they're out there somewhere. Don't let fear stop you like it did me."

Christopher nodded. "You take care."

"My fate is cast," said Claude Moravin, who closed the door and gripped the wall as he went back down the hall.

At the hotel, Christopher thought about what Claude had said about the answers being out there. Perhaps Mick Fontaine had died of natural causes. He had been an eighty-two-year-old man. Taking out a phone number, he dialed it and asked for Manon Valdon. A voice picked up, and Christopher told her his name and that he'd just spoken to Claude Moravin. "Never call me again," she said, her voice shrill, and the line went dead.

Looking at his watch, he had a few hours until the night shoot. Catching a taxi, he walked into the gendarmerie in Amboise, a rather bland building that looked like it was built in the fifties.

At the desk sat a man with closely cropped hair wearing a navy-blue jacket. Behind him was a map of Amboise. Christopher scanned the station looking for anyone about the right age.

"I'm shooting a documentary on Gemma Turner." While Christopher wasn't exactly shooting a documentary on this subject, it always seemed to give him an air of authority. People wanted to help people shooting documentaries.

The man looked puzzled.

"She was an actress back in the 1960s. I'm looking for an officer who might have been around then."

"An old one?" The man leaned forward in a conspiratorial whisper.

Christopher winked. "A really old one."

"Commander Lavigne," said the man with an eye roll. He picked up the phone and had a quick exchange, but he could hear the man shouting on the other end. Placing the phone in the cradle, the man looked up sheepishly. "He says that he does not talk about the case with filmmakers." The officer shrugged. "He asks that you leave or he will arrest you."

"A bit harsh," said Christopher, placing his hands in the air. "I'll go peacefully."

"That's a good idea. He isn't the most pleasant man," said the officer. "He would do it."

As he exited the station, he now had a name to work with: Commander Lavigne.

Later that night, as dusk was settling in the square in Amboise, he decided that he needed to see for himself the infamous "alley" where Gemma disappeared. It would be like a sacred pilgrimage. Perhaps he was just too sensitive, but he always felt that in places where history had *happened*, that you could still feel an energy emitting from the source.

It took him several false tries, and he almost missed it. Leaving the square, he found a rather unremarkable side street with exterior shutters all closed. The space, with litter and occasional loose bricks, was designed for pure efficiency—deliveries to the back of the houses, laundry. He wondered why Valdon had chosen this setting. Looking up, he thought it might have been for the controlled light, which cast a heavy pink hue at dusk. Taking a few steps, he saw wash hanging from an apartment above and thought how, after all these years, many people walked down past here never knowing about Thierry Valdon or Gemma Turner. Beneath him, the cobblestones were so uneven that Christopher couldn't imagine anyone running over them.

He walked to the middle of the alley before turning. He imagined the scene much as Gemma Turner did that night. Spinning around on the cobblestones, he took in every shuttered door and window, a few of them boarded up permanently. He wondered how many takes they did that night? Each doorway was a quiet witness.

But there was something. An energy vibrating off the bricks that beckoned to him. Perhaps it was hearing the stories about her, but he felt like Gemma Turner was close. Very close, if only he could listen carefully enough.

20

Gemma Turner
"1878"
Amboise, France

"Coupé!" As she said the word, Gemma looked around the room, wanting something to change and the scene to end. If she'd had the power to change the script, did she have the power to end it? "Coupé!" When nothing happened, she screamed, "Cut! Cut! Cut!"

Manon emerged from the kitchen in a frenzy. "Mademoiselle, what is wrong?"

Gemma slid back in her chair, feeling spent and numb. "Coupé," she said once more, quietly. Making her way back to her room, she felt itchy. For days now, she'd been wandering around the house, and the place was getting claustrophobic. At the typewriter, she struck the keys:

```
What next? I want to go home. I'm a prisoner here.
```

But the typewriter was silent, and she began to wonder if she'd imagined the writings that had come from it. Had she typed them in some fevered dream?

Then an idea struck her. The problem was this house. Paris! Yes. That was it. She had to go to Paris. If she could just get to Paris, there would be cars and phones and electric guitars, miniskirts and lipstick, just like before. This was like a closed set inside a studio. If she wanted to be free, then her world was in Paris! If Amboise was the problem, then Paris was the answer. But Bernard had said something about the roads to Paris being unpassable. That felt suspicious, like she was purposely trapped here.

She came running down the stairs the following morning. "I want to go to Paris."

Manon came in from outside, carrying a newspaper, and gave her a curious stare. "Why?"

"Shopping," said Gemma, thinking of something that wouldn't rouse suspicion. "I want to go shopping for new dresses."

"Today?" Manon's voice raised in alarm. "But the road to Paris—"

"Is unpassable?" She felt a wave of panic. If she couldn't go to Paris, she was afraid she was so fragile that she might shatter like Avril and Roman.

Manon eyed her warily. "I think I heard the road had been fixed. I'll just need to fetch Bernard. He'll have to take you since his boy is still not right from the... vampires." The maid shook her head each time she mentioned the killings, still not believing what she had seen with her own eyes. "How many nights will you be staying?" The woman began fussing around. "I'm sure the Grand Hôtel du Louvre will be able to accommodate you, but usually you give more notice for us to send word to them. This is highly unusual."

"I'll find somewhere to stay," said Gemma with a wave.

"In Paris?" Manon gave her a peculiar look. "You will not find a place in Paris, not a respectable one, I assure you. But Bernard will need to leave shortly to make the trip by evening."

She'd forgotten about the carriage ride. There were no airplanes or fast trains or even cars. Gemma ran up the stairs, then headed down the hall. In her room, she began searching for suitcases but didn't see any. After looking under her bed and in the closets, she came up empty.

"I hear you're going to Paris?" It was Bridgette, her worried voice already so familiar to Gemma. She was fresh from her sickbed and looking relatively unscathed.

"Oui." Gemma pulled out her own dresses, scowling at each of them.

"Today?" Bridgette's eyes widened in surprise. "But it will take you all day to pack. And the road—"

"Yes, I've heard that," said Gemma, cutting her off. "You wouldn't happen to know where I could find my suitcase?"

"You mean your travel trunk?"

"My trunk?" Well, that was unexpected. Gemma hadn't thought she'd need a trunk. Looking at the condition of her dresses, there were only a few that she wanted to take with her. "Oh, I just need a suitcase. I'll be buying more clothes when I'm there."

"But you will need the trunk, mademoiselle. That will take me several hours to prepare it."

"Several *hours*? I don't have several hours, and you are not well, Bridgette. Go back to bed. Bernard is bringing the carriage around."

"But that is not possible," said Bridgette, her face turning red. "It takes me a day to pack the trunk."

"And you are going to go back to your bed and rest; is that clear?" Gemma shooed her and threw open the armoire, plucking two dresses from their hangers. "Do we have a duffel bag?"

"A what?" Bridgette looked as though she'd been slapped—twice. "I have one, mademoiselle, but it is not proper for you to travel with such a bag as the duffel."

Scooting her along, Gemma waved her off. "I'll decide what is proper. Where is your bag, Bridgette? Come on, let's get you back to bed, and I'll borrow your bag."

The maid led her to her room and, from under the bed, pulled out a modest gray tweed bag. "Here you are, mademoiselle."

"You aren't using it?"

The maid tilted her head, showing the puncture marks still visible on her neck. "Is that a joke, mademoiselle?"

"No," said Gemma. "You might be planning a trip for a few days after what happened. You should, you know. After what happened to you, you could use the rest."

"Where would I go?" The maid looked exasperated. "Mademoiselle, I must say, you are behaving strangely again."

"These are strange times, Bridgette." Gemma snatched the bag out of her hand and lifted the bed covers, motioning for Bridgette to get under them. "Now, get back into bed."

"But I need to help you pack." That Bridgette was running around the house in her nightdress showed Gemma how her relationship with her staff had changed so quickly in a very short time.

"You need to rest," said Gemma, shutting the door behind her.

Back in her own room, she folded two dresses into the bag along with a slip, a corset (in case the maid at the hotel spied her things), and an extra pair of shoes. She chose one day dress and one evening. As she packed, Gemma felt foolish. She'd be back in Paris soon and wearing blue jeans, wouldn't she? They'd kept her from Paris for a reason. Nothing had been right since she'd arrived in Amboise in her own world. Her world was back in the City of Light; she just knew it. She had to get off this set.

Two hours into the carriage ride, Gemma finally understood why everyone had made such a fuss over her departure. Coach rides were not for the faint of heart—or back. As the carriage made its way over the rough road, Gemma was jostled around the thinly padded seat. Several times the road was so uneven that she was sure the carriage would tip over, sending her and Bernard spilling out into the forest. Sweltering in the midday heat, she kept sticking her head out the window, though she was already in a pool of sweat by the time they made a stop for lunch.

This wasn't exactly a rest stop like she was used to seeing off the highway. Instead, it was an old pub.

"It's the best we've got," said Bernard with a shrug.

Gemma tended to herself in a washroom and got some bread and chicken. Bernard stressed that they would be only stopping along the road for a late lunch and then another stop for dinner. As if all this jostling and stopping weren't enough, a fierce thunderstorm broke out that cooled the air but turned the road into a giant mud puddle, causing Bernard to have to slow down even more.

The new, unhurried pace gave her a chance to see that the outskirts of Paris were rugged places, not the neat suburbs that she was used to. There were no road signs pointing the way to Versailles. In fact, Bernard had mentioned that Versailles was in terrible condition, like all the other grand palaces after the Revolution.

Instead of feeling impatient as usual, she was glad she had time to sit quietly by herself as Bernard expertly navigated the smaller roads and then finally the grand avenues that Baron Haussman had built after the Commune.

She kept expecting to see lights or cars. Any sign of her world. With no road signs or even roads, she knew for certain that she had been transported *inside* her film, and a few days ago, with her maid and groomsman, she had killed the film's vampire villains. Yet, finishing the film had not earned her freedom. Perhaps there *was* no freedom. She couldn't walk off the set and back into her life. It all made her head hurt. Leaning her head against the window, she watched a totally unfamiliar city unfold in front of her.

When she finally arrived at the Grand Hôtel du Louvre, she felt like a Dickens urchin. Looking down at her bag, she realized that showing up at the most opulent hotel looking like a shabby housemaid was perhaps not the best idea she'd ever had. It had been a typical Gemma scheme—impulsive and rash. At heart, she was a bohemian hippie, but that didn't play well in this world or the time that this world was set in—1878 Paris. Would she be turned away from the hotel? Would the manager call Monsieur Batton and tell him that she was, once again, behaving erratically? She was quite sure that he would delight in sending her away to an asylum for women with "the fever," to quiet her.

As Bernard pulled the coach in front of the entrance, she saw two shiny carriages parked in front of them with a matching pair of ebony horses. She had yet to see a white horse in this world. Women, sheathed in cornflower-blue and chartreuse-green silk dresses with ornate beading, strolled on the arms of men in coats and top hats, looking like walking macarons. As she stepped down from her carriage, she gazed down at her own sweat-soaked dress. She turned to Bernard. "This was a bad idea, wasn't it?"

"You've had better ones, mademoiselle. And considering your last idea was killing vampires, that's saying something." He chuckled with a wink. "You are quite a wealthy woman. I know that Manon made sure that you have plenty of money. Plus, your father's name carries quite a bit of weight, probably in there at that front desk." He pointed beyond the lobby to an oak-paneled counter.

"I don't belong here, Bernard." While she knew he thought she was meaning this hotel, she was confessing something much larger to him. "Where will you go?"

"Oh, don't worry about me, mademoiselle. I will be staying in a little inn down the road if you need me. I have a favorite drinking spot and some friends I see there. I'll check in on you tomorrow, and you can leave word for me at the front desk when you want to go back home."

"Do you have money?" Not only had she not prepared well for

herself, but she worried that he hadn't had time to gather his things. She had been so stupid and selfish thinking that Paris would be different.

"Oui. Thank you for checking, mademoiselle." Bernard tipped his hat.

A bellman lifted her bag, eyeing it like it contained horse manure. She followed him through the hotel doors, entering one of the grandest lobbies she had ever seen. On the walls, red velvet drapes were interspersed between ornate sconces that beamed a soft light throughout the area. Above her hung four crystal chandeliers resembling bouquets that dangled on bronze filigreed chains. No expense had been spared in the creation of this lobby. Below her, her dirt-encased shoes stepped over an opulent blue-and-red runner that led her to the front desk.

"Oh dear," she said with a discouraged sigh.

"May I *help* you?" From an elaborately carved wooden counter, a man wearing a black coat with a trimmed beard gazed at her suspiciously. He braced himself like he was preparing to defend the hotel if it came to that.

"Pardon," began Gemma. "Excuse my appearance. It was a long ride. I am Gisele Dumas." The name felt strange on her tongue.

The man's face did not change with this new information.

"My father and I usually stay here when we are in Paris. As I mentioned, I've had a long journey, and I'm afraid I do not look my best." She smiled, motioning to her clothes.

"You would like a room *here*?" The man pointed downward with his finger for emphasis.

Gemma looked around the lobby. "It is a hotel, non?"

The man leaned over the counter to peek at her appearance, down to her feet.

Embarrassed, Gemma attempted to tuck her shoe under her gown. Feeling her face flush with anger, she stepped closer. "I'm in Paris to *shop*, monsieur."

"Is there a problem?" A voice behind her caused the front desk clerk to look up.

Gemma turned to find Bernard wheeling a stunning Louis Vuitton trunk into the center of the lobby. "My apologies that it took me a few moments to retrieve your bag, mademoiselle, but there was no bellman outside." He tilted his cap to her.

"This *shop girl* seems to want a room," said the front desk attendant with a snort.

"This is no shop girl, sir," said Bernard, removing his hat and scratching his head. "This is Mademoiselle Gisele Dumas, daughter of Roland Dumas of Amboise, who has stayed here many times with you in the past. With the weather, the trip was particularly muddy today. You know the road has been closed, and frankly it is still treacherous. Fortunately, I have Mademoiselle Dumas's trunk here. Now, where shall we place my lady's trunk?"

Gemma was beyond grateful to the man and the rest of her staff who had packed her luggage, knowing that she would not be well received at the hotel without looking like a proper lady. She grinned, realizing that she hadn't even noticed the trunk hanging on the back on the carriage.

"Mademoiselle Dumas usually stays in the Napoleon Suite, doesn't she?" asked Bernard.

"I'm sorry, but that room is occupied." The man was a little more contrite but pursed his mouth like the sight of Gemma was distasteful to his senses.

"Then she will take a similar room. The solicitor failed to send the letter announcing her arrival, but it couldn't be helped—he has the fever, unfortunately." Bernard turned to Gemma. "I will be back tomorrow to take you to Rue de la Paix. He turned his attention to the front desk manager. "I trust my mistress is in good hands. I hope that there will be no change in accommodations since the death of Monsieur Dumas."

Bernard waited until a bellman was summoned and a book was placed in front of Gemma for her signature.

"She will be in good hands," said the manager. "We have the Josephine room, if that is acceptable."

"That will work," said Bernard. As he turned, he winked at Gemma.

The bellman led Gemma down a grand hallway. When he opened the door to Gemma's room, she gasped at the grand suite with inlaid wooden panels, silk drapes and duvet, and an elegant velvet chaise. Pulling the curtain back, she surveyed Paris. While the buzz of the city was still present, this version of Paris was muted without the electric lights and the ever-ornate Eiffel Tower.

Paris had not changed anything for her.

After the bellman departed, Gemma sat on the edge of the bed, not sure what to do next. She undid the corset that Manon had made her wear and was relieved when the ties were undone and she could breathe again. Images ran through her mind: the last time she saw the Citroën following her down the alleyway, the lights cutting out, and then nothing. Then here. Where was here?

The knock at her door in the morning announcing the delivery of coffee and pastries was the first thing to rouse her. Numbly, she climbed into her bath.

"Your driver is in the lobby waiting for you." The maid, dressed in a crisp black-and-white cotton day dress, dipped in a curtsy before hurrying out the door. She'd pulled a few things out of Gemma's closet and surveyed them with surprise. They were not fine things that were usual for a lady of Gisele Dumas's stature.

Having no idea what to expect shopping, she selected the best dress that she had brought with her, but it felt too formal for daytime. If she was going to be in this world—wherever it was—she was going to have to fit in.

"How will I pay for the things I buy here?" Gemma whispered in Bernard's ear as she climbed in the carriage.

"Just have them send the bill to Monsieur Lafont in Amboise." Bernard hesitated. "He has taken over as your solicitor, I understand."

"Has he?" She raised an eyebrow, pleased that she might not have to see her old solicitor again. "What do you know of Monsieur Lafont, and where has Monsieur Batton gone?"

"He is Monsieur Batton's partner. Lovely man. I heard Monsieur Batton has traveled to Budapest to take the waters. His nerves."

"Vampires, more like it," said Gemma with a sniff.

They stopped first at the House of Worth on Rue de la Paix, where Gemma chose three dresses that would be cut specifically for her—a gold silk dress with a small train, a tulle neck, and embroidery on the bodice; an aqua silk dress with tiers of gold lace; and a dramatic black-and-white satin gown. Before putting her own dress back on, Gemma called to the attendant, a woman in a black dress with a severe bun. "Do you have anything that I could take with me today?"

Her face lit up. "I do, mademoiselle." She returned with a simple silk dress with a rust-colored skirt and ruffled silk blouse. "It was a sample for a fall day dress. It doesn't come with a jacket, but I think it will work," said the woman. The dress was perfect for late summer in stifling Paris. "I also have another." She returned with a taupe silk dress with a small train with black embroidery and short organza sleeves. "If you need an evening dress while you are in Paris."

"Merci," said Gemma with a sigh, grateful that the woman did not judge her shabby appearance. "My father died, and I just haven't been shopping in so long."

"Transitioning out of mourning clothes can be difficult," said the woman.

Next, she bought some Debauve and Gallais chocolates for Manon and Bridgette and a new silk hat for Bernard.

As she went through the motions of moving through high society, she felt like she was immersing herself in a part. And just like playing a part, she found this world exhausted her. It was dark and the smells were everywhere—horse droppings from carriages and donkeys carting flowers or food. Worn out, Gemma sat outside at one of the cafés to wait for Bernard.

"Why so glum, my dear?"

A curious-looking man with flowing brown hair and a long brown suit jacket stood above her. He wore round, wire-rimmed sunglasses, like the ones she always associated with Jules Verne. Strangely enough, he resembled Lord Byron. Two large terriers the size of lions stood by his side, affixed with golden leashes.

"Your dogs are lovely," she said. As she patted them, it dawned on her that she had met this man once before—in her world! This was the man from the Savoy, the occultist whom no one remembered.

"You?" Her eyes widened.

He appeared to blush with false humility and bowed. "At your service." He surveyed the scene with wonder. "I simply adore this world, don't you? We're out for a stroll in it." He gazed down the boulevard with the curiosity of a child.

"At the Savoy, they said I'd imagined you."

"Oh, I was there." He laughed. "Only you could see me."

"Like an imaginary friend? That doesn't make sense." Gemma shook her head.

"But you know what does make sense? This world. You should be quite proud. Every boulevard reflects your mind, my dear." He saluted her. "What a world builder you are! Of course, I did have to reject a few of your—duller attempts at storytelling!"

As he continued down the street, fussing at the dogs, Gemma sprang from the chair and followed him. "It was you on the typewriter?"

He bowed. "I am adding *director* to my curriculum vitae."

"All those retakes."

"Necessary, I'm afraid." The man held out his hand. "Althacazur."

Gemma extended it to be kind, but that name stopped her short. "Althacazur? From *The Damsel and the Demon*?"

"Is there another?" A deep guffaw emitted from the man.

"*The Damsel and the Demon*. It was my mother's favorite."

He looked down at the sidewalk in faux modesty. "Well, the subject is rather compelling."

"I... I slayed the vampires." As she blurted out the words, Gemma realized how ridiculous she sounded.

"Brilliantly," he said. "I was only bored once or twice, but we did a retake on those, didn't we?"

Emotion welled up inside her. This man—this creature—had the power to send her home. This was what she'd wanted. Her mouth felt dry and she twisted her hands, feeling herself wobble with nerves. "Well, it's just, now, I was hoping to go back home... to my world?"

He was silent. A long time.

Perhaps he hadn't heard her. She felt the need to tread carefully here, yet she felt herself breathing shallowly. She wanted—no, she needed—to get home. "This is not my world?"

"You're wrong." His answer was like a verdict. "This is precisely your world. One of your own making."

"But it's not the one I came from."

He gave her a quizzical look. "Why would you ever *want* to go back there?"

"Because it's my home." She bobbed her head a bit and clicked her heels. "There's no place like home."

A full belly laugh came from the man, causing him to bend over in apparent delight. "You grow more entertaining by the minute. Your home is your *mind*, my dear." He touched his temple. "Allow me to show you." With a flick of his wrist, he turned the sunny day to dark, gaslights igniting around them. Within moments, the skyline had changed. "You can do that, if you want."

The visual movement between what was there and its replacement made her woozy. This man was talking in riddles. Where was she now? Spinning around the new skyline, she recognized the familiar clock that sat along the river. "We're in London?" Her heart leapt. If that was Big Ben, then they were in London! Once this city had been her home. "London!" But out of the corner of her eye, she saw something that made her sink once again—a cab being pulled by two ebony horses. There were no cars here, no streetlamps, no telephones.

"Oh," he said, leaning in to inspect her expression. "My pet, you're crying?" He gazed up at the heavens in frustration. "I hate crying. Oh, please, please make it stop." He patted her on the head like a dog. "For a creature formed from Hell, I do detest sadness."

Turning away from him, she gave a quick nod.

He handed her an elegant silk hankie from his sleeve like a stage magician. "I'll never understand you humans and your fervor for your insufficient world. I would have thought that you of all people would have realized that place was a prison. All the suffering you endured there." He mocked her voice as he leapt on a nearby bench like he was Gene Kelly in *Singin' in the Rain*. "'All I want is to collaborate with someone on *L'Étrange Lune*,' you cried. And cried...a lot. Well, I am your greatest collaborator, and together we made a film that has transcended cinema. You made Gisele Dumas the heroine, exactly as you wanted." The two dogs, now free of their master, appeared bored and sat heavily until he stepped back onto the street, giving a little bounce as he landed.

"I miss home," she said, dabbing her eyes with the hankie. "I'm alone here."

"Had you stayed in that world, it would have broken you like it did everyone. It does nothing but break people. I gave you another option."

"You mean Aerin?" Gemma thought back to the story of *The Damsel and the Demon*.

"It broke her." There was a hint of something in his face. Regret.

"You sent all her suitors away. She was ruined."

"Out of love," he said, his mouth forming a small pout like a petulant child. "I couldn't bear anyone else to be with her."

Gemma thought it was unwise to say that his treatment of Aerin had been entirely selfish. She needed to keep her wits about her now and get home. "It feels like a prison here."

"It depends on your vantage point." He took off his glasses, and she could see his eyes were round and amber with horizontal slits for pupils. "You must trust me."

Gemma snorted with laughter at this preposterous idea. "You're the devil."

Althacazur's jovial exterior vanished. "I'm afraid he's not that creative, my dear."

"Can you tell me how I came here? One minute I was running up an alley, and the next I was here."

He pulled at his gloves like he was growing bored with her. "You were cursed."

At this Gemma blinked, suddenly clearheaded. "What? Who cursed me?"

Abruptly he placed his glasses back on his face. "I've said too much. I thought this was a more fitting solution for you than the other."

"What other?"

He ignored her. "If you insist on returning, you will need a key to get back to your world. It isn't as simple as just sending you back."

She had a feeling that she only had a few more moments with him. While she craved other answers—who had cursed her and why—she now knew it was possible to go home. "I just need a key?"

He sighed wearily. "What makes you so sure that the reality you know is the superior one?"

This stumped her. "Because…"

"It's home." He rolled his eyes, finishing her sentence.

"I'm lonely here."

"Weren't you lonely in your *preferred* reality? I remember your loneliness well."

He was right. Gemma looked down, recalling all the times she had been excruciatingly lonely.

"And in this *favored* reality of yours…'home'…did you have control over it? Sickness? Death? In this reality, the one you create, you cannot die. You cannot be sick."

"I miss my mother."

"Ah," he said thoughtfully. "I'm a motherless creature myself, so I am sympathetic. That is the hallmark of a demon, so that one I cannot help you with, although you could conjure her. Sadly, mothers die in that other world. One day, you would have had to learn to live without her there, as well."

In her head, she knew what this creature was telling her was crazy, and yet she'd ended up inside a horror film. She was outside the bounds of everything she'd once considered real and concrete. "You're saying I could re-create my own time and my own mother in this world. But would it not be hollow? Not reality, but a shadow?"

He smiled. "And you're so certain that you didn't live in shadows before? That you weren't a shadow yourself? In this world, my dear—you are the *sun*."

"This key. How do I find it?"

Sighing dramatically, he gathered the dog's leashes back up into his gloved hand. "You were given to me in a curse to do with as I wish. I wished this, but I grow weary of being a jailer. So the answer is that you don't find the key, my clever girl," he said. He snapped his fingers, and they were back in sunny, warm Paris, gazing out at the boulevard. He began talking to the dogs. "They never really listen to you after you say *key*, do they? I must change my approach." Facing her as he would a child, he steeled himself. "Now I must give you all the legal disclaimers related to a key. It's a new requirement." He began a long monotone ramble. "Be careful what you wish for. The worlds—or realities—are different, but one is not better than the other. Each has their own rules. Keys are not infallible, nor are they endorsed by the organization—that organization being Hell, of course. Please note that not all rules of time apply to each world. Check your time zone before traveling with your key." He breathed dramatically. With that, he disappeared.

She spun around looking for him, but both he and the dogs had disappeared on the street.

As she walked back to the hotel, her step was light and her head was racing. She could go back home with a key. Her mind raced. Where would a key find her? It was a curious statement. But for the first time since she arrived, she had hope.

Back at the hotel, her packages had arrived and had been placed in her room. Laying them out on the bed, she admired the tulle and embroidery. Yet, as lovely as they were, she had no one to wear them for. Tonight, she was here alone.

Curling up on the chaise, she leaned her head on the pillow and breathed deeply. She was desperately lonely. The man had said crazy things. Could she really conjure things like cities? Tonight, she was desperate not for a place, but a person. She focused on the face she loved so much, imagining the curves and lines. "I'm afraid," she said to the empty chair. A form appeared in the chair with the face of her mother, wearing the familiar flowered blouse and rust pencil skirt. The creature gazed at Gemma with the glow of a mother for her child.

"I'm here," said the form.

Once, Gemma had gotten lost in a department store. A kind woman had taken her to the office to wait while they searched for her mother. The office sat high above the aisles in the store, most likely so the manager could monitor for stealing. From her vantage point, Gemma watched her frantic mother appear, running up the paper aisle. Never had she loved or appreciated her mother more than in that moment, when she was sure she'd lost her. Gemma felt tears roll down her cheeks. "But you're not."

"Are you certain I ever was?" The form was kind.

Gemma shook her head, wiping her face with her palms. "I'm not certain of anything anymore."

In the morning, the chair was empty and the world still without light switches or the sounds of motorcycles and sirens. Pulling back the curtain, she saw carriages moving below her down the boulevards of Paris.

She sent word to Bernard, her only friend in this fugue state, that she needed to return to Amboise immediately.

There was only one thing she was certain of now, and it was that she was desperate to find the key.

21

Christopher Kent
January 7, 2004
New York

The knock on his door was unexpected, but then it was followed by a familiar pounding.

Opening the door, Christopher found his cousin's tall frame leaning against the doorframe. "I was in the neighborhood." Jason pushed past him into the living room. It looked like civilian clothes didn't quite fit his cousin anymore. Everything was too formal about his dress; his leather jacket hadn't been broken in, and the collar of his shirt was too stiff, like he'd just pulled it out of the packaging. "Your address changed. I thought you were still above the Thai restaurant."

"I moved a year ago." Christopher was trying to think if he'd missed a call about a planned trip. Jason had come back from Okinawa, where he'd been for two years. "Aren't you supposed to be in Florida? You aren't AWOL, are you?"

Christopher had gotten a mountain of publicity for the Rick Nash film. It had taken him two years of his attention to finish the feature-length film and edit it himself. It had just been selected for the Sundance Film Festival, and he was scheduled to be leaving in two days for Park City.

"I had a free week; thought there was no one I'd rather spend it with than my cousin who is now famous." Jason slapped him on the back hard, causing Christopher to wheeze.

So, he hadn't missed a call. Anxiety set in as he ticked down the interviews he had scheduled before he left. The attention for the film would make funding for his other projects much easier. That there weren't any other projects was a problem, but everything kept leading back to Gemma Turner as his next project. Claude Moravin had been right. Her story needed to be told. That Claude had not died immediately had also convinced him that talking to him wasn't a death wish. At least he told himself that.

Glancing around the small studio in SoHo with high ceilings, Jason gave out a whistle. "Pretty nice."

"No, it's not," said Christopher, aware that the loft was half the size of his previous apartment.

"No, it's not," said Jason with a wide laugh as he deposited a worn duffel bag on Christopher's dining room table, then opened his refrigerator door and took out a beer. "I met a girl; she's from Long Island."

So that was it. Christopher rolled his eyes. "You know that Long Island is big, don't you? She might live in the Hamptons, which is nowhere near here."

"Anyway," said Jason, settling on the sofa. "I got us dates for tonight."

"I don't know." It came out faster than he'd expected. Christopher just didn't do dating anymore. After Ivy, he'd had more than a few drunk hookups, but that was the way he liked it. Taking his cousin out for a beer was one thing; entertaining a date was not what he'd planned. "I've got a ton of work."

"Jessie works with me. She's home visiting her family this weekend. Her sister, Lindsay, will be joining us. I've seen pictures of her, and she's cute as hell."

"This Jessie doesn't think it's weird you followed her here?"

"I said that you and I had planned to get together. Called it a 'coincidence' that we were in the same city."

Christopher groaned loudly. The least he could do for Jason was to be his wingman. The guy never asked anything of him. Hell, he hadn't seen him in years. "You really like her?"

"Would I fly here if I didn't?" Jason put his legs up on the coffee table, a rustic industrial thing made of railroad ties and aged wood. "You've decorated the place."

"A little bit," said Christopher, who'd painted this apartment, purchased a sofa that wasn't a futon, and bought a decent bed.

"I see your girl is still on the wall." Jason pointed to the Gemma Turner photo that still commanded the place of honor over his desk.

"Always," said Christopher.

After quite a lot of back and forth, they agreed to meet Jessie and Lindsay at a little Italian restaurant on Prince Street. This involved Jason exchanging a half dozen phone calls with Jessie, who seemed reluctant to travel so far into the city.

"What does she do?"

"She's a JAG," said Jason.

"A lawyer?" Christopher's eyebrow rose.

"I think she likes me," said Jason with a wide smile.

At the restaurant, they were easy to spot. Jessie and her younger sister, Lindsay, were both athletic, compact women with strawberry-blond hair and freckles. Jessie, four years older than her sister, had less baby fat in her face, but they were nearly identical.

As they settled into their table, Christopher had never seen Jason trying so hard. Women came to Jason; he never had to work for attention. His cousin had matured from the kid with the comb in his pocket to a handsome guy with his mom's dark hair and his father's soft features. The military had polished him, but there were still hints of the goofy kid inside.

"Where did you meet?" Christopher prompted as he ordered a round of drinks. Based on Lindsay's knowing look, they both seemed to be aware of their roles of third and fourth wheels.

"We were in a pool league," said Jessie. "He's terrible."

"I pretended that I was terrible," corrected Jason.

"No," said Christopher. He met Jessie's eyes and they laughed. "You're terrible."

"Jason tells me you're famous," said Lindsay as she tasted her Pinot Grigio. He could tell she hated it but felt the occasion warranted something sophisticated, and she was trying to hang with her older sister.

"Do you want a beer instead?" Christopher pretended to pick some lint off his jeans and leaned closer to her.

She looked relieved. "I'd love one."

"He's totally famous," interjected Jason. "His film is being shown at Sundance."

That made both sisters perk up.

"Documentary," said Christopher. "No movie stars in anything I do."

"I don't watch those," said Jessie, "but I loved *Lost in Translation*." She had a harder edge to her voice.

"Oh yeah," added Lindsay. "That film is so cool. What do you think he whispered to her at the end?"

" 'I love you,' " said Jessie, laughing.

"No, no," said Jason. " 'Leave your husband and come with me.' "

"We aren't supposed to know," said Christopher. "The whole film is about their connection, and at the end, it is their intimacy and we're outside of it. What they actually say doesn't matter."

"Okay, then," said Jason, shooting Christopher a look. If Jason could have reached his leg under the table, he would have gotten a swift kick from his cousin. "Don't ask the filmmaker a question like that." They all looked at him like he'd spoiled the fun with some kind of film-theory gibberish. Feeling awkward, Christopher searched the room, hoping for an escape.

He found it. Out of the corner of his eye. Christopher noticed a woman sitting alone in the VIP booth, her head down. He was sure he knew her from somewhere. He continued drinking, but his eyes kept pulling back to the gray-haired woman. Finally, it hit him. That was Tamsin Goyard, the fashion designer with a storefront on Wooster Street.

Before that, she had been one of Charlie Hicks's lovers.

One of the prevailing theories that kept coming up in the notes from the Seventy-Five was that Charlie Hicks had killed himself in Amboise because he'd known more about what happened to Gemma Turner. If he was ever to do a documentary film on Gemma Turner—and that was still a big *if*—then he had to deal with Charlie Hicks both as Gemma's boyfriend and as someone who possibly had something to do with her disappearance. She was a fabulous source of material.

Over the years, he'd continued to write Commander Lavigne of the Gendarmerie Nationale in Amboise, asking to talk to him. At the same time, he'd tried several times to reach Tamsin, but she'd also never responded. In fact, no one ever responded, and that was part of the frustration around any film about Gemma Turner. After all these years, still no one wanted to talk.

Tamsin Goyard was now a top designer, but she'd once been a

groupie with the Prince Charmings. And there she was, sitting alone. This was an opportunity he couldn't waste.

His pulse quickened like it always did when he might get an interview. Looking down, he saw he was rubbing his hands on his legs. Lindsay said something, but he didn't hear her.

"I'll be back." Christopher stood up. "Someone I know is sitting over there. I'll be just a second."

Tamsin's designs were colorful, bohemian creations, and her store was like an art gallery, painted all white, letting the colorful pinks and pale blues of her dresses and pantsuits take center stage. Studying the small woman with a gray pixie cut, Christopher was sure it was her, but the black portfolio with sketches of dresses laid in front of her was confirmation. So engrossed was she in making notes on each sketch that she didn't notice that he was standing there until he cleared his throat.

She looked up, studying his face. "You don't give up easily."

"I haven't even introduced myself," said Christopher, puzzled at her comment.

Tamsin slid her glasses down to the end of her nose. "You're the filmmaker. You were recently featured in the *New York Times* style section for that documentary on Rick Nash, and in a few days you're going to sit in the Egyptian Theatre in Park City while people bid on the right to distribute your film. How am I doing?"

"Ouch," he said. "That's a little harsh. I've come by your store before."

"Three times, to be exact," she said, pointing a pink fingernail. "You were getting to be a problem, but I'll give you ten minutes. I'll only talk on background. You *cannot* quote me."

"I'm not a reporter," said Christopher with a laugh.

"No, you're a pain in the ass." She flipped another sketch over. "Nine minutes now. I have no idea what you think I know."

He slid into the booth opposite her. It was one of those contemporary contraptions with a high back that made you feel like you were dining in a clamshell. It took him a minute to settle himself. Now, with the woman sitting in front of him, staring at him, Christopher had no earthly idea what to ask her. Everything about this evening had been topsy-turvy, from Jason showing up to finding out he was on a double date to seeing this woman sitting alone in a booth.

"Eight minutes. We can keep doing this until the clock counts down." Her hand flipped another design over. "Or I can get back to my fall collection." She placed a pair of thick eyeglasses back on her head. "We're doing a few coats this year. Very long, military inspired, in blue wools. Feels very *Doctor Zhivago*."

Christopher peered over the table at them. At first glance, he'd thought they were dresses, but now he saw they were long coats with elaborate detail. "How did you get into design?"

She pulled a face. "You can read up on that in *Women's Wear Daily*. A million people have asked me that question, and it bores me." She motioned back toward his table, where Jason was glaring at him. "Give me something interesting or go back to your friends."

His face felt hot, and he became extremely thirsty. There was an extra water glass for a second place setting, and he grabbed it and took a huge gulp. "I want to know about Charlie Hicks."

At the mention of Charlie's name, Tamsin Goyard placed her pen on the table and met his eyes for the first time. "There's a name I haven't heard in a long while. Why on earth do you think that would I know anything about him?"

"You knew him, didn't you?"

"I did, once," she said, her voice falling flat. People often reacted that way when they had stories they didn't want to tell. From the silence, he could almost hear the weight of these memories in her voice. She sighed deeply and sank into the booth, ready to give up the memories. "In answer to your first question, I had a day job doing alterations at a dry-cleaning establishment in London for a few months while I was flat broke. I was quite good. I began to create clothes using marvelous material by repurposing old vintage items. Each piece was handcrafted. Wren Atticus met me in a vintage shop on King's Road. He took one look at the jacket I was wearing, a suede cape, and bought it off me. That cape became one of the most famous things he ever wore. He introduced me to Charlie Hicks, and then I started dressing him as well. I loved Wren Atticus. I owe him everything."

She motioned for a waiter and held up her highball. The table candlelight only illuminated Tamsin Goyard's perfect bone structure. Her signature was the pixie cut with bold lipstick. She was an elegant woman, no doubt a presence in every room she entered. She took a final sip of what appeared to be gin and tonic, and the ice clanked against the sides of the glass as she drained it. "Are you doing a film on Charlie or the Prince Charmings? I suppose it's time for them to have a revival."

"No," said Christopher. "Gemma Turner." As the words left his lips, he knew this was finally true. He'd been running both toward this film as well as away from it for years, but deep down he'd always known she would be his next project.

"Gemma?" Tamsin's eyebrows rose. "Another name I haven't heard in a long time."

"I'm trying to find out about Charlie and Gemma." He braced himself, knowing that he probably had five minutes left on her clock. "Why do *you* think Charlie killed himself?"

She looked like she had the weight of the world on her shoulders, then she glanced down at the floor. There it was! Her "tell." When people averted their eyes in the middle of talking to you, there was always more to the story. "Charlie was dying from the minute I met him."

"There are people who think that Charlie had something to do with Gemma Turner's disappearance. They'd broken up, and then she disappeared."

"Oh God, no." She scowled, rubbing the lipstick off the rim of her glass for something to do with her hands. She was nervous. "First of all, Charlie wasn't in Amboise when Gemma disappeared. He was in London, and I was with him, so those rumors are just that. You need to understand that after Gemma went to France, Charlie spiraled, and the Prince Charmings finally fired him, but it had been a long time coming. He didn't even finish the fourth album. It was around the same time Brian Jones died, so it was all the talk that two of the original creative geniuses had been scrapped from their bands. After they threw Charlie out, Wren struggled to keep the group together." For a moment she didn't seem to want to say something. "Without Charlie, the Prince Charmings had no soul. He was a lot of things, but he was the soul of that band. And for all his faults, Charlie felt Gemma's death deeply. Until he died, he blamed Thierry Valdon for her disappearance."

She recited these details like they were well-rehearsed facts, but he felt something was off with her account. Yes, time smoothed the edges, but it didn't eliminate empathy. While she was claiming to be nostalgic and going down memory lane with him, this felt like a cover story, something she'd rehearsed at one time in her life. Just tonight, she'd needed to use it.

"Were you in love with him?" He wanted to toss a question at her that she might not be expecting.

She nearly snorted and was forced to wipe her mouth with her hand. "You don't know?"

He gave her a confused look.

She tapped an accusatory nail on the table in front of him. "Let me give you some advice before you approach someone you've been hounding for an interview. Do your research."

His face turned red. She was right. The Charlie Hicks angle to Gemma's disappearance wasn't his favorite, so he hadn't spent much time reading about the guitarist boyfriend or her.

"Not only did I not love Charlie, I didn't even like him. My friend Penny and I moved in with Charlie after Gemma's death. I was in love with Penny, not Charlie. Penny was hell-bent on keeping him sober, but that was an impossible task. The three of us shared his flat in Mayfair after Gemma left. Penny was with him in Amboise when he drowned. Penny was the one who identified his body."

The waiter finally returned with another gin and tonic, taking the old one away, then dusted invisible crumbs off the pristine white tablecloth. She saluted him with the fresh drink. "These things will be the death of me. I gave up cigarettes in seventy-nine, but these..." She looked at the glass longingly. "Anyway, you should find Penny. She would know more about Charlie's state of mind. Sadly, we've not kept up." She shrugged. "It didn't end well." Her mouth turned up in a coy little smile, and she looked at her watch. "Your time is up. I must get back to work. I'm not sure I helped you at all."

Christopher wasn't sure, either, but like an obedient child, he scooted himself out of the booth.

When he rose, she looked up at him. "You are a rather handsome young man," she said. "Can I ask *you* something?"

"Sure." Looking back at his own table, he could see all three of his dinner companions staring back at him. No one was smiling. What they'd thought would be a momentary *hello* had turned into a long conversation.

"Why a film on Gemma Turner?" He could feel her studying him. "You're becoming famous in certain circles. You could be the next young thing. I've been that young thing, so I know. Your next move is important. Why pursue this little acre of ancient history?"

His answer was quick, and he was surprised by its simple truth. "Because no one else has done it, and she deserves answers."

She made a distasteful face that told him she found his answer to be mostly poppycock. "There has to be more than that, surely." He could feel her guard going down. "Look, after Gemma went missing, Charlie did as well, but it would take him another three years to die. If you have some romantic notion of this time in history, some misplaced nostalgia, just know the reality of it was a train wreck. I think of Charlie so often. My heart breaks for him. He was just a kid. We thought we were such adults. It's hard to watch someone kill themselves, you know?"

Christopher nodded. He knew that terrain well. "Yeah, I've seen it."

She smiled thoughtfully, then picked up her reading glasses and returned to her stack of sketches. He was dismissed. In fact, she waved her hand at him. "Find Penny, and she'll fill in the gaps for you."

Jason shot him an angry look when he got back to the table. "Isn't she a little old for you?"

Taking his seat, Christopher was weary. He simply wasn't up for this tonight. Not that he didn't love seeing his cousin, but nothing had gone according to plan, and he just wanted a break. "Sorry, that was Tamsin Goyard," he said.

Lindsay flashed a look of recognition. "The one who makes the beach dresses?"

"The very one." Christopher found his beer was now warm and slid it away.

"Do you know her?" It was Jessie.

"No," said Christopher. "I just had wanted to talk with her about..." He hesitated. "Someone she knew long ago."

"Not Gemma Turner again?" Jason rolled his eyes. While his cousin was always the extrovert, alcohol combined with nerves to impress Jessie had him speaking more loudly and dramatically than usual. He also didn't seem to like the attention both girls were giving Christopher, who was never the first choice of any woman when the two of them were together. "So, Christopher here is obsessed with this old actress from the 1960s. As a kid, he was a freak, staying in and watching all these home movies and then going back and forth to the video store to find these rare surf film videos. Let it go, man." Jason waved his arms theatrically.

"I think it's cool." Lindsay moved her chair closer. "Who was the actress again? Jemima?"

"Gemma," he corrected her, a little too quickly. "Gemma Turner."

"Why were you so taken with her?" Lindsay seemed fascinated.

Christopher didn't interact much with anyone anymore. He shot video, so he navigated film sets and film crews, but not actual people. He had no friends, so when Lindsay and Jessie asked him to tell them the story, he did.

An hour later, he still was going over the theories of her disappearance in detail. As he spoke, he was sketching out a potential script treatment. Was it Charlie Hicks, the errant bad boy? Was it a vagrant who spotted a ringer for his estranged girlfriend? Could it be the director who was in love with his starlet?

"Why would it be the director?"

He looked up to see the drinks were empty and uneasy glances were being exchanged between the three of them.

"I think we got it," said Jason. "You're a little intense, dude. Let's talk about something else, okay?"

So engrossed was he in the tale that Christopher didn't pick up on the fact that he'd lost his audience about thirty minutes ago. Suddenly, he hated himself. When he met with Elizabeth Bourget, they talked until the wee hours about the pros and cons of each little theory. He was so out of practice in social situations that he'd forgotten his audience. "I'm sorry," said Christopher, feeling his face burning.

"It's okay." Lindsay popped up from the table, placing her hand on his wrist. "This has been great, but I have a long bus ride back home." She glanced over at her sister, waiting for a response.

Jason's face showed alarm at the prospect that Jessie was going to join her.

"Me too," said Jessie. "I don't want you riding back alone." She looked down at Jason. "I'll see you back at the base. It was nice catching up with you."

Both girls nodded to Christopher awkwardly, like he'd soiled himself at the table. This was not the outcome that Jason had been hoping for, and he felt terrible for ruining his cousin's night.

When Jason returned from walking them to the corner, he plopped down on his chair. "God, you're a buzzkill. I mean, you sounded like a freak. What's wrong with you? Read the room, buddy. Look up once in a while when you're talking. Make eye contact." He pointed to his own eyes. "Jeez."

"So you said." That same feeling of not belonging set in. He could never hang with Jason, no matter how hard he'd tried. Once, as a kid, he'd tried really hard, but tonight he'd proven he wasn't fit to be around people.

"No." Jason's voice rose, and spittle had formed in the corner of his mouth. "You have no idea how out of touch you are with reality. Let me ask you a question. When was the last time you got laid?"

"That's none of your business." Christopher grimaced. "Do not go there, man."

"Ivy?" When Christopher was silent, Jason smiled triumphantly. "That was what, four years ago?"

"It hasn't been four years," said Christopher, feeling a misplaced point of pride at, what—six, or was it seven one-night stands? His sex life was an embarrassment.

"You do know you need to step outside of your shrine to Gemma Turner to get laid, right? Then you need to start talking to women—not about them, not racing off to chat with some old bat about something that happened before you were even born." His cousin gave a disgusted sigh and slunk down in his chair. "She'll never look at me again because of my crazy cousin."

Christopher had always felt grateful for this family who had rescued him. He'd adored the big brother that Jason had been to him in what was a time of need, but tonight Jason was stepping over the line. "Back off, okay?"

"No," said his cousin, the veins in his neck popping. "Maybe you're famous now, but you've turned into a weirdo, man. You live in a dream world, like your mother did." His cousin hesitated. "Do you know that when you and your mom would come to visit, that when you would leave, my mom would be in agony at the way you were living? You were a little boy who had to take on the care and responsibility of a grown woman. She neglected your schooling so you could tend to her every whim. It was my mom who had to step in."

"I'm grateful for your family," said Christopher, leveling his eyes at Jason as a warning. "You know that."

"Mom is worried you'll end up like your nut mother. She tells me to get here to make sure you're okay. I want to protect *my* mother. Do you understand? Because I can't tell her that you live in a shrine to a dead woman, you haven't been on a real date in four years, and you're incapable of having a conversation with normal people. Those women were terrified you were some kind of crazy man living in a shed somewhere."

Christopher was seething. "Really? I thought they were interested in the story."

"For ten fucking minutes, they were," said Jason, his voice booming. "Then they kept giving each other glances, but you never saw them because you don't see people." Jason pointed at his eyes, dramatically. "Then they started looking around, pleading with me for help. They even stopped you to order drinks, but, no, you kept going. Thierry Valdon did it... a vagrant killed her... maybe it was the boyfriend. Listen to yourself."

Humiliated, Christopher got up from the table, his face burning. Was Jason right? Probably. He could feel the pressure of tears welling up in his eyes, but he was damned if he was going to cry here like a ten-year-old boy. That child, vulnerable and alone, was never far from his exterior. "I love you and I love your mom. You're my family, but you really need to stop." He tossed Jason the apartment key. "You can let yourself in. I'm going to walk for a bit."

"You're becoming your mom." Jason took a big gulp of his beer. "You need to snap out of it."

Christopher pushed away from the table and stood up. While Jason could be annoying, he'd never had a greater desire to punch his cousin, so he thought it was best that he walked away before he said or did something he regretted. Heading up Broadway toward Midtown, he found another bar, where he sat in a dark booth and nursed a few beers until last call. His aunt and uncle had given him a home. That familiar coupling of gratitude and unworthiness had always tugged at him. Did he connect with Gemma Turner? Feel like they were both doomed creatures, marked by two distinct paths in their lives that neither chose? She could have left Amboise and gone back to Los Angeles and likely lived. His mother could have chosen another hotel, and their lives would have been different. He felt something catch in his throat. Recently, he'd found himself nearly doubled over with waves of grief, often being brought on by images in his head—his mom in the driver's seat, the sun in her hair, and the way she'd belt out songs, closing her eyes. And a boy, peering under bathroom doors to discover a limp arm on the dirty tile floor. His mother was the love he'd held on to for a brief moment, but she'd slipped through his fingers along with his childhood. Maybe with distance he was able to process his grief now, actually feel it in the safe space of adulthood. He got back to his apartment to find it empty. A note from Jason:

Chris:

Sorry for the things I said. I'm going to try to catch a flight back to Florida first thing this morning. This was a crazy idea, anyway. We all worry about you—Mom, Dad, Angie, and me. Finally I agree with Mom. Take the fucking photo of Gemma Turner down off your wall. Live in this world, man! Okay! Love you!

Jason

Never had Christopher felt so alone or so unsure of exactly how to live in this world.

22

Gemma Turner
"1878"
Amboise, France

Not long after Gemma returned from Paris, curious stories began to emerge from Amboise about young women disappearing near the river. There were always tales of strange disappearances in the forest, but they were vague stories from cloudy memories. This time the women vanished near the river, which was near the town, where it was supposed to be safe. While the Loire was untamed and could turn wild in the blink of an eye, the only occasional accidents involved fishermen. So, when the body of a girl was found floating near the boathouse, the villagers began to panic. This girl, the fifteen-year-old daughter of a local vintner, appeared to have drowned herself, yet her family was not sure the girl had taken her own life. There had been a mysterious boy she'd become enamored with in the days before her death, so the feeling was that he might have had a hand in it.

Another girl, however, had been missing for three days when her body was found caught under some rocks, not one mile from the first. A friend of the second girl came forward to say that the victim had also recently met a boy and that she had been smitten. When pressed, the friend said that the girl had been secretive about any details, meeting him clandestinely. The police were used to these kinds of stories, love gone terribly wrong or a girl "in trouble," so they began a quiet search, starting with the places the young lady had met this mysterious man. She'd been a server in Amboise. Strangers were suspected and lodgers were questioned. Yet, no traveler turned up.

The household, still reeling from the murders of Roman and Avril, was shaken by this news. Bridgette, always nervous about the stories in the woods, now refused to take the carriage past the river, so certain was she that whoever was killing these women would find her.

Within a week, two more girls' bodies were found winding down the Loire, bloated, their dresses in tatters. The river was low, leaving the girls sinking into the mud.

For the next few days, their deaths were all anyone spoke of. There was a killer living in the village among them. Who would be next?

It was only when Bernard began to talk about a second blood moon, and Gemma heard the words *l'étrange lune*, that she wondered if these events were connected to her. She kept this theory to herself, but if this world were truly a product of her own imagination—her own mind—was she creating these monsters?

"I've never heard of two blood moons happening in succession," he said. "It's never happened."

"It's the devil's work," agreed Manon.

"He's not that creative," said Gemma, recalling what Althacazur had said to her.

Villagers closed up their shutters as dusk approached, and the Loire River, normally bustling with evening activity near Amboise, was silent as a cold bath.

That week, Gemma's dresses arrived from House of Worth. Bridgette busied herself hanging them in the armoire, chattering away as she usually did. "I knew the second girl, Marguerite," said the maid.

"They're now saying that the last girl had her hair wrapped around her neck, strangled like—"

That detail stopped Gemma in her tracks. "What did you say?"

"They think it might have been the current that twisted her hair, but it was wrapped around her neck and she was strangled. They say it was a terrible sight. My friend Suzanne's brother is with the police."

"The police shouldn't be telling their sisters these stories."

"No, mademoiselle. They should. It's a warning to all of us." Bridgette rubbed her neck. "You don't think they're back, do you?"

"No. You're fine," said Gemma. "Avril and Roman are dead."

Bridgette nodded in reluctant agreement, but Gemma could see pools of tears forming in her eyes and dripping down the sides of her cheeks. She hugged Bridgette tightly.

"They said you saved me," said Bridgette through sniffles.

"We all saved you—Manon, Bernard, and myself." Gemma pulled the girl away and looked at her. "You are safe here, Bridgette."

"But the second strange moon?" The woman looked up at Gemma, her eyes pleading.

"It will pass," said Gemma, lying.

When night fell, the household came out to peer up at the sky. The moon was round and bright red like a child's ball taking shape, but the clouds hung thick around it like they were cotton bits stuck to it. And the night was not black as though it were devoid of color, but a deep velvet blue.

"It is, indeed, a strange moon," Gemma said aloud, recalling the title of the film she had starred in.

At the typewriter, she composed a note:

`Why am I creating monsters?`

The typewriter carriage began to move, then keys struck:

```
To rid yourself of them, once and for all.
```

She had been right. The monster had been created by her and could only be destroyed by her.

If a monster that she created was preying on women near the river, then she needed to go there. That night, donning a black cloak, she rode a horse down to the river, just past the graveyard. From the time she left the house, a thick, wet mist had formed around her. The nearby graveyard was old with small, faded stones and a broken iron gate. Whoever was buried in there had no immediate relatives left to patch the fence.

The moon was now strangely low in the sky, like a fake sun on a movie set. She reached up, sure that she could touch it, but it was an illusion beyond her grasp. Walking down to the edge of the water, she waited. An occasional fish leapt out of the river, its splash sending small ripples.

At first, it sounded like a whisper. She turned to look behind her, but there was nothing. She shivered and began to turn back. This had been a crazy idea.

"Gemmy. Is it you?" A voice first, and then a figure emerged from under the water, like a child coming up from the bottom of the pool.

She felt the blood drain from her face. It was *that* voice, deep and gravelly. It had been ages since she'd heard his rich voice. How many times had she hated the sound of it on the phone, and yet it had been so long since she'd heard someone say her name, her *real* name, that it was like she was being truly seen again. Without thinking, she ran into the river until the water covered her knees.

Standing in the water before her was Charlie Hicks.

23

Christopher Kent
June 10, 2008
New Orleans, Louisiana

It was a crazy idea. Dangerous even. He'd gotten the call that the screening would be at the Pantages Theater in New Orleans. What if he just got there early, staked out the place to see who delivered the film? Someone delivered it.

The Pantages was an old theater on Canal Street that had been shut down since Hurricane Katrina. The old box office, with its dramatic round facade, sat empty with its velvet chair still in the ticket booth, in hopes of one day coming back into service.

In the early afternoon, Christopher sat across the street at a run-down bar, his laptop open, watching the activity. A weathered old stick of a man opened the back door to the theater and looked around suspiciously down Canal before crossing the street. He slid up to the bar, placing an order for a shrimp po'boy.

Seeing his opportunity, Christopher gathered his stuff and moved two seats over.

The man leaned over the bar, nervously wiping his face with a handkerchief.

"It's a hot one," said Christopher. He motioned toward the old theater. "You opening it back up?"

"Nah," said the man, his eyes darting around the room. "Just for tonight."

"Private event?"

"You're awfully nosy." The man turned away, keeping his eye on the theater door.

"*L'Étrange Lune*?" Christopher watched the effect these words had on the man.

His head turned slowly, and his voice lowered to a whisper. The man's eyes were wide with fear. "What are you? Are you with him?"

Christopher took a chance. "Anthony?"

"The dapper dude," he said, his Cajun accent thick. "I don't know his name. He's like a dandy from the bayou. Told me to meet him in the St. Louis Cemetery."

"I know him," said Christopher. "Dangerous man. Be careful of him."

"You're telling me. I didn't want to be opening my damned theater again. The whole thing feels wrong, like I'm showing a snuff film. I'm not even allowed to have staff to run my projector. And it wasn't like I was really given an option." He eyed the baseball game on the television. "How do you know him?"

"I've been working in the same field for ten years," said Christopher. It felt like a truth.

"I don't want no trouble. But he looks unreal, like a doll who comes out for the night. Gives me the creeps."

The man's food arrived, and he took out his wallet and paid the bartender.

"You stuck there all day waiting?"

"Something like that." The man was done and held his food tightly, crossing the street and shutting the door behind him.

Christopher waited all day, but no one arrived at the theater. At eight, he needed to get back to his hotel to wait for his mask and gown to arrive. He considered that this had the exact effect of keeping him away from the theater while the film arrived. The call came at ten thirty to look outside his door. Opening it, he knew he'd find a box in the hallway.

As he walked through the theater's front doors, however, he spotted the familiar shape of Ivy Cross. Though she was wearing a mask and a robe with a hood, he would have known her anywhere.

He slid into the aisle next to her and studied her hands. They were the familiar fingers with one exception, a large princess-cut engagement ring perched on her left ring finger. He knew it would eventually happen, and frankly he'd assumed she'd already gotten married, but seeing a ring on that finger made him realize what he never would be able to give her.

In the second row, he spotted a tall, erect woman whom he knew to be Elizabeth Bourget. As always, notebooks, pens, cell phones, cameras, or recording devices were all forbidden. They would get one showing to pick up the differences of twelve minutes that had been added between this version and the last one, ten years ago.

Elizabeth had said something curious yesterday: "The first film, you're disoriented and you have no idea what you're seeing. In the second, you'll remember more than you know. Focus on any changes. Those of us who have seen several films—three for me now—will note the additions. Get ready at the end. That is where the big changes usually happen."

Adrenaline shot through his veins as he gazed up at the blank screen in anticipation. The last year had been the worst, just waiting for the film to materialize again. "I didn't think you'd be here," said Christopher.

"Ditto," said Ivy. "I didn't realize you'd actually earned your own spot."

Oh, how wrong she was. Yes, her father had gotten him the first ticket, but Christopher had earned the spot in this viewing entirely on his own. She had no idea that in ten years, he had become one of the foremost experts on the film outside of Elizabeth Bourget.

"How are you doing?"

She glared at him through her mask. "You don't care, so don't ask. Let's just watch this damned thing again in silence. Okay?"

"Okay," he agreed. And he was sweating, nervous about what he was about to see. Elizabeth said the second screening changed everything.

"You'll see the changes for yourself. The effect of the impossible is rather shocking. How can someone so long vanished be on-screen with new footage?" she'd said. "So, either the film will get you in its grip like it has all of us, or you'll give up your ticket and wonder what all the fuss was about."

"People do that?" At the time, he couldn't imagine giving up his ticket. He was desperate for the second one.

"A few decide they don't want anything to do with it."

As he wondered which camp he would fall into after the screening, the candles extinguished, and the film began.

24

Gemma Turner
"1878"
Amboise, France

Charlie Hicks stood in waist-high water.

"Charlie," she said breathlessly. "Is it you?" She put her hands to her face and began to wade farther out to him, the desire to touch him so strong that she fought the current just to reach him. "I knew that someone would come for me. I just knew it." Was Charlie the key?

He was dressed oddly—a flowing white shirt and breeches, like a movie extra from a nineteenth-century period piece. It could be expected that he had been outfitted for this strange time as well. "Come out of the water, Charlie." The mud was making it hard to reach him, and the riverbed was uneven. With one wrong step, she'd slip and drop two feet. Her dress was like a weight around her waist, threatening to pull her under.

"They said you were dead, Gemmy," he said with a conspiratorial whisper, his eyes wide with wonder like a child at Christmas.

"Who said I was dead? No, Charlie. I'm not dead. I've been here."

She looked at him curiously, wondering where *here* was, exactly. Had she been wrong? Was this what death felt like?

His hair was the same golden mop, the scar around his cheek clearly visible. As he turned toward the moonlight—the red moon—she saw there was a shimmer to him, like the sheen of the minnows she'd seen in the creek as a child. Just like how she'd conjured her mother in the chair, she knew Charlie wasn't real—he was like a collection of something—particles in the air that formed into a creature that looked like Charlie.

The creature resembling Charlie brushed the hair out of his eyes and reached out to her. As he moved, his arm shone with a translucent quality before filling in solid again. For a moment he studied his own fingers, and Gemma could see water dripping from them like a faulty faucet. Those fingers had been out of the water long enough to be dry. This detail caused her to step back.

"You disappeared during the filming," he said, a strange tinny quality to his voice, like it was a recording of one of the old 1930s crooner albums her mother played on the antique phonograph. "They looked everywhere for you. I came a few days later and had a big fight with that frog. I punched him."

Hearing these details rattled her. They thought she'd disappeared. Of course they did. She had disappeared from the set that night. But to hear it was like listening in at your own funeral. She could imagine the panic that must have set in, just like it had done for her as she searched for phone lines and light switches. There was no doubt that Charlie would have made a big production and shown up to declare himself. That was why she'd been so surprised when no one had come to rescue her. And yet, it appeared Charlie, despite their rocky history, had tried to find her. With this revelation, she felt a wave of gratitude for him.

"But I'm here, Charlie. I've been here. I don't know what happened or how it happened. One minute I was on the film, and the next I was here. I'm not sure where *here* is, though."

"You're dead, Gemmy." There was a certainty to his voice that frightened her.

"No, Charlie. I assure you, I'm not." With a key, she knew she could go home. Dead people didn't have that option. "At first I thought I was kidnapped or in a coma." She shook her head at the memory. "Come out of there, Charlie." Her dress had snagged on a rock, and she was unable to move farther forward. "Come home with me."

"I can't, Gemmy." The corners of his mouth turned up.

In that moment she forgave him for those awful last minutes with those two girls—how hurt she had been with the constant parade of his lovers and his cruelty. He was here now. "What on earth are you talking about, Charlie? Of course you can. Here." She put her hand out for him. Their fingertips almost touched.

"I need you to come in *here*," he said. Shifting on the rocks, he looked exactly like the man who had stopped the band at the Whisky a Go Go to ask her name. "I need you to come to me."

She was so captivated by his face, by his presence here—finally someone came to rescue her—that she found herself swaying in the water as if in a trance. "You're wrong, Charlie. I'm not dead. This is my story."

"Just come here... to me. It's been so long." His arm extended out toward her.

It had been... so very long. He was from her world. He called her name. Despite everything between them, she longed to slide her arms across his chest and entwine herself with him like a tree taking root.

Yet, her head snapped up, and she focused on his words, not his face. This time she heard the tone. There was something ominous about the way his voice cracked as he spoke.

"You look beautiful in that dress." His head cocked at that sexy angle she always loved. His mop of messy hair blew and shimmered again, reassembling itself. He reached for her again. "Come here to me."

"It's ridiculous, Charlie. I want to go home. I want out of here. This water is cold."

Warily, she stepped back, a threatening feeling washing over her. This was, after all, still a horror film. She could not forget that. While this looked like her Charlie, something told her to run in the other direction.

"I know. I just want things the way they were before." Tears flowed freely down Charlie's cheeks. "I love you so much, Gemmy. I couldn't get through. I thought I could. I tried, but without you none of it made sense."

"What did you do, Charlie?"

"I think I drank too much, maybe took some pills. I sat down by the banks of the Loire. I figured that you were there. I felt so close to you. I don't know why, but I felt the river calling to me, like a promise that it would reveal itself and show you to me again. And look," he said, his arms out wide. "It did." He looked up at the red moon. From his fingertips, water flowed as though he were a fountain. "It's a beautiful moon, Gemmy. Let's see it together."

"Come with me, Charlie. You're talking madness." She backed up another step, her foot catching on a rock, and she panicked as she struggled to free herself, unsure if it was her boot or the hem of her dress holding her in the water.

"I can't come with you, Gemmy. I am a creature of the water now. I live *here*."

"You can't live in the Loire River, Charlie. That's impossible." Gemma laughed, but Charlie made no move toward her. Something was terribly wrong.

"How did you know it was me?" His voice held no malice, but it wasn't as childlike as it was before. "Who killed the women?"

She looked down at the dark water beneath her. "The woman who was strangled with her hair," said Gemma somberly. "It reminded me of 'Porphyria's Lover.'"

"My song," he said.

"Yes," said Gemma, recalling his song "And Yet God Has Not Said a Word."

"I can't help it, Gemmy."

Gemma felt her heart break. "You're not a monster, Charlie. Tell me it wasn't you. Say it. Say it wasn't you."

"But I am a monster, Gemmy. You summoned me." A sad smile formed on his face, but he didn't speak. Even though she'd hated him so much in those months before their breakup, being here, she realized that she missed his face and his voice, an echo from a distant world. Seeing him standing there with his broad shoulders and wet blond curls, she remembered the man with the guitar slung over his arm. That man had taken her breath away. Even in this world, declaring himself a monster, he still did.

Her stomach twisted at the truth of it. Tugging hard on the dress, she worried for a moment that it wouldn't come free, until she finally felt it rip. Her heart racing, she nearly ran to the riverbank.

"I don't know where this place is and why you're here, but all I wanted was to see you again, so I came when you called." He placed his hands out. "And look at you."

"What is this place, Charlie?"

"I don't know. I don't think it matters, Gemmy."

"It matters, Charlie. You're killing women, and I've disappeared from the world we know. Aren't you curious?"

"I was obsessed with it, Gem. I couldn't write. The band dumped me. Only Penny and Tamsin stuck with me."

Gemma didn't recall who Penny or Tamsin were, and they didn't matter.

Gemma tried not to panic. Everything she believed she knew was upside down. Her last memory was running down the alley, but what if that was wrong? What if she'd been killed and had no memory of it? But that didn't feel right.

"I don't think anyone killed me, Charlie."

"Come back." He held his hand out for her to come to him. Water trickled down his face, turning his skin luminous as the light hit him. Was Charlie real or was he simply a manifestation, like her mother had been in the hotel? Gemma looked up at the sky, the stars and the ominous red moon of yesterday being replaced by the shining orb above her. Was he the key? Or was he simply a ghost haunting her?

She had no idea what he was, but it didn't feel like he was so different from her. They were similar creatures now, and she'd missed him so desperately. He understood her loneliness in a primal way. As awful as he could be, those edges had softened. If he had become a monster to find her, at least he had come—no one else had made the journey.

Still, she hesitated. If she went with him and he killed her, at least they would be together. These were crazy thoughts, but her head was spinning. She waded out a few more steps.

Even though he looked translucent, like he was made of water, his hand touched hers and it was surprisingly solid, his fingers folding around her own, like he'd done so many times. The memories warmed her. Instinctively, she reached around to hug him, to hold him tight, to take herself wherever he had come from, just anywhere not to be alone anymore.

She looked up at him and knew without him telling her that he killed the women with his kiss. "You drowned them?"

He nodded, water dripping off his eyelashes. "I don't mean to. I just want to kiss them. I'm so lonely, Gems."

She knew this loneliness, felt it deep inside of her as well. For a moment, she wondered what it would feel like to touch his lips to hers and to take in water until she passed out in his arms, until she floated down the river.

She studied his face and touched the scar near his eye. "Sing something for me," she whispered near his ear, the feel of his wet flesh under her fingers. "I miss the music most of all."

Holding her steady on the riverbed, he began a few lines of a song she hadn't heard before, a haunting melody about a lost love. Tears flowed down her face, the agony of a world lost. Like an inherited truth and sorrow, she knew that she would never see *that* world again. She was ready now. She leaned up to kiss him, expecting, even anticipating what came next. If this kiss was the end of her, then she would go willingly. Except it wasn't. Gemma's lips touched Charlie's, and instead of him flooding her lungs with his watery essence, she inhaled him easily, as though he'd turned to a sweet mist, the essence of him returned to her.

As Charlie's eyes fixed on her, there was a look of peace as he shifted and began to disperse into a thick vapor. The shape of him clung to the water's surface as though wishing to linger, to regard her for a few moments more before it folded into the dark Loire.

She reached out, and her fingers ran through the remnant mist of him, like he was a cloud. The sad reality was that he had been nothing but a manifestation of her mind.

"Charlie?" She looked out at the dark water to find herself alone. "Charlie?" A wave of despair came over her. "No. Please don't leave me."

Gemma's hand remained in the water, reaching, hoping he might be able to grasp it once more so she could drag him from his watery home. On her hands and knees, she crawled to the bank of the Loire River and collapsed, alone.

25

Christopher Kent
June 10, 2008
New Orleans, Louisiana

What Christopher was witnessing on-screen was impossible.

Charlie Hicks had never been a part of the cast of *L'Étrange Lune.* Thierry Valdon had banned the lead guitarist of the Prince Charmings from the set. Tamsin Goyard confirmed Charlie was in London during the filming. Then how was this scene happening?

As Charlie spoke from the river, he called her *Gemmy*, his pet name for her, rather than her character's name, *Gisele.*

At this detail, the audience gasped.

As the scene continued, a member stood up and walked out, muttering, "This isn't funny anymore."

While Christopher tried to focus on the film, he couldn't help but notice that everyone in his row, Ivy included, was on the edge of their seat.

The last twelve minutes were strange, and it seemed to Christopher that what they were witnessing was no longer a horror film in the traditional sense, but a larger horror. The two people on-screen were not in character anymore. Gemma Turner, not Gisele Dumas, seemingly desperate for connection, walked into the river, preparing herself to be drowned by Charlie Hicks. As she drew him in for a kiss, the loss and passion between them was palpable. Instead, it was Gemma who absorbed Charlie, turning him to a mist that she seemed to inhale before their eyes. In the final scene, Gemma Turner lay on the banks of the Loire River, sobbing and alone, once again.

It was a breathtaking performance, but was she acting?

As the film made a screeching noise as though it had been ripped from the projector, the audience jumped.

"My god," said a voice behind him.

And then something happened that had not happened before. At least Christopher had never heard of it happening. It began with a few members in the front row who stood, but like a wave, it rippled as row after row stood and the applause began.

The lights went up and he scanned the room, looking to see anyone who might look like Anthony A, but the masks and robes cloaked everyone into simple shapes. The group seemed divided into old and young, the older members' robes moving uneasily back and forth on old joints.

"What the fuck did we just see?" Ivy was shaking. "Charlie Hicks didn't film those scenes. In that thing"—she pointed up to the now darkened screen—"he knows he's dead. We just witnessed a ghost." She raised her mask and looked up at him, wild and defiant.

"Or two." Christopher *needed* to talk to Elizabeth. She'd told him in their first meeting that she feared what they were watching was a film that came from Hell itself.

"Come with me." He took Ivy's arm. "Put your mask back on; you're drawing attention to yourself, to us."

"Who cares?" She pushed him away.

He leaned down. "It's very bad to draw attention to yourself here. Put the mask back on."

Reluctantly, she did as she was told until he led her out the door, where once again, the mask and gown were collected.

"I don't want anything more to do with this shit," she said.

Christopher, used to her outbursts, calmly walked her to the next block. "Yes, you do."

Shaking him off, she spun on the street and studied his face. "You aren't surprised by what we just saw."

"Of course I am."

"No." She stepped closer, scrutinizing him. "I know you and I can tell that you're not. What has happened to you, Christopher?"

"It's just something that I heard about the film once."

Her eyebrow rose. "Do enlighten me?"

Ivy seemed different. Physically, she was unrecognizable from the black-clad woman with the Louise Brooks haircut. The graveled voice was still the same, as though she'd been up smoking and drinking all night, but she now had long, straight chestnut hair. Her face was narrower, more chiseled. The one-upmanship seemed to have disappeared. While she might wax on about how wonderful Los Angeles had been, he could see by the way she held herself, the shoulders a little more rounded and the shine that had been extinguished from her eyes, that she'd experienced disappointments. This Ivy paused to gauge reaction; the old Ivy had charged in without looking.

"I heard once that what we're seeing is a film that came from Hell itself... or something like that."

"That is seriously fucked up." She threw her hands in the air and began pacing. "It's like a virus. I feel like I've been infected by something yet again. You know it took me months to shake it the last time. Why did I do this to myself again?"

It was true. The melancholy that blanketed him for nearly a year after he'd seen the film the first time was beginning to wash over him once again. His mother's memory was close now, cutting at him, the images of her both beautiful and grotesque, like a constant feed in his mind. "Your dad warned you something was off about this film. Why are you shocked now?"

She considered his words for a moment. And it was just as Elizabeth Bourget had predicted. The second time you experienced the film was pivotal. Either you walked farther down the path toward obsession, or you turned away from it. "I'm getting married next month—to a fabulous man."

"Trent?"

"No." She rolled her eyes. "*Sam* is an entertainment lawyer in LA. I don't need this negativity in my life."

He processed what she'd just told him. He was shocked that he felt something stirring in him upon hearing that she was getting married, just like the tug when he'd spied her ring. It could have been him. Right now, instead of scribbling notes about a film that could come from Hell, he could have been planning a wedding and riding a convertible down Sunset Boulevard. But he'd made his choice long ago. He swallowed, and it came out a little too quiet. "Congratulations, Ivy."

"Thank you." Her voice softened again. "He's wonderful. Really. I'm thirty-two. I need to make some changes in my life."

"Then why did you come here?" He stood there in the street with his hands in his jean pockets. In twenty minutes, he needed to meet Elizabeth Bourget.

She looked up at him but said nothing.

Then he knew. She'd come for him. His response came out unexpectedly, like he'd been kicked by the truth. "Oh, Ivy."

Her shoulders lifted as she shook with spasms. Then a fury of tears erupted, and she began poking him in the chest. "I swore I wasn't going to do this. Maybe it isn't the fucking film that infects me, maybe it's seeing *you*. The hell with you, Christopher Kent. I came here to see you. I wanted to be happy with *you*. I loved *you*, but you're empty where it counts. You're an empty, empty person. The truth is that you don't love *anyone*. You're not capable."

Rarely was Ivy wrong, and she wasn't wrong now. He'd missed something early in his life. As a child, instead of love, he'd been focused on survival. Love had been a luxury. While he missed his mother dearly, she'd never taught him how to love. He didn't need scores of therapists to point that out. How could he possibly describe his formative years to Ivy? Living in one motor lodge after another, he had been babysat by off-duty prostitutes who were paid by his mother with reds or whatever drugs she had on her in the morning. He never wanted anyone's pity again, so he just shut them away. But in shutting them away, they had taken a part of himself with them. Somewhere, a portion of Christopher tended these bad memories, like a gardener. He knew she had terrible memories of her own mother, but she didn't let them define her. This was the line between him and Ivy. Perhaps that was why he knew that after seeing *L'Étrange Lune*, he was headed farther down the path, not away.

"You deserve better than me," he said, believing it now more than ever. For she was wrong about one thing, despite how fucked up it was. He did love something more than anything. He loved *L'Étrange Lune*. He loved its mystery. The lore of the film drew him in. Never had anything beckoned him like this film.

"I love you," she said. It came out more of plea. "But I'm so tired of it being one-sided."

What came next, he needed to do. For her. She needed to go forward and embrace her new life fully and let him go. He inhaled. "This is hard for me to say, Ivy. But I don't love you. Not in the way you want, and not in the way that matters. Everything you just said is true."

He looked down at his Dr. Martens just so he could avoid her stare. He could see her jaw tighten. Then her palm connected hard with his left cheek, snapping his head to the side. It had been so quick he'd never seen it coming. Without another word, she crossed the street quickly, falling in behind a couple as she headed toward the crowded safety of the French Quarter.

And as he watched her walk away, he knew he'd lost something, something he never deserved to have.

Elizabeth Bourget sat at the bar with what looked like a gin and tonic in front of her. In all their meetings in the past ten years, she was always early and always waiting on him.

He slid onto the open stool next to her.

"Thank God you didn't bring *her*," said Elizabeth. "I was worried you would." She turned to look at him. "Have you been snuffling?" She scowled. "Oh, don't tell me you *miss* her?"

"Stop it," he said. Unlike Jason, he never minded Elizabeth needling him. Her advice, when she gave it, was like a precious gem.

"Oh my," said Elizabeth, twisting herself further. "Let me guess, she's getting married. You're about that age."

He inhaled sharply. "Beer for me."

"And you regret letting her go." She smiled wistfully.

"She wants nothing to do with the film."

"That's an interesting answer," said Elizabeth with an exaggerated cock of her head. "About the film, she's wise." She fingered a tray of nuts that had been placed in front of her.

Christopher's beer arrived quickly, and he took a too-large sip, knowing that he was going to get really drunk tonight and this was just the start. "Were you surprised?"

"I thought I'd seen everything," she said quietly. "I was wrong."

He slid his barstool closer to her. As he spoke, he rolled up the sleeves of his black long-sleeved shirt. "The first time that I met you, you said what we were seeing was possibly Hell itself. At the time, I thought you were exaggerating. But you weren't."

"That film tonight was the most disturbing thing I've ever seen."

"Elizabeth, I can't sit here with you tonight and go scene by scene like we do," he said. "This film was different. Gemma was in pain. Real pain."

"She's not real, Christopher. She's an illusion you're seeing on film. Don't go down that rabbit hole. Don't go crazy." She waved her hands.

"How do you know she's not real?"

"Because if she's real, then we're truly dealing with evil. I know what I said about a film from Hell, but to really have that be the case..." She didn't finish her thought.

"Wasn't that always on the table?"

"We sound crazy." Her shoulders stiffened.

Christopher considered whether to delve into his past, but he felt he needed to explain his connection to someone who just might understand. "My mom struggled with her mental health, and we were on the road a lot when I was a kid. When I was ten, she got this month-long singing engagement at some hotel outside of Pittsburgh. They were going to put us up. I could see a normal life for us, or at least I had hoped. I thought things could be different."

"This story doesn't have a happy ending, does it?" She motioned to the bartender for a second gin and tonic.

"The hotel had these old celebrity photos on the walls...you know,

Cary Grant... Audrey Hepburn... Sophia Loren. And there was this photo, a black-and-white, but it was different than the rest. It was a photo of Gemma Turner at the Savoy hotel in the Monet Suite."

"Rick Nash," she said, with a smile like pieces of the puzzle were fitting together. "So that explains your film about him."

"Well, my mother took one look at it and she completely lost her shit, destroying the picture, the frame, the carpet, the wall. Hell, she trashed the entire hallway. Two days later, they took her away in an ambulance. She never recovered." It was like a weight off his shoulders to finally tell that to someone. "I had forgotten about the picture that caused it and Gemma Turner, until years later. What I'm trying to say is that my entire life just may have been a course charted toward this film."

"And Gemma Turner." She gave him a knowing, sad smile and shook her head.

"Maybe," he said, suddenly very conscious that he had possibly shared too much. He felt vulnerable.

"Said by a little boy whose mother abandoned him. You're looking for connections to *her*, not this film." She reached over and touched his arm. He respected Elizabeth's opinion. He'd worked hard to earn her respect. "Don't confuse this film with real life. Don't get blurry."

"You got blurry."

"Don't *become* me, Christopher. I'm a lonely woman who has a beautiful Paris apartment and two cats. I'll turn fifty-seven on my next birthday, but my longest relationship has been with *L'Étrange Lune*." She played with the glass in front of her, and he could tell she was considering something. "I have my own story with her, you know."

Something stirred in him, recalling the look on her face ten years ago when he suggested that le Soixante-Quinze were possibly connected to Gemma Turner.

"My mother owned a hotel in the Latin Quarter. Before Gemma sealed her fate by going to Amboise, she stayed with us in Paris. It was a turbulent time during the riots, and an explosion happened in front of our hotel. I thought my mother was dead. Gemma found us. I recall her asking my name." She smiled at a memory. "My mother called me Bette. Gemma carried me through the streets in a sheet they used as a makeshift gurney. Gemma Turner saved our lives. Like you, when I heard what had happened to her, I felt that I needed to do something. I *have* done something. I've talked to everyone who will speak to me, created the only forum we use to communicate, but still it hasn't been enough. We're no further in this mystery, and the film keeps upping the ante, getting stranger, more inexplicable. And I'm weary."

Christopher saw the connection between them. He placed his hand on her wrist. "It has been enough."

"No," she said. "I fear we're just chasing ghosts. You hinted at it that first day I met you. God, you were an arrogant little fuck, but you were right. I think we've been handpicked, which isn't necessarily a good thing. Look at us. It's driven us mad. Hell, you're my only friend."

"That's why we need to lift the cover off, lure whoever is doing this out in the open. Don't you want to know?"

"Of course," she said. "But..."

"You're afraid."

"And you should be, too," she said with a firm shake of her head.

"If we're handpicked, then we have roles."

She let out a snort. "We just don't know what they are."

"I'm going to announce that my next film will be a Gemma Turner documentary. I've been sketching it out for years. I'll cover her early career, her romance with Charlie Hicks...and, of course, *L'Étrange Lune* and her disappearance."

"Might I point out something obvious?" She popped another nut in her mouth.

"That everyone who talks to me on film dies."

She nodded.

"I didn't say I was actually going to make the film. You know I've been back and forth for a long time on the Gemma Turner project."

"Wisely so," said Elizabeth, who was never supportive of his making a film on Gemma.

"Whoever is behind this film loves theatrics," he said. "I can't think that they won't reach out to either talk to me or stop me." He purposely left out that he'd gotten a description of the man, Anthony A, from the Pantages Theater owner.

"You're making yourself bait." She met his eyes. "You realize that you're quite possibly talking about antagonizing the devil himself?"

26

Christopher Kent
July 20, 2008
Amboise, France

The heavy bag hit the ground with a thud. All the years of carrying unwieldy film equipment had caused compression between his L1 and L2 vertebrae, but Château d'Amboise wasn't dolly friendly, so Christopher and his PA had been forced to drag their bags up the stone stairs.

Movietime Online had been eager to hear about his next project, so he'd given a few interviews about his next film, called *The Star and the Strange Moon*. Of course, there was no project per se other than his rough treatment and video from Mick and Claude, but anyone interested in the film would be paying attention to a new documentary on its principal star.

Over the years, he'd formed an almost comical relationship with Louis Lavigne, the commander of the Gendarmerie Nationale in Amboise. Every few months, Christopher would send a note asking to speak to Lavigne, who would send word that no one from the Gendarmerie Nationale would speak to him.

Until last week, when Christopher received a mysterious request from Lavigne to meet with him.

The trip came at a perfect time. The recent screening of *L'Étrange Lune* had gripped him fiercely, sending him on a road trip to a hotel near the Pittsburgh airport to quell a childhood demon. Taking the address from the old bill, he nearly missed the turnaround in what was an unremarkable hotel that hadn't been updated since he'd been there in 1986. The once imposing fountains now looked dated, and the elevator was out of order, and after getting a room on the sixth floor, he pulled his suitcase down what felt like a much smaller hallway with cheap botanical prints now hanging on cheaper wallpaper. The Hollywood star photos were long gone. Why did this place have such a hold over him? It was ridiculous nostalgia. Yet, he stood at the door where it all happened, resting his fingers there for just a moment, trying to feel if the ghost of his mother was still there somewhere in the grain of the wood.

Now he was in Amboise, and he arrived at the gendarmerie offices to find another young man at the desk.

"Christopher Kent here for Louis Lavigne."

The man picked up the phone, and within moments, a thin, gray-haired, uniformed officer came through the doors, looking irritated.

"My pen pal," said Christopher, extending his hand.

The man spoke little English, and Christopher was grateful for all his French classes at the New School. He directed them to a room more suited for meetings than interrogations.

"All of this is off the record, no filming," said Lavigne as he took his seat. "I'm retiring in a month, so I'm happy to have a coffee with you and talk history, but nothing more. I also have a meeting in fifteen minutes." He motioned over to a Nespresso machine that looked nothing like the terrible pots of coffee Christopher had seen at other police stations. He motioned for Christopher to go get a cup.

The Nespresso looked tempting, so he went over to fumble with the machine, irritated that he'd come all this way to have Lavigne giving him time parameters. "You reached out to me."

The man clicked his pen nervously. "Do you want to hear the story you've been bothering me for all these years?"

The espresso machine roared and nearly drowned out Christopher's "Oui."

"I was in my second year as a constable when my boss got a call that we had this missing actress, and everything just shifted to finding her. It was the only time that my boss and I walked out of our little police station to find a sea of reporters. For that one moment, Gemma Turner was more famous in Amboise than da Vinci."

Sliding back into his chair, Christopher pulled out a notebook. "Do you mind? Just for background?"

Lavigne gave an irritated nod before continuing his story, his nasal voice clipped and his words spare. He was a man used to getting to the point. "No one believed that Gemma Turner disappeared into thin air. As a policeman, I knew this was not possible. Fortunately, we had a witness, the cinematographer, but what he told us was nonsense."

"But she did disappear."

"Gemma Turner *did* appear to vanish," he conceded, folding his arms. "You'd have to file a request if you want to see the actual photos of the video. It's a cold case now, so I can't see that it would be of much consequence, but I can confirm that we did have still photos of each video frame. Gemma Turner is running down the alley in frame 400. I still remember the number after all these years. Then, in frame 401, she is gone. Of course, this is impossible. I have no explanation for it, but my job was to find answers rooted in fact, not fantasy. So, for the next six months, we followed every lead. We sent the film out to see if it had been tampered with. The findings were that the film was intact. There was no explanation for Gemma Turner's disappearance on film."

"What other things did you do?"

"We searched the Loire River several times. Finally, we got a lead on a man who had been spotted in the area that week. That man, Jean-Michel Caron, was a known vagrant who had been arrested in Nice for assault on his girlfriend, leaving her badly beaten. The girlfriend did resemble Gemma Turner, so we thought it was plausible that it was a revenge attack, and he was seen around the area and had no account of himself for that evening. We held him for two days but let him go when the evidence did not materialize. As you can imagine, this was an unfortunate outcome."

"That's it?" Christopher was annoyed that he'd come this far for information he already knew.

"What were you expecting? I don't believe in this disappearing nonsense, but I have always had a feeling that it was Jean-Michel Caron who was responsible. We just never found her body."

It was the word *body* that struck him. This theory from the police, while not surprising, was cold and clinical. He never thought of Gemma Turner as a body.

"There's one more thing." Lavigne picked at a fingernail like it was difficult to utter what came next. "There is the business of this camera."

"What camera?"

"*The* camera."

"Claude Moravin's camera? But he's been dead?"

"For five years... I am aware."

The room was silent while Christopher waited for Lavigne to connect the dots for him. This was why he'd been summoned.

"When we didn't hear from Moravin, we threw the camera in the trash." Lavigne tapped on the table, his leg shaking.

"I'm not following you."

"I have thrown that camera in the trash six times. Each time, it is back on the third shelf in the evidence room in slot 652, where it has always been since 1968. My officers won't go into the evidence room alone anymore. They say it has become... haunted."

"But you don't believe in fantasy?" His voice rose in a tone that he knew would irritate Lavigne. As the man's lip quivered, Christopher felt a small sense of satisfaction.

"Well, my officers are a different story."

Lavigne rose from the chair in one brief movement, as a soldier would. "Can I give you the camera? You are a filmmaker. If you believe in such things, you've been pestering me for years, and the camera has been plaguing me for years. Perhaps you belong together." Without waiting for a response, the commander left the room and returned holding a small box.

Inside the box was a small leather bag.

Christopher went to unzip the bag, but Lavigne stopped him, placing his hands over the zipper. "Not here, s'il vous plaît." He motioned toward the door. "Take it away. I hope to not see it—or you—again."

Christopher hoisted the box up and carried it out of the station, noticing fearful glances from behind desks as he passed. Outside, he walked across the street away from view and unzipped the bag to find a classic heavy steel Arriflex 16 BL "Blimp" body camera inside.

"You've been causing problems." Pulling it out of the bag, Christopher steadied the instrument in his hands. It was heavy like a machine gun, with a textured black body. In filmmaking history, this was rather famous for being one of the first quiet cameras that could capture sound and images simultaneously without clunky noise or workarounds. Never in his life had he held a fabulous piece of equipment like this. "You were the last one to see her. What secrets do you have?"

As a kid would, he turned the camera over and over, marveling like he had with his grandfather's old video camera. "You're magnificent."

Opening the body, Christopher noticed it was missing Eastmancolor film in the chamber. The gendarmerie had taken the film years ago.

Back at his hotel, he dialed Elizabeth Bourget to tell her about the camera, but his call went straight to voice mail. He'd been worried about her since the last film. She had seemed more and more enveloped by sorrow.

The following morning, Christopher was back in the square filming B-roll of Amboise to re-create the set of *L'Étrange Lune* from 1968. Scanning the village, trying to see the frame through Valdon's eyes, he knew it had been a perfect location, one that the director had known well. Like so many old cities in France and Italy, the streets and castle were made of stone, and the inner walls could substitute for a small village in the nineteenth century.

On a whim, Christopher had brought Claude's Arriflex camera. There was something about the beauty of this camera that left him unable to leave it behind in his room. It hadn't returned to Lavigne's evidence room, and he had a sense it belonged to him in some cosmic way. The power cord for it still worked, and Christopher had rented a generator. Film was another matter. No one made Eastmancolor film anymore.

Something about the need to re-create that scene gave Christopher a momentary idea to look through the lens. Lifting the Arriflex up on his shoulder, he thought about what it might be like to be Thierry Valdon. Feeling the weight of the camera on his shoulder, he peered through the viewfinder. Then he pulled his head back, unsure of what he was seeing.

"That's not right," he said with a quizzical glance. Looking into the viewfinder once more, he spied them—horses—dozens of them, all black, on the street in front of him, some pulling carriages, others supporting a single man on their backs.

Yet, when he looked up, taking his eye away from the camera's viewfinder, there wasn't a single horse to be found on the streets of Amboise, only tourists bustling about, as well as flower shops and postcard turnstiles and a steady stream of cars.

What he was seeing in the camera was not there in front of him.

27

Christopher Kent
July 21, 2008
Amboise, France

Christopher left Elizabeth several urgent messages, telling her about the Arriflex and what it was able to do. This was bigger than either of them had imagined. "Call me," he pleaded.

A daily email notification chimed. Yes, he kept a Google alert on for *L'Étrange Lune*. Usually the feed was empty, but today's news stopped him cold:

Prominent Film Critic Elizabeth Bourget Struck and Killed in Paris

Christopher stared at his computer screen in disbelief. Scrambling through various websites, he tried to find additional details to confirm the news, anything to tell him this couldn't possibly be true. As he pulled up page after page, each a version of the original article and providing no additional detail, he slumped in his chair. "Not you, too."

Needing more details, he phoned a journalist he knew in Paris and found out that Elizabeth had been struck by a truck while crossing

Rue des Écoles in front of Les Deux Magots. She'd lingered a day without regaining consciousness before dying of head injuries. The police report ruled her death an accident—a man had failed to see her in the crosswalk due to the bright afternoon sun—but the report contained a curious detail: The truck had been transporting wine to Montparnasse restaurants from the Loire Valley—*from Amboise.*

Checking his email, he found three messages from a strange account—Bette Bourget. The three emails each contained a video. One had an email:

Christopher:

I can't shake this melancholy. It's worse this time. Trust me on this, don't see the film four times! It's not good for your health. I keep coming back to our conversation that night. You were right. We can't hide in the shadows any longer. I've recorded three videos for your documentary idea. While I'm sure I'll be fine and we're both paranoid, I'm sending them to you for safekeeping. In the unlikely event that something happens to me, you know what must be done with them. We need to draw the attention of whoever is doing this, so I'm doing it first. Make the film.

—E

In the three videos, Elizabeth told the story of everything they'd discussed over the years, from her connection to Gemma to the first time she'd seen the film and her last, all their secrets that they had been prohibited from sharing with the world. As the video stopped, freezing on her final frame, Christopher closed his eyes. "Elizabeth, what did you do?"

He put his head in his hands. She'd done exactly what he'd prodded them both to do. Driven by melancholy, she'd set out to light a match and drive whoever was behind this film into the light. If he'd had any doubt before, he now knew: Mick Fontaine's and Claude Moravin's deaths were not a coincidence. Anyone who spoke on film about *L'Étrange Lune* died.

Suddenly, he couldn't breathe, needing to get out of his hotel room. It was a stifling-hot night in Amboise. Walking the streets, he couldn't imagine ever talking about the fucking film to anyone again. She'd been his confidant and partner in this strange mystery. How could he possibly go on without her? As the moon shone brightly above him, he found himself wandering down along the bank of the Loire River where Charlie Hicks had drowned. As though something were circling in the air, he could almost channel the despair that Charlie had felt the night he plunged into the black water. Did sorrow cling to things like the rocks and the water? Listening to the movement of the river, he put his head in his hands and began to sob.

Elizabeth would never know what he'd found. She would have *loved* the discovery he'd made today. "What would you tell me to do?" With that question he began to really feel the weight of her loss, the number of conversations they would never have again. He knew this well-trodden path, conversing with ghosts, looking for hints and shadows. "Just give me a sign," he used to say, but that was all bullshit, and all he ever did was feel lonelier when nothing ever came.

Was the mystery of *L'Étrange Lune* just a salve for his loneliness? Had he found another tortured soul in Elizabeth who also needed the mystery to fill a void? Was Aunt Wanda right all along? *Live in this world, Christopher.*

Wiping his face, he spoke to the river. "You'd tell me to start with the camera. As a film scholar, you'd remind me that people used to believe that cameras could steal your soul. Is that what this camera had done to Gemma Turner?" He stopped, thinking of Elizabeth's fate. "And your camera stole your soul as well, my friend."

The next two days were a blur of alcohol and crying.

On the third day, he woke up furious with Elizabeth. "You were fucking irresponsible and should have called me before you shot a fucking film." The momentary anger fueled him to take the Arriflex out to the square, glad he'd spent so much time as a kid learning how to rig the Yashica video camera. While the Arriflex seemed to show another world through the viewfinder without the power button being on, he turned it on just to see if it made a difference.

A sense of wonder struck him as he gazed through the viewfinder. Like a silent film playing in front of him, he saw people in dressed period clothing walking in the same square he stood in. There were horses and carriages. He moved the camera around the square and noted all the different shops and storefronts. Instead of a tourist gift shop, there was a tobacco shop. A cobbler instead of a bar.

Until the power ran out, he stood for hours just watching the people's movements and catching the rhythm of their day. Was it a gateway to another dimension or time? If it was powered on and filming, did it have the power to transport its subject into this other world? Is that why Gemma appeared to vanish into thin air? A thought struck him. If Gemma had been sent to another world using this camera, then she had been unable to return. He kept coming back to the old superstition. Had the camera stolen Gemma's soul and sent her there? The implications of that theory were awful, because it meant she'd been a prisoner over there for more than forty years.

The next day, to test his theory, Christopher took a Coca-Cola bottle and set it in the square. Powering on the Arriflex, he focused the viewfinder on the bottle and hit record. There was no film loaded into the camera, but he wasn't sure the camera needed it. Peering over the camera's body, he saw that the bottle was now gone from his world. Shutting off the record button, he looked through the viewfinder to find the bottle sitting on the other side and missing from his world.

The blood rushed to his head, and his fingers tingled like he was going to pass out.

Had he just sent a soda bottle to another dimension?

His heart was racing, and he couldn't get his breath. Sure, he'd thought up all these wild theories, but had he really *believed* any of them? Did anyone believe wild theories, really? Things like this didn't happen to ordinary people. They didn't *stumble* upon other dimensions. This should have happened to a quantum physicist, not a filmmaker. Feeling extremely inadequate for the task, he thought he might throw up. "Oh fuck!"

But could he bring the Coca-Cola bottle back? Well, that was an intriguing idea.

The camera could probably work the same in the other dimension, but you'd need it to go with you.

"You are not going to do this." Christopher wiped the sweat from his face. Jesus, it was hot here in July. Elizabeth flashed through his mind. The courage it had taken her to record a video knowing she was putting her life in danger. "Yeah, I'm going to do this."

Placing the camera on the tripod, he turned his body so that he was directly in front of its viewfinder, careful to hold on to it as he turned. Closing his eyes, he steeled himself to see if he had the courage to push the record button.

"Do not be a baby right now," he said out loud. His finger hit the record button, and he felt a rush of air. He opened his eyes to find the square in front of him had changed—the cobbler and tobacco shop were in front of him, and the clothes people were wearing looked like costumes. The place had a strange hue to it, like a color television with increased saturation.

"Where'd you come from?" A man on a horse had to veer out of the way to avoid him. "You could have been killed."

Christopher held tightly on to the camera. The fear that he had no idea if he could get back suddenly hit him.

The man looked at his hands curiously, eyeing the camera. Then he frowned at Christopher's jeans and T-shirt. "What are you?"

"I'm sorry," said Christopher, scurrying out of the street, moving to the alley, taking the tripod and camera with him. As he'd turned to the alley where Gemma had disappeared, he saw the man watching him suspiciously. He needed to be more careful with the camera, so it wasn't damaged. Flipping on the camera's power button, Christopher looked through the camera onto the square.

And then it was modern-day Amboise again, but nighttime. The square was empty.

"Holy shit," said Christopher. "It *was* the camera." Bending over, he felt nauseous, and he ran back to the alley and threw up.

The night sky above him was disorienting. Looking down at his watch, he saw that it had stopped. While Christopher had been on the other side for what seemed like minutes, the clock in the square said one in the morning?

Buzzing with adrenaline, he surveyed the square, wondering if anyone had seen him materialize. He needed to be more careful if he was going in and out of worlds.

Tucking the camera under his arm, he headed back to his hotel.

Tomorrow, he'd use it to try to find Gemma Turner.

28

Christopher Kent
July 26, 2008
Amboise, France

Christopher made a list of the things he would need to travel: period clothing and currency of some kind. Visiting a costume shop, he found a period suit that could blend in, although it was a little snug on his tall frame.

Taking his list, he visited a pawnshop and antique shop looking for gold jewelry, old coins, anything that he could use for money in 1878. While debating doing it, he decided to trade the Tag Heuer watch that Ivy had given him in exchange for a pouch full of gold rings and pins that he could pawn on the other side for money. The most prized of the lot was a Victorian sapphire ring. If he got in trouble and needed a larger sum, like having to bail himself out of jail, for example, he now had some reserves.

With the hat and the addition of fake sideburns, Christopher could have passed for an extra in *L'Étrange Lune.*

There was the issue about time. In the antique store, he'd found a small brass hourglass. While he thought he'd been gone five minutes, fifteen hours had passed on this side. He'd need a place to put his luggage and video equipment. If his calculations were roughly correct, if he stayed three hours it would be almost ten days over here.

If the films were any clue to her whereabouts, his best bet for finding Gemma was at the Château Dumas set at Château Verenson. Operating purely on adrenaline now, he took a cab to the edge of the property, telling the driver he was part of a period film. There was a bit of truth to the tale, and the driver didn't seem to care and left him off without a word. As he crept through the woods, he knew that Manon Valdon had made it clear she didn't want to talk to him and would have him arrested—or worse—if she saw him.

Carefully, he placed the camera on the tripod and turned on the power. Granted, it was probably not the best place to cross over. It was a forest without landmarks, so it wasn't like there were horses or carts around, like at the town square. He placed the camera in the leather duffel bag and unfolded he tripod, placing the camera on it. From this distance, he could see the clearing where the lake formed in both worlds, a pungent, almost savory smell in the area where the pines stood.

In the distance, he saw the brick house that was Château Verenson. In this angle it was every bit the imposing Gothic mansion. There was thick mist clinging to the ground, giving the place an eerie, haunted feeling that gave him the shivers. "You're just being paranoid," he said, flicking on the power button, placing his duffel bag over his shoulder, and carefully hitting the record button with both of his hands on the Arriflex. He didn't need to know he'd crossed over. The thick mist was gone, replaced by a tranquil sunny afternoon. The sound of horses' hooves attached to a black carriage driving past only confirmed his arrival to the world of the film.

Placing the camera back in the bag, Christopher headed up the path to the front of the house. He knocked, and after several moments of painful waiting, a dour woman with gray hair in a neat chignon opened the door wide. He recognized her from *L'Étrange Lune*. She was the housekeeper who had killed the vampires with Gisele.

"May I help you?" Her tone was so frosty that Christopher took off his hat and placed it over his chest, like movie cowboys did to honor the dead.

"I am looking for Mademoiselle Dumas."

"She is not home." The door began to swing closed.

He put his arm out to block the door from closing. He hadn't factored in her not being at home, but at least she was there. His heart was pounding furiously. "Has she gone in town to Amboise?"

"Non."

"Mademoiselle Dumas will want to see me. I *need* to see her."

"Well, here I am," said a pleasant voice behind him on the terrace.

It was that voice from the film—and yet it was different—deeper, more playful, almost like it had sounded in the interviews on *The Mike Douglas Show.* No matter many acoustic advances had been made over years, Christopher always thought sound recordings lacked the timbre or texture of the real thing. He turned slowly, almost hesitantly, not knowing what to expect. It felt like slow motion seeing Gemma Turner—the disappeared film starlet—the woman from the photo of his childhood—standing on the terrace, holding a basket of white asparagus in her arm. The sun was in her eyes, and she held a hand up to shield them to get a good look at him. "How can I help you?"

Surely his eyes betrayed him. They had to be deceiving him, because the vision in front of him could not be real. She looked like she'd stepped out of the film. He began to stutter. "It's you. It's really, really you."

Christopher had never fainted in his life, but his legs were buckling now. After all the years of looking at a black-and-white photo of her, it took him a minute to adjust to the scale of her. She was taller and thinner than he'd imagined. Standing in front of him was a woman who would never look entirely like her two-dimensional image, because she was flesh and volume. The dissonance between those two women was both exhilarating and disturbing.

But beyond her physical appearance, this was a woman who had disappeared forty years ago. She should be sixty-two years old, yet she didn't appear to have aged a day. Stumbling and trying to find his feet, he was so overcome that he exhaled and placed his hand to his face to make sure that he was still flesh and bone.

"You're American." She looked at him peculiarly, a smile forming on the corners of her mouth.

"It's *really* you." Those were the only words he could muster, and they came out as breaths.

"I tried to get rid of him," Manon deadpanned.

"Where are you from?"

"Yes, well, that's a complicated answer."

"Is he a salesman?" Manon studied him with an air of curious disdain.

"Let's just say I'm from Pasadena." He let the last word linger.

"Not another cousin," said Manon wearily.

But Gemma's smile had faded with that word. "Pasadena?" The basket dropped from her hand, and he saw her legs wobble.

"Mick Fontaine sent me on a quest to find you." As he spoke her agent's name, he watched the change in her features. Inhaling sharply, her smile grew wide. He felt a little guilty using Mick's name, but he needed her to understand where he had come from and not throw him off the property.

"Oh my god," she said with sharp cry. "You found me."

They stood there, looking at each other in disbelief. Then in one swift movement she bounded toward him, hugging him tightly. He could feel her body shaking. "You've come for me. You've finally come for me."

"What have you done?" In a shot, Manon was at her side, a lock of hair tumbling loose from her tight bun. She held on to Gemma's shoulders.

"No," said Gemma, her hands sliding down from Christopher's shoulders and taking the maid's hand. "He's come for me." The desperation in her face was heartbreaking. "You have, haven't you?"

Christopher had never expected this—any of this. The confusion registered on her face was heartbreaking. This poor woman had been stranded here with no way to get home. With seventy-four other people, he'd watched films starring her; all the while, she'd been a prisoner. He wanted to vomit. "I've come from your world."

"And you're not dead? You're not a ghost like..." Her eyes were pleading, searching, clutching Manon's hand for strength.

"Like Charlie," he said, finishing her sentence.

"How do you know?"

"I'm very much alive, but I don't have much time."

Understanding that he had to talk to her privately, she turned to her housekeeper. "You can leave me, Manon. This man is indeed a cousin—a *real* cousin. I am quite safe with him. I would like some tea, however, for myself and our guest. S'il vous plaît."

Reluctantly, Manon moved but paused at the doorway. "Are you sure?"

"Allez," said Gemma, shooing the housekeeper away. "I'm fine."

"Please sit." Gemma pointed to an iron chair on the terrace, taking a seat opposite him.

"My name is Christopher Kent," he said. "I'm a documentary filmmaker from New York. I'm not really your cousin, but you know that."

"I only have one cousin," said Gemma with a sad smile. "And his name is Oliver."

His hands began to shake, so he rubbed his palms on his thighs to calm himself. "I'm sorry, I'm kind of emotional. In a way, I've been looking for you for a very long time."

"Am I dead?" The dread in her voice told him she might not want to hear the answer.

"I don't think so," said Christopher.

"I guess that's reassuring." She laughed bitterly. "We could walk, if you're up to it," she said, fidgeting like she needed to keep moving. "The path is lovely, plus we get away from Manon's prying eyes. She'll have tea for us when we return."

Removing his jacket, Christopher stood and offered his hand, noticing that Gemma was wearing an odd cotton short-sleeved empire-waist dress. He'd taken a costuming class as an undergraduate and had written a final paper on women's fashions of the late 1800s, and knew this dress would not be in fashion for at least a few more years.

"What are you looking at?" Gemma looked down, alarmed.

"You're dress. It's not correct for 1878."

"Have you *seen* the way these women dress in this oppressive heat?" She tugged at the bodice. "I took most of the dresses and had Bridgette make them short-sleeved and removed those ridiculous bustles. I have two *fashionably correct* dresses if I need to go into Amboise."

"I can sympathize." He laughed. "Did you see my suit coat? I almost melted."

There was a slight breeze, but it was warmer here than it had been on his side. Christopher rolled up his sleeves, wishing he'd brought a T-shirt.

"I must warn you the staff thinks mysterious things happen in the woods here." She cleared her throat and then clasped her hands in front of her as she walked down the path. "You said you're a filmmaker."

"Yes, I do documentaries, not the kind of films you did."

As a filmmaker, he was always looking at light. Dramatic shadows bounced off the trees and the lush field with tall, swaying grasses as they walked to the edge of the terrace. He'd seen pictures and film of this side of the house and its grounds, but it had never looked like this. In front of him were nearly one hundred twisted oaks forming a long canopy. Turning to look back at Château Verenson, he couldn't believe he was standing inside the actual set of *L'Étrange Lune*.

Like a tour guide, she pointed things out to him as they walked. "Chenin Blanc grapes are over there and white asparagus here. There are pear trees there."

"I didn't know you were a gardener."

"I wasn't," she said. "But I rather enjoy it. I get up early, before the sun becomes too oppressive, and weed. I worry when we've had too little rain or too much sun, but enough about that." She turned to face him and walked backward on the path. "How did you find me? I want to hear everything."

"I warn you, it's complicated."

"You can start at the beginning." She stepped onto a stone walk. "What happened to me?" The easy manner had fallen away; her brow was furrowed, and she'd folded her arms waiting for his reply.

"The beginning it is. On the night you vanished, you were running down an alleyway on the set. One minute you were in the frame, the next minute you were not. It was as though you disappeared into thin air. This is purely a theory, but from what I've been able to make out, you were transported into the film *L'Étrange Lune.* Who is doing this, I don't know."

Her mouth drew and she bit at a fingernail, like he'd just confirmed terrible news. "I have a director."

That was news to him. "Who?"

"Name is Althacazur, made famous from the book *The Damsel and the Demon*. I read it as a teenager."

"I have your book," said Christopher, shocked at the information.

"My book?"

"*The Damsel and the Demon* with your notes. It was in your possessions when you disappeared."

"Althacazur is not just a fictional character. He's very real and told me I was cursed and brought here. Fancies himself a director, and if he doesn't care for a scene, we replay it the next day. I get helpful notes on my typewriter, like spirit writings." She pointed to the house. "None of them have any idea that they've done the same things the day before. It's quite lonely being the only person who knows the plot."

"He makes you reshoot scenes?" That made sense with the new footage, but it was macabre. Christopher debated whether he should tell her the next part, but she had a right to know. "The film plays an updated version every ten years. It's become kind of a cult film, like *The Rocky Horror Picture Show*."

She stared at him blankly.

"But you don't know *The Rocky Horror Picture Show*, do you?"

"I don't." Her jaw tightened as she processed what he'd just told her. "He'd referred to the audience, but I thought he was kidding. You mean he shows me in this world?"

Christopher raked at his hair, wishing he'd gotten a haircut before he came here into the oppressive heat. "After you disappeared, Thierry Valdon finished the film, but he died without it ever being shown, and no one knew what had happened to it. Then, ten years after it was filmed, *L'Étrange Lune* was delivered to a theater in Tours for one screening only. It's always a small audience of seventy-five people."

"What do you mean, ten years after it was filmed?"

"The film arrived in 1978," he said rather weakly, knowing where she was going with this question and wondering how to explain the differences in time to her. "Every ten years there is one screening, and the additional scenes—the retakes you do—are edited into the film. Then it disappears between showings. It evolves, like you're still being filmed." He looked around, wondering if there were cameras in the trees. "In this world."

"And you've seen this film?"

"Twice."

"When?"

He swallowed. "First in 1998 and then this year." He put his hands in his pockets and looked up at the sky for courage before meeting her eyes. "There's no easy way to say this to you, but time has continued on my side, but it doesn't appear to have done so on yours. If he wants to retake scenes, then it appears it moves so slowly here that it's almost imperceptible."

Turning, she faced the field, almost appearing to brace herself. "What year is it?"

"2008."

"Oh." Clutching her stomach, she bent over like the breath had left her. "No, that's not true, I've only been here a few weeks. It can't be 2008 at home." There was a wild, desperate look in her eyes, almost challenging him that he had gotten the time line all wrong. "It can't be."

Reaching out, he tried to steady her. "You've been here for forty years."

She shook him off and began to walk in circles, rubbing her neck. "You're wrong. Fall hasn't even come yet. It's been summer since I got here. I've only been here a few weeks. And what about Charlie? What happened to him? He was here." She was desperate for it not to be true.

Christopher paused, dreading the idea of giving her more bad news. "He died in 1971. Either he drank too much and waded out or purposely drowned himself in the Loire Valley in Amboise in despair over your death. I know about him in the river. I saw those scenes."

"They were filmed?" A moan came from her, deep and low like a wounded animal. She bent over again.

"They were."

"That bastard," she screamed into the woods. "Charlie was a ghost then. I thought I had conjured him."

"I don't know what he was, Gemma. He knew things that only the real Charlie would have known. You might have conjured him, but I do think he was a ghost that you were able to channel somehow."

"My parents?" By now, she was defeated, swaying a little. "What do they think happened to me?"

Jesus, he didn't want to tell her all of this in one sitting. This news was too much. He could lie to her, but given she'd been held here for forty years, he wasn't about to deceive her. "They had you declared dead. Your father died two years ago. Your mother, well, she just died recently."

At this news she put her arm out and backed away slowly, but she was shaking. "I need a minute alone."

"I'm so sorry," he said, reaching for her, but she shook him off. Standing in the path, he watched her wade down into the field, where she sat staring out at the tree line. He took in the scenery; the green was... well, *too* green... the lake *too* blue, as though a director went through and turned the knob on the television making the hues deeper. Had someone told him that a set painter painted each and every tree leaf, he wouldn't have been surprised. Giving her time, he walked back to the house and waited at the terrace step for her.

What had he expected? To waltz in here, and she'd be so grateful, like he was a knight rescuing her? His plan had been a poor one. If he was honest, he had never expected to find her. How did you prepare to find a wrinkle in your dimension? Things like that only happened in movies. Instead of helping her, he'd given her one piece of bad news after another. All his presence seemed to do was destroy every bit of hope she'd been clinging to. Guilt smothered him.

"Elizabeth, what would you do?" He wasn't sure she would have handled it any better, but she was more elegant about everything, so who knew. In this journey, he was alone.

Gemma returned a while later and sat down next to him. "Like a fool, I thought I'd been kidnapped."

"I'm so sorry for coming here."

She shook her head and reached for his hand.

"I think you *were* kidnapped."

She looked off toward the lake, and her jaw tightened. "How did you find me? Why did no one else?" There was bitterness in her tone.

Sliding his duffel bag, he pulled out the Arriflex. "This is the camera that was filming you the night you disappeared. It can open another dimension. This is probably the source of the curse. The camera had been in police custody since you disappeared, so no one was looking through it; they thought the film inside was what was valuable. Through trial and error, I found another world in the viewfinder—this world. I think you were transported here. When you hold on to the camera while it's seeing you through the viewfinder, it sends you here."

With a burst of excitement, she grabbed his shirt and shook him, nearly lifting him off the step. "Then I can go home."

Tucked deep in Christopher's duffel bag was the hourglass. When he'd stepped foot in this world, the first thing he'd done was turn it over and secure it so it wouldn't move. He could turn it twice more, but then he needed to leave. Out of the corner of his eye, he could see it emptying out its final grains of sand. This side of the camera tricked you. While Gemma didn't age on this side, he had a theory that she would on the other. "I'm not sure you can."

"No," she said, her voice nearly a shout. "You're wrong. The man said that I needed the key to leave. The camera is the key." She looked over at him with a new sense of wonder. "No. The key is a person. *You're* the key."

Her face fell. There was something so primal about her grief, like a starving prisoner sent back to the cell block. "Why wouldn't I be able to leave? You're here."

"Time works differently on each side. If you were to come to the other side in 2008, I believe you would revert to your original age. Like you never left."

"So, I'd be, what...sixty-two? Do you know that for sure?" But then something struck her and her face fell. "The disclaimer."

"What?"

"Althacazur read me a disclaimer about the key, saying that I..." She struggled to remember. "Needed to check the time zones before traveling. I thought he was mad."

"I think he was warning you that once you cross over, you'd age rapidly. Gemma, what has happened to you is horrible, and I'll take you back if that's what you want, of course, but you should know everything before you cross. The decision is yours."

She laughed bitterly. "So, my choices are, I can stay here, or I can go back but I'll lose forty years of my life in an instant. Everyone I know is either dead or..." She didn't finish the sentence. "What about Mick?"

Christopher looked down at the ground, watching an ant make its way. God, this was awful business. Leaning over, he clasped his hands. "He died in 1998. I was one of the last people to talk to him."

"Oh," she said softly, processing the news. She looked up at him, her brown eyes wet with tears.

He touched her arm lightly, feeling an electricity. He'd *found* her across time. And yet, he felt like he'd failed her. "I'm so sorry to tell you all of this. That was too much for you; I shouldn't have—"

"No," she said, cutting him off defiantly. "Thank you, Christopher Kent, for finding me. No one else cared enough to try."

"Well, that's not necessarily the case, Gemma. I'm not sure anyone else knew where to look. I had help." He thought of Elizabeth. "When you were in Paris during the riots, you stayed with a woman and her daughter.

"The girl. I think you knew her as Bette. I knew her as Elizabeth. She was my closest friend, and she helped me find you. She died a few days ago." He could feel his face flush and knew that tears would follow.

"I imagine that looking wasn't easy, was it?" She met his eyes.

It hadn't been easy finding her. Good people had died in the quest, people like Elizabeth and Mick Fontaine. "It was Mick who sent me on this path. He told me about the screening of the film and that if I figured out who was showing the film, I'd find you. People tried to find you, Gemma."

The truth had taken a toll on her. Her face, which had been so animated and excited when he first met her, was now pale, and the lines on her face looked more defined, like he'd aged her ten years in the hour that he'd been there.

Manon came to the door. "Is he staying for dinner?"

"I have only two hours before I have to get back to my side."

She leaned over, taking his hand and squeezing it. "Then let's have dinner together before you go." Leading him inside the house to what appeared to be a parlor opposite the dining room, she busied herself behind the bar. "Would you like wine? I have a hearty Cab Franc from one of the local vineyards."

She was putting on a brave face, proceeding with dinner. While her external veneer was cool as she fussed over wineglasses, he could see grief in her eyes and the tight pull of lips when she thought he wasn't looking. After dinner, what would happen? He would go back to his world with the mystery solved, and what? He would leave her here, heartbroken. God, it couldn't end like this.

"That would be lovely," he said, knowing nothing about this situation was lovely.

Behind the bar, she poured him a glass.

Bridgette, the maid, popped into the room for a moment, a garment in her hand. "Oh," she said, shocked to find the room occupied and attempting to back out through the door. He noticed that the maid was also wearing a sleeveless gown. "I did not realize you had a guest." She did a little curtsy like Gemma was the queen.

"Is that it?" Gemma studied the maid's hands. "Bring it here."

"Oui," said Bridgette, who held up a small garment. Her face flushed.

"My bathing suit," said Gemma, beaming. "Toss it to me."

Bridgette seemed confused, and Christopher motioned for Bridgette to throw the garment to Gemma.

"I will not be swimming in the lake in a *dress*," said Gemma, making a face.

"It's not a dress," said Bridgette, hurling the garment across the room.

"It has bloomers?" Gemma's voice was a squeal as she caught the small maillot. She turned it over. "This will work wonderfully."

"No one must see you in it," whispered Bridgette.

Gemma rolled her eyes.

The maid threw up her hands and headed back into the kitchen.

"She's an excellent seamstress, but such a rule follower," she said, tucking the bathing suit under her arm. "Let me change," she said, excusing herself. "It will only take a moment."

Christopher hadn't even finished a third of his glass when she returned, completely transformed. Dressed in a sapphire-blue silk gown, she wore a crocheted gold jacket that matched the detail on the bodice of the dress like the two pieces were companions, the colors accenting her shiny hair, which, in the light, was a deep rust. Until that moment, he didn't realize how stunning she truly was. The camera adored her, but it never did her justice.

On cue, Manon opened the doors to the dining room. The tabletop was adorned with dramatic hydrangeas with candles. They started with a salad, artichokes, asparagus, and parsnips served on exquisite aqua-and-gold china plates. He recognized the asparagus from the basket she'd carried in her hands. He took his seat opposite her.

She poured herself a rather large glass of wine, waving off the butler, who was offering to do it. "I'm stuck here forever?" She sank into the chair, looking small and a little lost.

"You *can* go back with me. The choice is, of course, yours."

"Not much of a choice, is it? I think we both know I'm not going to step into that world again." The sadness in her face gutted him.

"You said Thierry Valdon died. When?"

"In 1972."

"Four years after the film ended?" Her voice had a curious tone to it, and she drummed her fingers on the table, like she was working out a riddle. "Hmmm."

"After you disappeared, he became a recluse. There were rumors his wife had destroyed the film after he died."

"That wouldn't surprise me one bit. She hated me, thought I'd stolen the role from her." She snorted. "God, I wish she'd have taken the fucking role instead of me."

Trying to change the subject, he took a generous sip of his own wine. "You like it here?"

"I do, but it's like vacation. You get bored. I miss London. I miss Paris. I miss California. It isn't places, though. I miss my time."

"I suppose you could travel. You've altered the script already quite a bit. What's to say you don't travel to Paris?"

"I went to Paris, mistakenly thinking if I could get out of here—this house—that I could get back home." She leaned forward, all business. "Tell me about the film. You said it is strange. How? I want to know everything. It might help me understand why I'm here."

"It's kind of like *The Truman Show.* You're constantly filmed, and then a new version is shown every ten years."

"Harry Truman had a show?"

"Oh." He laughed, forgetting that she never saw the Jim Carrey film. "There was a movie in the 1990s. It was about a man whose entire life was filmed and he didn't know it."

She sliced her asparagus a little too eagerly. "I bet he was fucking pissed when he found out."

"He was."

Doors opened, and the staff brought the next course: salmon with a beurre blanc sauce, and button mushrooms with sorrel sauce. As he bit into warm, rustic brioche, he thought it was perhaps the best bread he'd ever eaten. As each course emerged from the kitchen, Christopher felt like he was at a Michelin Star restaurant. Each flavor was fresh and pungent, like it had been captured at its peak ripeness.

"Wait until you see the tarte tatin," she said with a throaty laugh, appearing to forget her situation for just a moment. And then it hit him. All those years ago when he'd been so lonely, he'd stared at this woman's photo, and all he'd wanted was to be the one making her laugh, and now he was.

The pressure of tears welled up in his eyes as a wave of nostalgia washed over him.

"Don't you start or I'll start," she said softly, turning the wine bottle with her hand.

After dinner, they settled with a glass of Madeira in the garden overlooking the lake. From a distance, he could hear a guitar playing something familiar. He tried to find the source of it, so beautiful and atmospheric was it. While the melody was the same, it was being played by someone who had never heard the original, so the translation wasn't a copy. "Is that...?"

"It's the gardener. 'Love Me Do.'" She laughed.

"How many Beatles songs have you taught him?"

"I've hummed about ten of them. He catches on quickly."

Looking around, he took the entire scene in. "What you've done here is remarkable." He leaned over toward her.

"I've tried to make the best of it and have a little sense of humor." She motioned toward her sleeves. "I wonder who did this to me?"

Feeling like a detective, Christopher ran through the cast of characters. "If you were cursed, then we should start with the video camera. Who had possession of it?"

"Claude Moravin...Thierry...Manon Valdon?" She shrugged. "Half the crew, really."

"I'm not sure about Manon Valdon. Your leaving did her more harm than good."

She sniffed. "How did my leaving do Manon more harm than good?"

"Thierry went mad."

She cocked her head in disbelief. "He was dying from cancer."

"He committed suicide. You're sure he had cancer?"

"I'm not sure of anything," she said with a shrug. "That's why I asked you when he died. He didn't think he'd live to finish the film. That he lived four more years was not something he expected."

He swirled his wine. "Then he's the most likely."

Gemma nodded slowly, like her thoughts were far away. Then she refocused on him. "Enough about me. What about you? Is there a Mrs. Kent?"

"No," he said rather sheepishly. "I hear that I'm emotionally unavailable."

She stared at him, a blank expression on her face.

"It's a term people use for someone who is—" He searched his brain for the right word.

"A jerk?" She placed her hand on her chin.

"Yes." He laughed. "I hear I'm a jerk."

"I know a lot about jerks," she said with a sly smile.

He focused on the stem of his wineglass, feeling like she was flirting with him. He liked it. He pulled at his shirt. Was it hot? Of course it was hot, it was eighty degrees outside this evening. Even this sun going down wasn't lowering the temperature. Christopher heard himself chattering. "My mother raised me. We moved around a lot. She was a musician of sorts. A singer. You might have known her. Pamela Kent."

She considered it. "No. I'm sorry, the name doesn't ring a bell."

"Oh," he said, surprised that while Gemma had caused such an emotional reaction to his mother, she had no knowledge of Pamela Kent. Had his aunt Wanda been right? Was his mother's relationship with this woman only in her imagination? "I moved around with my aunt and uncle."

"Your father?"

"Never knew him. I went to Columbia film school in New York City. Made some small documentary films, lots of acclaim but not a ton of money. I also got an invitation to see *L'Étrange Lune*. It changed everything for me."

"Yes, well, it changed everything for me, too." A wry smile formed on the corners of her lips.

His duffel bag was on the stone beside him, and he looked inside to find the hour was almost gone.

"I see you looking at that. What is it?"

"An hourglass." He held it up. "I only have one more turn, and then I have to go." He supposed he could stay a little longer, but he had deadlines for editing jobs and rent to pay back in New York.

"Then tell me what I've missed in forty years. What is the world like?"

Gazing up at the sky, he tried to answer the question. How did you boil down forty years in a few words? He told her about the world, including the wars, presidents, and what had happened to people she'd known. As he spoke, he found himself looking out toward the lake to avoid her eyes, like a teenage boy with a crush.

"What is film like?"

"There was the creation of the blockbuster in 1975 with the film *Jaws*. My favorite film."

"What is a blockbuster?"

"A film that shows at a bunch of movie theaters on an opening day. Malls have these ridiculously large theaters. You can order wine and food and sit in lounge chairs. They're usually big-budget films, lots of action."

"You said that *Jaws* was an example of this and is your favorite film. What's it about?"

"A shark that terrorizes a small New England town. And blockbusters usually come in threes because the studios want to get the most money they can out of the franchise—that's what they mean by all the merchandise surrounding a film. So, there's the film, the sequel, and then the 'final countdown' or 'showdown' to end the trilogy."

"A trilogy?"

"Most blockbusters come in threes."

"*Jaws* is your favorite film? Not *Citizen Kane* or *Vertigo*?"

"Sadly, no." He laughed.

She cocked her head. "You have a great smile. You remind me of someone. And your hair... Women would kill for those waves."

He looked down, embarrassed. Was she flirting with him?

They talked until Christopher's voice was hoarse. Both watched as the hourglass neared the end of its sand. Christopher looked out at the lake, thinking how peaceful everything was. The faint sound of automobiles wasn't humming like it did in his world. There was something about the soft focus here—the slow, quiet, deliberate movement within it that was intoxicating. It was as though movements were at half speed and everything from the food to the music and the grounds were to be savored.

"Can I ask you something?"

"Of course."

"What do they say about me? My legacy. It's all that is left of me over there."

"That your performances were better than you were given credit for at the time. You were a trailblazer."

She nodded, satisfied. "You need to go, don't you?" she asked, a choke in her voice.

"Don't you start or I'll start," he said, reaching for her hand.

As the soft breeze blew, he held on to her, and then she leaned close and he pulled her forehead to his and they stayed that way, clinging to each other, like the need to do so was primal.

"You can go with me," he said, his voice a whisper.

She pulled away but met his eyes with an intensity that he had never experienced, like a door opening between them. "My world is gone. You must understand, to lose forty years. I would be lost. I don't belong there anymore." Looking out toward the lake, she closed her eyes like she was steeling herself. "I will make peace with this place."

Reluctantly, he picked up his duffel bag and he began to chew on the inside of his lip. Leaving her felt wrong, but he couldn't stay. He had no idea how long the batteries would last on the camera, and given he was in some version of 1878, he had no power outlet. He didn't know the rules of the camera yet, and he didn't want to make a mistake and get stuck.

"I'll walk with you," she said.

They made their way through the trees beyond the lake. Night was coming, and the trees cast gorgeous shadows as the birds called to one another, and something, locusts perhaps, came in and out in waves of sound. He could not imagine a more perfect evening. The smell of warm grass mingled with the scent of the occasional wildflower.

At the right spot, he set his bag down, pulled out the video camera and the tripod, and opened it up, placing the camera lens facing away from him. Away would focus on the other world.

"It was the camera?" She stared at it like it was a dagger drenched in blood.

"Yes," he said, flipping on the power button, relieved to see it light up red.

"Why?" She wiped at her face. "Who hated me so badly?" Almost pleading with him, she looked up. "I hate to see you go. You've reminded me of who I am... who I once was."

There was a visible charge between them; perhaps crossing over dimensions had given him energy. He took her face in his hands and leaned over, kissing her forehead. As he did, there was a current that ran between them. With any electrical charge, the air around it sacrifices itself to feed what's growing. At the touch of his kiss, she leaned toward him, almost as though pulled by invisible hands. In his life, Christopher had never felt so intimate with anyone and a sense of such pure emotion. "I will find out who did this to you." It was a promise that he meant to keep. Knowing her now, he felt a renewed purpose in solving the mystery of *L'Étrange Lune*. He had more pieces of the puzzle now, but there was so much more work to do.

"I wish you didn't have to go, Christopher Kent." Her eyes were locked on the camera. She was considering going with him, but then her stare broke, and she looked up at him, a sad smile on her face.

He considered his words carefully. "I will come back to you."

"Why, Christopher Kent, I've gotten rather used to you already."

He exhaled like it was his final breath, unable to break his stare, memorizing every curve and hollow of her face. "God, I hate to leave you when I just found you."

She took his hands in hers. "You cannot stay and I cannot go. Thank you for what you did in coming here."

"Are you sure you won't go?" His voice was tentative. It was the last moment before he left, and he needed to know her decision.

"What would you do if you were in my shoes?"

"The choice isn't a good one." And the truth was, it was impossible to put himself in her shoes, but he was also a poor judge. He knew his world, and half the time he didn't want to live in it.

"But it is a choice," she said, her chin raised. "You gave me that, and I'm grateful. Althacazur says that you don't die or get sick here, so that is something at least, right?" She embraced him tightly. Then Gemma pushed away. "I cannot watch you go, Christopher. I'm sorry."

She waved before walking back toward the house and away from him. Then her walk became a run. The sight of her getting smaller as she moved through the forest tore at his insides, but he had to go. He didn't belong here. But then again, neither did she.

The camera was still a solid red, and he took the bag in his hand and stood facing it. Holding it with one hand, he turned the record button on. It was the sound of a faraway truck on the highway that told him he was back in his world. He turned the record button off and let go, feeling a wrenching sadness that both Gemma—and her world—were gone.

29

Christopher Kent
August 5, 2008
Amboise, France

A door opened, a car engine started, and Christopher heard the roar of a dog coming toward him, and then a shot went by his head. That's when he took off running toward the road.

"Don't come back," said a woman's voice in French. He cut a corner briefly to see Manon Valdon standing near the lake with a shotgun in her hand.

Strangely, he was winded. As he got to the road, he touched his face and realized he had stubble, at least a week's worth. Walking the rest of the way to town, he saw a newspaper. It had been ten days since he'd crossed over. Exhausted, he got a room for the night in Amboise. His cell phone had been long dead, so he plugged it into an outlet and found that he had twenty new messages, and his mailbox was full. Several were from Ivy, which was odd, but two were from Aunt Wanda and Uncle Martin. He played the first one:

Christopher. It's your aunt Wanda. Call me, please.

That was dated nine days ago.

There was another that day from his cousin Jason.

Christopher. Dude, I don't know where you are, but you need to call me.

The next call was Ivy, four days ago.

Where are you? Everyone is looking for you. Your aunt Wanda called me frantic. I said you don't call me anymore, anyway, but I think something is going on. She's desperate to find you. Quit being a shit and call her back. Okay? Are you alive? If you're dead, I'll feel bad for leaving you this voice mail message. If you're alive, you're an ass. I'm getting married this weekend; I don't have time to deal with your shit.

Another call from Aunt Wanda dated three days ago:

Chris. I don't know what has happened to you, but I need to talk to you. I'm sick. Please call me.

The desperate sound of her voice sent Christopher's stomach twisting into a knot. The next phone call was left yesterday, from his uncle Martin, who never called.

I don't know where you are, but your aunt is in the hospital. She's been diagnosed with a glioblastoma. Jesus. Has something fucking happened to you? Call me.

Immediately, Christopher dialed his uncle's cell phone. When he did not pick up, he tried his cousin Angela next. She answered on the second ring.

"Where the hell have you been? You asshole. We've been sick with worry with Mom, and we didn't need to worry about you, too."

"I was on assignment without access to a phone."

"You could have told someone that before you left." It was odd to hear anger in Angela's voice. Then he remembered what Jason had said. They all worried that he was going to end up like his mother, who went missing for months at a time only to show up strung out and in trouble.

"I'm so sorry. I didn't know I would be gone that long." It was the truth, but it didn't make the situation any easier.

"You need to get here quick. Mom's been sick for a few weeks, but they just diagnosed her a few days ago. It's aggressive, so she's started treatment, but she's been crazy with worry about you. Nothing new there; she's always worried about you."

It was a rather cutting statement. The joke between Jason and Angela was that Aunt Wanda liked him better than her own kids. He knew that it came from the fact that Christopher had no one else, so his aunt had showered attention on him. That he had let her down when she'd needed him was unbearable. He caught the train to Paris and then flew to Newark and then on to Las Vegas.

Arriving sixteen hours later, he went straight to the medical center. He found his cousins camped out in a waiting room. To his surprise, Jessie was sitting beside Jason, her hand lightly rubbing his back. Angela had a man sitting next to her who introduced himself as Steve. When they saw him, all four exchanged glances, like he'd been well discussed.

"Hey," said Angela, her voice detached.

"Finally," said Jason, sitting back in the chair and folding his arms.

"I'm sorry," said Christopher. "Like I told Angela, I was on a film shoot and my phone wasn't working."

"Whatever, dude." Jason shrugged.

"He's here now," said Jessie, shooting Jason a look as she tried to smooth the situation.

"Dad is in there now with her." Angela pointed down the hallway. "She had her first chemotherapy treatment to shrink it. Then they'll see if they can operate."

"It's aggressive," said Jessie.

It felt strange to be among his cousins, his family, and feel hostility. He could never tell them where he'd been, but even if he could, they wouldn't believe him anyway. Leaving his bags in the room with them, he walked down the corridor until he found her room. The door was open and he stood there, struck by his aunt's tiny frame in the bed.

Uncle Martin spotted Christopher and gave him a smile. At least one friendly face. He braced himself, needing to get over the shock of seeing Aunt Wanda's newly fragile appearance. From a distance, she resembled a woman much older than she was. In fact, she looked like his mother in those months before her death.

What he hadn't been told by anyone was that she was now blind. That had been the symptom that had finally sent her to the doctor. At first, he thought it was just that she didn't recognize him, but when he spoke to her, the delight on her face made his heart break.

"You came," she said, holding out her hands toward his voice. He took her cold, tiny hands in his own—they felt bony, like a pair of talons. Angela had said that she'd been unable to hold food down for three weeks.

"I'll give you a minute," said Uncle Martin with a nod.

"I was gone on an assignment for a film; I'm so sorry. I had no idea that I was going to be gone so long."

"You had said you were traveling for a film. I must have forgotten." Aunt Wanda squeezed his hand, then patted the top. "It's all okay. You're here now." It was strange that she looked beyond him. Her stare was usually direct and fierce.

"I should have been with you," he said.

She tried to follow his voice, and a sad smile formed on her lips. "I wish I could see you, Christopher."

He took her hand and put it to his face. "How do you feel?"

"Don't tell them, but I feel like I'm dying, slipping away. It's not unlike a beach ball deflating. I know that it isn't good."

Closing his eyes, he squeezed her hand, and she squeezed back. He couldn't lose her, too. He wasn't ready to. He had a thought of taking her from this place and flying her to Paris and then driving to Amboise to put her in the other world, where it appeared you didn't age. "What if you could live forever?"

She coughed. "Are you offering?"

"Maybe," he said, recalling what Gemma had said just before he crossed over, that you didn't get sick or die on the other side.

Her voice dropped, concerned. "What are you up to, Christopher?"

He shrugged nonchalantly. "Research for a film."

"Be careful," she said, wagging a finger. "Soon, I won't be here to worry about you. Besides, I wouldn't want to outlive you all, tempting though it sounds."

"Now it's time that I worry about you," he said. His aunt pulled a face. Locating a folding chair in the corner, he moved it close to her bed—it was a tiny, low bed, like a child's, with a sign that read FALL RISK above it. The place had that antiseptic smell that mixed with the very scent it was trying to mask.

"When you didn't call anyone back..."

"It reminded you of Mom."

She nodded.

"I assure you I wasn't strung out somewhere. I was in France."

Christopher stayed for an hour, until he saw that she looked fatigued. Angela had said with the treatment she grew tired easily, and he was happy that she'd been good for an hour.

"I'll come again tomorrow," he promised.

There was a crack in her voice, and she held on to him as he stood up. "You're the only one I can talk about this with. I feel the end coming. Where will I go, Christopher?"

So honest was the question and so frightened was she that he looked up at the ceiling and tears rolled down his cheeks. He was so glad that she couldn't see his face this one time. Trying to lighten the mood, he smoothed her thinning hair. "Oh, there are volumes written and paintings galore that ponder that eternal question, Aunt Wanda. None of us knows." But in fact, he'd seen things—things that had defied what he'd thought the universe had been about. "I've never been one for religion; you know that."

"It was awful trying to get you to church." She smiled at the memory.

"This film I'm working on. Let's just say I think there is more to the universe than I originally thought. I've seen things I can't explain."

"I can hear it in your voice," she said. "A sense of wonder that wasn't there before. You were so broken once, but I heard something that has changed in you."

He hadn't thought someone could so clearly read him from something as simple as his voice. "I think I have a mixture of sadness and wonder."

Her voice caught. "When you're young, you think that you'll be ready for death when the time comes, spent from living. Here's the dirty little secret—you aren't." She shook her head slowly. "I was naive to think that I'd be ready for this. Fuck acceptance. I can't tell them that—but you..." She gripped her chair with her hands.

He waited until she had finished. "Aunt Wanda."

She followed his voice.

With tears in his eyes, he rubbed them. "You saved my life." With Elizabeth, then Gemma, he now knew how important it was to tell a person how important they were to you.

"No, my dear," she said. "It was *you* who saved mine. Promise me something," she said, holding on to his hand tightly. "Live in this world, Christopher. I worry you're slipping away."

As he turned toward the door, he found that he couldn't leave her. He stood in the hallway watching her breathe. He could see her chest still rising and falling. So tempting was it to wake her up one last time, just for a few more minutes of her. But there would never be enough time with her.

He forced himself to finally leave. He took one last look at her before he made his way out through the doors.

Within a week, she had slipped into a coma, never getting to radiation therapy. Angela commented to anyone who would listen that she'd held on for him, the prodigal son, to return.

In another week, she was dead.

30

Christopher Kent
August 24, 2008
New York

On the heels of discovering another world, Christopher Kent came home to face the rather heartbreaking yet mundane fact that on this side of the world, you died.

Routine got him through the difficult weeks following his return from Amboise and the deaths of Elizabeth Bourget and his aunt Wanda. In fact, he wasn't sure when he woke up in the morning who he would be mourning. His aunt Wanda always tugged at him because she would no longer be a phone call away. Mourning Elizabeth was twofold: She was gone, but so was the mystery. He now knew what he was watching every ten years, and the idea sickened him. It was a bad day when all three of these losses hit him at one time.

He had a lot of bad days.

So, feeling a need to do things, Christopher joined a gym, running six miles each morning on a treadmill. Since he'd been back in New York, he'd picked up every job he could to keep busy. He had no new film projects of his own; he was too lost to try to create something new. To pay the bills, he edited other people's projects and put the money in an account to pay his rent and utilities for when he disappeared for six months or a year. He'd made Gemma Turner a promise that he would return.

The special project—gathering sheet music and creating a series of mixtapes on an old Sony Walkman—took up most of his afternoons. On the cassette tapes he'd included every song he'd sang to her. In the grocery store he saw a book called *Last Fifty Years of History* and picked it up, thinking it would be a nice way for her to see what had happened. The box for Gemma grew to two boxes then to three.

Above his desk, Gemma Turner's photograph still hung on his wall, but it didn't have quite the same haunting pull as it once had. He was interested in the woman now, not the image, not the mystery. He knew the freckles that dusted her nose, the feel of her skin, and how she bit her lower lip when she was contemplating something.

After hanging up the phone, he checked his watch. He'd be catching a flight tomorrow back to Las Vegas to help his uncle Martin clean out the house. In what everyone thought was a rather sudden move, his uncle Martin had decided to sell the house and move to a condo.

His plane landed at McCarran close to dinnertime. When he got to the house, it was evident that his cousins had been there a few days earlier and claimed their belongings with neat piles of clothes and used, dirty, and undesirable toys in the garage destined for Goodwill.

He and Uncle Martin went for dinner at a local brewery. The older man seemed out of sorts, almost confused by everything, so Christopher drove. He'd always been grateful to his uncle. They weren't blood relations, and while his aunt Wanda had some familial obligation, this man did not. He'd often wondered if the man had resented taking him in. If he had, Christopher never felt it.

They ordered beer and wings, and his uncle stared off at the television.

"I don't think I can manage the house without her," said Uncle Martin. "I know your cousins want a place to call home from time to time."

"But you have to live here day to day."

"And I can't bear it without her." Uncle Martin met his eyes. "They'll get over it...Jason and Angela. They loved you, but they resented that she had a different relationship with you than them."

"I should have gotten the call and been here."

"You were here," said his uncle. "You were always here. Like I said, they'll cool down. They're angry about their mother and you're an easy target, but you saw her at the end. Forgive yourself."

After dinner, Christopher walked through the garage and nearly tripped on a box with old shoes. The pair of wedge heels that his aunt Wanda used to wear with her summer dresses was on top.

"She'd be happy that someone else will be getting her things," said his uncle.

"Yeah," said Christopher wearily. It felt too soon to be doing an accounting of her things, but no one was going to help his uncle get everything organized, and the man didn't look capable of doing it on his own. "There are more boxes upstairs in the attic. Some of them are your mother's."

Christopher smiled. This meant that the attic needed clearing out.

The next morning, Christopher made coffee, and his uncle kept remarking how much the pot tasted like his wife's. He wondered how the man would fare now, trying to make a new life for himself with a new reality of living without his spouse of thirty-five years. Christopher patted his uncle on the shoulder before grabbing a mug and heading up to the attic. "Later, let's go to the Strip for blackjack."

As usual, the attic was oppressively hot, which was why his cousins had left the job for him. Christopher brought stacks of boxes down to the bedroom and began to go through them where it was cool. Several were boxes of clothes that he recognized from the old videos of his mother and Aunt Wanda. There was a heavy box with water damage and a layer of dust on it; the tape that held the cardboard together was nearly rotted. The bottom gave way, and several canisters scattered.

They looked like film canisters. Opening one, he realized that they were reel-to-reel tapes, not film canisters. The labels were *C&P—Find My Way Back Home.* There were three others also labeled *C&P.* On the side of the box was written *Charlie and Penny Master Tapes.*

Like pieces of a puzzle, the final image came into focus very clearly. He laughed out loud. "I'll be damned."

Penny. No wonder no one knew where to find her. Penny couldn't talk to anyone anymore. She was long dead.

Penny was Pamela Kent.

Penny was his mother.

If Mr. Barnhardt was still around next door, he would have an old reel-to-reel tape player. Grabbing a handful of tapes and a new cup of coffee, he went down the cul-de-sac to the end house and found his uncle's neighbor out on his lawn in his bare feet, trying to get a sprinkler head to launch. "Young Kent, you've grown up," said the man without looking up. "I hear your uncle Martin is moving to Bridge Cove."

"He is," said Christopher, looking at the stubborn sprinkler head. "Can I help you with that?"

"Oh no," said the man, who was now on his knees tightening something. Suddenly, a steady spray of water emerged from the clogged sprinkler. "Aha!" Mr. Barnhardt's red face registered delight. He turned to Christopher. "What do you have there?"

"Reel-to-reel tapes," said Christopher. "I think these are my mother's. Do you still have that old tape player?"

"Best place to play my Benny Goodman music." The man motioned for Christopher to follow him. Mr. Barnhardt led Christopher down the hall to his study, a room he knew well. It had been here that Christopher had lost his virginity to Debbie Barnhardt, the daughter. It was no surprise that the velvet chesterfield sofa that was the spot of Christopher's deflowering was still here.

"Do you mind if I don't stay?" He pointed out to the yard.

"Of course," said Christopher. Suddenly, he had an urge to tell someone about the humor of this situation. The first person that came to mind, simply because he knew she would love the story, was Gemma.

Left alone in the study, Charlie noticed a photo of a dark-haired woman on Mr. Barnhardt's desk. The woman was seated next to a man and had two small children—he recognized one as Debbie. Smiling, he turned on the power and unwound the big band tape that was on the player and turned it on and cued up the first *C&P* tape. There were three tapes, featuring one song each, and the longest was thirty-three minutes. He hit the play button, and the tape began to rotate, but no sound came. After fiddling with the receiver, sound filled the room—laughter. Christopher sank onto the sofa. It was his mother's laugh—the wild, infectious laugh that had convinced him so many times that she was all right. It had been so many years since that wonderful sound filled his ears. He closed his eyes, imagining her still with him. "Mom," he said, tears filling his eyes.

Stop it, Charlie. You have to change the chord, or it won't work. Here.

Inaudible mumbling.

It wasn't shite. It was good. Let's do it again. Please?

And then simple chords came from an electric guitar. From the sound, he knew it was a Charlie Hicks guitar intro. The melody was moody. His mother's voice started first. It was gut-wrenching to hear that voice, lost to him so long ago. He was instantly transported to happy times with her—the Lithuanian ballroom where she sang in New Jersey and how the women made a fuss over him, the little boy that accompanied the singer. He must have been five, and they fed him pierogi with sausage and sauerkraut. He remembered being so happy sitting in the front row, eating the most delicious thing his child palate had ever tasted, while he watched his mother sing with a band in front of hundreds of captivated people. After the performance, she was surrounded by a small mob of well-wishers extolling her talents. He'd been so proud of her. He was so proud of her now. This song was *good*. Had this song been released, it would have been a hit.

A second voice joined on the melody. They achieved a perfect harmony, and he felt like he was listening to recorded intimacy. So loving was the exchange that he felt himself looking away from the reel-to-reel machine. He didn't know what had driven Charlie Hicks to the banks of the Loire River, but from the sounds of the real affection between them, Charlie Hicks and his mother were a couple very much in love. Despite everything he knew that would follow, in this outtake of a moment in their lives, his mother and Charlie Hicks were laughing; the joy in their voices as they worked out a different version of the song and their process—and their relationship—were recorded for history.

It was as though he were seeing the outlines of his mother for the first time. She was taking shape right in front of him. Of course, she'd hated Gemma Turner. His mother was no groupie; she'd had loved this man and written songs with him. Good songs. Songs that, had the circumstances been different, might have turned into hits. Pamela Kent had seen a future with Charlie Hicks. But that all changed when Charlie went to Amboise and drowned in despair over another woman.

"Oh, Mom," said Christopher, feeling the weight of this pain—her pain—like an inherited memory. He experienced the weight of Charlie's death as she had. His mother would have felt like she'd lost him to Gemma. But then she lost herself. Never had he felt closer to her than now. The haunted eyes, the promises broken. His mother had done her best, but she couldn't live in this world. Her world had gone with Charlie Hicks, and for that, she'd blamed Gemma.

But his aunt Wanda had been wrong. There had been so much more to his mother's story. Studying the box, he found that while it had rotted, it had never been opened. His aunt Wanda had never really wanted to know her sister. But the interesting thing was who had mailed the box.

It was a familiar name: Tamsin Goyard.

31

Christopher Kent
September 10, 2008
New York

He probably should have called Tamsin Goyard first, but he wanted to surprise her this time—the way he'd been surprised—the way she'd allowed him to be surprised.

A woman with a bright silk scarf and beige dress looked up from the cash register.

"Is Tamsin here?"

"Who shall I tell her—?"

"Penny's son," he said, cutting her off. When she paused for clarity for a moment, he was firm. "Just tell her."

A few moments later, Tamsin emerged from the upstairs office. Her short, perfect gray hair had been recently sprayed, and her pink lipstick was perfectly applied. She wore wide-leg camel wool pants and a white shirt. "Come on," she said.

He followed her slowly, trying to set the pace. "You knew who I was."

"Good Christ. Can we at least get out of the shop, Christopher?" The elegant woman turned, her hands in her pockets. When he didn't move, she shrugged and breezed past him. "Well, of course I *knew* who you were."

"Why didn't you tell me?" He followed behind her like a sullen child out onto Wooster Street.

She spun, facing him. "Because it was better that *you* find her. That you learn who *you* were. You needed to get to know her, like I knew her. Your mother wasn't a groupie. Hell, I sent the tapes to your Aunt Wanda addressed to you. I tried to put you in the right direction toward Penny. She'd been a *brilliant* musician. Had Charlie had any sense, he'd have seen that she was the collaborator he'd always longed for, not Wren and certainly not Gemma. But Charlie was a fool. That broken ghost who haunted those low-rent hotels and sang at those dive bars was *not* your mother."

"I'm sorry, but I beg to differ. That was my childhood, and if I remember, she was there alongside me."

She frowned. "You know very well what I mean."

"Why didn't you just tell me when I walked up to you at that restaurant?" He thrust his hands deep into the pockets of his leather jacket.

"I didn't *want* to." She turned to face him. He could see her straighten her spine to gain height and stature. "So, if you're going to be pissy, then I'll make my way over to the Starbucks without you. If you'd like to have an interesting conversation about Penny, then I'm all ears."

She pulled the collar of her coat tightly around her neck and crossed the street, her ankle boots wobbling precariously with each step.

The dots began to connect, and he remembered what she had said to him at the restaurant. Christopher darted after her. "You loved my mother."

"She was the love of my life. I still feel the loss of her, probably as great as you do. I found Charlie a drag, but Penny adored him, so I tolerated him." Finally, she stopped walking, needing to clarify. "I mean, that's not entirely true. At the beginning, he was exciting—a rock star and all—but he was a *child*. After Gemma, well, he just descended into a black hole of depression. It was too much for me, but it seemed to fuel your mother. She took his care upon herself like she was possessed. I was scared for her, but I loved her, so I stayed. I stayed far longer than I should have. Charlie began to compete with me for her attention." She placed her hand on the door. "But she stayed with him until the very end."

"There was a photo of Gemma Turner. My mom completely lost it, destroyed it and the frame. That was the last day she was ever any good."

"I see," she said. "And you've somehow attached meaning to that episode?" She lowered her head, waiting for a reply.

"Well, who wouldn't?" He moved his messenger bag around for something to do with his hands.

Tamsin held up a finger for him to hold his thought as they ordered their drinks. Taking their coffees, she walked them over to an uncomfortable-looking Danish table.

"She hated Gemma." He said it more to himself, bits of knowledge finally collecting.

"If she did, it was sadly misguided. Charlie could never love the person in front of him. He loved the idea of Gemma certainly more than he'd ever loved the woman herself. Broken people do that to other people. Then Charlie overdosed and drowned. I think Pamela thought she'd failed him and that somehow Gemma had won, as if that were logical. That's only a guess. Your mother never spoke of him again. Kept that cornicello necklace of his around her heart for the rest of her life."

Christopher recalled her pawning everything they owned at some point, except the necklace, which they'd given him before they closed her casket.

Leaning in close, she wiped her lipstick from the lid of her cup. "I knew your mother for twenty-five years before she died. God, she could be so full of life, but then she could spiral. Wanda and I agonized over whether she should have custody of you, but neither of us could bear to rip you from her. It wasn't your fault. It wasn't my fault. It wasn't Charlie Hick's fault, and it *certainly* wasn't Gemma Turner's fault. It wasn't even your mother's fault. She was sick, and in those days, there wasn't the help, not like there is today. You, however, have attributed mysterious things to what was a medical condition she had, Christopher. It was a *medical* condition and nothing more. Stop torturing yourself."

Tamsin let this sit with him and leaned back in the chair. "You have all these romantic notions of her, but they're all false. You had a better life with your aunt and uncle than you ever would have had with Penny...and believe me, kid, it pains me to say that. I guess I have romantic notions of her as well from time to time. I get very nostalgic for her, but I had enough time for all the sides of her to settle. I have a more complete version of Penny than you do. That's why I wanted you to dig a little and see her as the complex woman she was."

Recalling the beautiful facility in Atlanta that now he knew no one in his family could have afforded, he smiled sadly. "You took care of her. That hospital in Atlanta."

She nodded. "I thought they could help her. I wanted her to have the best, and I could afford it."

"And my tuition at Columbia?" The shape of Christopher's life slowly shifted with each revelation.

She squirmed in the chair uncomfortably, a confirmation.

"And the video camera when I was fifteen." He'd recalled the rather expensive gifts, while his cousins got baseball gloves and Magic 8 Balls.

She smiled sadly. “Wanda and Martin weren’t always able to help you financially. They said you were a fabulous student...and your aunt told me about how much time you’d spent getting Penny’s old videos running. I wanted you to take new videos and create fresh memories.” She shrugged. “Now you know everything.”

“Not everything,” he said. “Do you know who my father is?” He kept thinking about the missing variable that Ivy was always looking for.

She gave him a curious look.

He ran a shaky hand through his hair. “The math doesn’t add up for Charlie Hicks. He was dead five years before I was born.”

Something about him caught her eye, and Tamsin squinted. “I didn’t until now, but seeing you, I might have an idea.”

32

Gemma Turner
"1878"
Amboise, France

After Christopher Kent left Château Dumas, a melancholy set in for the entire staff, even though he'd been there for less than one day.

Manon found Gemma sitting out in the field. "He was quite a handsome young man," said the maid. "Like a rascal I once lost my heart to... that shy smile. And he's so tall."

At the memory of him, Gemma closed her eyes. There had been a kindness to Christopher that Gemma had never experienced with another man. He'd crossed time and dimension to find her.

"He did have a magnificent smile, didn't he?"

"That he did," said Gemma.

They sat side by side gazing out at the lake where Christopher had disappeared. "You said he came a long way to find you? From the window, I saw that you could not bear to watch him leave, but I must tell you it was quite something. He was there one minute, and then the next he was gone. As you know, I'm a religious woman. It's like something they describe in the Bible."

"Yes, I guess it is," said Gemma, not fully comprehending everything that she had learned from him. It would take time to process the answers. "I come here to sit a lot. I can imagine that I'm home here. It reminds me of a field we had when we lived in Colorado. I can pretend for a minute."

"You really *aren't* from here, are you?" Manon looked at her curiously, a hint of a smile.

Gemma faced Manon, the stern house manager with the gold cross. "No, I am not from here, but this is my home now. I cannot go back." Over time, Gemma had begun to feel like Château Dumas was her home and the staff were her family, even Manon.

"Monsieur Kent called you Gemma." The maid's lips turned up at the corner.

"My name is Gemma Turner."

The woman stood and brushed off her skirt. "Mademoiselle Turner it is, then. I'll get lunch started."

As Manon started back toward the château, Gemma wondered if that exchange between them would show up in a future screening. How was the scene being shot if there were no cameras around? While there had been so much devasting news that Christopher had given her—she wasn't going home—time had moved on—her family and closest friends were dead—it was that every movement was being filmed that made her furious. Who had the right to intrude on her intimate moments like that? Curse or no curse, the fact that people watched her heartache for entertainment was repulsive.

Gemma's thoughts were interrupted by a commotion on the terrace—Bernard could be heard shouting. "What now," said Gemma. She ran up to the house a little uneasily, not sure if she'd find another set of vampires, maybe Frankenstein this time. Instead, a horseman had brought a curious package to the door.

Bernard opened the bundle. "What the—?"

"What is it? Gemma peeked over his shoulder.

"A puppy." Bernard pulled a chubby little brown-and-black rough-coated dog from the basket, then passed a note to Gemma. "It has your name. 'Hope you enjoy him. —A.' "

The dog was like the one Althacazur had walked in Paris. Gemma lifted the puppy, solid and heavy like a Thanksgiving turkey. "This looks like a puppy version of his dogs." Was it an apology, something to make the melancholy easier? Well, she wasn't accepting the apology, not when he was behind this circus.

"Strange. Did the man know your name?" Bernard was always on guard now after the cousins.

"Oh, Bernard. This dog is the least strange thing that has happened here of late." The puppy licked her nose. "What shall I call you?" Taking the puppy in her arms, she headed toward the house. "I will call you Elvis."

"You don't want the dog in the stables, mademoiselle?" Bernard seemed concerned. "They pee."

Gemma laughed. "I will be keeping him with me for now, but thank you."

If the puppy wasn't enough to send the staff into a bit of an uproar, the arrival of a strange man that afternoon had everyone in the household peering around corners and whispering to one another. The gentleman was handsome, with a solid build, brown hair, piercing blue eyes, and the assurance of a man as comfortable with the outdoors as he was in a country office. She noticed he wore good-quality boots, but they weren't overly shiny.

"Mademoiselle Dumas?"

She nodded, her arms full of the squirming puppy, Elvis. The name did not translate to the staff, who mistook it for *Elves*.

"Beautiful dog," said the man, lifting the puppy's paw to inspect it. "Is it an otterhound? Quite a strange animal. I've not seen this dog."

"And you are?"

"My apologies." He smiled, taking in the canopy of trees around him. There was an enveloping comfort about him, like a warm breeze. "I am Monsieur Lafont."

"My new solicitor?" She'd heard about this man, replacing that toad Monsieur Batton. If there was choice between the two, then she definitely preferred this man. "Are my affairs all in order?"

"Oui," said Monsieur Lafont. "I should have sent word I was coming; I do apologize. I do have a final transfer of the house in your name. Since we had not met, I thought it better that I come here rather than sending you into town."

"That is very courteous of you. And how is Monsieur Batton?"

"He is still taking the baths in Budapest, I fear."

"Good," said Gemma, not hiding her disdain for his predecessor. "I see you are also a dog lover. That speaks well of your character."

A wide smile crossed his face. "I have my own broken-haired dogs—hounds. They are low to the ground, fabulous for hunting, but this is an unfamiliar breed you have here."

"I believe this one came from London," said Gemma.

"That makes more sense," he said, rubbing the little dog's chin.

"I was just headed to the vineyards." Gemma motioned toward the door.

"I'll join you if you are amenable, mademoiselle." He paused to wait for her agreement. At her nod, his boots squeaked as he turned on his heels to follow her. "I didn't know you had vines here."

The stroll to the vineyard involved traveling over an overgrown path where small, rugged hydrangea bushes and sculpted boxwoods separated Château Dumas from Monsieur Thibault's house as well as a high stone fence. There was a sliver of an open space to slip through where a hedge had rotted away.

Upon inspection of a Chenin Blanc vine, Monsieur Lafont offered his thoughts on their condition. "I grew up with these plants. It's been a warmer summer, so you must look for rot here," he said, pulling a leaf from the bottom.

"You're quite the gentleman farmer," said Gemma.

"I dabble," he said. "A remarkable wine, really. Goes so well with the herbs and the vegetables here in the Loire, softens them."

"Those trees are curious," said Gemma, gesturing toward a line of tightly packed evergreens that blocked what had once been a pathway between the two estates. Gemma peered between the trees onto Monsieur Thibault's property.

"As your solicitor," he said, about two steps behind her, "I must advise against trespassing. It is my understanding that Monsieur Thibault does not take kindly to it."

"You know him?" Gemma spun on her heels, causing Lafont to stop abruptly to avoid bumping into Elvis.

"My... my father knows him. Very bad man. People go missing on his property all the time. You don't want to tangle with him, I assure you." He lowered his voice. "I must insist that you turn back."

"Yes, yes. I keep hearing about strange disappearances in the woods."

"You would be wise to heed the warning." Monsieur Lafont stumbled over his words, gazing at the sky for a moment like he was waiting for a line prompt from a faraway script.

Two steps beyond the line of trees began endless rows of impeccably tended grapevines.

"Those vines," said Gemma, still trying to get a good glimpse. "They're magnificent."

"World renowned," said Lafont, "but he won't sell wine anymore."

"So, what does he do with them?" Gemma began climbing the wall, her shoe finding a crumbled stone to secure her footing. "Come on. Give me a push."

"This is very unwise," he said. She felt a little shove and then was over the other side, the rows of vines even more precise from this vantage.

Lafont was over the wall in one swift leap. He surveyed the neat rows. "These vines are magnificent. They look unreal." His eyes lit up. "Petit Verdot!"

"You know that it is a Petit Verdot grape just by looking at it?"

Lafont plucked a ripened black grape and rolled it between his fingers. Something about this scene felt familiar, and it seemed like he was about to pop the grape into his mouth. She thought about warning him, but then had the opposite thought. If he was a creature created by her mind—perhaps in response to loneliness—then she could compel him to eat it or force him to throw it on the ground. Wanting to test her theory, she thought about what he should do next. As if on command, Lafont stopped and studied the grape as if he was awaiting instruction.

"Taste it," said Gemma, wondering if this act would draw Thibaut out into the open.

His eyes lit up as he chewed. "It is, indeed, a wonderfully ripe Petit Verdot." He took her arm. "Yet, I must insist you head back over the wall. There are strange stories about this place, and I cannot abide something happening to my client on my first day of managing her affairs." He put his hands down for her to step on them so he could hoist her back over. "Please, mademoiselle, I insist."

Frowning, she gazed over the vines as she was lifted over the wall.

As she landed back on her side of the wall, she heard Bernard's voice. "What on earth were you doing over there, girl?" As Lafont's steps landed on the ground, Bernard sized him up. "And who are you?"

"I am Raphael Lafont, the new solicitor." The man put his hand out but pulled it back when Bernard grunted and turned back to the house, shaking his head.

"Well, you should have known better than to let her go there." Bernard wagged his finger. "Mark my words, no good will come from you messing with Monsieur Thibault's vineyards."

Gemma had a sinking feeling Bernard's warning would come back to haunt her.

33

Christopher Kent
March 6, 2009
New York

I don't tend to talk about Charlie Hicks, you know," said Wren Atticus before taking a large, foamy sip of beer that ended up on his fingers. He shook it off. "I was surprised to hear from Tamsin. She said you were working on a new project. I saw your documentary on Rick Nash. You know I knew him well. He did the photo of the band for the cover of our fourth album."

The two sat at the packed bar at the Soho Grand. Tamsin had bent the truth a bit to get Wren to talk to him. There was no project. Oblivious to signs forbidding smoking, Wren Atticus lit a cigarette, and Christopher looked around the bar to see if anyone would dare stop him. Dressed in a black blazer with black leather pants, the man had the entitled air of someone who had once been famous, but the thin fabric at his elbows also said the money that had come with that fame had been fleeting.

Christopher placed a tape recorder between them. This was all theatrics. It was too noisy in here to pick up anything, but he wanted to recall what this man said. "Mind?"

"No," said Wren, looking slightly uncomfortable.

"You have to talk about Charlie," said Christopher. "You know that, right? If you're not willing to talk about him, then I don't think we can do this. I heard you have songs that didn't make it onto the fourth album. Why not rerelease them like some extended album? There is a lot of money in that kind of thing."

Wren Atticus was a good businessman, everyone said that. Yet, in this case, it was something else that was keeping him from releasing those songs. Pure jealousy and hatred for Charlie Hicks. Wren's eyes were gray daggers, as though he were trying to pierce Christopher with them. This man was not used to being challenged. "They weren't in the style of the Prince Charmings."

Atticus's complete denial of anything related to Charlie Hicks had been a blind spot. For a moment, Christopher wondered what the Prince Charmings would have been had those songs made it to the fourth album.

"We didn't need him in the band, you know. Our first manager brought him over from America. We'd have done just fine without him."

"Niles Tarkenton thought he could blend your style with that of the Americans. It's what the Beatles and the Stones did. It helped them evolve."

"We didn't need him," said Wren, like the topic was closed for discussion. "It wasn't our style," he said distastefully. "I *knew* our style. Charlie just came crashing through the studio, telling me that nothing I created was good enough. Then after he dismantled *my* damned band"—he pointed to himself—"he became a self-destructive asshole. What he did to Gemma Turner was nonsense. I thought he was going to kill her the night she left him to go to France."

At the mention of her name, Christopher felt his chest flutter. "Did he love Gemma?"

"He was sure obsessed with her, but I wouldn't call it love."

"What about Penny? Did you know that Charlie and Penny wrote songs together? I have tapes of music that they did. They were good."

"Ah, Penny and Tamsin," said Wren. "It's like a walk down memory lane. I discovered Tamsin. I'm not sure where she picked up Penny, but they were tight. Now, there is someone you should talk to about Charlie Hicks. Penny's your source."

"Yeah, that would be great," said Christopher, his jaw tightening. "Do you keep in touch with her?"

"Nah," said Wren, straightening himself in the booth. "Don't think I've seen her since seventy-five or seventy-six, I guess."

"What was she like? Penny?"

The man looked confused, like he was trying to recall the name of his first-grade teacher. "Penny? Not much to tell, really," said Wren. "She came along after Gemma disappeared. She was always in Gemma's shadow. We used to joke that it took two of them—Tamsin and Penny—to replace Gems." At that, he laughed.

Christopher felt his face flush. No wonder his mother had resented Gemma.

"Do you think Charlie loved Penny?"

Wren squinted in disbelief at the question, like Christopher was the town fool. "How the fuck would I know? Charlie Hicks loved himself. Ain't you listening? No one else, not even his beloved Gemma, rose to the level of love Charlie had for himself. He made her life a mess. Last time I saw Penny was like the third anniversary of Charlie's death. She was distraught and really had started drinking too much. We got wasted. I think we ended up sleeping together, but I can't recall. I will say this for Pens, she was no groupie. She sang vocals on our last album, not the fourth one, but the one that the studio scrapped."

"I hadn't known that." This information was like a punch in the gut. One more disappointment his fragile mother had endured.

Wren kept talking. "We were all disappointed, but I think Penny was hoping it would lead to something bigger. I was hoping I could hold on to something. We all were." There was bitterness in his voice. Wren took a final drag of his cigarette. Had sleeping with Wren been as close as his mother could get to Charlie once he was gone? Was it her last attempt to hold on to that time?

Everything finally seemed clearer than ever. His sweet and gentle mother had gotten on a bus with ambition and hope, not to mention a lot of talent, and had been used up by this lot. Wren wasn't a bad man; he just bumped into people without realizing the damage he'd done. Charlie, too. He resented Tamsin for, once again, knowing that he would come to the same conclusion that she had. She kept leading him around like goddamned Yoda.

One look at Wren Atticus told him everything he needed to know. From Christopher's mouth, his voice, his gray-blue eyes, to his height and his hair color, he was a walking imitation of the man, only with Pamela Kent's curly hair. All the missing variables were right in front of him. This *was* his father, who couldn't even recall if he'd slept with his mother. How disappointed he was with this news. He might have preferred *unknown* than this man sitting next to him. Christopher cut the interview short, not caring if it was rude, and stood up abruptly.

"Penny was my mother," said Christopher. "And while I should talk to her, I can't. She's been dead for years."

"Ah," said Wren. He turned to face Christopher and studied him. Unless the man was blind, he'd see the resemblance.

There was a sudden heaviness in the air.

Placing his cigarettes in his jacket pocket, Wren threw a twenty-dollar bill on the bar. "Fame is fickle. You court her like a lover, but never know what little turn you make that causes you to lose favor with her. Pens wasn't lucky. Neither was I. For that, I'm sorry, kid. It's a shit legacy we gave you."

Wren Atticus stepped away from the bar and put his hand on Christopher's shoulder, letting it rest there for a moment. It was all the man could do for him. And in that moment, it was enough.

Finally, he had answers. The missing piece of who he was finally snapped into place. Had the knowledge changed him in any way? Often, he'd felt like he was made of paper, a cheap imitation of a real man. Everyone else seemed to know their place in the world. While the documentary had given him some measure of fame, it was finding Gemma Turner that had given him more purpose than anything else. So what if Wren Atticus had been his father? That mystery was a footnote in his life. He knew that now.

And the other thing he knew was that what would define him would be crossing over to another dimension to do right by a woman who'd been connected to him from the very beginning.

34

Christopher Kent
March 10, 2009
Amboise, France

The taxi driver was confused when Christopher asked to be let off outside the gate to Château Verenson, but he relented, finally leaving him in the middle of the country road, sticks breaking under his feet as he navigated the path. His backpack was enormous, threatening to topple him over with books and mixtapes and batteries—lots of batteries. Ducking through the trees, he moved toward the lake. Hearing sounds from the château—doors opening and shutting and the sounds of staff calling to one another, he hunched down.

He'd been drawn here. He'd fled here, needed to see her, needed to escape to her world.

He pulled out the heavy camera from its own bag. Facing it, he adjusted the strap on his backpack, then flipped on the power switch.

The woods were silent.

Waiting for a beat, he leaned over to study the camera to make sure it was working properly. From the thick forest, he couldn't exactly tell if it had worked, but it was the barking of a puppy that caused him to release the camera and hit the power button. He reached into his pocket to make sure he had the hourglass.

"Elvis," called a familiar voice.

Christopher put down the heavy backpack and realized he was out of breath.

"Elvis—" Gemma stopped in her tracks. His eyes met hers, the joy in her face so raw when she recognized him. "You came back?" She started with a run toward him, grabbing him and pulling him into a tight embrace.

He pulled her close, folding his arms around her slight frame, and held her, speaking softly in her ear. "I told you I would."

Pulling away, she gave him a good look up and down. "Men say anything. But not you. You do what you say you're going to do." She held on to his shoulders and looked him in the eye. "Something happened over there, didn't it?"

He smiled sadly but didn't answer.

She was quiet as they made their way to the house. "I'm hosting a dinner tonight."

"A dinner? Am I invited?" He suddenly felt a moment of panic as he looked down at his costume. "I don't know if I have the right clothes for a dinner."

She made her way ahead of him, ducking under trees. Since he'd last seen her, her clothes looked like she was making more of an effort to fit in with the times. The ripped sleeves had been replaced by elegant silk-capped sleeves in turquoise and gold. "I brought you tennis shoes." He looked down at her boots. "You can just say they're American. Anything strange, just say it's American."

Her laugh was a mischievous cackle and it was wonderful, like it came from her soul. "And I bought you a suit." She turned back and raised an eyebrow. "So, you'll be dressed for tonight."

He smiled. "You knew I'd come back!"

"I'd hoped," she said quietly.

Bridgette showed him to his room. Even Manon seemed thrilled to see him this time, offering to launder his clothes. Once in his room, he was careful to take out the special twenty-four-hour sand timer that he'd had specially made. It had cost him six hundred dollars, but it wasn't practical to keep turning an hourglass every sixty minutes. By his calculations, he could stay three more turns of the hourglass, four at most. On the mantel, grains of sand dripped down, marking time until he had to return. He supposed he could flip it when it emptied and spend another six months here. The thought was tempting. What did he really have to go back to? An empty apartment in SoHo? Since he'd returned the last time, he'd made sure that his rent was automatically withdrawn from his account, as well as all his utilities. Royalties from the documentary still went into his accounts, and he'd finished three editing jobs. His life could run on the other side without him for a year if it needed to. Subconsciously, it was as though he'd been plotting and planning to come back here. Each step, the move was for "convenience," he'd told himself. But now he realized that like a snowbird who escapes to Florida when the weather turns, he'd locked his house back in "that world" for the season.

From his room, he could hear the staff moving downstairs with the air of duty. In addition to Bernard, Manon, and Bridgette, there were several faces he did not recognize who were busy polishing silver. He could hear pots clanging and smelled garlic cooking.

Inside his wardrobe, he found a black, surprisingly light wool three-piece suit with two shirts. The silhouette of the suit was narrow with the long jacket. He hadn't worn anything this elaborate since the prom. Holding up the white silk shirt with matching white bow tie, he wondered just how formal this dinner was.

There was a knock on the door. He was surprised to find her standing there.

"I don't know what to say." She leaned against the doorframe.

He motioned for her to come in. "You don't have to say anything."

"I meant I don't know what to say, but you desperately need a haircut." She held up shears in her hand.

In his thoroughness to take care of everything on the other side, he had forgotten to get a haircut. The last time he'd been to the barber was almost six months ago, when he'd crossed back to his world. Even then, the haircut hadn't been very good, and he knew he looked shaggy. She motioned to the chair near the window.

He smoothed his errant auburn locks protectively. "Do you know what you're doing?"

"I cut Charlie's hair all the time. My father's, too." She lifted a lock of his hair. "My own hair doesn't grow over here. It has stayed this garish color as well."

"I can bring you hair color the next time. Oh," he said, holding up his finger. "I bought you something at a thrift shop." Reaching into his duffel bag, he pulled out a stack of items and presented them to her. "I have it on good authority that the blue jeans are from 1968, the top, too. I think they're your size. I erred on too big, figuring you could take them in."

She touched the two pairs of jeans and the top like they were sacred objects. Unfurling them, she saw they were the wide-leg jeans that were so popular in her era.

"I mean, you look so uncomfortable in those dresses." He sat heavily in the upholstered chair in front of the mirror, like a child. "I'm ready now."

She put the clothes down and put her hand to her mouth. "This is the most thoughtful thing anyone has ever done for me. I just missed my world so much."

They stared at each other through the mirror that hung over the dresser. From the open window next to them, a curtain blew with the soft breeze, and he slid his hand up her forearm and held it there. "You're going to a lot of trouble for this party."

"It's going to be the event of the season in Amboise. I'm embracing my life here. Next week, I'm conjuring up Paris from the front yard. I'm told I can do that." She glanced over at the hourglass. "How much time had passed when you got back?"

"Ten days," he said. "No one knew where I was. I had messages telling me that my aunt was dying."

"I could tell from your face that something had happened." She began tugging gently on his hair with a comb that she was wetting in a cup. "It felt like a week at the most. And that device over there?" She pointed the comb toward the hourglass.

"Measures one day here," he said, looking over at it as she guided his chin back toward hers. "And six months there. Approximately."

There seemed to be something on her mind, something she wasn't saying. "You didn't have to come back," she said. "You gave me the choice to go with you. You didn't owe me anything more. I just don't want you feeling obligated." She turned his head back to face the mirror.

A lock of long auburn hair fell to the wooden floor. "There is no way I wouldn't have come back. I have my affairs set up so I can be here.... My rent is paid up.... I finished all the work that I had. I have no one back there who will miss me, really." The truth of this hit him. He felt some guilt about Jason and Angela as he said it, but he didn't talk to either of them much anymore. His friends had all dropped away to become occasional beers. There was a world where he could be gone for a year before anyone would notice. When he thought about it, he realized his life was rather sad. He wasn't essential to anyone.

"That sounds like a lot of trouble to go through." She'd stopped clipping, stepping back to look into his eyes.

He wasn't sure what she was saying. Did she not want him here? Did he remind her of a world that was lost to her? She'd bought a suit for him; surely that meant she wanted him here. He took a deep breath. "Do you not want me here?"

She leaned forward, their faces side by side in the mirror. "I was afraid to hope you'd come back." Gemma was so close that he could smell a gardenia soap.

"I will always come back." Then he turned to face her, needing to tell her—the only person who would truly understand—who he really was. "I found out my mother's relationship to all of this—to Charlie Hicks—and the Prince Charmings and to you." It was like a weight had left him. "I'd wanted to tell you about it so badly. Remember when I said my mother's name was Pamela Kent? You knew her as Penny."

There was a beat before recognition registered on Gemma's face, and he could see the corner of her mouth turn down.

"She was Charlie's girlfriend after you. Of Tamsin and Penny."

"Oh," she said, looking both curious and hurt at the same time, something that only Gemma seemed to be able to do. She looked down at the floor and pushed a lock of hair around with her foot. "I did know your mother, but it wasn't in the greatest of circumstances, I'm afraid." There was a hesitation. "Do you really want to know?"

"Yes," he said, ready for truth about his mother after all these years.

"The morning I left for Paris, I walked in on your mother—and Tamsin—with Charlie. They were in bed together. God, Christopher, it feels like that just happened a month ago, but..." Her voice fell away.

"It was forty years ago," said Christopher.

"I had a thought to just go and give Charlie one more chance. I went to his apartment, and well, let's just say he'd replaced me already." There was a bitterness to her voice that surprised him. He had a tinge of jealousy for Charlie and the emotion he caused in both Gemma and his mother.

"I don't think she ever replaced you," said Christopher. "I spoke to Wren Atticus, and he said that the joke had always been that it took two of them to replace you."

"That was an awful thing to say to you."

"When he said it, he didn't know I was her son."

"Wren wouldn't have wanted to hurt you. He was the best of them all, really." She tousled a bit of his hair to see how it lay. "This party is a stupid idea. If you want to stay up here and…just tell me to fuck off about it."

"Wren is my father." It was the first time he'd said the words. They felt strange on his tongue.

Christopher caught a flicker of something in her eye.

"Wren." She smiled wistfully. "The girls all fell for him. I can see the resemblance."

Christopher rolled his eyes.

"Wren is handsome; everyone thought so. Take the compliment, Christopher."

"Wren was handsome forty years ago," said Christopher, not realizing what he was saying. Her face stiffened. "I'm sorry. That was a terrible thing to say. I wasn't thinking."

"It's cool," she said.

Gemma twisted her mouth as if debating what to say next. "Wren isn't who you think he is. He was good to me when Charlie left. What is it that they say? The enemy of my enemy is my friend. That was Wren and me." Gemma turned him around and started to comb his hair. "I saw women come and go. I'm sorry if that hurts you. I don't say it to make you feel bad, but only to point out that their behavior shouldn't take anything away from your mother. I fled London to get away from *that* scene. They used everyone up, even each other. I remember hating Charlie just because the value of a person was what they could give him. We all gave out," she said with a weariness in her voice, like the memory had taken something out of her. She tugged on his hand. "I'm sorry that I got out and your mother did not."

He snorted. "You're trapped in your own horror film and yet you think *you're* the lucky one?"

She shrugged, looking around the room. "Don't you?"

He debated whether he should say what was on his mind. "You asked why I came back. The truth is, I couldn't *wait* to tell you things... things about my life that only you would understand. People only you knew. I even wrote them down." Reaching in his back pocket, he pulled out a folded scrapbook paper, containing lists and photos, like a precious offering.

She opened the paper and read a few lines and smiled. "What is Apple? Like something you eat? They've changed those?"

"No," he said, shaking his head. "It's a phone that you carry with you."

Crossing the room and depositing clumps of his hair on the floor, he searched through the bag and pulled out the Walkman, hoping there wasn't some strange magnetic force here and that it would work. Placing the headphones over her head, he secured them and pushed the play button. He could hear the faint bars of Roy Orbison emitting from her headphones.

She touched the Sony Walkman, her smile wide. "This is lovely. I can let the harpist listen to it."

"The what?" Christopher's face twisted in confusion.

"The harpist...tonight...at the party." She smiled, talking too loudly. He pushed the stop button and showed her how it worked. "I brought you five packs of batteries."

She turned the Walkman over in her hands, the corners of her mouth turning up. This time, there was a pull to them; their glances lingered longer, and there was a need he felt to look away, to break what was a brewing intensity.

Reaching over to his backpack, he pulled out two books, *Popular Piano Songs*, volumes 1 and 2. "Give these to the harpist. It has everything you missed, and some of the stuff is on the three mixtapes I made you. You won't have to hum as much if they can read music."

"What is a mixtape?"

"It's kind of a thing that someone does for you, an intimate gesture. I have the Cure's 'Lovesong,' Roy Orbison's 'She's a Mystery to Me,' and my favorite, God Within's 'Raincry (Submerged).'" He felt uncomfortable, itchy even, telling her this. "All the songs that I told you about so you can listen to them yourself. I've made you two, the ones that I like and the ones that remind me of... well... you."

"Why?"

He stumbled for words, realizing he'd never made a mixtape for anyone, even when he was a lovesick teenager who should have done such things.

She gazed at his lips, like a poker tell of what she was thinking that caused him to lean over just enough to see if she would stay put. Her hand changed position as though it was conscious of the connection. They separated slowly, both studying their hands. Then he slid his around her neck and drew her to him. Their lips met softly. He pulled her close to him and felt her sink into him.

She drew away. "I have a party. And you... need a haircut."

Walking around him, she clipped locks of his hair. She'd done an expert job. It was a closer cut than he was used to, but oddly it had a modern feel to it, like he was an art director on a job interview.

When she finished, she laid the scissors down on the dresser and leaned back on it, her face serious. "Can I ask you a question?"

"Of course." He turned in the seat to face her.

"Was it worth it?"

She didn't need to clarify; he knew what she meant.

He inhaled loudly, not sure where to begin. "When I was ten my mother destroyed a photo of you in a hotel hallway. She struggled with drugs, alcohol, mental health, you name it, but that day she didn't recover. When they came to take her away, we were presented with a bill for the cost of replacing the poster of you—it had your name on it—and I spent my life trying to find the connection between the two of you. Maybe it was a simple thing, and another boy would never have pursued that quest, but I did. There are people on the other side who think I don't live in my own world or think I'm obsessive about you or about my mother."

"I never knew... that she destroyed my picture."

"Until I pieced it all together, I didn't really know what I was looking for, but it led me to you... here. I found you, but I found myself in the quest. There are a lot of people who would tell you it wasn't worth it, but I'm not one of them."

"How long are you—?" When she didn't finish her sentence, he noticed her face fell a little.

He nodded to the hourglass on the dresser. "I can turn that thing two more times."

She stared at the hourglass like it was a dagger. "It's never enough, is it?"

"No," he said. "It never will be."

"I need to go." She leaned down to kiss him. "See you at seven."

After she left, he had a long bath, scrubbing two worlds from his body, then he dressed for dinner. That time moved slower in this world was palpable. There was a calmness like the place was a living yoga class; each and every moment was savored. Gazing at his reflection, he thought the suit fit him perfectly. He spent some time attempting to shine his black shoes to make them somewhat presentable.

The clock struck seven. Descending the stairs, he found the house transformed. There was a stir of voices and activity that gave the room a charge, like the vibe at the most desired restaurant in town. Plates dropped, glasses clinked. As he entered the parlor, four women who had assembled silenced their conversation as he passed by. From the corner of his eye, he could see them straining to figure out who he was.

"You look as out of place as I do." The voice belonged to a solid, athletic man. "Raphael Lafont." The man extended a warm, if slightly clammy hand, and Chris shook it. He was dressed in a similar three-piece suit as Christopher, except this man's ensemble had a gray evening jacket made especially for a country dinner party, like something he donned following an afternoon of hunting.

"Christopher Kent."

"You're American?" The man looked at him curiously, like he was a rare object.

"I am," said Christopher. "New York."

"We don't see many Americans here. How do you know Gisele?" He opened his hands like he also felt some obligation to welcome people to this party.

Something about the man's tone gave off an air of possessiveness, like he was owed an explanation. How had this man entangled himself with Gemma enough to feel a sense of propriety over her? Pascale had been a ridiculous character that Gisele Dumas would never be interested in, and Roman had been a vampire. This man, however, was a different story. This was a formidable leading man. What had he expected? The look on Gemma's face when he told her that he could stay two or three more days here. He couldn't very well expect her to not want a man who was living in her world. Christopher was seized with jealousy at the thought of this man with her.

"We're old friends," said Christopher. "You?"

"I'm her solicitor." The man scratched his chin, like he was contemplating something.

"I thought her solicitor was Monsieur Batton?" This name he knew from the films.

"Oh, she fired him." He smiled like it was an inside joke.

"Yes," said Christopher. "The cousins."

He felt a small sense of relief that Gemma had *hired* this man. He was an employee, nothing more.

"The what?" The man seemed perplexed.

"Time of the Season" by the Zombies began to play on the violin outside on the terrace.

"Gisele has such interesting taste in music," said Lafont, squinting his eyes to place the song. "She teaches those people songs. Odd songs, yet they're surprisingly catchy. Don't you think?"

"I do," said Christopher, marveling that she'd managed to create some Laurel Canyon commune inside an 1878 French horror film set. A type of pizza went by on a silver platter. None of the parts made any sense, yet they worked together wonderfully.

The sunlight was dimming, and torches had been placed in every corner. On the terrace, guests marveled at the taste of red sauce slathered on a piece of bread with cheese and prosciutto. They gathered to form a line dance as the band changed to a familiar folk song that they all seemed to follow. It was like some complicated square dance.

And then he spied her, moving through the guests—there had to be nearly thirty people, filling every corner of the house. A gold brocade train followed behind her with cascades of chiffon at the tail. Soft gold chiffon pieces crossed the dress and were affixed with silk appliqué flowers in pink and green, her hair long and shiny, in stark contrast to the women who had their hair twisted and knotted. He did spy one or two women attempting to imitate her, their hair down and brushed straight with bangs. Yet, she was unique with her laugh, hearty and rising above the dainty titters emitting from the women around her.

"You two," she said, lifting her dress to cross the lawn. "You're being antisocial."

"No, we aren't," said Lafont with a protest. He pointed to Christopher. "We found each other."

She met Christopher's eyes, and it took every ounce of restraint not to reach out to her. "I love your haircut," she said with a sly smile. Close-up, it wasn't just the hair that invoked her real time; she'd drawn the line of her eyeliner outside of her eye in the sixties "cat-eye" look.

"A new lady did it," he said, raking his hands through it. "You think I should go back?"

"Definitely."

"Oh, did you go somewhere in Amboise?" Running his hand through his own hair, Lafont looked back and forth between them, trying to gauge what he was missing. "I'm in desperate need of a haircut."

As nice as he seemed, the idea of Gemma circling this man with a pair of scissors in what he'd found to be a very intimate act made him want to punch Raphael Lafont in the face.

"I need a drink," said Gemma, trying to change the subject.

"I'll get it," said Lafont quickly. "What do you want?"

"Chenin Blanc," said Gemma, never once breaking eye contact with Christopher.

They watched him head toward the bar in a fast clip, eager to return.

"You don't approve of him," said Gemma.

"It's impossible to dislike him," said Christopher, cocking his head and feeling a bit catty. "And yet, I hate him."

"I knew it," she said with a wry laugh.

Waiters circled with silver trays as guests milled around tables stacked high with cheese and fruit. Finally, Christopher recognized "Yesterday."

"Dance?" He held out his hand.

"Out here?" They were beyond the guests, near the lake.

"It's rather perfect."

"Perfectly scandalous, you mean."

He motioned for her to follow him and took a bit of delight to find Lafont standing there with two wineglasses searching for Gemma.

Stepping onto the clearing where guests were dancing, she held him at arm's length, more in the style of dance in 1878. They twirled, and he noticed that she was avoiding his eyes, self-conscious as he was about the energy brewing between them. Her hand was small, her fingers long, as they wrapped around his own.

As they moved, he was surprised by the song. "It isn't really 'Yesterday,' is it?"

"Marcel is quite gifted. He arranges them differently, and somehow it feels better, like they are unique to this place." She turned her head back to the guests. "Now I'll have them listen to your devil's device."

"You're happy here."

"I'm homesick, but we both know that world is lost to me, so I've made the best of this one. I'm not happy, but I'm not unhappy, either. Have you learned anything... about who did this to me?"

"No," he said, ashamed that he hadn't made progress there. The smells of a long, hot summer day filled his nostrils—the grass, the flowers. From a distance, the crowd of guests broke into laughter, causing them to stop dancing.

They faced each other, feeling the eyes of partygoers on them. Smoothing his suit, she smiled shyly at him. "It fits you perfectly. I'd kiss you right now, but it isn't done."

"It's enough to know." He brushed a lock of hair from her face before letting go of her with a bow. "You need to get back to your party."

He watched her walk back into the crowd of admirers. Raphael Lafont's eyes followed her as well, and he took the first opportunity that she was free to give her the glass of wine. The party went to the wee hours of the morning. If he had any notions of formality from 1878, it seemed people partied like rock stars in that time as well.

Hours later, finding he couldn't sleep, he heard a soft knock on his door. Opening it, Gemma stood there in her party dress.

"Are you giving out haircuts again?" A bit groggy, he must have nodded off in his suit pants, and the ruffled shirt was now untucked and half-buttoned.

"Very funny," she said, shimmying past him through the small space between him and the door.

Looking back over her shoulder at him, he recalled the research he'd done for his documentary. *That look.* It was the same glance for the perfume ad that had driven Valdon to dump his wife for the lead role in *L'Étrange Lune.* Had there been no perfume ad, would he be standing here now? Their fates were so entwined he didn't know where she ended and he began.

She pulled him toward her, and they both fell on the bed. He kissed her forehead and then her lips, feeling the warmth of her and realizing there was no space between them. All of the one-night stands were hollow imitations of this intimacy he now felt. Running his hand lightly over her hip, he whispered, "I have no idea how to get this dress off."

She laughed, rolling over to expose her back, and nearly rolled herself off the bed. "I think it has hooks."

"They don't have zippers?" he asked.

"They haven't invented them yet."

"Can't you just imagine them? Or, I'll have to bring some the next time I come," he said, unhooking her dress to her lower back.

As she turned back to face him, her face softened. "You *will* come back. When you say things like you dream of me, I don't know what to do with it. You're like a sailor who is heading back out to sea again. And I'll do what? Wait? I'm not good at waiting; I never was."

He stroked her face. "I will always come back. If you'll have me."

She shook her head. "You don't need—"

He stopped her from finishing her sentence by pulling her toward him and kissing her. He slid the dress over her hips and heard it fall heavily on the floor. Now he could see why period films always showed women pulling up their skirts in moments like these. He pulled off his shirt, and it was just the two of them, their bodies pressed together, him moving inside her.

They never slept that night.

When the light began to filter through the curtain, she looked over at the hourglass again. "I want every minute that you can spend," she said, a slight break in her voice, her skin pressed against his. "Knowing you're leaving is breaking my heart." Her voice was melancholy and flat.

"It's breaking mine as well," he said. "Every hour, just know that every moment I'm not with you, I'm trying to find a way to get back here to you." He kissed her temple, thinking that he could easily turn the timepiece over and over. They watched the sunrise with dread, lingering in his bedroom. She rolled on top of him one last time, and he wished they could be fused in time and space as well as body.

Two days later, she didn't follow him down the path. They kissed and pulled away from each other several times, him making several attempts to leave the room and finding himself in tears. He felt raw, and he could see the toll his visit had taken on her.

On what he knew had to be his last moments with her, he drew her close. "I will be back."

When the time came to leave, he took his backpack and the Arriflex and walked to the site beyond the lake. Setting up the tripod, he sighed heavily, wondering if he had it in him to cross again. Before he took the camera in his hands, he looked back for one more glance. From a distance, he could see her staring out the window. He wished she'd look away before he disappeared.

As if she could read his mind, she turned as he placed his hands on the metal sides of the camera.

And he was gone.

35

Gemma Turner
"1878"
Amboise, France

The morning Christopher left, the staff steered clear of her, sensing her sadness. She wondered if there would ever come a time when he would stay permanently. She could never ask him. It was too much, but she hoped there might come a day. In the time between his visits, there had been some more fine lines on his face, like he'd aged a few more years in what seemed like days on her side.

As she stepped onto the terrace, she heard Bridgette gasp and her arms grow tall with description. "Come quick. There's a giant thing in the field."

"Not to worry," said Gemma. "It's just the Eiffel Tower."

"The what?" Bridgette gave her that look like she might have the fever, except there was now an iron tower sitting in the field beyond them.

"It's in Paris." Tut-tutting her, Gemma stared at her creation with admiration. She was getting better at conjuring worlds that she wanted and had taken to turning the field into a variety of cities. She'd even made Piccadilly Circus appear, complete with black cabs, but only for a minute.

"I've never seen an Eiffel Tower in Paris." Bernard had come around from the stables to gawk.

"Well, it hasn't been built yet." Gemma squinted at it, making sure it was correct. "Give it ten years."

"That makes no sense," said Bernard.

"Gemma isn't from here." It was Manon who quieted them with a new air of authority of all things related to the mistress of the château. "Let her work. I will say that I don't much relish living in Paris, so consider that before you change our entire surroundings."

With the wave of her hand, she sent the tower back to somewhere else. As she walked farther from the house, she noticed a thick mist clung to the twisted oak path. "What are you up to?" she shouted to the trees. "Lovely fog, Althacazur. Very spooky, indeed; I'll just keep walking this way."

Halfway down the path, she spotted something weaving in and out of the trees. It emerged to stand at the end of the row of trees, blocking her way. It wasn't a thing, but a man, wearing the head of an animal. Gemma shook her head, thinking she had to be seeing things.

"What now?" She squinted to get a better look. Was the thing wearing a costume? It reminded her of those ridiculous paintings where the head of a dog sat on the shoulders of a general.

A cold thrill zipped down her spine as she realized who this absurd creature might be. "Monsieur Thibault," she called out. "Is it you?"

Without responding, he turned and walked briskly toward his château.

Gemma ran after him, slowly at first, but gaining speed as she realized he was traveling at a fast clip toward the forbidden grapevines. When she reached the stone wall, he was gone. Running her hands down the seams of the mortar in the stone, she searched for a doorway. Nothing.

When she arrived back at the house, there was a buzz in the kitchen.

"First Eiffel Towers in the field, and now another strange blood moon is coming," said Bridgette in a dramatic whisper. "This is the third one."

Christopher had told her that cinema loved blockbusters now, and they were made in threes called a trilogy, with the last one being the "final showdown." This was the third strange moon.

"This just came for you." As if on cue, Manon handed her a letter.

Mademoiselle Gemma Turner

This was a curious development. Whoever wrote this letter knew her real name. Then it occurred to her that perhaps Christopher had left this for her. Was he saying goodbye and had chosen a letter to break the news to her? Ripping open the envelope, she found it was not a letter from Christopher at all.

Mademoiselle Turner,

A few days ago, you and a companion entered my forbidden vineyard. To add insult to injury, your companion, Monsieur Lafont, tasted the grapes. Your presence is requested at my home this evening at eight. Come to the end of the canopy of oaks. I will meet you there. We need to discuss how you will make recompense.

Monsieur Thibault

"How dare he?" Gemma threw the letter on the table, but it had unnerved her. What could he mean by recompense?

Manon took the letter and read it. "You must be careful. He is dangerous. You know that he has no workers in the vines. Everyone disappears. They say they are tended by the devil himself."

Gemma snorted at Manon's wild tales, yet the sight of her strange neighbor had only piqued her interest more. Dutifully dressed for what she assumed was dinner to sort this matter out, she set off down the path at five minutes to eight. For the occasion, she'd chosen a sapphire-blue gown with gold embroidery—she wanted to look her best for battle.

Walking through the trees, she could see the sun setting a little more with every step. At the appointed spot, she waited. The nocturnal creatures were beginning their nightly duties—the frogs and locusts weaving a complex song that was oddly reassuring.

"You are here," a voice said from the shadows of the woods. She turned to see the man emerge from the tree line wearing the head of a lion. With the twisted oaks around him and the mist, he looked preposterous, like he was wearing a Halloween ghoul costume.

"How could I pass up such an enticing invitation?" She folded her arms, mostly because she was shaking and didn't want him to see that she was a bit frightened. Like the scene with Charlie, this was an entirely new script and one that she didn't quite know how to play yet. No doubt these were scenes for the next viewing of *L'Étrange Lune.* That thought caused her to gaze around the trees, wondering if there were cameras she couldn't see.

"Come," he said, motioning toward his château.

She hesitated.

"I won't ask again," he said sharply, yet his voice was muffled behind the mask.

"How dare you," she said. "I'm not going *anywhere* with you."

"I think you are, Gemma."

The sound of her name stirred something, but still she didn't move. "Who are you?"

"I will give you answers," he said. "This way."

Then a sickening thought occurred to her. Was it a real animal head that this man—that this creature—was wearing, not a costume? If she turned and left, no doubt there would be another envelope for her in the morning. This was her next chosen foe, another monster. She wondered if she'd conjured this one up as well. Considering her options, she followed him down a path to a secret opening in the wall. As she walked through it, she wondered, if she disappeared, would anyone know where to look? She'd heard the whispers that no one invited to Monsieur Thibault's château ever returned, yet no one seemed to recall anyone who'd gone missing, like the information just appeared in the script somewhere. Like everything with Thibault, everyone was frightened, but no one really understood why.

Flaming torches lit the path to a large wooden door. As she entered, it shut tightly behind her with an ominous thud.

The house was something out of the set of *Dracula*. In fact, it *was* the set of *Dracula*. She'd watched the film more than a dozen times. The stone steps where Bela Lugosi had descended were exactly in the same spot. The house was damp and cold, and immediately she felt goose bumps on her arms. The house had a pungent smell of animal fur or hides mixed with a little metallic smell, possibly blood. She held her hand up to her nose and found she was gagging.

Thibault led her to a formal dining room with a ten-foot table, illuminated with gold candelabras. At each end of the table was an elaborately carved chair.

"Please," he said, pointing to a chair. "Sit."

Eyeing him warily, she made her way to the far side of the table, where a silver-plated dome hid the first course. She slid into the heavy chair and attempted to pull it closer to the table.

"Enjoy," said the man with a nod toward her place setting.

"You're not eating?" The idea of eating anything in this macabre house sickened her, and she was terrified to look under the dome. The smell of the place alone was enough to kill her appetite.

"I don't require such things... anymore."

"Then what do you require?" As the question left her lips, she wasn't sure she wanted to hear the answer.

"That is irrelevant." He slumped sideways in his chair like the head was too heavy.

A grim servant dressed like an undertaker pulled back the silver dome to reveal a porcelain china dish with a fresh garden salad of arugula, white asparagus, and truffles. She breathed a sigh of relief.

"It's from my garden." The man sat back in his chair, looking at her plate like he was admiring an art object.

Apprehensively she picked up her fork, and as she did so, a strange feeling of déjà vu washed over her. Something about the way he spoke...she'd heard this line before. An odd thing about this world was that the longer she stayed, the more details about the other world were beginning to get hazy. If pressed, for example, she wasn't sure she could name all six of her films, and certainly none of her costars, with a few exceptions. It was as though that world was sailing away, getting smaller on the horizon. As if forty years *had* really gone by.

He cleared his voice. "You have been called here because you came to my garden uninvited, and your friend ate the forbidden grapes."

She put down the fork. Was this a trap? There was something about the tone of the man's voice; somewhere in the attic of her memory she knew it, that clip of authority with more than a hint of indignance.

Then the idea hit her. She knew this man's identity. "Thierry?"

He ignored her like he was reciting a line. "There are consequences for scaling the stone wall and stealing fruit from my vines."

"Yes, yes," she said, waving him off. "Thierry Valdon!" It wasn't really a question this time. She was up out of the chair and around to where he sat in seconds, peering at him. "It's you, isn't it?"

The animal head looked up at her rather pitifully. To her horror, up close she realized that it was, indeed, a taxidermied head of a real lion. Thierry's hazel eyes peered through two holes at her. The feral animal smell was stronger now that she was closer, and she felt bile rising in her throat. How could he stand to be inside that head?

"What *happened* to you?"

He turned away and spoke like he was dictating a letter, his voice mechanical. "As recompense for your theft, you have a choice. Since you are a principal in this film, I am unable to harm you, but either you must remain here with me or Monsieur Lafont must die. It is your choice."

He looked so preposterous that she laughed. "Stop this now. What are you talking about? This isn't *Beauty and the Beast*, Thierry."

"I assure you, it's not a laughing matter." His voice rose, the lion's chin lifted.

She moved to remove the lion head. He winced and was up out of his seat, like a rabid dog. "Don't touch me. Don't *ever* touch me."

Gemma swallowed and steeled herself. "Instead of making a bunch of threats, why don't you tell me how I got sent into your film? It was you, wasn't it? You just said something curious. I am one of the principals of this film? You know the rules, don't you?"

He gave a nod. "You and I are, indeed, the leads of this world."

Gemma felt flushed as she finally knew who had sent her here. It was so obvious now. "It was you who cursed the camera?"

"The camera?" He looked confused, and the animal head cocked heavily to one side.

"The video camera was cursed. It sent me here."

"The camera, of course." He gazed off in the distance like the details were finally connecting for him. "Oh, Gemma. After I talked to you that day in the cave, I met a man at the Amboise Hotel bar. He was like a man from another time, with flowing hair and wire-rimmed sunglasses. He spoke strangely."

"Althacazur," said Gemma.

"I was in a state of despair over my health, my mortality," said the creature, winding up for a monologue. "Quite frankly, I was drunk. This man asked me what I wanted most in the world. I'd just read the notes that you'd written on my script, the one you'd slipped under my door. How I hated you then. You were always thrusting them in my face." The head looked down at the floor as though he were ashamed. "Your version of the film was better than mine."

Gemma strained to hear him, so muffled was his voice inside the head.

"There was an air about him—something told me that this man could alter the universe. I know that sounds strange now, but I needed to confess to him my fears, so I did. I told him about dying and you besting me with your version of what should have been my story and mine alone. My legacy."

"You were jealous?" Gemma pulled back to take him in. "Of *me*?"

"You had life and talent. Everything that was slipping from me."

"Oh, Thierry," said Gemma, wanting to hate him, but finding the whole spectacle pitiful.

"I asked him to let me finish the film. I may have mentioned something about wanting to live forever. You can't blame me, with the death sentence I was given. I also might have told him that I wanted you to go away."

"Let me guess... you added *forever*?"

The silence affirmed her suspicion.

"I see," she said. Surprisingly, she was calm listening to this news of how he had doomed her. This man had been stupid. "What did he ask in return?"

The creature sat there. Mute.

"You don't know, do you?"

"It's a little fuzzy."

"I'll fill you in. In addition to me being part of the deal, he also took your film." One thing Gemma still recalled clearly was how she'd wanted to be this man's Josette Day. She wanted to write her own film, and it seemed she'd gotten her wish as well. Now they were acting a scene from *Beauty and the Beast.* Althacazur certainly had a sense of humor.

She poked his shoulder, hard, nearly taking her fist out to hit him. "You stupid, stupid man. Look what you've done to us."

He endured her pummeling, like he deserved it. "I never thought it was *real*! I thought he was as drunk as I." He shook his raggedy lion's mane. "Who would ever think it was a real ceremony?"

She pulled back, her eyes wide. "What do you mean... *ceremony*?"

"I cut myself," he said. "I cut myself on the wineglass." His voice became clearer as he recalled old memories. "My blood dripped into the glass, and he...he *drank* it. How could I have forgotten that detail all this time?" He looked up at her. "It's like you've awakened something in me."

"That creature, Althacazur, was not a drunk in a bar. He was a demon. You sealed the curse," said Gemma, "and then I disappeared."

"At first, I thought you had left or had been abducted."

"Abducted?" She looked at him incredulously.

"Well, I didn't know what to believe. No one did. We all walked around the set not knowing what to do. But the longer it went on, I *knew* that I had been responsible for your disappearance. For months, I went back to the Amboise Hotel to find the man again, but he never reappeared. I convinced myself that he hadn't been real and that you had just left." Thierry fumbled with his hands almost nervously. Finally, he stood, trying to compose himself, and walked over to the fireplace in what appeared to be an attempt to get warm.

It stung, that he could so easily arrange her out of his mind for his convenience. "Well, you managed to finish the film without me. It was a horrible film, you know. I told you that from the beginning."

There was a flash of something in his eyes, contempt for her yet. "I know what you told me about the script. By this time, the frenzy over your disappearance had begun to die down. I hoped the film would just disappear. And I waited to die—strange as it sounds—I was finally ready. The guilt of you was too much, but death didn't come."

"Well, you'd asked to live forever."

It was hard to see him pitying himself while he'd been safe in their world and she'd been wandering about Château Dumas in a bewildered state.

"I didn't leave the house for years, waiting for death. Instead of being a masterpiece, my film was cursed.... Everything that touched it was tainted. In the end, though, I got my wish. I got to live forever."

He took the animal head off.

The smell of rot and putrefying flesh overtook the room, and Gemma found she was woozy from the stench. Once again, she put her hand to her nose to shield herself from the odor. At the sight of him, Gemma gasped. That Thierry had been felled by a gunshot wound was clear. One side of his head was open and oozing thick, dark blood as if the wound was fresh.

"What happened to you? Were you shot?"

"Isn't it obvious?" he said with a sad laugh. "I have become my monster. The wound never heals. I crave blood all the time to replace what is lost. This odd man, this master of our entwined fates, well, he didn't specify *how* I would live forever. When I died over there, I found myself here. A living hell is what it is."

"The people in the village who don't return..."

"It's true, they are buried in my garden," he said. "And it grows beautifully for their sacrifice."

Thinking that she had almost tasted asparagus from his garden, Gemma nearly retched, wiping her mouth.

"But the blood is never enough. I need more and more." The taxidermied lion head fell to the floor, and Thierry put his own damaged head in his hands and began to sob. Abruptly, he stopped and seemed to compose himself. He lifted his finger. "Monsieur Lafont ate one of the forbidden grapes, and so he must die. It is required. You can, of course, save him by staying here with me for eternity."

"This is absurd, Thierry. I owe you nothing. We aren't characters in a Cocteau film."

"Oh, but we are, Gemma," he said flatly. "If you will not stay, then he must die."

"No," said Gemma, growing impatient with Thierry and his self-pity. "He will not."

"Then you must live with me."

"No," she said, thinking she could not stand the sight or smell of him. "I will not do that, either. After what you've done, I owe you nothing. We're even."

He sighed. "Gemma…do not argue. This is how it must be. This is *my* story."

Gemma turned to walk through the doors and leave the house, but she stopped at the last minute and turned to charge at him like a bull, suddenly infuriated. "How dare you threaten me after you condemned me to live in this hell because of your petty jealousy?"

"And my film—my legacy—was ruined because of it."

"My *life* was ruined. Am I supposed to feel bad for you? This hell is entirely of your own making, not mine. You do not get to make *any* further demands on me."

She walked out the door, finding the stone path and secret door with ease. Finally, she had the answers she'd wanted. She was damned if she would buckle to Thierry Valdon again. They were equals here, and he had no right to make demands on her.

At home, she collapsed into her bed, exhausted.

The next morning, she was awakened by a frantic pounding on her bedroom door. "Mademoiselle Turner." It was Manon. "Come quickly."

Disoriented, Gemma sat up. Her room was still dark, but she could see a glimmer of light through the curtains. Dressing quickly, Gemma rushed downstairs just as she heard screaming out by the path.

The entire scene felt unreal. From a distance, she saw a man hanging from one of the big oak trees. Like a slow-motion film, Bernard raced ahead of her carrying a tall ladder. Manon held it as Bernard attempted to cut the man down. Bridgette stood in the center of the pathway screaming, but Gemma couldn't hear her. She couldn't hear any of them.

She didn't need to wonder the man's identity. Thierry had warned her, but foolishly she had not heeded his words. Not only that, but she'd also compelled Laftont to eat the grape. For what reason? To awaken the monster? Well, she had succeeded there. When she got to the tree, she saw Raphael Lafont lying motionless on the ground.

"He's been drained of blood," said Bernard, pushing his cap back from his sweaty head, alarm in his voice. "Are the cousins back?"

"No," said Gemma, pushing past them and making a direct path toward Monsieur Thibault's château. From a distance, she could hear Bernard telling her not to go there.

Sweet Raphael Lafont was not a character from the original script. She had created him as a friend to her in this world, and it was her fault he was dead, and she had killed him. Thierry had no right to condemn her—or anyone who was her friend—to anything. He'd gotten them all in this mess. "You selfish bastard," she screamed, loud enough for him to hear.

The stone wall was cleverly built to hide the secret passageway, but as the sun began to rise, Gemma could see the outline of a door. Finding no handle, she pushed through it, surprised that it gave way so easily. She made her way to the house, deceptively sunny and inviting within the lush forbidden garden. Monsieur Thibault stood at the door. Today, he was wearing the head of a bull.

"I warned you," he said, like he was reciting a rote weather prediction. "But you didn't listen."

"You are not a monster, Thierry." She brushed past him, recalling that not too long ago, she'd said the same thing to Charlie in the river—and she'd been wrong then, too.

"How wrong you are." The man's voice was flat. "I am the *very* monster in my own film. One should really read the fine print on all blood oaths."

This entire thing was so preposterous that it had to be a dream of some sort. Perhaps she'd dreamed everything—the cousins, Charlie in the river—even Christopher. She circled Thierry as he stood in the foyer, like a child taunting another in the schoolyard. "You know they show the film, don't you? Every ten years. They add to it and show it to seventy-five people. This whole charade you've created has become high theater."

Thierry turned his head, awkward with the weight of the bull's skull. "I never wanted the film to be shown. Ever. Not the way it was."

"Oh, but they do. You did more than sign yourself up to be a monster...you gave *him L'Étrange Lune* to do with as he saw fit. So, yes, you are indeed a monster in your own film. And now everyone will see it. Everything around us"—Gemma gestured wildly—"is filmed. Including this scene." She took a deep breath, trying not to cry. Pointing at herself, she said, "I am to blame for Raphael Lafont's death, but you won't kill another person, Thierry Valdon. Not in *my* story."

"I cannot help it," he said. "It is the thirst."

Realizing that she was still in her nightdress, Gemma backed away from him. "I'm assuming my debt to you has been paid in full."

"Sadly, yes," said Thibault. "For what it's worth, I took no joy in it. I drained him before I hung him there. It was quick."

Gemma thought she would vomit. "No, Thierry, it *doesn't* make it better."

"It's madness," said Manon.

"He will kill you," Bridgette squealed.

"Yes, yes," said Gemma, pushing back her morning coffee, barely able to hold it down. The servants now gathered with her each morning for breakfast. The idea of sitting alone in that room had seemed increasingly ludicrous, so she'd changed it up and instated a morning meeting to ask everyone for daily ideas about the house.

"Monsieur Lafont was a good man," said Bridgette with a shake of her head.

Gemma closed her eyes, the guilt of Lafont almost too much to bear. Could she just conjure another? Somehow she felt she could, but he would be a copy of a character, a recast.

Footsteps on the floor announced Bernard's arrival. He threw several pairs of silver animal shackles on the table.

"They're perfect," said Gemma, looking from the shiny chains to her groundsman. Picking one up, she pulled on it, judging its strength. "Thank you."

Bernard shook his head gravely. "Don't thank me, mademoiselle. This is a very bad idea."

"Tomorrow is the strange moon," said Bridgette. "You will need to be careful."

Bernard scratched his head. "Why Monsieur Lafont?"

"You saw us scale the wall, and Lafont ate one of his grapes," said Gemma, waiting for the wave of judgment across the faces of the staff. Instead, they looked down at the floor. She heard Bernard snort.

"I know, I know," said Gemma, holding her hand up. "You told me."

Bernard shook his sunburned head. "How many times, mademoiselle, have I warned you to stay away from there?"

"Bernard," said Manon, her voice rising. "You forget your place. She is your employer, not a child, and certainly not *your* child."

"She is to me," he said. "Gisele, you are like a daughter to me."

"Her name is Gemma," said Manon, her eyes meeting Gemma's. "Gemma Turner."

Touched by his words, Gemma reached over and squeezed his Bernard's hand. "I will be careful. He cannot touch me."

"He lies," barked Bernard.

"Oh, that he does," said Gemma. "But in this case, he is not wrong. We are the principals."

"You're what?" Manon leaned forward. Gemma noticed that she was wearing the crucifix again.

"It doesn't matter." Gemma stood. "I have a plan."

"Hope it's better than the last one," said Bernard under his breath but just loud enough for everyone to hear.

If what she knew was correct, then she had a secret weapon. The poetry of it was delicious. The others would be worried about her, but they didn't have to be. Now that Gemma knew the truth, she couldn't let him continue. That night, on the very typewriter that Thierry had used to mock her, she wound a new clean sheet of plain parchment. On it she keyed:

> To his surprise, on the night of the blood moon, Monsieur Thibault felt strangely compelled to visit the wine cave near Château Dumas.

Satisfied with the typed lines, Gemma made her way back down to the foyer and out the door. She hurried past the grass outline of where

Raphael Lafont's body had lain. At the wine cave, she found a puzzled Thierry Valdon standing at the entrance, donning the head of a goat. A rush of satisfaction hit her as she knew he would never have come if she'd merely asked. This *was* her story, and he was a character, nothing more.

"I felt strangely compelled to visit the wine cave," he said, confused. "I didn't even know where it was. This is most peculiar, but it's..."

"Over here," she said, pointing helpfully.

He stopped, something that looked like nostalgia overtaking him at the sight of the grass-covered mound. "Our old world has gotten fuzzy. I have forgotten much of Château Verenson. Has it happened to you?"

"It has. Forty years have passed, whether we know it or not. Lately, I've been searching for memories. But do you recall how you told me you hid here in the war?"

"I do," he said. He was lost in thought, his eyes moving to the places where, as a child, he'd hid while the other children counted aloud.

As she pushed open the door and ducked under the cave's entrance, the smell of smoke still lingered from their attempts to burn the cousins with fire. But just as he could not kill her, she could not kill him, so she would have to try another tactic. Taking a torch that she'd lit earlier, she used it to light the candelabra on the table. Beside it were two glasses. "Tell me that you still drink wine?" She held up a bottle.

He hesitated. "I can tolerate it. Sometimes, I do quite enjoy a good vintage. I miss it."

Taking the opener, she began to work the cork out. For a man who loved food and wine so much, to be condemned to drinking blood like an animal must have been a terrible form of hell. She sat and poured two glasses and studied the white stone walls. "Why is it that I got the wine cave and not you? It was yours, after all."

"It wasn't a divorce," said Thierry with a hint of sarcasm in his voice. "I don't understand any of this." He'd taken a seat and looked uncomfortable. In their original reality, he had always been certain of his place in the world. He'd charged about barking orders, comfortable with his power. This creature had been stripped of that confidence.

"And you will kill tonight?"

Removing the goat head, he placed it on the seat next to him, his once glorious hair missing in places and the rest matted to his head. "You are safe. I cannot kill you, and you cannot kill me."

"Why do you wear those?" She gazed over at the now discarded head. His own head was heavily bandaged.

"I cannot stand the way I look," he said. "The bandages soak through."

"What happens if you don't eat?"

"I don't know. That isn't an option." He sat up in the chair, his voice very matter-of-fact.

"So, you will just claim *another* villager tonight?"

"This is a *horror* film, Gemma," he said, his voice rising. "It is called *The Strange Moon*. Tonight, there is a *strange moon*, so, yes, that's exactly what I plan to do."

She stood up to light another torch, and his eyes followed her suspiciously. "I always knew we were destined to be together." Sitting back down, she poured them both another glass.

"And together we are again," he said with a pathetic smile. His hand slid toward hers like he was attempting to touch her affectionately, before pulling back. "If I recall, the last time we were here, you ran out."

"It seems like a lifetime ago, doesn't it?" She studied the man in front of her and found him hollow, like a dead tree. Even Charlie in the river, made of water, had been more animated. She'd been so thrilled to see Charlie despite all the complicated feelings she'd had for him in the end. But try as she might, Gemma couldn't conjure any feelings for this man.

"Oh, shoot," said Gemma. "That torch doesn't want to stay lit."

"Leave it," he said, growing agitated.

"But I like the flame." Taking another torch, she fussed at the candle. When she went past him, she leaned down to whisper in his ear. "What you forget, Thierry, is that this is my film now. Not yours." With a snap, she affixed the single silver shackle to his wrist.

He roared, jumping up from the chair, just as she shackled another to his leg. Yanking hard, he realized it was affixed securely to a hook in the wall of the cave. Tugging on the two chains, he growled. "How dare you! Get me out of here."

"No," she said. "This will be the film where I slay Monsieur Thibault."

"You can't slay me," he said triumphantly. "I'm a principal."

"How do you know that?" she spat.

"Because I've *tried* to kill you." His eyes met hers, and she saw the hatred in them. "So many times."

Fury welled up inside her. He'd tried to get her to pity him, and yet, given the chance, he'd have slit her throat again. It wasn't enough to send her away. Gemma recalled the scratches outside her bedroom door. "It was you at my door all those nights."

He smiled at her. "And I couldn't breach the threshold."

"The difference is that I'm not actively attempting to kill you. I'm just blocking you from existing."

"Which will destroy me."

Gemma shrugged. "Tomato, tomahto."

He lunged for her, but the chains held.

"You won't be alone. I'll stay here with you for as long as it takes."

For hours, he yanked on the chains, and Gemma feared they would give, but Bernard, who had affixed four chains to the cave wall, had assured her even a bull couldn't pull them out. She'd worried that Thierry had gained supernatural strength along with his immortality, but the two hooks she managed to get on him held.

When morning came, he began panting like a dog, the bandages now soaked through like a red headband. "I'll give you anything… anything," he said.

She looked up, having occupied herself with a copy of *The Count of Monte Cristo*. "I'm listening."

"I can send you back. I know I can."

"I know how to do that already," she said, sounding bored.

"The man who created the curse. He comes by to see me."

Gemma raised her eyebrow and snapped her finger. "And we can just go back like that? Back to the way we were?"

"Yes," he said, growing paler by the moment. There were deep hollows under his eyes. "Well, you can go back. You didn't die. I fear I'm in hell here. This is my afterlife. It's just your… well… your life."

"You mean my prison?"

"Tomato, tomahto." He laughed maniacally. "Let me go," he said, spitting at her with fury.

She pretended to consider it. "No."

"Hello?" There were voices coming from outside the cave. Gemma had a guess as to who would have come looking for her. She found Bernard and Manon standing outside the cave in the midday sun.

"I knew it," said Bernard. "You've got Thibault in there with you."

She folded her arms. "Well, it wasn't a stretch, Bernard; I had you install hooks in the cave, and you gave me the shackles."

"You did what?" Manon turned to Bernard, wide-eyed.

"Let me guess." Gemma rolled her eyes. "I can't kill the neighbors?"

Manon took a step forward and peered into the cave. Once she saw Thierry, she stepped back, scowling. "I think if you disposed of him, the village would thank you."

Cries emitted from the cave, and Gemma motioned for them to stay back. Inside, she found Valdon slumped over the table, his breathing shallow.

"Gemma, I beg of you, please take pity on me. I never meant for any of this to happen. The pain is too much. Do you want me in pain?"

She leaned over him. "You've caused nothing but pain. I'm sure Raphael Lafont felt agony. Your feelings are of little concern to me."

He gave one more surge toward her, screaming. He got within inches of Gemma, but the hooks held. Bernard, hearing the commotion, rushed in.

Pulling Gemma aside, he whispered, "I don't like this."

"I don't, either, but it must be done. He and I have . . . history."

"Manon brought cheese and bread for you," said Bernard. Gemma sighed. That was a good idea, since she didn't know how long she'd be babysitting this monster and how long he could exist without blood. "I'll be right outside if you need me."

"It is the strange moon," said Gemma. "You both go back to the house and lock yourselves in. I don't want either of you outside of this cave. Do you hear me?"

"This history with him," said Manon with a nod into the cave. "It's from your world, isn't it?"

"Oui. He's the reason I'm here."

They looked at each other and nodded wearily, before walking back toward the house.

As the sun set, Thierry began to sweat, his wound bleeding profusely and his face becoming as white as bone, except where streaks of crimson blood rained down. "Take pity on me."

"I do pity you, Thierry, surely you see that. You should want this to be over."

"You hypocrite," he said jeeringly. "You want to destroy me, and yet you will continue living on here forever?"

"I didn't get us into this mess." Her eyes never left her book, and she turned another page.

His jaw jutted out, and she could see the fury. "Do you remember the last time we were here, and I told you I could see our future? First this film and then after." Pinkish spittle ran down from one corner of his mouth onto his chin.

"I remember it well," she said, feeling a brief wave of nostalgia for that girl and an ache for that world, but it was like thinking of a child. Gemma wasn't that girl anymore. That girl ran out of this cave. If only she'd kept running like she'd wanted to, back to Los Angeles. She shook the thought away. No sense in thinking about a life she would never have.

"I lied," he said. "I just wanted to fuck you in this cave. You thought you were something special, but you were just another piece of ass to me." With one last tug, he pulled on the hooks with all his strength, and to Gemma's horror, one gave out and went sailing across the cave.

Like a wild animal, his eyes met hers, and she knew he was imagining the ways he'd kill her. Then he began to work on the leg shackle, hitting it with the arm shackle to bust it open.

The breath left her. If he got free, he'd kill her staff, anything to make her miserable in his hell. She needed to act fast. Spying a heavy magnum bottle, she grabbed it while he was busy and hit him over the head. At first, it didn't seem to affect him, but he went wobbly and finally slumped to the ground. Warily, she approached him, giving him a kick. While she thought she'd landed a good blow, she couldn't be sure that he wasn't pretending. Carefully, she tugged at the loose shackle. She'd had Bernard install four hooks, thinking that she could use all if she needed to, but she'd only managed to hook two shackles. Finding another hook that Bernard had installed closer to the ground, she attached the other leg shackle. Fully restrained, Thierry was now splayed on the ground.

He awoke screaming when he saw his new chains. "When I get out, there won't be a person in this village that you love who will remain alive."

The energy that it took to finish that sentence seemed to be the last he had. His breathing became more labored, and he threw up old, dark blood. By now the entire area around him was a puddle of red waste. While the grotesque sight disgusted her, she needed to stay there until the job was finished. She hadn't known this cruelty existed inside of her, and it scared her.

"I'm sorry, Thierry. If it helps, I take no pleasure in this." His own words being served back to him. "You need to go on to wherever that may be and be free of this hell."

Lifting his head, his dry and cracked lips formed his last few words. "You American bitch. Fuck you."

It would take another four hours in the middle of the most beautiful blood moon that Gemma had ever seen for Thierry Valdon to finally leave his mangled body. His moans faded to breaths that seemed to drain him. Within moments of his last exhale, the director's body began to turn to dust, sifting and billowing out of the cave.

Bending over to touch the now-empty shackles, Gemma spied the goat head rolled against the corner. She was briefly overcome with a wash of what could have been in another world and another time.

"I hope you're finally free. Once upon a time we could have made a good film together, Thierry," she said to the cave, hoping that somewhere he could hear her.

Picking up the animal head, she made her way out to the moonlight.

36

Christopher Kent
June 2010
New York

When he'd returned to his world, Christopher had been gone for nearly seven months. His savings had barely covered the extra month, and he was frantically doing editing jobs to restore his nest egg for his next visit, and he'd forgotten about taxes entirely.

In a strange twist of fate, Christopher learned that while he was in Gemma's world, Wren Atticus had died suddenly of pancreatic cancer. His father's death—and it was still hard to think of Wren Atticus in that way—was an interesting development, and even more so since Wren gave his control of the Prince Charmings' entire catalog to Christopher.

"There was no note," said the attorney. "He said you'd know why. Something about a shit legacy."

He was in editing mode at 2:00 a.m. when an email arrived:

Christopher:

I have a preview of the next showing of *L'Étrange Lune* if you want to see it. The Howard Theatre, T Street, Washington, DC, tomorrow at 4:00 p.m.

—Anthony A

He stared at the sender's name. "I'll be damned.... You've finally come for me," said Christopher. Sitting back in his chair, he wondered what Elizabeth would have thought about everything he'd found. He put his head in his hands, thinking about the journey he'd been on both with Elizabeth, and now, without her. "I miss you, old friend."

When he arrived at the historic theater in Washington, it looked to be tightly shut up, yet a man stood in front of the entrance, wearing sunglasses on a cloudy day. Dressed like he was headed to a steampunk conference with a long morning coat and vest, the man carried a walking stick like he'd stepped out of 1878 and landed here on Seventh Street.

"Christopher Kent," he said, extending his hand.

"You must be Anthony A.... Or do you prefer Althacazur?"

"Althacazur will do just fine." With a wave of his hand, the door to the theater swung open slowly. His stick tapped as he led the way to the art deco lobby lined with vintage photos of Washington, DC, and all the acts that had played here. Sliding into a booth in the back of the main theater, he motioned for Christopher to sit. Despite being set up for what looked like a dinner event, the screen was open on the stage.

"This theater is one of my favorite places," Althacazur said. "In the 1950s I saw Sarah Vaughan here." He pointed to the projector, and the room dimmed. "I thought this would be a good place for you to preview the next viewing of *L'Étrange Lune*."

"That's eight years from now?"

"Consider it a sneak peek." He winked.

A feeling of dread washed over Christopher as he turned toward the screen. From the projector room, the film warbled and then rolled smoothly like it had not been fed properly into the projector. Althacazur winced as the video and audio faded in and out until it caught.

L'Étrange Lune began like normal. Gemma pulled herself on the riverbank after Charlie. But then the plot got more interesting.

"We've got thirty additional minutes this year," he said with a smile on his lips. "As the director, you can imagine my excitement. We've also got several new cast members."

In the next scene, Christopher appeared, video camera in hand, telling Gemma that she had disappeared. It was strange to see himself on film with her. Those intimate three hours—scenes no one else should have witnessed—were on display for everyone, Gemma's pain reduced to entertainment. Then Christopher set up the camera and touched it, leaving her behind. The camera cut to her, and he saw the effect his leaving had on her, and he had to look away for a moment. The film showed her meeting her new solicitor, Raphael Lafont. He felt his heart lurch when he saw the joy in her face directed toward another man.

"Well, that's a love triangle if ever I saw one," said Althacazur, settling into his seat.

In the next scene, Christopher was back. He was struck by how clear it was, from the intimate scenes of his haircut to his bristling encounter with Raphael Lafont, that he was watching himself fall in love with Gemma. Then they made love. He lowered his eyes and felt his face flush; the film didn't shy away from the details, which Christopher found humiliating.

"My, my...fortunately we don't have children in the audience." Althacazur chuckled.

"What is this? *Mystery Science Theater 3000*? Enough with the comments."

And then he left Gemma's world again. This time, she watched him go. He hadn't known that detail. None of these next scenes were ones he knew. Raphael Lafont was hanging from a tree, and Gemma was in the house of Monsieur Thibault, who was revealed to be Thierry Valdon. Christopher felt his head begin to pound, and his hands were clammy. He sat on the edge of his seat. "Is Gemma all right?"

The sight of Thierry Valdon would have sickened anyone, but the film left little mystery. Thierry had cast a blood curse and doomed them all, but Gemma starved him, extinguishing him from her world. "You can't show that film. You can't. You're filming someone's life. It's an intrusion."

"Yes," said Althacazur with an eye roll. "She said as much, claiming she's tired of my direction and the reshoots that a good film requires. A real diva that one."

"It's not a film," said Christopher. "It's her life. You're holding her prisoner."

"Oh no," said the creature, holding up a finger. "You were the key. She could have come back with you, but she chose not to."

"That wasn't a choice."

"Incorrect. It wasn't an easy choice," said Althacazur. "But it was a choice, nonetheless." He drummed his fingers together like a movie villain plotting. "I'm still editing the last bit of film."

"But you can't—"

"It's my film," said Althacazur, cutting him off. "I can do what I want with it. It's a masterpiece."

Christopher leaned forward in the booth. "You *can't* show it."

"Don't threaten me." Althacazur turned suddenly, his voice booming.

For the first time, Christopher realized that while the creature appeared jovial, there was an evil corked inside him, just waiting to explode, so he needed to try a different approach. "What I mean is, if this version gets out, then everyone will know what happened. The Soixante-Quinze will know."

"Let me tell you something," said Althacazur. "Thierry Valdon was not a very interesting man. Considered himself a genius, talked a lot. While it is claimed that I confused him and he was in a drunken haze, he was quite clearheaded. He was dying. He wanted to finish the film, and he was ready to make a deal. He wanted me to spare his life and take hers. He gave me her writing—her notes—and a lock of her hair that he'd pulled the first night he saw her at Château Verenson. That's all it took to seal it. The camera did the rest. It was no drunken bargain. He came prepared to sell her soul. Do you understand what I'm saying? She was to be sacrificed, and he didn't care what I did with her if he could live."

Christopher's eyes widened.

"Missed that in your little investigation, didn't you?" Althacazur gave a little snort. "Well, souls are my business, so to speak, and I was interested, to a point. I love film; I love recordings of any kind. We went through millions of years with no real idea of how people lived, but that all stopped with film. It's a living time capsule of your tiny little moment on this planet. Thanks to recordings and film, as a creature collective you are now knowable...the way you spoke, dressed, fucked. Whether you're worthy of all the film you take up, well, that's a different question entirely, but it's all there for the future, who never have to wonder about you. So, I demanded the film and gave him his life. You know, vain creatures are the worst; they'll give anything for very little. He got to live and finish his pathetic version of the film. But I got his star and the final edit—the true director's cut—on his film. I got the better end of the deal, by far. You're a filmmaker, so you must agree that you waste your film stars. This crazy world you live in destroys the best ones. Imagine if Marilyn Monroe or Carole Lombard could live forever on film, never aging. I did that for Gemma Turner. I liked her. She'd written a screenplay."

"*The Damsel and the Demon.*" Christopher remembered her notes in the margin of the book.

"Very good. What can I say, it caught my attention. And she wanted to collaborate on *L'Étrange Lune*. It was a fair deal. I let her live."

"You can't show the film."

"Say it again and I'll kill you." Althacazur lowered his glasses, and Christopher saw the odd creature's eyes. "I've dabbled in the arts before, you know. Your Rick Nash? I collaborated with him. Nora Wheeler? Another of my stars. For someone not human, I adore watching the audience watch the film... our film—Gemma's and mine. It is my greatest entertainment. My proudest achievement, you could say." He looked away wistfully. "And it doesn't matter what I show in eight years." He smiled. "They won't *believe* it."

Christopher cocked his head, confused.

"They'll simply cling to their pet theories. No amount of logic will change their opinions... special effects, Gemma had a twin, Thierry was still alive somewhere... blah, blah, blah. Now, *you* will be a different story, unfortunately. It's going to be tough for you, answering all those pesky questions about the video camera. And of course, everyone will be upset that you kept the Arriflex to yourself. Tsk, tsk. They'll all want that machine, for sure. I assure you, the fallout from this *truth* will be far worse for you than me." His tone had the feigned innocence of a cartoon villain just before the knife was inserted.

"You called me here. You must want something."

"Can I ask you something first?" Althacazur folded his hands in front of himself innocently.

Christopher fiddled with the saltshaker that sat on the made-up round-top table, his mind racing, trying to figure out how to stop the film. The film he was *starring in*. "Of course."

"What were you planning to do when you 'found all the answers you and Elizabeth Bourget were looking for'?" He mocked the tone he knew they'd used as they'd conspired. "Did you *plan* to tell the world that the film was produced by a demon with a cursed video camera? *Weekly World News* can't wait to meet you."

"I didn't know." God, what hubris he'd had in approaching this film. Such arrogance. Lowering his head, Christopher felt ashamed. He'd just rushed in with no plan. Then again, Althacazur had made it difficult to form a plan, keeping the film hidden in shadows.

"You didn't know," said Althacazur with a cackle. "Of course you didn't. But you were so self-righteous, seeking answers, *stomping* around France interviewing everyone. Killing them when they spoke about the film, of course. Claude Moravin and Elizabeth Bourget had seen the film. They'd bled when they'd placed the mask on their faces, so they'd broken the contract of silence. Mick Fontaine died of natural causes, though. You weren't responsible for that one. All the kale juice in the world wouldn't have kept that man alive. Did you even prepare yourself for the consequences of those answers once you got them?"

Christopher was silent.

"Stupid boy," he said. "No one really wants the truth regardless of what they claim. Le Soixante-Quinze will always have their theories, but you? You've kicked up a shit storm you weren't prepared to deal with."

"Why me, then?" Defiantly, Christopher looked up, furious. "If I'm so stupid, then why did you choose me? And you did."

"I've brought you a little relic." Althacazur had a coy smile, like he was sharpening a knife. "Something I took to fuel you on a bit. I must say, I think even then, I knew we'd meet." In his palm, Althacazur held a little blue hippopotamus finger puppet.

Christopher couldn't believe his eyes. Like his own film playing in his head, images came rushing back to him: his mother singing "Happy Birthday," her handing him a map in the car, the car as it pulled into the hotel, the elevator doors as they opened onto the sixth floor, and the photo...always the photo. Christopher gripped the puppet like he did when he was ten.

It confirmed everything that Christopher had thought about *that* moment in his life. The one that had mattered the most. "Can I ask you a question? In that hotel in Pittsburgh in 1986. What photo had originally been hanging on that wall? Because we both know that it hadn't been a photo of Gemma Turner. You put that photo there because you knew what it would do."

"Good boy," said Althacazur with a coy smile like a cat's. "Elizabeth Taylor, I believe. The *BUtterfield 8* one."

"Was my mother collateral damage, then?"

"Oh, silly boy, had it not been a photo on a wall, it would have been a plate on a table or a posy in a vase. Pamela Kent's path was already well trod. But I needed a key. I'd promised Gemma a key so she could get back. Always a man of my word, I made one in you. In fact, I made seventy-five of them."

"Le Soixante-Quinze?"

He gave a nod. "All of you had some connection to Gemma, whether you knew it or not, but only you had the mettle, the obsession to find her. Of course, the gendarmerie hiding the camera was a little wrinkle, but you were on a tear for answers. I created a monster with you."

"Thanks," said Christopher bitterly.

Althacazur put his elbow on the table and rested his chin on his hand. "Right now, you're wondering if you had any free will, or did I, clever demon that I am, cast the die so much in my favor that your life was but a manipulation."

Christopher stared at Althacazur, feeling his cheeks flush. It was exactly what he was thinking.

"Seventy-four other people chose a different path from you." Pausing, the creature stroked his chin. "Well, seventy-three if you count Elizabeth Bourget. She matched you in obsession. Had you not found Gemma, my bet was on her. I mean, Zander Cross worked with Gemma and lived next door to her agent. Why not him? No one was a match for you for the task. No, Christopher, I humbly provided the kindling, but it was you who burned down your own village."

Christopher's contempt for the creature was visible. "I hadn't thought that I'd *be* in the film when I crossed over. You have the power to edit the film."

"I could."

"You *knew* this would happen."

"I did."

"Valdon is gone now; isn't the curse done, too?"

"He wasn't the only principal in the curse. The other—"

Christopher finished his sentence. "Is Gemma." His stomach felt like it had sunk to his feet. Was the creature suggesting that Gemma had to die to destroy the curse?

"Even with Thierry gone now, if the camera exists, then the curse continues and the camera films. I cannot undo a curse once I've bound it. There are rules. Airtight. Hell is a rather bureaucratic enterprise, I'm afraid. " Althacazur spread his palms wide and shrugged.

Christopher ground his back teeth. "But you have a solution, don't you?"

"I always have a solution," Althacazur said with a smile. "But you won't like it."

Christopher found he couldn't speak.

"Destroy the camera and you destroy the curse."

He wasn't expecting this. "But if I destroy the camera, don't I destroy Gemma's world—and Gemma with it?"

"Oh no. Despite her tantrums of late, I rather enjoy her. No, she'll stay safe in that world under my protection, but the camera, curse, and the film will all be gone, but—" He had a look of surprise.

"But I can't go back to her world once the camera is destroyed."

Pushing himself out of the booth, he adjusted his coat. "You're a smart man. You'll think of something. This film has sent you on an amazing journey, but life comes down to choices, Christopher."

"I destroy the camera, which ends the curse and this intrusive filming."

"And saves your ass at the same time. Let's not forget that."

"But I lose the woman—"

"—that you love." He finished his sentence. "Or you keep the camera and continue to see her, but she'll keep being the subject of new and exciting versions of *L'Étrange Lune*, and you'll face an awful fallout—one I'm not sure you'd recover from. If the camera exists, then *L'Étrange Lune* continues."

The walking stick clicked as he strode over to retrieve the film canister from a man exiting the projector room. "There is a third choice, however, but I'll leave it to you to figure out." Turning, he winked as he left the theater. "I have a feeling you'll make the noble choice."

Christopher thought this was a curious thing for him to say, but then it occurred to him that he'd known exactly which choice he would make in the end.

The door opened and then closed, which was just for show. If Christopher walked out on the street right now to try to flag him down, Althacazur would be gone.

37

Christopher Kent
June 10, 2011
Amboise, France

It had to be this day. Forty-three years to the date. Christopher stood at the edge of Manon Valdon's estate with an oversize backpack, hoping he'd planned enough.

Taking out the tripod, he sat the camera on top of it and positioned everything. Already, he had broken out in a sweat and wondered if he could live in a place without air-conditioning. This trip had taken so much out of him. He looked older than his thirty-four years. Christopher wondered if he would, eventually, regret his decision, yet the clarity that he'd found in preparing for this crossing made him sure that he'd never fit in in his own world. With Gemma, he was free, which was funny if you thought about it, as she was now imprisoned in a script, a movie, a set, likely in Hell. But then weren't we all imprisoned in our own worlds? The world didn't matter. The life you lived in it did.

"What on earth are you doing?" It was a woman's voice, in French.

He turned to find a woman in full hunting garb, pointing a rifle at him. With the elegant boots, jodhpurs, ruffled blouse, and perfect ash-blond bob, he knew that he was standing on the other end of Manon Valdon's shotgun barrel.

"I'm Christopher Kent," he said, holding out a hand. "You've shot at me before."

"I know. You were trespassing before," she said, keeping her elbows high. "I ought to try again."

He motioned for her to look. "Certainly, you can shoot me, but I'd kindly ask that you give me two minutes, and I promise I won't bother you again."

"You keep showing up." Her tone was flat.

"Well, it's easier to get there from here." Christopher motioned for her to peer into the viewfinder. "This is Claude Moravin's camera. But look. You can see it's different in the viewfinder." He stepped away from the camera.

As she lowered the gun, he noticed the elaborate carving on the side of the maple stock. Circling the camera warily, she leaned over and peered through the camera. Looking through the viewfinder, she stepped back like it had burned her. "Mon dieu! There is a horse in my roundabout." Her eyebrows rose, looking at the field of space in front of the camera, which was horseless.

"I know," he said.

"What is that?"

"That's *L'Étrange Lune* there."

"The set?"

"Oui. That camera sent Gemma Turner in there."

"And you're going in there?"

"I am... if you don't shoot me first."

She laughed. It was a throaty, hearty laugh. "I'll be damned. He was right. The bastard never told me he was dying, you know," she said, rolling her eyes. "Three years later, after locking himself away here to edit it, he came to me sobbing about what he'd done—told me everything about the curse, but I thought he was mad."

"Oh," said Christopher. "You knew?"

"He told me that he had received news of terminal cancer and that he'd bargained with the devil to finish his film. The arrogant bastard wanted to live forever, yet when he didn't die and found his career was ruined, he began wailing that all he wanted to do was die. 'Well, make up your mind,' I said. When he told me what he'd done—sacrificing Gemma for that awful film—there was no remorse." She looked down at the rifle in her hand. "The next time he began wailing that he wanted to die because his career was over, I helped him along. . . . I made it look like it was his idea, though."

Christopher's heart skipped a beat. "With that gun?"

She nodded. "I found the whole thing disgraceful. So, I gave him his final wish."

"He ended up in Gemma's world." He nodded toward the camera.

"Good. I hope he is miserable," she said, pulling the gun closer to her. Manon cocked the gun, causing him to jump in the air. She walked coolly past him. "If you're still here in two minutes, I'll shoot you as well."

Gripping the body of the camera, he took a deep breath and flipped on the power button.

38

Gemma Turner
"1878"
Amboise, France

The moon washed down on her, glorious and low, just like it had been the day that she'd kissed Charlie in the river. She took the animal head in her hand, like an offering, and made her way to the path.

"Where are you?" Her voice echoed among the trees. She held the severed head up like a warrior. "He was your proxy, wasn't he? I know the mask you wear, but this is you, isn't it? Come out and face me, Althacazur."

From the mist, she could see the outline of him. It wasn't the handsome Victorian visage he often used, with its tousled curls and sunglasses. This was his real face, the one with the horns and the eyes of the goat, and he was a size and a half larger than she was. His form towered over her, like a tree.

"How dare you summon me."

"How *dare* you hold me prisoner here."

"I think I've made myself clear on the matter. The blood curse was signed by Thierry Valdon."

She tossed the head at his feet. "I vanquished him. Now I want my freedom."

"Your freedom?" He stepped forward. "I sent you a key. You've been free to leave."

Gemma never felt more feral in her life. Shaking her head slowly, deliberately, she hissed. "I've been robbed of my life. There is nothing to return to, but you knew that. Just another trick, because that's what you are."

The creature's head dropped. "We all live in prisons, me included."

"I gave you a trilogy. First the vampires, then Charlie, and now Monsieur Thibault. This is the final showdown, Althacazur; either destroy me or free me from this film, but I'm tired of the retakes and the notes. I don't want to see another strange moon. I want to be free of this film, of your direction. I've earned it."

He lowered himself to face her. Their eyes locked. Those peculiar amber eyes with pupils like dashes that never exactly met your gaze. Like the *Mona Lisa*, it was impossible to read him. Once, Gemma had feared things, stupid things like speaking up for herself or asking hard questions. Oh, the time she'd wasted being frightened. Then, here, she had been afraid of Monsieur Batton and his threats, of her staff tattling on her. This time, Gemma Turner didn't back down, didn't take one single step backward. If her existence ended right here, she was ready for it.

"I underestimated you." The creature's head moved, like a viper before it strikes.

She leaned back a little, bracing herself like the condemned awaiting the guillotine's blade. She said her final words: "You weren't alone. Everyone underestimated me."

"Gemma." The sound of her name sounded so strange in this moment. She peered at the creature, wondering if it had come from him.

"Gemma, don't." The sound was coming from behind her, but it was getting closer. She turned to find Christopher Kent standing in the path.

She put her hand up to stop him. "Stay away, Christopher. This ends with him now."

Like a cat would toy with a baby mouse, the creature lifted Gemma from the ground with the subtle raise of an arm. Suspending her high above the oak trees, he slammed her body against a tree, the branches shuddering and sending debris raining all around her.

"Jesus," said Christopher, rushing over to her, but she was back on her feet quickly, staggering back toward Althacazur.

"That's it," she taunted. "Kill me. I'll take that before I remain your prisoner here."

"It can be arranged." The creature snorted.

"Anthony," said Christopher. Gemma thought it was so strange to hear him called *Anthony*.

The creature shook his head. Something Christopher was doing was confusing him.

She turned to warn Christopher to stay back. Out of the corner of her eye, the creature's arm rose in front of him, and she saw the clutch of his hand and felt her throat tighten. The air was gone quickly. The grip tightened. He was strangling her.

Momentary panic washed through her, and her arms tried to peel his claws from her just enough. As she began to lose consciousness, she realized she had been very much alive. Christopher was shouting, "Anthony." The bones in her throat were still shattering, crumbling, and her neck began to twist at an awkward angle. And it hurt.

It was the strike of metal that stopped the pressure, and Gemma fell to the ground, choking, but her battered neck repaired itself in a moment.

It was a curious thing to behold. Christopher had taken out a hammer and begun to strike the Arriflex, which seemed to have an effect on Althacazur, who had returned to his human form.

"Very clever," said Althacazur, the ruffled collar blowing in the wind. He looked like a Victorian poet standing in the bloodred moonlight. "You won't be able to go back, you know."

Gemma was confused.

On his haunches, Christopher stopped hammering to look back at Althacazur. "You knew I'd choose this."

The creature shrugged.

"I don't understand." Gemma had picked herself up.

"The key has decided that if he cannot take you back into his world, that he will stay with you."

Gemma shot Christopher a look, and her heart leapt. "Is this true?"

The hammer was in his hand poised to strike again. He nodded, and their eyes met. "I had planned to stay this time—*for good*."

She had longed to hear those words from him, and yet, it was too great a sacrifice, no matter how much she wanted him to stay. "No." She wrestled the hammer from him. "You should go back now and forget me."

Christopher Kent gave her that crooked smile, the one that melted her. "I don't seem to be able to do that."

"Oh, please." Althacazur rolled his eyes.

Christopher gazed up at him with irritation. "But that's not all, *Anthony*, is it?"

"Anthony?" Gemma searched Christopher's face to understand.

"My human nom de plume, so to speak. The key is about to destroy the camera, which is the cursed object."

Christopher lifted the video camera just in case Gemma had any question about the cursed object in question.

"When he succeeds," said Althacazur, "he destroys the curse. In choosing to destroy it on this side, you will both remain here. And you are free."

She let that sink in and then rose and held her hand out for Christopher. Looking back over her shoulder at Althacazur, she shouted, "I want to hear from you that there is no trick."

The creature placed his sunglasses on and took two steps toward them. "As you have pointed out, we created a trilogy. And while you're now convinced you're Coppola, it is rather annoying to admit that your work as my creative partner is now finished. You may remain here as my guest. You were a worthy producing partner, but I do find I'm bored with the screen. Perhaps I should turn my attention to the music industry."

"Unharmed?" Gemma touched her throat, which still felt the twinge of pain from him trying to crush it a minute ago.

"Of course unharmed," said Althacazur indignantly with an eye roll. "I'm not a barbarian."

"And the filming ends?" Gemma raised her voice and turned her body toward him, ready for another battle if that was what was necessary.

He spoke like he would to a child. "Well, if there is no camera there can be no filming, can there?"

"The filming ends?" Christopher stood.

Althacazur gave a heavy nod. "With the destruction of my beautiful instrument, filming ends. You are free of the curse." He turned and put his hand up. "I cannot watch it." As he walked into the mist, he was muttering about the work that would never be seen.

Gemma knelt beside Thierry Valdon's cursed camera and took the hammer firmly in her hand. Gazing up at Christopher, she said, "Are you sure about this?"

"I've been looking for you my entire life."

Gemma raised the hammer, but Christopher held her wrist. "You're the heroine who deserves the ending she wants. Is this what you want? We can cross over and destroy it there or stay here. The choice is yours."

Gemma Turner didn't move for a long time. Then she brought the hammer down on the camera once, causing a piece of it to propel.

Satisfied, she delivered three more blows to the camera before it broke apart. Crouching down, Christopher pulled out a yellow Bic lighter from his pocket. Then, gathering some sticks and leaves, he placed them around the camera to create a pyre. Within minutes of them lighting the leaves, the camera parts were melting. Still, he took a few more hits with the hammer himself.

Under the glow of the strange red moon above them, soft pieces of the exposed camera mechanics melted, a satisfied grin spreading across Gemma's face.

Sitting back on her heels, she took it all in.

Gripping the hammer, she took one final blow and shouted through the trees. "Coupé."

39

A Few Moments Later
"1878"
Amboise, France

In Château Dumas, upstairs in the old wing, in Gemma Turner's room, the typewriter carriage began to move. Its keys clacked furiously.

`Perhaps our film was a love story, after all!`

`Coupé, indeed.`

`—Althacazur`

EPILOGUE

Ivy Cross
June 10, 2018
Los Angeles, California

For seven years now, she'd often taken the letter out of her top drawer and read it, looking for clues, hidden meanings, anything to give her answers. But today, when no call came, she finally felt the full weight of the letter's contents and a swelling pride for what he'd managed to do. She knew the note by heart, but reading, she always heard his voice, felt the loss of him.

Ivy:

While I fell short of being the man you needed in this life, I hope you'll know that I never meant to hurt you. You're the only person in this world who I entrust with these tapes of my mother and Charlie Hicks. They are my most treasured possessions, my only legacy, and now they are yours. It seems Wren Atticus was the missing variable. I believe there is a story here, and you'd tell it brilliantly. As I often did, I stumbled into the secret to L'Étrange Lune, *and if I succeed in my plan, you'll never get another invitation to that horrible film again. It needs to end, but you know that. It also means you probably won't see me again. While I have no right to ask it, if I am able destroy it, please let my family know that I did one good thing. While I didn't follow their advice to live in this world, I found my way home. I wish you every happiness, Ivy. You are a remarkable woman!*

With love,
Christopher

The years had been a mix for her; she'd gotten divorced after only ten months, and then the following year, her father and Vera were killed in a plane crash, leaving her half brother, Zeke, in her care. She adored the boy and reflected often about her unexpected role as keeper of legacies, her father's and Christopher's. Wren Atticus had left the Prince Charmings' catalog to Christopher upon his death, who had, in turn, entrusted it to her. In the years since, she'd gotten their fourth album rereleased with the four missing tracks written by Charlie Hicks, as well as the three tracks that Pamela and Charlie had created together. *Rolling Stone* had called the remastered album a "necessary final chapter in a hardworking band that had always known its place behind the Beatles and the Rolling Stones...but this new material gives them new consideration as a force in British pop. Had these songs been included in the original album, who knows what the Prince Charmings might have become."

Yet, the dread of this date had been like a cloud hanging over her for years. When the phone failed to ring and no invitation to the screening came, today's precious silence meant that she could finally move on. Whatever he had done, Christopher had ended *L'Étrange Lune*.

But there was one more thing to do. Picking up the phone, she dialed the number, not sure what she'd say. How did you convey things that couldn't be explained to rational people? And *L'Étrange Lune* could never be explained in rational terms.

The voice on the other end picked up.

"Jason?"

"Yes?" There was hint of alarm, as though she might be a telemarketer or the bearer of bad news.

"It's Ivy Cross. . . . I'm not sure you remember me, but do you have a minute to talk? It's about Christopher. . . ."

Acknowledgments

When I was doing research for *A Witch in Time*, I came across a rather haunting photo of a woman who, I would learn, was the actress Françoise Dorléac. The red-haired, older sister of actress Catherine Deneuve, Dorléac was tragically killed in 1967 while rushing to catch a flight out of the airport in Nice. She was only twenty-five.

Years went by and I sought out her films, watching her in François Truffaut's *The Soft Skin* and starring with her sister in *The Young Girls of Rochefort*, her performances leaving an indelible mark on me. For me, it's that way with books especially. Something—usually an image—grips me and begins the germination of an idea. Readers often ask me who I'd cast to play a particular character. For this book, every scene I created for Gemma Turner, I saw Françoise's face. She is Gemma for me and the inspiration for this book, and I hope it honors her memory.

To my exceptional team at Redhook, thank you for finding my work so many years ago and giving it life: my editor, Nivia Evans, who as she often does, encapsulated this book's direction with a few perfect words at the exact right time to help me see it so much clearer; Angelica Chong, whose keen eye and great instincts are reflected on every page and took this book across the finish line; Bryn A. McDonald, a magnificent wrangler of words who will unfortunately have to edit her own thank-you as well as my poor French; Lisa Marie Pompilio for another stunningly beautiful cover; and the incomparable

Ellen Wright for the tireless job of getting these books noticed in a world overflowing with content.

I owe a great debt to Roz Foster and the folks at Frances Goldin Agency. Editor, therapist, and cheerleader, Roz is so much more than my agent. I'm not sure that either one of us saw where this journey would lead, but I'm so proud of what we've accomplished together. My sister, the brilliant editor, Lois Sayers, took early fragments of ideas and malformed chapters and helped me see the story underneath it all. I love and thank you for often reading my mind.

Special thanks to the Sandra Dijkstra Agency team of Andrea Cavallaro and Jennifer Kim as well as the BookSparks team of Crystal Patriarche, Taylor Brightwell, and Hanna Lindsley. You're a stellar team of collaborators, and you make this process fun.

Research for this book included *The Secret Life of the Savoy: Glamour and Intrigue at the World's Most Famous Hotel* by Olivia Williams (Pegasus Books, 2022); *Hammer Films: An Exhaustive Filmography* by Tom Johnson and Deborah Del Vecchio (McFarland, 2012); *A Wine and Food Guide to the Loire* by Jacqueline Friedrich (Henry Holt & Company, 1996); *François Truffaut at Work* by Carole Le Berre (Phaidon Press, 2005); *Truffaut: A Biography* by Antoine De Baecque and Serge Toubiana (Knopf, 1999); *A History of the French New Wave Cinema* by Richard Neupert (University of Wisconsin Press, 2007); and *Brian Jones: The Untold Life and Mysterious Death of a Rock Legend* by Laura Jackson (Little, Brown UK, 2011).

Considering this is a book "mostly" set in the Loire Valley, I would be remiss in not thanking my travel and life partner, Mark, who drove us on a weeks-long journey through the winding roads of France. Sadly the "you speak French and I'll drive" deal didn't work out so well for you, but it was during this trip that I found the inspiration for Château Verenson among the wine caves. Thank you for always reading.

To my wonderful family and friends: my brother-in-law, Daniel Joseph; my brother, Leslie Sayers, and sister-in-law, Ellen Sayers; my former husband and occasional reader, Steve Witherspoon; my fabulous friends Laverne Murach and Betsy Barin Keiser; my nephew and fellow *Sabrina* and *Wednesday* fan, Joshua Sayers; my boss, Tim Hartman (has it been twenty years?); and Andrew Werner, who is always first in line to listen!

During the writing of this book, I lost my mom, Barbara Guthrie Sayers. While she'd been slowly slipping away from us for years, it was an unbearable, final grief, and I found so much truth and comfort in writing Christopher's story. Like him, I will forever be searching until I find her again.

Meet the Author

Tyler Hooks for Laura Metzler Photography

CONSTANCE SAYERS is the author of three novels, including *A Witch in Time* and *The Ladies of the Secret Circus*. She splits her time between Alexandria, Virginia, and West Palm Beach, Florida.

Reading Group Guide

1. Gemma faces obstacles as a woman in Hollywood in the 1960s. How does this illustrate the challenges women faced in the 1960s? Is she able to transcend these obstacles in her new reality in 1878? Does she thrive?

2. Gemma faces a choice: She can return to her world as an old woman or remain at Château Dumas and never age. What do you think of her choice? Which would you choose?

3. How does Gemma evolve from the time she enters the film until its conclusion? How does she adapt to her new environment? How do her interactions with the supporting "characters" who inhabit the film change as the book progresses?

4. How does Christopher change (or not change) throughout the book? Ultimately, do you think he was happy with the answers he received regarding the connection between his mother and Gemma?

5. Gemma battles several "monsters" in the film: Roman and Avril, Charlie Hicks and Monsieur Thibault. What do each of these monsters represent for her? How do they strengthen her resolve?

6. How did you feel about the romance between Gemma and Christopher? Do you think he made the right choice in the end?

7. The book blends multiple genres: magical realism, horror, romance, and thriller. Did this mash-up of genres work for you?

For the first time in a long time, Beatrice's gift will be called on to help someone in need. But the ghosts have taken on an even darker edge—and there is something sinister lurking in the shadows. Beatrice may not be enough to stop what's coming for them.

1

Beatrice, The Island, 1977

The seascape beyond the cottage window was beautiful in a monochromatic way. Tarnished silver clouds drifted in a somber sky, and pewter water shivered under restless whitecaps. Sparse evergreens framed the pale scene with their dark, slender trunks.

It was a charming vista, but a painful reminder of how dramatically Beatrice's life had changed. San Francisco was all color, pastel houses marching along the steep hills, scarlet trolleys rattling along their rails, wisps of fog slipping through the vivid orange girders of the Golden Gate Bridge. The island was nothing like San Francisco, and it didn't feel like home. She had to remind herself that she had been here only six weeks. It would take time.

She liked the cottage well enough. She had bought it sight unseen, but it lived up to the real estate agent's description as a "charming woodsy getaway." The door from the wraparound porch opened into a well-appointed kitchen, separated from a dining area by a short bar. A forties-style archway led to a small living room, where wide windows afforded a view of the water. The outside walls were a muted blue-gray, in keeping with the coastal setting. Thick juniper bushes curled along the foundation. The interior walls were cream and rose and butter yellow, warm colors for a cool climate. A short strand of beach, featured prominently in the real estate photographs, ran below the porch, linked to the cottage by a steep stony path.

The photographs and the descriptions had somehow failed to mention one significant detail. Steps from the cottage, a small cow barn nestled among the pines and firs, an unpainted lean-to jutting from one side. Beatrice couldn't decide at first if the omission was an oversight or a deliberate effort by the sellers not to introduce a detraction. She doubted many buyers would see the barn as a bonus, nor would they be happy to learn about its occupants.

In any case, the purchase hadn't disappointed her, even though her ownership felt temporary. It felt pretend, like setting up a dollhouse, or like playing hide-and-seek, which was a better metaphor. The cottage—indeed, the island itself—was Beatrice's hiding place. She was an animal gone to ground, a wounded creature seeking respite, pulling folds of solitude around herself for comfort.

Beatrice was unused to isolation. She had chosen this loneliness, and it brought relief of a sort, but it was the kind of relief that comes from the cessation of pain. She was learning that the absence of pain left space for other discomforts, like the weight of unrelenting silence and the yearning for places and people she loved.

The worst was missing Mitch. At night, in her sleep, she often turned to reach for him. When her groping hand found nothing but a cold pillow, an unused blanket, she woke, and lay aching with loss.

She doubted that Mitch, safe in their blue and yellow house above the bay, felt anything like she did. He had neither written nor telephoned. She could only assume he was still angry.

In fact, the heavy black telephone on the bar had rung only once since she moved in, and that was to remind her that the store at the ferry dock would sell any milk she couldn't use.

Milk, for pity's sake. Who would have thought?

Beatrice moved close to the window to watch a single intrepid boat, bristling with fishing gear, plow its way through the frigid waters of the strait. It was too far away for her to see the people on board, so it didn't trouble her to watch its progress. It trailed an icy wake as it circled the distant silhouette of the big island and disappeared.

Thinking how cold those fishermen must be made Beatrice shiver and turn to the woodstove that dominated her living room. It hummed and crackled, filling the cottage with the spicy fragrance of burning pine. The fire was comforting, but the stove consumed an astonishing amount of wood. The cord stacked against the side of the cottage was shrinking with alarming speed in the face of the cold snap. She really shouldn't put off calling Mr. Thurman to ask him to deliver more, but she dreaded doing it.

Mr. Thurman was a pleasant man. When she called him with her first order, he had rattled and jounced up the dirt road, the bed of his ancient Ford pickup piled high with logs. He had greeted her cheerfully and made quick work of the chore, accepting her payment with a tip of his flat wool cap.

But he hadn't come alone. He would never come alone. Seeing him—them—had ruined what was left of that day. Remembering it, Beatrice pressed a hand to the base of her throat, where the borrowed misery lurked.

Regardless, she would have to order more wood. The radio said tonight would be even colder than the night before, which had glazed the boulders on her bit of beach with ice. She crouched beside the stove to stir up the embers and lift in fresh chunks of pine. She had just closed the glass-fronted door when Alice's commanding call rang out.

Smiling for the first time that day, Beatrice straightened and leaned to one side to look through the archway. Through the window half of the kitchen door, she saw Alice and Dorothy standing below the porch, the two of them gazing expectantly up at the cottage.

Dorothy was tall and rangy, white with splotches of black on her sides and her crooked nose. Alice was tawny and petite, with big dark eyes and long eyelashes. She was considerably smaller than Dorothy, but there was no doubt that she was in charge. At this moment she clearly considered it her duty to inform the new dairy farmer that milking time had arrived.

Beatrice adjusted the stove damper, then crossed into the kitchen to pull on the rubber milking boots left by the previous owners, as well as the secondhand red-and-black Pendleton jacket, her last purchase in San Francisco. She had not expected cows, but she didn't mind them. A woman alone could do worse for company than two easygoing cows.

The elderly couple who sold her the cottage were fortunate in their buyer. Beatrice had grown up in South Dakota. Her father had been a country GP who often helped out the local ranchers when the vet wasn't available. Beatrice had gone with him on house calls from an early age, and sometimes their patients had not been people, but horses, cows, or the occasional pig that had cut itself on barbed wire. She was used to livestock.

She said, "Good evening, ladies," as she stepped down from the porch and crunched across the graveled yard to the little barn. Her voice creaked, reminding her she hadn't spoken aloud all day. As she set Dorothy and Alice to munching hay in their stanchions, she chatted to them, just to hear herself.

She started with Alice, who would stamp and low if she didn't.

"You must have been reading Betty Friedan," she said, as she slid the milk bucket beneath the cow's udder and sat down on the three-legged stool. "You're a bossy little bossy, but that's okay. I like that in a cow." Alice gave a small, bovine grunt, and Beatrice took it for agreement.

For all the times she had helped her father treat animals, she had never actually milked a cow, though she had seen it being done. Now she found herself in possession of two of them. No one knew what might have become of the cows if she had refused to keep them, but she hadn't done that. She had figured out how to accomplish the task of milking through trial and error, aided especially by the patient Dorothy. Now the chore went smoothly for the most part. If it didn't, Alice never failed to apprise her of her errors, swishing her tail so it stung Beatrice's cheek, or overturning the bucket with one impatient hind leg.

Beatrice appreciated Dorothy's compliant ways, but she and Alice had more in common.

After the next morning's milking, Beatrice eyed the supply of milk and cream that had accumulated in the refrigerator and made a face. There was no excuse for not taking it down to the store. She had already managed that twice, after feeling guilty for letting a gallon of good milk go sour.

The experience hadn't been too bad. The nun who managed the store and the tiny ferry terminal called herself Mother Maggie. She had accepted the milk and filled Beatrice's grocery list with a minimum of questions, evidently unbothered by Beatrice's reticence. She was far from young, perhaps too old to be operating a ferry dock, but she had a kind face beneath her short black veil. Even better for Beatrice, Mother

Maggie's ghosts were mercifully pale with age. As long as she was the only person in the store, Beatrice wouldn't mind the chore.

She showered and changed. It felt good to put on something besides the wool pants that had gotten too big and the cable-knit sweater she had borrowed from Mitch and neglected to return. She wondered if he knew she had it. If he did, he would understand why she had kept it. It might even make him smile. She missed his smile. She missed his unlikely dimples.

She put on a fresh pair of slacks and a clean sweater, and took up her scissors to hack off a few strands of hair still straggling into her face. She had cut off most of her hair soon after she arrived on the island. The long dark strands lying on the floor around her—to say nothing of the ragged look of what was left—had put a period to what remained of her life. Her hair looked pretty rough, but there was no one to notice. Most of the time she covered it under her knit hat.

One of her patients had made the hat for her from leftover bits of yellow and purple yarn. It was a curious-looking creation, but the knit was smooth and regular, and the hat was warm enough for the damp cold of the island. Every time she wore it she thought of the young people she had worked with in the Haight: homesick kids, stoned kids, frightened kids. She cherished the hat, odd though it was, because it reminded her of them. They were sweet, but so hurt and confused, flower children struggling to accept that the Summer of Love wasn't what they had imagined it would be.

Beatrice pulled on the hat and her secondhand Pendleton, wrinkling her nose at the clash of red plaid wool with yellow and purple knit, deciding it didn't matter. She packed the bottles of milk into a straw-lined basket and set out in the crisp winter air for the hike down the hill.

Mother Maggie was the leader of a handful of nuns who made up a tiny island monastery. She took grocery orders and sometimes delivered them in the nuns' dusty yellow station wagon. The other sisters taught in the little school and took occasional shifts with the ferry ramp. Their brown habits were familiar to everyone on the island, but tourists smiled and pointed at the unusual sight of nuns as ferry operators. They took snapshots with their cameras, as they might with wildlife or historical buildings.

When Beatrice emerged from the quiet of the woods into the clearing around the terminal, she wished for the thousandth time that she had succeeded, in the face of her disability, in developing a strategy for dealing with people. It was what she expected her patients to do, build tools to handle their challenges, but she had failed to do it for herself. She remained raw and vulnerable, and though it hurt her pride, she had fled her problem instead of solving it.

She was glad to see that it was Mother Maggie operating the ferry ramp, which meant she was also working in the store. She wouldn't have to meet someone new. The ferry was churning its way back out into the bay as the nun trudged up from the dock, an orange safety vest zipped over her billowing habit. She caught sight of Beatrice and waved a welcome as she went into the store, leaving the door ajar behind her. By the time Beatrice reached it, Mother Maggie had shed the vest and exchanged her rain boots for Birkenstocks with thick gray socks.

"Good morning, Mother Maggie." Beatrice set the basket on the counter beside the cash register. "Six quarts here."

"Good morning to you, Beatrice," Mother Maggie said with a smile. "We'll be glad to have the milk. Are you settling in all right?"

"Fine, yes."

"The groceries you ordered are in. I'll bag them for you."

"Thank you."

The nun turned to put the milk in the big refrigerator behind her, saying over her shoulder, "Won't you stay for a cup of coffee? I was just about to make some."

Beatrice found, to her surprise, that she liked the idea of sitting down for coffee with Mother Maggie. She hadn't been in company for weeks, and the shades that trailed behind the nun were so faint as to be nearly invisible, their energy almost spent. She could surely ignore them for a little while.

She said, "I'd love some coffee."

"Good. Go grab a chair. I'll just be a few moments."

There were three wooden tables in the back of the room, arranged around a potbellied stove that hummed with warmth. Beatrice pulled a chair close to the stove.

She sat down and started to shrug out of her coat just as the door to the store clicked open with a jangle of its welcome bell. A tall, slender young woman stepped through.

Beatrice froze, one arm still in the sleeve of her jacket.

The woman wore an expensive-looking camel's-hair coat, a creamy cashmere scarf around her throat, and a pair of elegant leather boots. She had fair hair tied back in a low ponytail and a shining leather handbag on a shoulder strap. She was exceptionally beautiful, with long legs and smooth skin, but her slender shoulders hunched as if she were carrying a burden.

As in fact she was. Two burdens. Beatrice saw them distinctly.

One, hovering above her like a storm cloud, was a threatening charcoal gray so dark it seemed lightning might flash through it.

The other clung to her legs, tiny and tragic, the lavender and indigo of confusion and grief. It was accompanied by the faint sound of a child weeping. Beatrice's throat throbbed suddenly, painfully, choking her with anxiety.

Hastily, she thrust her other arm back into her jacket and blundered her way through the tables toward the door. Mother Maggie was saying to the newcomer, "Oh, hello. You just got off the ferry, didn't you?"

Beatrice didn't hear the woman's answer. She was already out the door, abandoning her basket, forgetting her groceries, having not so much as nodded to the woman who had come in, nor said goodbye to Mother Maggie. Her mouth dry and her throat aching, she stumbled toward the forest path that led to her house. She fled.

She was ashamed of it, embarrassed by it, but she was helpless to do anything about it.

Most people saw their ghosts in the dark of night. Beatrice saw them in broad daylight, and it was intolerable.